SHADOWS
AMONG US

ISBN:978-1-7336701-5-9

Cover Design:

Giovanni Auriemma

Developmental Edit/Line Edit and Manuscript Evaluation:

Ann Castro, AnnCastro Studio

Proof via Editorial Lens:

Emily Dings

Interior Design and Typeset:

Mallory Rock

This book is a work of fiction. Though some situations in this book are based on actual events, such as the Vietnam War, the situations in this book are purely fictional, and any resemblance to actual persons, living or dead, events, or locales is entirely coincidental. *Shadows Among Us* contains adult themes and is recommended for a mature audience.

For Gar
My partner in crime

"*We serial killers are your sons. We are your husbands. We are everywhere. And there will be more of your children dead tomorrow.*"
—Ted Bundy

AUTHOR'S NOTE

Shadows Among Us contains numerous references to the Vietnam War, which began in November 1955 and ended with the fall of Saigon in April 1975. Though the Vietnam references in Shadows Among Us are loosely based on truthful accounts of wartime occurrences, all other identifying aspects have been fictionalized. There is no "Bravo Company, the 4th Battalion of the 10th Infantry, Ground Assault Division" or "Cam Chi" village; however, the emotional fallout experienced by the characters is no less real.

It is my hope that this story will encourage readers to learn more about the Vietnam War and its enduring impact on all those involved, many of whom continue to be haunted by what they witnessed, what they experienced, and what they were called to do.

AFTER

CHAPTER ONE

(MONDAY, SEPTEMBER 24, 2018)

I spot Dakota at the distant end of the cereal aisle between the Rice Krispies and Raisin Bran, rising up like an angel from the stark-white floor. She's taller and thinner. Her hair longer and less bubblegum pink than I remember.

But of course, she's different. She would be.

It's been 766 days since I last saw her. That's a lifetime in kid years. And I'm different too.

Changed.

Though that seems too soft a word for what's happened to me. For the total obliteration of my old self. The nuclear fallout that's left me pushing this sad shopping cart of cheap vodka, Oreos, and boxed mac and cheese. An ironic six-pack of Diet Coke. And a sack of Alpo, which Gus will begrudgingly gobble only because he's

1

long given up on waiting for the overpriced organic crap I used to buy.

I linger near the Fruit Loops, awaiting confirmation as she raises to her tiptoes and cranes her neck at the top shelf, her contortions both strange and familiar. I grip the front of my shopping cart with quiet desperation, willing my legs to remain upright. The hairs on my arms prickle with recognition. A sob catches in my throat. Or is it a scream?

Whatever it is, I swallow it. I don't make a sound.

As she turns to go, Cheerios box in hand, I see it there on her right shoulder, bare beneath the thin strap of her tank top. The tiny inked cage with its open door, the tiny inked bird flying just beyond her scapula. I'd raged at her when I'd first seen it, demanded to know who and where and why. And then I'd spit nails down the telephone line at a man who called himself Bull and claimed to be in charge.

What kind of backwoods operation tattoos a fifteen-year-old girl? You know it's illegal here, right, moron?

Now, I'm grateful for Bull. For that tattoo. Because it's irrefutable evidence.

I know. For certain.

It's her. Somehow, it's her.

Behind the white bone fence of my rib cage, my heart shudders to life, sputtering like a half-dead thing awakened.

I barely breathe. I measure every movement, wheeling my cart with the slow precision of a hunter belly-crawling through the grass. She's a miracle—a forty-five-point buck, with antlers stretching to the sky—and I don't want to spook her. I can't lose her again.

I follow her as she walks on, oblivious to my silent stalking. Past the slabs of bloody meat resting in their tidy Styrofoam packages. Past the shrimp and the lobster and the crawfishes' filmy black eyes. Past the decapitated heads of broccoli and the bruised, too-ripe peaches. She skips, light-footed even in dime-store flip-flops.

I notice the gentle swish of her hair—almost audible beneath the drone of the grocery store soundtrack—remembering how it felt between my fingers. First, her soft blonde baby curls that darkened to the color of my own cinnamon brown. Then, pigtails and ponies and braids I'd twisted myself. Bows I'd pinned to the top of her head. Tangles that had brought us both to tears. And then, finally, the what-the-hell-did-you-do-to-yourself pink. It stained the towels a pale red that never did wash out.

Now, I'd dye it for her myself if she'd let me. If I could.

I will her to turn around and look at me.

Look at me!

I need to count the freckles on the bridge of her nose. To watch the light catch the flecks of gold in the green eyes she got from her father. To notice the thousands of other things I can't forget but can't quite remember. The things lost in the ether of the in-between world I inhabit, the one where I'm not quite alive, not yet dead.

But she won't look at me. She's leading me somewhere. And I'm as helpless. Panicked, nearly. My breath comes in shallow little gasps. Still, every few steps, relief grips me by the neck, shakes me. And I laugh out loud.

Bouts of panic and relief. This is motherhood. I slip back into it like an old jacket—a straitjacket—its bindings as brutal as they ever were. No wonder my own mother had fucked it up so royally, and yet, somehow, no worse than I had. Was there any mother anywhere who really believed she'd gotten it all right? Who didn't want at least one do-over?

The thought of it—my second chance—nearly overwhelms me. My eyes well until the aisles go blurry, but I don't stop.

At the front of the store, Dakota's pace slows a bit. I match mine to hers, holding back near the overripe strawberries, big and bursting as babies' hearts. She's looking for someone, I think.

For me.

"Mom . . ." She speaks that holy word. The word that summons me back to her from the edge of the earth. The rest is meaningless.

3

Though I can barely stand, my body knows what to do. I shuffle toward her, spin her around by the shoulder. Already the tears are coming, hot and fast and endless. It's a wonder there are always more.

"Dakota?" The name is a wound to my throat.

And now, with her captive before me, it's my world that's spinning, spinning, spinning. Knocked off its axis and careening toward another galaxy, light years from where I'd started.

Because if I had drawn this face, I would have scratched through it with heavy strokes and crumpled it into a ball and tossed it into the trash and said to myself: *Wrong.*

Pouty little upturned lips—where my Dakota had the mouth of a poet, serious and wistful. Sleepy gray eyes—where my Dakota's were bright and clear and moss colored. My Dakota had a strong chin, teeth made straight with braces. An elegant nose she would've grown into. Not the bulbous button flaring its nostrils at me.

All wrong.

But the tattoo? The tattoo!

The girl cries out as I claw at her right shoulder, searching. My nails leave tracks on her skin, otherwise unmarked.

There is no tattoo.

Half words stutter out of me, halting and crippled. Small peg-legged men that can't quite stand on their own. And this girl—this wrong girl—stares at me, with a gaping hole of a mouth I want to shut with my fist.

I turn tail, pushing past the wide-hipped woman who must be her mother. Through the doors that sense my coming and part for me, giving me a generous berth.

Later, a pimple-faced stock boy will sort through my abandoned cart, reshelving its contents, wondering about the crazy lady who left it there. But for now, it's stranded behind me, a symbol of the ordinary life I once claimed as my own. The life I took for granted.

Outside, in the parking lot, I blink against the violent brightness of the sun. It stuns me, and I wobble there, slow and confused, like a creature emerged after too long a sleep. My shoulders, heavy; my spine, a wet noodle. I collapse under the weight of the cold, hard facts. Of what I've known all along. Of the truth that prowls the dark cave of my mind, its teeth razor sharp and always at my neck.

That girl is not my Dakota.

That girl is not my daughter.

My daughter is dead.

CHAPTER TWO

I drive through Napa in a half-dazed stupor, the way a drunk man would flee the scene of an accident. White-knuckling the wheel, tapping the brake pedal, trying to hold it steady. To keep it between the lines now.

My eyes dart to the rearview mirror. As if not-Dakota might follow me. But behind my cranky old Jeep—the one I'd refused to part with even after Cole bought me the Range Rover—there's only blacktop and the purpling twilight. Two shades of the same nasty bruise. I grip the wheel tighter to stop my hands from shaking.

Dead.

I let myself think that word, and now it's all I can think. Even with Iron Maiden blasting on the radio. One of my schizophrenic patients had told me heavy metal drowns the voices best. But not this voice—my own.

Not this word.

Dead.

But not just dead. Four weeks dead by the time they'd found her scattered in the woods by Lake Berryessa. By then, my girl was all parts: one fractured humerus, half a rib cage, a pelvic bone, one femur, three phalanges, and an intact mandible with teeth perfected by orthodontia.

Cole had been the one to call the dentist, to get the records, to go to the station. He'd been the one to bear witness to the remains of our daughter. Then, I'd simply felt grateful one of us could stand upright, could speak without sobbing. But after, it became another regret on a long list of them. Maybe if I'd laid my eyes on her bones, I'd stop seeing her. I'd stop imagining they'd gotten it wrong. Stop hoping for a miracle.

Don't ever hope. Hope is an empty box wrapped in shiny paper. It's a gift from the devil himself. I should know.

I turn down Highway 29 and fall in line behind a row of brake lights, inching along in the Monday evening traffic that's part daily commuters, part tourists here for the annual grape harvest. I'd planned on stopping off at home before group to let Gus out and drop off the groceries, but that's moot now, and I'd only spend the time holed up in the mausoleum of Dakota's room sniffing her pillows, sucking up every lingering trace of her.

So I take the long way, past Napa State Hospital with its blank-canvas buildings and sterile offices, one of which I used to call my own. Along with a full caseload of criminal crazies who I'd abandoned just like that shopping cart. Because when they find your daughter murdered, you turn into someone else. Your heart bloats, decays, liquefies, right along with your PhD and your doctorate-level compassion. You say things like *fuck you, you sick pervert* to the people you're supposed to be helping. And then, they seize your employee ID and walk you off grounds like a pariah. Which you are now.

Dr. Mollie Roark: a childless, divorced pariah.

Fittingly, Bruce Dickinson lets out a primal shriek—arguably, the best scream in heavy metal—as I pull into the parking lot at Napa Valley College where I facilitate the Grieving Parents group every Monday. I certainly didn't volunteer for the gig. I could barely stomach the hour-long pity parties myself. I'd been nominated by my fellow sad sacks and basket cases as the obvious choice when our fearless leader, Sandy Hooper, took a counseling job in Hawaii. Apparently, grief is better with hula skirts and mai tais. That makes me Lead Basket Case now. The one who tells the other basket cases when to speak and when to shut up and when it's time to go home. They don't even pay me to do it.

With twenty minutes to spare before the masochism commences, I close my eyes and crank up the volume. Bruce is wailing now about his warped mind and the fire and the way it's hard to tell sometimes whether life is real or just a bad, bad dream.

The phone buzzes on the passenger seat. I already know it's Cole. He always calls on Mondays, and I always let it go to voicemail. Where he clears his throat and uses his doctor's voice, the one that means he's delivering bad news, and spouts some variation of I feel sorry for you. *Just checking on you, Mol. Hope you're alright, Mol. Call if you need anything, Mol.* But I'm sure he doesn't mean it. That his weekly check-ins are only a salve for his guilt. So I never answer.

I can't let him off that easy, though. Not today. I kill the radio and slide my finger across the screen.

"Hi, Cole."

Five seconds pass. Five sweet seconds I savor, picturing him open-mouthed in his white coat and wire-rimmed glasses. "You—uh—you answered."

I allow myself a smile. Maybe he's not incapable of shock after all. Even if I had called him the Tin Man on more than one occasion. "I did. Now what?"

His laugh is unexpected too. The laugh of someone I don't know anymore. Maybe that's what happened to our marriage. We both turned into different people.

"Well, I'm not exactly sure. But I think this is the part where we make awkward conversation. You know, you tell me how you're doing, how the dog's doing, and I—"

"Did you forget? Did you actually *forget* what today is? You're unbelievable."

I wield my voice like an axe sunk deep into his chest. I doubt he feels it. He's all ice. Which I suppose I should've figured from our first date at Bistro Jeanty when he'd told me he'd just finished his residency in pediatric oncology. At the time, I'd oohed and aahed and branded him a saint when I really should've been asking *who chooses a job like that?* A job with a body count. Someone with an essential piece missing. Obviously.

"God, Mol. Of course, I remember. I just don't feel the need to relive it every goddamned second of the day. What good does it do? We can't fix it. She's gone. She's not coming back. And I'm not sure we'll ever have any answers."

I imagine him dismissing our daughter from eight hundred miles away, and my chest tightens. Cole thinks I need to move on. He'd actually had the audacity to tell me that before he'd packed a U-Haul with his cancer books and his dad's stethoscope and his overpriced golf clubs and driven to Seattle to start a brand-new life. Like a real Doctor McDreamy. I sharpen my teeth on the memory.

"You act like our daughter never existed. Like our family was nothing more than a speed bump on your way to claiming your precious chief oncologist gig."

In the long pause, I hear all the things he doesn't say. All the things he's already said. The things I've said too. Nails we've both hammered into our marital coffin. None worse than the spike I'd driven ten days after Dakota went missing: *Did you have something to do with this?* He'd fired back with a vicious nail of his own: *You sound just like your father.*

"Is that really how little you think of me?" He sounds tired. Of me. Of this. "Never mind. I already know the answer. Just remember I'm not the one who gave up."

"Gave up?" The words are on fire, and my throat burns. This is why I still need Cole, why he still needs me. He makes me angry enough to feel alive. And my anger deems him worthy of martyrdom. "You've got some nerve saying that after what you did. Besides, I badger Detective Sharpe at least once a week. I pay for the billboard. I'm *here*. And what the hell do you do? You try to save other people's kids."

"Yeah, I get it. *Saint Mollie.* But if you really want to play this game, don't forget it's my alimony check that pays for the billboard. Along with the mortgage for that mansion you live in."

I say exactly nothing. Because the sound of it is better than *you're right.* Cole must really feel sorry for me because he doesn't even rub it in. When he speaks again, his voice is soft like a lover's.

"I meant you gave up on us. On your job. On life. On everything. You're stuck. You're stuck back there. And Dakota wouldn't like it any more than I do."

I catch my own eyes in the rearview. There's a rare flash of brightness there, even if it is a lit fuse. "Fuck you. You don't get to say that. You don't get to claim her anymore."

"Neither of us do. She's dead, Mol. But you won't let her go. You're obsessed. She's all that's left of you. And that's sad."

I hang up fast, feeling outed. Publicly flogged. A stoning in the middle of the town square. I think of smug Cole, throwing his rocks at me from behind the safety of his desk at Seattle Children's. So far away her ghost can't reach him anymore. He doesn't drive to Napa Prep forgetting Dakota won't be there. Or pass the billboard on I-80, the one with the Crime Stoppers phone number and the garish headline: *Do you know who killed me?* He doesn't see her loser ex-boyfriend's mother duck out of the post office to avoid an awkward conversation. Or pause at her room every night, certain he hears her giggling behind the door.

The famed Karl Menninger, a shrink himself, had said it best. A free fish can't hope to understand a hooked one. And while I'm flapping around with a nasty barb in my gullet, Cole is swimming the blue waters of Lake Washington.

"Give up, my ass." I tell it to the radio, in the middle of my new theme song—"The Unforgiven"—because surely Metallica would understand. "If anybody catches the bastard, it's gonna be me."

****

I jolt awake, eyes flying to the window. Luciana's there knocking, her blood-red lips smiling down through the curtain of her shiny black hair. She laughs at me. For an agonizing moment I'm convinced I dozed right through group. The Lead Basket Case caught sleeping on the job. That happens to me now. I sleep everywhere but in my bed. Everywhere I'm not supposed to. I'd stopped taking the trazodone a year ago, stockpiling the white bottles under the sink. Because when my head hits the pillow, body exhausted, my demented little brain punches its timeclock on the workday that always starts the same: *Who killed my daughter?* I need to be sharp for that.

Luciana raps again on the window. "Wake up, chica sueño. Five minutes till roll call."

I groan at her and shake my head, still buzzing with the sting of Cole's judgment and the ominous chords of Kirk Hammett's guitar solo. There is no roll call, of course. Only a pathetic round-robin game of tell us your name and the sob story of why you're here.

She leans forward to peer at me, sticking out her tongue, and her oversized bag slips from her shoulder and spills onto the pavement. "¡Mierda!"

Serves her right. As she chases down a rogue tarot card that's caught the wind, I crack the door and reach down to gather her hair brush and grocery list that fell on the pavement near my feet. Apparently, Luciana has the same low-budget, high-carb taste in food as I do now. She stuffs it all back into her bag, haphazardly, and tugs at the zipper until she gives up. Curses again. Shrugs. And we both laugh.

"Did anyone else see me sleeping?"

I step out into the warm night, shedding my thin sweater as we walk. It's as warm today as the day they found Dakota. Heat does unspeakable things to dead bodies. And in Napa, September has a way of clinging to summer, of digging its claws in.

"If by anybody, you mean Sawyer, then no. He's not here yet." She gestures over her shoulder to the parking lot, empty, save for my Jeep and Boludo, her beat-up Honda Civic with its duct-taped side mirror and *Trust Me, I'm a Psychic* bumper sticker. Its nickname inspired by the ex she'd stolen it from. "But he will be. And it's a good thing, too. You've had a rough day."

"Are you reading group members again, Madame Luci?"

She wiggles her fingers at me like she's casting a spell with those long black nails, that skeleton bride tattoo on her ring finger. "No need, mi querida. The circles under your eyes speak to me as clearly as tea leaves. I passed Sawyer and his pickup truck at the gas station around the corner looking muy guapo as usual. Besides, I don't serve the dark side, so I'd never read you without your permission. You know that."

The steady *twack* of heels on concrete builds to a crescendo behind us, and we both turn our heads.

"*Her* on the other hand . . . *sangrón.*" Luciana grinds out the word—her typical insult—from between her clenched teeth as Jane Wiederman strides past, clad in her standard snob's uniform. Pencil skirt by Theory. Heels by Manolo. Bag by Louis Vuitton. I wait for her artsy husband to follow in her wake, nervously tugging on his goatee, but tonight she's alone.

Watch this, Luciana mouths to me. A phrase I recognize as the preamble to trouble. "Hey Jane, where's Scott this evening?"

Jane turns to us, tight-faced, and I wave at her, offering an apologetic smile. Because once upon a time, I'd been more like Jane than I care to admit. My own Louie retired to the back of my closet, along with the tailored slacks and the pointy red-soled shoes that now seem nothing more than an elaborate costume. The Range Rover sold off for a bargain-basement price on Craigslist.

"He couldn't make it," Jane says, her voice more clipped than usual. "He's photographing a gala at the Ford Coppola Winery."

"¡Qué sofisticado! And he didn't invite you?"

Tears fill Jane's eyes, and she spins away, her ponytail whipping behind her like a horse's mane. "It's a work function, Luci," she says to the bathroom door before ducking inside.

Luciana raises her penciled eyebrows at me, ignoring my disapproving frown. "Mentirosa. Liar. They're done. It's just her and King Louie now. You wait and see."

"Luci . . ."

"Yes, mi querida?"

"That wasn't very nice."

She shrugs. "Lucky for me, *nice* is for white girls. Jane should try it."

I don't argue. Because she's not wrong about Jane. Last December, she'd earned the distinction of Luciana's mortal enemy when she'd asked why a psychic couldn't predict that her own loser boyfriend would shake her little girl so hard, she'd lapse into a coma and never wake up.

I was crazy high on meth back then, Luciana had confessed to me later. *My spirit guides were all out to lunch. Muy loca.*

All I could think: *Where were my spirit guides? What's my excuse?*

Luciana walks on ahead without me into the student break room, the site of our planned commiseration. I spot her through the small window, feeding change into the temperamental vending machine. On a bad day, it steals your quarters and dangles your M&Ms in a pinch grip until you kick it into submission. On a rare good day, you feast on two of your chosen delicacy.

A hollow whack from Luciana's foot tells me what I already know. Today is decidedly bad. I wonder if it's too late to bolt, if anybody will notice if I cut and run.

I glance over my shoulder at the door where the exit sign beckons from above. When Sawyer pulls it open, I spot the sliver of night sky behind him, feel the rush of open air. It's a vortex. I can barely keep my feet planted to the floor. This happens to me now too. A desperate need to take flight.

"Plotting your escape?" Sawyer asks. His work boots leave dusty prints down the hallway like a marked trail for me to follow. And his easy swagger says he'd come with me if I asked him to.

"How'd you know?"

"You've got that look."

"And what look is that?" I ask, avoiding his eyes. He's beside me now, smelling of freshly mowed grass and sweat. His usual cologne during tourist season since he never has time to shower after finishing up work as the groundskeeper at the Blue Rose B&B on the other side of town. It's the sort of rugged, earthy smell that makes no apologies, and I don't mind it. Mainly because it's nothing like whiney Cole's antiseptic soap.

"The scared shitless look of a boot about to drop into a combat zone."

A dissonant laugh clunks from my throat like a single note played on a poorly tuned piano. "You're right. It's a support group. It's not like I'm parachuting into a war zone crawling with Taliban."

Sawyer's face is unexpectedly grim as he points to the break room. "Have you met Jane? Luci? Bin Laden's got nothing on them. I stashed a spare flak jacket in my truck if you need to borrow it."

He's joking. But I feel my knees buckle anyway. I should've known this would happen. Should've seen this day looming weeks ago and canceled tonight's group. I should've called in sick, invoked the phone tree. Or had Luciana fill in for me. I should've driven straight home after I'd practically assaulted not-Dakota in the grocery checkout line and spent the night bingeing on peanut butter from the jar.

Sawyer nudges me with his elbow, and I flinch. "Hey, I was just teasing. Say the word, and I'll pull the fire alarm. We'll blow this popsicle stand."

I ponder the small, red rectangle on the wall, my heart pounding like a fist in my chest. Surely, this counts as a fire. I imagine how relieved I'd feel to get back in my car and drive away from this place where I can't escape who I've become. Where I have to speak it out loud and pretend that I'm okay.

"Is this where the Grieving Parents group meets?" The woman addresses me like I'm in charge. Like I know what the hell I'm doing. Like I'm the Lead Basket Case.

I nod at her. "Right in there. We'll be starting soon."

Sawyer holds the door as I follow her inside.

****

Luciana pops a blue M&M into her mouth, crushing its fragile shell with her teeth. That murderous crunching is all I can hear even as I talk over it.

"Since we have a few new members tonight, I'd like to do introductions and revisit the two group rules. They're fairly simple but very important for the success of the group. First, this is a confidential environment. That means what gets said in this room stays in this room. No exceptions. Second, we treat one another with respect."

Jane eyes Luciana. And Luciana eyes her right back, making another well-timed sacrifice. Yellow, this time. Down the hatch.

"A few months ago, the other members asked me to keep the group running smoothly until we find a new facilitator. I'm trained as a psychologist, but I'm here mainly as a participant. My daughter, Dakota, was murdered just a short while after her fifteenth birthday. Her body was so badly damaged the police couldn't tell exactly when she died or how. As of today, the investigation is ongoing."

There. The hard part is over. Somehow, I'd coasted through on autopilot and made it look easy. A credit to my Napa State Hospital days. Because even Luci and Jane can't compete with the ten murderous psychotics who'd semicircle around me every Monday, Wednesday, and Friday at Napa State Hospital, my state-issued alarm clipped to my waist. If I could handle those overmedicated bodies slumped in their chairs with their poor insight and their bad hygiene and their occasional need to whip it out and jack off right there in front of me, this should be a cake walk.

I smile as if I didn't just splay my chest wide open and let these strangers have a look inside. Then I gesture to Sawyer sitting at my right.

"Grant Sawyer. But everybody calls me Sawyer—or *One-Armed Jack.* Cyborg works too." He chuckles as he pulls up his left shirt sleeve, exposing the sleek metal of his prosthetic. But his grin falters, flattens. "My son . . . his name was Noah. He drowned in our pool back in 2010. I was supposed to be watching him. I come to this group because losing Noah is a million times worse than any war wound. And the only people who get that are sitting in this room. You've all been downrange with me, right there in the foxhole."

I start to do it then, as unfair as it is. The ploy I'd never let my Napa patients get away with. I call it the comparison game, and it goes like this: At least Sawyer *knows* what happened to Noah. At least it wasn't violent.

Jane sits up straight, rigid in her seat, holding King Louie on her lap. It's her turn.

"My name is Jane Wiederman, and my husband, Scott, and I have been coming to this group for a year now. Scott couldn't . . . he isn't . . . he won't be coming anymore."

She lets out a tearful gasp, and Luciana winks at me. I shake my head at her, Jane's tears a solid confirmation of what I've known for a while now. No marriage can survive this. Not Sawyer's. Not Jane's. Not even mine. This is a tsunami. And marriages, even the best of them, fall like houses of straw in its wrath.

"We separated last week. He blames me. Oh God. Of course, he does. It was my fault. I-I-I . . ." The rest of it is stuck in her throat, like a toy caught in a baby's windpipe, and her face reddens with the effort of expelling it.

"She forgot their kid in a hot car," Luciana finishes for her. "It was supposed to be Scott's turn to take her to day care, but he had an early morning photo shoot. Right, Jane? *Pobrecita.*"

"Luci, let Jane tell her own story. As much or as little as she wants to."

Two green M&Ms and a roll of the eyes, and we're back on track. Sawyer was right. This is flat-out psychological warfare. And in my own battlefield, the comparison game rolls on: At least I didn't *forget* my child.

"I hadn't been sleeping well," Jane admits. "I mean, who does with a new baby? And she was so quiet. So quiet. I was supposed to turn right at Cambridge and drop her off at daycare. But I didn't. I turned left and went to work instead. One wrong turn. That's why I'm here."

In the pin-drop quiet that follows, I gesture to the first newbie, a dark-skinned woman with red-rimmed eyes. "Hi. I'm Debbie Baines, and it's my first time here. Malcolm . . . he was my boy. A good boy. Not into drugs or gangs or any of that shit. He played football for a J.C. in San Francisco. A couple NFL scouts even went up there to check him out. He had real big dreams. Anyway, three months ago, he and his friend got shot outside of a nightclub in the Tenderloin. I told him so many times not to be hanging out with that kid. He was bad news. And you know what happened? Jalen ended up with a flesh wound. My Malcolm took a bullet to the head. Last week, they arrested some gangbanger. A case of mistaken identity."

Debbie finally pauses, releases a shaky breath. "I didn't expect to say all that. It's not the kind of thing you can tell most people without scaring them away."

"Well, we're glad to have you here," I say as Luciana squeezes her hand. I think: *At least she knows who. She can stop searching. At least she has a face. A real name. Not a stupid moniker.*

The man next to Debbie looks up, slightly stunned, as if he's surprised to find himself here in this room full of basket cases and sad sacks. He brushes his hair back, fiddles with a silver thumb ring, and rubs a patch of waxy skin that stretches from his hand to his elbow. A burn, I assume. He catches me looking and tugs at the arm of his long-sleeve Star Wars T-shirt.

"Boyd Blackburn," he says, with a bitter laugh. As if he's knows I'm pondering the irony of his name. "Do I have to talk about myself?"

"Not if you don't want to," Jane tells him, still sniffling. "I didn't say anything at first. Scott did all the talking."

"Alright, then. Maybe next time. I do have a question though."

The room waits in silence, and Sawyer shifts in his seat, his knee nearly knocking into mine. *I don't trust quiet*, he'd told the group a while back. *It usually ends with a big fucking boom.*

"Fire away, buddy," he says. "You're makin' me nervous."

"Oh. Sorry. I was wondering if it's against the rules if I know . . . if I *knew* . . . one of your children. Would that be a problem?"

Sawyer is right. Boyd's question detonates through the room with the force of an IED, leaving everyone staggering, slack-jawed, and speechless. Everyone but me. The woman who'd once broken up a fistfight between two men at Napa State, each of whom had been convinced he and he alone was Jesus.

"It shouldn't be," I say. "This is an informal support group, so we don't have any rules about knowing each other or spending time together outside of this space the way a more formal therapy group might."

And thank God for that. Because in forty minutes I fully intend to shove my tongue down Sawyer's throat. Again. If he'll let me. At least the day won't be a complete loss.

"With that said, it might be easier to answer if you could be more specific. Who is it that you knew, Boyd?"

"I knew her. Dakota. I knew your daughter."

Sawyer had said he remembered every bit of the explosion that took his arm. The eerie calm before the blast blew all the windows out of the Humvee and ejected him onto the road where he laid in shock, unable to look away from the shard of smooth, white bone protruding from the spot where his elbow used to be. For a solid eight hours after, he'd heard nothing but silence.

That's how it is for me. I see Luciana's mouth move—¡*Ay, Dios mío!* Watch Sawyer's feet shift toward me. Eventually, he touches my arm.

I speak too. Murmur some exclamation of surprise. But all I can hear is the staticky *whoosh* of panic beneath the throbbing beat of my own dark heart.

CHAPTER THREE

THE parking lot is deserted. "Crazy Train" is blaring on my radio. And I'm slouched in the back seat of the Jeep, taking a hit of Sawyer's medical marijuana, my blouse disheveled from round one of our post-group make-out sesh. This isn't a midlife crisis. It's a no-holds-barred breakdown. The sort of thing that happens when your reservoir of healthy coping skills goes bone dry.

"Are you sure you don't want to talk about it?" Sawyer asks, running a hand through his scruffy hair. He keeps it a little long because he can. No more army regulation haircuts. Or as he had put it: *I answer to myself now.* The same reason I stay in my sweatpants most days and eat all my meals from the processed food group.

"What is there to say? He knew Dakota. His sister took AP English with her freshman year. It's no biggie."

Sawyer cocks his head at me. Apparently, I'm not a convincing liar when I'm stoned.

"You freaked out in there, Mollie. You went blank for about thirty seconds, and then you just acted like nothing happened. Business as usual. I'm no psychologist, but I'm sure as hell an expert on PTSD. And that was dissociation."

I laugh, and I hate how it sounds. Petulant and pathetic rolled into one. And high. That too. "My whole life is an exercise in dissociation. How do you think I get through this damn group every week?"

"Ouch." He stiffens and looks away from me. His discarded prosthetic rests on the floorboard. It turns out you don't need two arms to fool around.

"You know what I mean."

"Why'd you agree to do it if you hate it so much? I'm sure Sandy could've found someone else." When the answer doesn't come to me right away—*did weed get stronger since the nineties?*—he levels another blow. "Why do you come here at all?"

"Why do you?"

He sighs, and I feel guilty. I'd never let a patient get away with that. Answering a question with a question. A total cop-out.

"Because it helps. And because my ex-wife voluntold me to. Also, I've got a crush on this gal, misguided though it may be, and she refuses to see me outside of the confines of this parking lot."

"That sucks." I sling one leg over his lap and kiss his neck. His blond stubble prickles under my lips in a good way. I rub my cheek against it.

"Yeah. But you know what I learned in the Rangers . . ."

"Embrace the suck," I repeat Sawyer's motto.

He pulls me closer, flush against him. "Roger that," he whispers.

****

This is an all-time low. That's my first thought when the cop car pulls up alongside us, its lights casting a strange blue glow on Sawyer's bare chest. My second thought: *Where's my top?*

21

Sawyer swears under his breath and tosses me his Blue Rose work shirt. I slide my arms inside and do up a few crucial buttons as the officer raps on the back window. The *shush* of the opening window is the official anthem of my shame.

"Good evening, folks. Officer McGinnis, Napa PD." As if sitting in the back seat of a car, half-dressed, is a perfectly respectable way for two forty-somethings to spend a Monday night. "You mind turning down the radio and stepping out of the vehicle?"

I do mind, but I'm fairly certain a polite *no, thank you* is not an option, so I slide out, bare feet to the pavement with Sawyer behind me. I instantly register the barking dog in the back of his cruiser. I have a sinking feeling I'm about to set the bar of my all-time low even lower.

"Whose vehicle is this?"

I raise my hand, head hung.

"You two been smoking tonight?"

"No." As soon as it's out there—my blatant lie—I flash to my first year at Napa State Hospital when I'd caught a patient drinking pruno in the laundry room. The odor of alcohol had wafted from him even as he'd shaken his head and insisted I was wrong. But I understand it now. That childish knee-jerk reaction. I guess a man with a badge turns us all into three-year-olds.

"Look ma'am, this can go one of two ways. You can be honest with me, and I'll do my best to work with you. Or you can keep right on lying. I smelled marijuana as soon as you opened the window. My dog will find it whether or not you fess up."

"Officer, I'm not—"

Sawyer stops me with a touch and gently moves me aside. "It's mine. I was the one smoking. I have a prescription."

Why does he have to do that? The gallant hero thing. The *shirtless* gallant hero with the body of an Army Ranger. Which he is. *Was.*

"That's not exactly true," I say. "I smoked too. I've had a bit of a rough night."

Officer McGinnis nods, pleased with the results of his interrogation. A full confession. "Alright. See. That wasn't so hard, was it? Now, let me get your IDs."

He shines his flashlight on the front seat while I paw through my cheap bag—Louie's antithesis—and produce my driver's license. Before I hand it over, I glance at the photo. It's me but not me. It's the old me. The me who had a husband and a daughter and a plan.

"Mollie Roark." Officer McGinnis reads my name aloud and frowns. "Doctor Mollie Roark?"

"Yes, sir."

"The Mollie Roark who lost her little girl a couple years back?"

I feel like I might be sick. "That's me. We were here tonight for a support group. Grieving Parents."

He returns the license to me, and I tuck it in my pocket. I don't want to look at *her*. "You probably don't remember, but I was there that day. We canvassed that whole road, that whole neighborhood. I thought for sure we'd find her alive. What a goddamned shame. Are they still thinking she's one of the Shadow Man's?"

What can I say? Certainly not what I want to. Dakota is not a number. She's not just one of the gang. A notch on the bedpost of a serial killer. She's my daughter. "That's the working theory."

"Listen, I'm real sorry about your loss. I hope we finally catch that SOB. It's been way too long. His time is up." Officer McGinnis waves Sawyer back to his pickup and turns to me, reaching into his pocket. "Take my card. If you ever need anything, give me a ring."

"So we're free to go?" I ask.

"If that happened to my kid, I'd be doing a helluva lot worse than weed and heavy metal. Just get home safe—and consider this a warning."

I wait until he's gone to tug on my flats, retrieve my crumpled blouse from the back seat, and head to Sawyer's truck, his work shirt and metal arm in tow. He chuckles when he sees me. "I've got to *hand* it to you, Mollie, you sure are *handy* in a sticky situation. Without you, I'm half a man . . . well, three quarters I guess."

I give him a playful shove. "Thanks for trying to take the rap." He grabs my wrist and tugs me toward him.

"Thanks for not letting me." His voice is light and teasing, his hard kiss anything but. "Maybe next week we can grab dinner before we get arrested."

My skin buzzes with an inexplicable jolt of panic that sobers me up. He must sense it, because he doesn't wait for my protest or my lame excuses. "Alright then. At least let me pick the music."

****

My lips still taste like the minty smoke of Sawyer as his taillights linger at the exit. I wave him on, suddenly eager to be completely alone. To make the lonesome trek across the parking lot back to the Jeep. To remind myself I don't need rescuing.

It's almost peaceful the way the asphalt shimmers in the glow of the lampposts. The distant hum of traffic reminds me of a mother cooing to her child. *Probably the weed*, I tell myself. Even though I know it's Sawyer. Somehow, he unloosens the knot inside of me, the one that's been twisting and tangling and snarling since long before I lost Dakota. Cole had only made it tighter with his perfect hair and his God complex and his mountainous expectations. And that's why I'd married him. To prove something to somebody. Maybe my mom, though she'd been dead ten years by then. Or my dad, though he'd hardly cared, mailing the invitation back to me. Return to sender.

I sidestep a puddle of oil pooling in the spot where Luciana had parked Boludo hours ago. She's going to be *muy furiosa* since she paid a pretty penny to overhaul the transmission last month. I touch a finger to the spot, and it comes back sticky black. Another bad sign.

Then I see it beneath the Jeep. Even from here, I know exactly what it is, and I shiver. One of Luciana's tarot cards from the deck she keeps stashed in her purse just in case. Because there's a sucker born every minute. Or as she says, *a la ocasión la pintan calva*.

24

I walk to it, dread curdling in my stomach like sour milk. It lies faceup just inside of my front tire. A pale horse with a skeleton rider wielding a sickle, the word DEATH printed black as the oil on my fingers. I can't bring myself to pick it up, to claim it. So I snap a photo of it instead and fire off two back-to-back texts to Luciana.

You know I don't believe in this crap, but you lost one of your cards. Should I be worried?

BTW Boludo has sprung a leak.

I leave DEATH where I found him. But I look both ways once and then again before I merge into traffic, the bloodshot eyes of the cars in front of me glowing as they lead the way.

****

I'm nearly home when I realize. *Gus.* I totally forgot about him.

Shit. Literally. *Shit.*

Eyes already tearing, I speed down the dirt road. My wheels spitting gravel as I make a hard turn into the driveway. Of everything that's happened today, this is the worst. Because it's indisputable proof. I am a bad mother. Hell, I'm not even a mother anymore. I lost my child. *How can somebody lose a person?* But not just any person. The most precious one.

And now, I forget my dog. *Her dog*, really.

Dakota had begged for years until Cole finally relented on her twelfth birthday. We'd spent the entire day at the pound, because picking a dog is a lot like adopting a baby or buying a purse. That's how Dakota had put it.

This one, she'd announced, pointing to a yellow Lab making sad faces at her from the front of his cage. She'd christened him Gus while Cole and I'd exchanged a private *whoop* of relief that she'd finally made her selection. *He looks like a Gus, doesn't he?*

And he did. With his warm eyes and his easy canine grin. His tail that seemed to never stop wagging.

I hear him whining through the door, and I hurry to fit the keys in the lock. I'm already crying.

His head is lowered, half shamed, half confused, his urine puddled near the door. "I'm so sorry," I tell him. "It's okay. Go on out."

Permission granted, he darts straight past me and into the yard. I swear I can feel her there with us, chiding me, telling Gus he's a good boy. That he'd held it as long as he could.

My tears pick up steam, but I manage to soak up the puddle with a handful of paper towels from the kitchen before I slide to the floor, sobbing. Gus is back there in an instant, nudging me and licking my face, my gross neglect instantly forgiven.

An excellent choice, the woman at the shelter had told Dakota. *Labs make great first dogs.*

The first in our pack, Dakota had said, grinning at us mischievously. What would she say now if she knew I'd nearly given him away a hundred times, a surrender by owner? That I'd blamed him, reviled him. Barely tolerated the sight of his lolling tongue and his smooth white belly. I'm embarrassed to admit I'd even thought of dropping him on the side of the road. Because Gus didn't save her. He didn't save our girl.

"I forgive you too," I tell him, rubbing the sweet spot behind his ears. He leans in as if to say, *it's about damn time.*

****

Three hours later, my brain is back on the job, and I'm staring up at the ceiling, Gus in the bed and curled at my feet for the first time in two years.

I reread the texts from Madame Luci—they'd come in rapid succession, seconds apart—as we wait for the clock to show midnight. For this cursed day to be over.

¿Muerte? He's not as bad as he looks. He's a man of transformation sent to tell you a part of you must die so another part can live.

Besides, don't you think you're due for a change?
I thought you didn't believe in this crap anyway.
Damn Boludo.

I imagine DEATH standing over me with his sickle glinting in the moonlight. Lopping off the festering parts of me—all the bad memories—with one clean slice.

This is where I'd start:

I'd been in the cereal aisle when I'd gotten the call from Cole. Because even when your kid goes missing, you can't just lie down and die like you want to. You have to buy milk and bread and laundry detergent.

Come home, Mol. Already I'd knew. I knew they'd found her. I knew it was bad. Probably, I'd already known in some deep-down part of me. In that underbelly of the brain where unspeakable truths spring up like poison weeds. But the whole drive back, I'd clung to that shiny box of hope anyway, cradled it on my lap eager as a kid at Christmas. Until Detective Sharpe ripped off the lid with four words, each innocent in their own right. *We found a body.*

At 12:01 a.m. I release a shaky breath. I made it. It's already tomorrow. It's already *not* the anniversary of the day they found my daughter.

CHAPTER FOUR

(TUESDAY, SEPTEMBER 25, 2018)

AT 12:02 a.m. I swing my feet off the bed, determined. My brain has its own agenda, and it's useless to resist. So I traipse down the hallway to Dakota's room, Gus at my heels.

I pause at her closed door, studying the PRIVATE: KEEP OUT sign she'd decorated with glittery pink skulls. *That's my Dakota.* Skulls and glitter.

The knob feels ice cold in my palm. But the oak slab behind it seems to throb with warmth. With life.

Once, before he'd swam for open waters, Cole had caught me knocking on it. My face burned when he'd regarded me with the same wide and wary eyes that he usually saved for stories about my Napa patients. *Total nutjobs*, he'd pronounced them. And maybe

I was a nut job too. Because I'd half-expected the door to open, for Dakota to answer.

Gus nudges his wet nose against my leg, and I startle, opening the door before I lose my nerve. I wait for the obnoxious click of cheap plastic: The Mardi Gras beads from Dakota's New Orleans–themed freshman dance she'd slung on the coat hook and forgotten about. Those beads are a relic of my real daughter. The girl with the friends and the grades and the swim team and the dream of being a writer. *An investigative journalist, Mom. Like Lisa Ling.* Not the smartass rebel she'd turned into that summer she'd gone missing.

I enter the darkness, welcome it. Let it envelop me. I feel at home among the shadows. I'd live under their cover if I could.

A thin blade of moonlight cuts through an opening in the curtains, spotlighting the photo on Dakota's nightstand, and I'm drawn to it the way I always am. The three of us at the Petrified Forest, perched on the trunk of a giant Redwood turned to stone by a volcano long ago. Thirteen-year-old Dakota sits between Cole and me, leaning her head slightly toward my shoulder. Cole's arm is wrapped around us two. And I look unabashedly, stupidly happy.

I pity myself in that photograph. Because I've got no clue what's coming. I'm a deer in the forest, frolicking, even as an unknown stranger sights me with a rifle, godlike. Just the way my father and I had done at Putah Creek when I was a girl. *Wait until he's broadside,* Dad had said, coaching me through my first kill. A six-pointer. *Then aim for the shoulder and take your shot. Steady. Steady now.*

I don't touch the picture's sterling silver frame. Or imagine Dakota unwrapping it on her birthday, the photo already carefully inserted. I don't linger, gazing at it with longing. Because I could sit—*I have*—for hours with the irony. Our family, frozen, preserved just like the fossils around us. The victims of a massive eruption. A cataclysm.

Instead, I turn away from the photograph toward Dakota's Great Wall of Books, a massive shelf stacked from floor to ceiling.

I crouch down to the third row and run my hand along the well-worn spines of her favorites. *Harry Potter* and *Hunger Games*. *Pride and Prejudice* and *Catcher in the Rye*. Down, down, down I go, to the end, where the covers are as black as the night sky.

The third shelf is also a timeline. A timeline with a hard stop at the end. A bright blue Post-it, folded and pressed between pages fourteen and fifteen, marks the very last words Dakota had ever read in Thomas Harris's *Silence of the Lambs*. Cole hadn't approved, but what the hell did he know? By Dakota's age, I'd already read *Lolita*, the beat-up paperback copy I'd smuggled out of the Allendale Public Library while my father had waited in the truck. Dad didn't believe in things like library cards. *Don't want nobody from the government knowin' our business*, he'd said. Which was just as well because that meant I could keep it.

Dakota's last book beckons to me, and I answer its call, tugging it free, holding it tenderly. I scan the bookmarked page. The start of chapter three, where six-fingered villain Dr. Hannibal Lecter meets noble heroine Clarice Starling. Surely, I'd read that page hundreds of times now, not counting the last time with Detective Sharpe when he'd asked me to show him Dakota's room again. Or the first, when I'd holed up in the UC Berkeley library stacks, devouring it straight through. Or the time in-between, when I'd left the book on Dakota's desk with a note tucked in-between those pages: *Do not read at bedtime.*

Returning Lecter and Clarice to their resting place—a perfectly sized tomb between *Mindhunter* and *The Stranger Beside Me*—I shake my head at the memory. My old clueless self again. Imagining I could protect her from the world. That the only monsters who could get to her were the ones she conjured in her head. Not mere mortals like the men I'd therapized every week.

I find what I came for resting on the bottom shelf. Dakota's freshman yearbook. And I start to hurry, feeling newly energized.

I slide it out, blow a thin layer of dust from its leather cover, and fling it open, flipping through the Bs like a woman possessed.

Cara Banks.

Joey Bates.

Benjamin Beatty.

Michaela Bishop.

Zoey Blackwood.

Graham Broomfield.

My heart quickens. No Blackburns. I knew it. But it's a hollow victory. Because Cole's voice is already in my head, admonishing me. *What does that prove? You're paranoid, Mol. You're delusional.* He's probably not too far off the mark. But paranoia seems completely reasonable to me now. Same for soul-splitting grief. Murderous rage.

Satisfied with my discovery, I tuck the yearbook back in its place and walk toward Dakota's bed, preparing to commence my usual routine. The pillow-sniffing. The picture-ogling. The exact opposite of moving on.

But I stop—I freeze—when I spot Gus snuffing at the floor.

"Leave it," I say, my voice firm. Hard as a slap to his nose. He looks up at me and whines before he backs away reluctantly.

I drop to one knee and examine the business card that's fallen there. WHITETAILS AND WHOPPERS: GUN, BAIT, AND TACKLE SHOP. ALLENDALE, CALIFORNIA. The familiar logo, a rainbow trout with antlers, had always made me laugh.

But now, I stand up fast and stagger back from it. It's been so long since I thought of that place. Longer still since I was seven years old, gazing up at that strange fish and my father, a giant towering beside me.

I poke at the card with my foot like it might bite and take another look. Sure enough. It's what I thought. The idea of Dakota touching it, slipping it inside her yearbook, unnerves me more than scythe-wielding DEATH on his creepy white horse.

I toss it into her desk drawer and slam it shut so quickly Gus bolts. And I'm right behind him.

Breathing hard, I press my back against the wall opposite the doorway. The drawer stays shut, but I know the past is alive inside it.

It's unburied now. And it may as well be a hand clawing up from its shallow grave to seize me by the throat.

CHAPTER FIVE

AS soon as it's light out, I walk down the path to the guesthouse Cole had converted into an office for me. Because after I'd gotten the axe from Napa State, I couldn't do it anymore. *It* being much of anything. Getting dressed. Driving. Sitting in the mind-numbing funeral procession of traffic with nothing to do but think (before I discovered the magic of heavy metal). I didn't tell Cole I couldn't be a therapist either. Not even here. Steps away from my front door. But after the office had been empty for months, he got the idea.

My skin hums with that early morning buzz as I unlock the door and cross the threshold. That chronic-sleep-deprivation-two-shots-of-espresso-empty-stomach high. And it hits me like usual. The smell of paint and new carpet and overpriced furniture. Like the regal leather sofa in the corner that regards me with contempt. It understands why Cole left me. *You didn't even try*, it says.

I make my way to the unfinished room in the back—my real office—empty save for the one unopened box I'd brought from Napa State and the two-thousand-dollar ergonomic chair Cole had insisted on. I'd wheeled it in from the office the day after he'd split. The day after he'd found me here at 2 a.m., muttering to myself like one of my patients.

I can't sleep anyway, I'd said. As if that explained it.

There's not much space left on my wall of suspects, but I find room at the periphery between photos of Tyler—Dakota's jock ex-boyfriend—and Cole. As cruel as it had felt to post it there, to watch Cole's eyes well when he'd sighted it, then harden to ice, I had my reasons. Never mind that the police had ruled us both out. I know better than anyone. The cops get it wrong sometimes. Way wrong.

I tack up the note I'd scrawled early this morning—*Boyd Blackburn, Grieving Parents Group. Says his sister knew Dakota from AP English*—along with the public records report I'd uncovered online, after forking out thirty-five bucks. Turns out Boyd is likely a thirty-two-year-old student at ITT Tech who lives in Cuttings Wharf with a fifty-eight-year-old woman named Martha. His mother, I'm guessing. According to Facebook, he has exactly twenty-three friends—none female, with the exception of the aforementioned Martha—and is employed part-time at Reptiles 'R' Us. Photo evidence indicates he'd attended Comic-Con 2014 dressed in full Stormtrooper regalia. Which makes him awkward and lonely and, therefore, a prime suspect. I never said my methods were logical.

I sigh and plop down into the gel seat that's supposed to keep my butt extra comfy while I ponder which of these assholes killed my daughter. But I can't look away from the Shadow Man. Because most of the wall is taken up with him. Whoever he is.

A few months back, I'd even paid off an administrator at Napa State to find me a copy of the 1989 psychological profile created for the FBI by our former chief psychologist. It told me Shadow Man was a white male between the ages of twenty-five to forty. Possibly former military or police. With unbridled rage toward women that he probably managed to conceal well in his day-to-day life. So, in other words, any number of men. What a waste of five hundred dollars.

With a firm push, my chair rolls across the smooth hardwood and stops with a *thump* against the wall. I reach up and snag the last article, published eight months ago in *The Napa Valley Register*. Eight long months. Cole had been gone for twelve. Life marches on for everyone but me. The caught fish, skinned and mounted, glass eyes affixed in dry sockets. With nowhere to go and nothing to do but read the same speculative bullshit the detectives expected would satisfy me.

The Shadow Man Returns After Twenty Years, Claims Another Victim

In a statement to the media on Friday, the Napa County Sheriff's Department, accompanied by agents from the Federal Bureau of Investigation, confirmed long-standing speculation that the 2016 unsolved murder of fifteen-year-old Dakota Roark is being investigated as the work of the Shadow Man, the prolific serial killer who terrorized the Napa Valley throughout the better part of two decades. Authorities had speculated that the Shadow Man, who has been linked to the murders of sixteen young Caucasian women between 1976 and 1996, was deceased or incarcerated due to his lengthy cooling-off period. Other experts posited he may have changed his patterns, targeting victims like runaways or prostitutes, victims who would not be missed.

Peter Jacoby, Chief Psychologist at Napa State Hospital, which houses the criminally insane, said, "It's unusual to see a cooling-off period of this length, but it's not unheard of. For example, Dennis Rader, known as BTK (Bind, Torture, Kill), committed ten murders during a span of approximately thirty years. Joseph DeAngelo, the Golden State Killer, was arrested more than thirty years after his last known murder. We don't yet fully understand this peculiar phenomenon, and it certainly flies in the face of what we do know about most serial killers. They are often compulsively driven to kill and to kill again."

Investigators cited key similarities between the Shadow Man's early crimes and the Roark murder, including the location of the young girl's body, which was discovered in the same forested area of Lake Berryessa as Susanna Donnelly, the Shadow Man's first known victim. All of Shadow Man's victims disappeared from Napa or Solano Counties, and many of the bodies were recovered in varying states of decay near Lake Berryessa. Autopsy results indicated victims' bodies, including Roark's, had been burned following death. Detectives declined to comment on additional similarities due to the sensitive nature of the ongoing investigation.

I stab the pushpin back through the widening hole at the top of the newspaper clipping—*take that, Dr. Jackass*—and tack it back to the wall. Peter Jacoby had walked me off Napa's grounds himself and sent me on my way with a patronizing *I hope you get the help you need, Mollie*, his sweaty little hand resting on my arm like a warning or an invitation. Because I'd tried everything to feel alive again. Even self-destruction. Screwing Peter in his office or in the staff dormitory where he'd stayed when he was on call. Of course, Cole had other words for it when I'd confessed to him. Most of the four-letter variety. As if he had the right.

I stare at my suspect wall until the ink blurs. Until the whole damn thing is a shadow man. Luciana's voice teases me, mocks me: *Don't you think you're due for a change?*

My face flushes, and I start to sweat. Lungs clamp shut. Brain goes on lockdown. Everything stops but my heart, which scampers on without the rest of me to destinations unknown.

Out. I need out.

I lumber past the disdainful sofa and across the haughty wool rug with its pretentious hand stitching. And finally, through the front door and into the glorious air, which I suck up unapologetically.

I'm still taking it in like a starving child, too fast to savor it, when I hear the growl of a motor up the drive. The separate drive Cole had graveled for me and marked with a fancy sign pronouncing me ROARK PSYCHOLOGY SERVICES. The drive that's never been traveled by me or anyone else. Except maybe a fox or two.

Too weak to move, I sit on the front step and wait for whoever it is to turn around.

But now I'm nose to nose with a brown Cadillac and its old-man driver. Beneath his cowboy hat, his face is more stricken than mine. Gray and swollen, the same as my mother's at the very end. He pushes the door open, and his snakeskin boots meet the ground. A strange thought passes through my head like a cloud over the sun. *He probably skinned that rattler himself.*

"Are you lost?" I ask him, hearing myself from a million miles away. I sound almost normal.

"Don't think so, Doc," he says, leaning against the door to stand. "But I don't feel so good. I haven't driven in a while. Usually, I take that Senior Shuttle."

He staggers toward me, a tired wind-up cowboy. One step, then two. Then one more. He reaches out a shaky hand before he quits entirely, bends over, and upchucks right there on Cole's quarry stones.

I should help the old guy. Make sure he's okay. But I can't stop looking at the hood of the Cadillac. The ornament there. The red-and-yellow crest between two crescent halves of a wreath.

Because when you squint it's not a wreath anymore. It's a sickle.

CHAPTER SIX

THE old man's black Stetson sits on one side of the leather sofa, resting peacefully as a cat. On the other side, the old man himself. He downs a gulp from the cup of water I'd retrieved for him, wiping his mouth on his shirt sleeve. Every time he moves the smell of vomit and chew tobacco wafts my way. I have no doubt the sofa doesn't approve. So I stand in the doorway, just beyond the reach of its judgmental gaze.

"Better?" I ask, hoping he'll get to talking. Get to telling me what the hell he's doing here. And get to leaving. Soon.

He grunts and runs a hand over his liver-spotted head, which gleams under the lamp light like the surface of the moon. With only a wisp of white hair to cover it.

"Are you sure there's no one I can call for you?" He'd already blatantly refused an ambulance. "The Senior Shuttle, maybe?"

He straightens up and pins me in place with his rheumy blue eyes. Underneath that filmy wet is something sharp. Something that bites. It darts near the surface, then disappears again. "You're Mollie Roark, ain't that right?"

I nod. Unfortunately, I have to claim her.

"Then I'm exactly where I need to be." And I believe him, even if it makes no sense. Even if his certainty discomfits. Even if my stomach flip-flops like a fish out of water when he smiles, revealing a dilapidated fence of stained and broken teeth.

"I'm afraid there might be a misunderstanding. I'm not seeing patients right now, Mister . . ." I flounder, realizing I haven't even asked his name, partly hoping I wouldn't need to.

"Wendall Grady," he pronounces himself, extending his hand.

I don't particularly want to touch him—not after he's barfed up his breakfast all over my drive—but I step forward and surrender to those long fingers, let them swallow mine. If he's contagious, I'm done for anyway.

"Pleased to meet you, Doctor Roark. And I hope you might kindly reconsider. I'm a special case."

"I'm sure you are." *Aren't they all?* "But I haven't practiced therapy since—" How long *has* it been?

"Since you lost your little girl." Not a question. But a statement of fact. I recoil from it. From him. From the naked truth of words I hadn't planned to say. And the shameless way he'd said them. "I am aware of your situation. In fact, that's why I've come. I think you can help me."

I lean against the doorframe so he can't see my legs wobble. *Am I dreaming?* This old man can't be real. He's just a figment. A puff of last night's marijuana smoke. An insomniac's hallucination. I squeeze my eyes shut and open them again, but he doesn't disappear. He leans back, comfortable now, and spreads his gangly arm across the sofa's back, revealing a smattering of scabs on

40

his crepe-paper skin. I can practically feel the sofa shrug him off, disgusted.

"Why me?" Two words that seem to sum the last few years perfectly. Even though I know it's not personal. I'm just another ball of atoms bouncing around in the universe. Some bouncing balls crash through beach waves. Others end up flat as a pancake under the tire of a big rig.

"Who else *but* you?"

"I don't understand."

He puts those eyes on me again, and I try not to squirm under their weight. "Stage two non-small cell lung cancer. That's the name of the devil sent to end me. And I've got a few heavy stones to push off my chest before I go. I was hoping you might help me lift them."

In my head, the stones are craggy and moss covered, nearly impossible to move, like the ones around Lake Berryessa. The ones I thought of as gravestones scattered in the clearing where they'd found her. His breastbone would snap like a cracker beneath them.

I frown and swallow hard, uncertain how to let him down easy. I'm not strong enough to carry anybody else's burdens anymore. I can barely manage my own.

"Don't go feelin' sorry for me now. Some sorta devil comes for all of us eventually. I reckon you should know that. Sometimes he's one of a goddamn million cells, just multiplying faster than a rabbit in heat. And sometimes he's a man, slippery as a shadow. Either way, I think we'll find some common ground. Help an old man out, won't you?"

As he struggles to his feet, he reaches for his Stetson, sets it atop his head, and nods at me like a haggard John Wayne. With a hitch in his step, the wind-up cowboy comes to life again and makes his way around the sofa.

I realize I've left the door to the room with the suspect wall gaping, but his eyes gobble it all up before I can rush to slam it shut. I mutter an apology, my breath unreasonably loud like static in my head.

"I'll swing by next week. Same time, same place. If you're not here, I'll just mosey on my way."

I follow him to the front door. He opens it and pauses there. Just beyond the threshold, I see the Cadillac, those dueling sickles.

"Maybe I can help you too, Doctor Roark."

I want to ask him what he means, how he found me, and how he knows about Dakota, but all I manage is a polite murmur.

"I'll have to think about it," I say, finally. But I already know if and when Wendall Grady comes back, I'll let him in.

****

Wide-eyed, Luciana shovels in the last bite of a fish taco and swivels on the barstool to face me, dabbing at a drip of sour cream on her bottom lip. We've been making the trek to Fairfield for cheap Tex-Mex at Picante Cantina every Tuesday night since we'd first met at group, but this time is different. Because it's only noon—*I couldn't stare at my suspect wall one second longer*—and I'd already knocked back a vodka, neat, instead of my usual watered-down margarita, and started on round two. And because I'd felt pulled to take the shorter route here, the way I never go, up I-80 and past the billboard of Dakota's smiling face. Hence, the vodka.

"¡Qué locura! I told you the cards have power. The goddess is giving you a nudge."

"Yeah, yeah, yeah. Cards schmards." But I can't shake the thought of that skeleton man atop his alabaster horse. Or the other card that fell into my path early this morning, the one I'd shut away in Dakota's desk drawer—out of sight, not mind. "You really believe the goddess wants me doing therapy with an old cowboy? He's the earth-shattering change I'm due for?"

I don't tell Luci I'd spent the last two hours holed up in my "real" office, googling Wendall Grady within an inch of his life. Because to her, I'm still the normal one, and I like that more than I care to admit. I'd lost my share of friends in the last two years.

Nothing runs them off quicker than a dead kid. At least with Luci, I don't have to explain why something as simple as a kids' movie on the marquis leaves me teetering on the edge of a black hole.

Grainy photos from the annual Yountville Vietnam Veteran's Association Picnics, Chapter 702, are all I have to show for my efforts. It's the same chapter my father claimed way back when. When he could still be bothered with conventional obligations like picnics and a nine-to-five job and his only daughter.

Luci shrugs and laughs at me. "The goddess works in mysterious ways, muchacha. And I never ignore a jumping card." Apparently, that's psychic-speak for one that falls from the deck with a mind of its own.

"Maybe DEATH was meant for Boludo," I say, trying to change the subject. "He's in desperate need of a tune-up."

"Please, that car has had one tire in the grave for years now. He's about as useless as the pendejo I stole him from. And you had two jumpers in one night. They say if it falls on the floor, it's at the door, you know?"

"What does that mean? DEATH is at my doorstep? Comforting, Luci. Really comforting."

"Are you actually asking for Madame Luci's professional opinion?"

I shrug, because I can't bring myself to say yes. Or no. Before I decide, Luci squeals and rubs her hands together. There's no stopping her now.

"When a card comes out of the deck, it usually represents something that will happen very soon. Muy próxima. DEATH could signal a change, like we discussed. But it could also mean letting go of the past."

She raises one eyebrow and stops speaking long enough for my stomach to clench tight, my hands to ball in fists at my side. All of me wound as tight as the vise grip I've got on the past, on Dakota. I don't say it out loud, but we both know I won't let go. I can't. The goddess would have to pry Dakota's memory from my rotting fingers.

"And my other jumper? Whitetails and Whoppers? What does Madame Luci have to say about that?"

"Well, it's technically not a tarot card, but the goddess is unpredictable. You said that place reminded you of your dad, right? And you haven't seen him in a while . . ."

She doesn't call it what it is. Total estrangement. But I know she understands. Her dad had spent twenty-five years in San Quentin as a shot caller for the Mexican Mafia. *Muy complicado*, she'd told me when I'd asked if they got along. But I'd take Juan Castillo and his teardrop face tattoos any day. Sometimes the devil you don't know is better than the one you know too well.

"And you mentioned the old cowboy is your dad's age. Maybe the goddess is telling you it's time, mi querida."

"Time for what exactly?"

"Abre la puerta. Your father is at the door, and you need to open it."

I roll my eyes as hard as I can muster and take a long sip of vodka. I hold it in my mouth and let it pickle my tongue to stop the chill racing up the back of my neck. Because I'd already decided to make the drive to the junkyard in Allendale the moment I'd quarantined that business card in the desk drawer.

"Well?" she asks, preening. "Am I right or am I right?"

I knock back the rest of my glass, savoring the burn. "Does Madame Luci give refunds?"

****

When I see the dead squirrels hanging on the fence line, their mud-brown pelts shivering in the wind, I know my father still lives here. *Here* is Mol's Junkyard, my namesake, though the sign had tumbled to the ground years ago. And it's never been more apropos. As if my dad had somehow known, even then, what a wasteland my life would become.

I'd been seven years old when I first came to Mol's to live with my father. After the court had declared me a liar and my mother unfit. Back then, this place had a heartbeat, a vital kind of magic. With rusted-out cars for hide-and-seek and old engines my father brought to life again, wielding his tools like a wizard, his hands mucky with grease. *Where there's muck, there's brass,* he'd say.

I park the Jeep in the gravel turnaround outside the chained gates, next to my dad's ancient rust bucket—4 SALE $100 painted on the back window—and tap the horn. The sound splinters the stillness, sudden as a starter's pistol. A few blackbirds scatter from the refuse, taking flight with an urgency I fully understand. I watch them with envy as they disappear into the grove of sycamore trees.

There's no sign of Dad. Even the dingy beige curtains he'd sewn himself are pulled across the windows of the Terry travel trailer, as stiff as if they'd been starched and ironed. The silence feels unnatural too, and I can't stop thinking he's watching me from behind them. Rust stains the trailer's exterior, its wheels like roots sunk into the earth. No one would know it had another life, cavorting cross country to Badlands National Park, where I'd celebrated my fifth birthday counting prairie dogs instead of candles. Then Mom and Dad divorced, and the trailer anchored itself here like a statue, a monument to my father's despair.

I open the car door and call to him. But my voice sputters, dies out, like one of his hopeless cases. The engines he couldn't save that he'd lined in a row in back of the trailer, where they'd rested in their own pitiful graveyard. I try again, louder this time, but the only reply comes from the crickets, desperately flinging themselves out of my way as I trudge like a giant into the tall grass.

The mailbox attached to the gate tells me what I need to know. It's not stuffed full, but it's not empty either. Inside, I find a sportsman's catalog and a check from the VA, both postmarked three days ago and addressed to Victor Krandel, my father.

I exchange a wink and a nod with the familiar NO TRESPASSING signs as I avoid the gate entirely, making my way around the side where there's a hole in the fence. The same hole I'd slipped through at fifteen, when I'd run away from Mol's and back to my mother's, just in time to watch her sicken with breast cancer and die. Long after the heart of this place had ground to a stop and the magic turned black and my father became a dark wizard who went off his meds and talked to himself and drank too much and shot the squirrels that nested inside his precious rust buckets, marking his kill count on an old steel drum until he'd run out of room.

The break in the fence seems smaller than I remember—the whole place does. But I manage to squeeze through on my hands and knees without snagging my sweater on the torn end of the chain-link.

Once I'm inside, I move like I'm on enemy ground. Like I'm making a slug trail through the jungles of Vietnam. The way my father taught me. Most of it is still here, exactly as we'd arranged it, but the weeds have grown into thick camouflage. Better and denser than any we could've made ourselves.

Near the gates, to the right of the burned-out jalopy, I spot the booby-trapped plyboard with the 16-penny finishing nails my father had hammered in as I'd watched. *Just in case Charlie tries to sneak up on us at night.* It wasn't until seventh grade—US History—I'd realized Charlie wasn't one person but a whole army of them. The Viet Cong.

I creep over the air-horn trip wire that runs along the perimeter of the trailer, marveling at how well it's concealed. He must've finally invested in the USGI snare wire—the cheap fishing line we'd strung had always stood out like a sore thumb. The thought makes me shake my head in dismay. It's no surprise I'd never fit in with Cole's friends and their Stepford wives. Even with my Louie and my Manolos, my degree, and my put-on sophistication. *You can take the girl out of the junkyard, but . . .*

I survey the rest of the lawn, if you could call it that. The skeleton frame of a tattered recliner stands guard like a scarecrow at the periphery. Otherwise, it's a jumble of beer cans, car parts, and cigarette butts set atop a blanket of dead leaves. Same as it ever was. The steel drum is there too, overturned and red with rust, and for a moment, I'm a girl again, awakened at dawn, terrified by the sound of my father's voice barking one of the army's drill slogans, "Kill! Kill! Kill! To kill without mercy is the spirit of the bayonet!" as he etched another mark in the drum's cold flesh.

Just beyond the kill-count barrel, the front door. Dad always set a trap there. *The last line of defense*, he'd called it. Usually an Altoid-tin alarm system he'd rigged like a regular MacGyver. I never knew whether to be worried or impressed.

"Dad?"

My voice echoes in a way that convinces me I'm the only person left alive on the face of the earth. Me against the world: the fantasy of a survivalist, especially a paranoid misanthrope like my father.

I take another step—the trailer's within reach now—and cry out as I fall. Straight down and hard through the leaf cover. My foot lands in a hole clear up to my knee, my body vibrating with the impact.

Damn it, Dad.

I suck in a breath and wait for the searing pain. For the sharpened spikes to gouge my foot the way my father must've intended. The same had happened to him when he'd stepped into a punji pit in Vietnam. He'd shown me the quarter-sized scar where the bamboo had gone straight through. But I don't feel a thing. And I'm afraid to look down.

My foot sticks a little as I haul it back to solid ground, and I stare at my sneaker in horror. The spike pierced the toe box, narrowly missing flesh and bone. Infuriated, I poke at the pit, watching the rest of the thatched twigs and leaves tumble to the bottom. Four rows of sycamore sticks, filed like spears, point up at me, the intruder, with their accusing fingers.

He's gotten worse. I'd been right not to let Dakota anywhere near this place.

I test the door, jiggling the handle—so far, so good—and open it a crack, waving half of a discarded car antenna inside. With all my limbs intact, I give it a gentle push, and it swings open, wide and beckoning.

My father could be inside. I'm not sure what frightens me more. That he is. Or that he isn't. But it's the portal to another life, one I thought I'd left behind forever, and I'm sucked right in, powerless to resist it.

I breach the threshold and call for him again, certain he'll answer now. Because the place reeks of him, that nauseating fragrance of malt liquor, mildew, and anger I'd grown accustomed to at the end. He's probably sleeping one off in the pullout bed in the back.

I swipe at the half-eaten can of Beanee Weenees attracting flies on the kitchen counter. There's at least two months' supply of them in the pantry, the ones we'd pack for hunting trips and spread on saltine crackers with a pinch of brown sugar. *A hillbilly's delicacy,* Dad would tease.

The flies disperse, then circle back for more, and the memory of that sweet, salty taste coats my tongue in a nauseating instant. I bend over the sink and seek relief at the faucet, scooping the water from hand to mouth. It's warm and slightly musty, but I swallow it down anyway, grateful the damn thing still works.

I pick through the top layer of paper on the dining table— mostly delinquent bills and unread newspapers—and make my way to the beds in the rear of the trailer, which is only a few steps further on the cracked vinyl.

His bed is empty and unmade. The pillowcase stained an unhappy yellow. The sheets rumpled and cast aside in the kind of fitful sleep he'd awaken from, screaming. He'd always fall right back under, leaving me huddled in my burrow, mouth dry and heart pounding.

Resting on the floor within his reach, a half-empty bottle of risperdal—the antipsychotic medication my father had always insisted was manufactured by Charlie himself—and an open can of Olde English. Chasing one good decision with a bad one. That's classic Krandel.

A fat black horsefly flits from the can's mouth to the pillow and past me, landing on the lower bunk nearby where it sits, watching me with its alien eyes. I walk to shoo it, and it takes flight again. But I'm fixed here, staring at the bunk I'd called mine as a girl.

It's littered with the debris of twenty-some years. At the center, an open photo album with a glossy 8x12 splayed like a body at a crime scene. It's Dakota's freshman yearbook picture. I steady myself in the narrow hallway, leaning against the bathroom door and gulping up the stale air like my life depends on it.

"Put your goddamn hands in the air where I can see 'em." I haven't heard that voice in years—that razor-toothed bark—but it belongs to my father. Of that, there's no doubt. "And turn around real slow."

"Jesus Christ, Dad. It's me. *Mollie.* Your daughter."

He's backlit by the late afternoon sun streaming in from the open door, looming so tall on those stilt-like legs of his, it's a wonder he can stand upright in here. The light plays tricks, and for a moment, I'm a kid again. And he's the man who can catch a fish with his bare hands and lift me onto his shoulders like a sack of deer feed and fix anything with duct tape. The man who would never hurt me no matter what my mother had convinced me to tell the judge. But as he steps toward me and into the shadows, his jack-o'-lantern grin reveals itself as a grimace, and his skin turns to worn leather, deep lines etched in sun-spotted earth. The .22 rifle in his hand becomes undeniable. It's pointed right at me.

"I don't care who you are. You're trespassing on private property. And you know my motto. Kill anything that moves."

I don't mean to laugh—a short burst of bitterness—but it comes out anyway. "I came looking for you. And I nearly got a spike in my foot." I point my toe at him, and he nods like he's proud of himself. "Now you're gonna what? Shoot me?"

"Good ole punji pit woulda served you right. This ain't your home no more. You made that real clear a long time ago." But he puts the gun down at least, leans its slim body against the kitchen counter, and I see what he's brought with him, strung up over his shoulder on his game carrier. At least six rabbits, fur slick with blood.

I look away before I get sick. Or cry. I won't let that happen.

"Where'd you get this?" I ask, pointing to the photo. I can hardly look at it. Here. In this place. Where I'm already so raw.

He shrugs. "Showed up in the mailbox one day. Figured you'd sent it. You used to send 'em to me. Or did you forget about that?"

"You never wrote back. Or called. Or said thank you. I didn't think you cared. You didn't even come to her funeral."

"Yeah, well. That's how you wanted it. That's how you always wanted it. Still a teenager and thinking you knew better than your daddy. You got yourself emancipated. So you ain't my problem no more."

"Can you blame me?" My question is rigged, as booby-trapped as the junkyard itself. Because we've never talked about the night I ran away. Not from Mol's per se, but from my father. The man I've spent a lifetime trying to make sense of. But he's smart enough to sidestep my punji pit.

"No. I blame your mama. She fed you all kinds of BS about me. Tried to turn you against me. Had you spouting her little story like a goddamn parrot. Hell, she tried to get me locked up for touching you inappropriate. You remember all that? You remember when that judge said you was a liar?"

Coached. That's what the judge had said. I'd been coached.

"He said I was a victim of the alien syndrome."

I laugh again, this time unabashedly. Even if it is at his expense. Maybe especially so. "You mean Parental Alienation Syndrome, Dad. And it's junk science, you know that."

"Don't go thinkin' you're smarter than me. I've got a college degree too, ya know?" And he did. An associate's in automotive technology, paid for by the GI Bill. And a doctorate with honors in changing the subject.

"I know you do. But that's beside the point. You can't blame mom. She lost custody. And I lived with you for eight years. Whatever happened between us, you messed it up yourself."

50

"So is that why you showed up here, trespassin'? To give me the old laundry list of what I did wrong? Because you can just ride out on your high horse exactly the way you came."

He unhooks the rope carrier from his shoulder and deposits the rabbits on the counter in a lifeless heap. "Unless you want to stay for dinner. I'm partial to fried rabbit these days."

He wants me to look. I know he does. *They didn't feel a thing*— one of his favorite hunting sentiments. But as hard as I'd tried for him, I never had the heart for it. "I came to ask you something."

"Well, go on then."

I tread carefully, measuring every word. "Do you still go to that store, Whitetails and Whoppers? The one with the half fish, half deer on the sign?"

"That sign always did tickle you, didn't it?" His face is hard to read under all his camouflage: the wiry gray mustache, unkempt; the soiled baseball cap; the eyes so practiced at avoiding mine; the inevitable silence. Finally, he breaks the stalemate. "Here and there. Why?"

"Did you ever see Dakota there?"

He frowns, blinks, and stretches his head back, shocked. As if I'd grown a third eye right there in front of him. "What kind of damn asinine question is that? You know I ain't never even met Dakota. You made sure of that. You and Cole, that well-to-do husband of yours. *Cole*. That's a soap opera name if I ever heard one."

"We're divorced, Dad."

"*Hmph*. Can't say I'm surprised. You always were a handful." He shrugs out of his corduroy jacket—the same one he'd draped over my shoulders when it got too cold at the lake. The cigarette burn on the sleeve is a dead giveaway. Tossing it behind him, he opens the fridge and pops the top on another Olde English. "Want one for the road?"

Over his shoulder, I spot the oversized duffel where the jacket landed. The bag that had always been too heavy for me to lug myself. I can't help but think he did it on purpose. He remembers the night I ran. How could he not?

I snatch Dakota's photo from the album and push my way past him. Past the rabbits' slender bodies, probably still warm.

Down the step, around the pit, and through the hole in the fence. Eyes straight ahead. I don't even glance back. But I hear him though, shouting after me.

"You can't outrun your own shadow, Mollie girl."

****

I peel out, spraying gravel from my tires. Thoughts racing. Skin radiating heat. Blood thrumming through me like electric current.

The Jeep seems to have a mind of its own, driving me north on the 505 toward the easternmost edge of Lake Berryessa. I roll down the windows and scream like a once-caged animal, now freed and on the loose. The wind whips at my face, and I stick my hand out in the stream of it, wishing I could catch it under my wings like the bird Dakota had inked on her shoulder and let it take me far from here.

The tears come later. Hysterical laughter too, when I rehearse the text I'll send Luciana:

Some doors are meant to stay closed. And I'm nailing a board over this one.

The Jeep comes to a rest at the overlook near Glory Hole— that's what the locals call the massive spillway in the middle of the lake that drains into Putah Creek below. Dakota had been enchanted by it, the plunging falls of water infinitely streaming down, down, down. Even Cole had perked up a bit, leaning over the railing to get a better look. But it always unnerved me. Probably because Dad had once called it a wormhole, a shortcut through space and time. A direct route to the devil's lair. He'd tossed a beer can into the water and grabbed me as we'd watched it go over the edge. I'd squealed with terrified delight, believing every word of his story.

I stare out at the mossy green lake that's growing darker as the sun plunges toward the craggy hills. Soon, the water will be obsidian black, Glory Hole lit up by a sliver of moon. Or the hellfire down below.

They found Dakota's body not five miles from here.

I remember the picture then. I'd tossed it on the passenger seat in such a hurry, it slid down to the floorboard faceup.

There she is. My girl.

I turn it over, half-expecting to see my father's chicken scratch. Or nothing at all. Just the unmarred white canvas of photo paper.

But the handwriting is loopy cursive. Just two words. And those two words snap shut around my heart, piercing it through and through like one of my father's sycamore stakes.

To Grandpa, it says.

CHAPTER SEVEN

(SATURDAY, JULY 2, 2016)

DAKOTA sat cross-legged on the bottom of the swimming pool, opening her eyes to the shimmering surface. She blew a trail of bubbles and watched them float to the top without her. She preferred it down here, where the world above remained both vaguely recognizable and strangely distorted. A lot like her life lately.

Lungs burning, she counted in her head. *Fifty-seven, fifty-eight, fifty-nine, sixty, sixty-one*—she'd done it! Broken her own personal best. So what if it came nowhere near the female world record holder's 18 minutes and 32.59 seconds. Eighteen whole minutes underwater. Dakota could hardly imagine it.

Her muscles began to tense, and the urge to breathe became unbearable. Panic seized her, shook her like a pair of strong, violent hands. *Ted Bundy's*, she thought, stretching her arms and pushing off the bottom. She gasped the moment her head broke the surface, blinking and breathing—nothing more—until she stopped seeing stars.

That's what it's like to be strangled. She didn't know for sure, of course. She'd never actually been strangled. But since she'd started reading *The Stranger Beside Me*, the creepy book she'd found packed away in her mother's things from college, she'd imagined it plenty of times. Her mom called it a true-crime classic. Her dad, sensationalist garbage. One thing they both agreed on: It was a phase. Her serial-killer phase. And she'd grow out of it. At least she'd gotten them to agree on something.

"What the hell, Dakota?" Tyler's voice startled her, and she realized he'd been staring. Her other friends too. They'd gathered at the edge of the pool, pointing down at her. "You're being weird," Tyler said, frowning with such intensity she had to look away. But a second later, he started laughing when Eric snuck up from behind and shoved him in.

Dakota turned away, only partly to avoid the swash of water. *I am being weird.* Weird, meaning different. Weird, meaning not a total clone. Weird, meaning an embarrassment to *him*. Tyler Lowry. A rising senior lacrosse phenom who'd asked her to the prom in April. Since then, they were sort of a thing. Which she was supposed to be *like excited* about. And she had been. Once upon a time. But lately, that felt like a monumental ask. Especially the way he'd been acting. Reminding her he wouldn't wait much longer.

"I'm okay," she said, watching the waves ripple the surface like aftershocks. But they'd already moved on, laughing along with Tyler as he splashed like a deranged orca in the shallow end. Eric tossed a floaty at his head. It missed and dead-ended against the pool's concrete edge.

Dakota's legs felt heavy as she swam to the steps and climbed out, suddenly conscious of her body, exposed and dripping. She had broad swimmer's shoulders and was shaped like a board. Nothing like Hannah, who hosted her own beauty vlog on YouTube and dressed up as a sexy panda last Halloween. Only Hannah could pull that off.

Ignoring the roughhousing in her wake, Dakota walked away from the pool and tugged on the jean shorts and T-shirt she'd left in a pile on the lounge chair. Her bikini top made wet spots on the front—two bullseyes for Tyler and his jock friends—but it felt better to be covered. Especially with Hannah prancing around like a *Sports Illustrated* swimsuit model. Everyone said she looked like Kate Upton. And her mom had actually worked as a catalog model before she became Nurse Montgomery at Napa Children's Hospital. The same Napa Children's her dad disappeared into most days, spending his time with sick kids who thought he was a superhero.

"What's up with you?" Hannah took a swig from a bottle of Gatorade that didn't smell like Gatorade at all. When she offered a taste, Dakota took a sip, forcing herself to swallow.

"What do you mean?"

"You're acting all emo. Like you don't even want to be here. You've barely said two words all night."

"Actually, I said four words just now, so don't exaggerate."

Hannah rolled her eyes. The perfect cat-eyes from her last makeup video tutorial. Dakota suspected that's why she'd avoided the water. Just strutted around in her bikini and short shorts, preening. As hard as she tried, Dakota couldn't remember when Hannah had turned into this person—the old Hannah was addicted to SpongeBob and thought high heels were an especially cruel form of torture—but it had happened so gradually, she'd hardly noticed. Somehow her best friend had risen to the top of the Napa Prep social strata, towing little ole Dakota behind her like a glamorous tugboat.

"Whatevs. It's your prerogative if you want to ignore your totally hot senior boyfriend. But don't be a biatch to me too. What have *I* done?"

"I'm not being a biatch." Dakota hated the sound of that word as it left her mouth. "And he's technically not my boyfriend."

"He won't ever be if you keep acting like a biatch. You unfollowed Faces by Hannah. And you haven't slept over since—when was it? Prom? That was ages ago."

Dakota knew precisely how long it had been. Two months and three days. But Hannah was right. It felt like ages. The Middle Ages with its Black Death and Hundred Years War. "Look, I'm staying over tonight. And I told you my dad's on a kick. I guess he thinks too much screen time is corrupting my mind."

Dakota left out the other part. About how her parents had practically diagnosed her as depressed. They didn't exactly say it to her face, but she'd heard them discussing it. And since they were both doctors, they always got it right. What a sham.

"Well, he's not wrong." Hannah smirked at her, and Dakota understood all had been forgiven. At least for now.

Hannah's eyes widened, her mouth a little red *O*. Dakota spun around, saw what she saw. A light had come on in the house behind them. And then another, a bright naked bulb on the patio. It bore into her, and Dakota felt stunned. Zapped with a proton beam like one of her father's patients. She'd had that feeling a lot lately. Since the incident. That seemed like a safe word for it. A word without emotion.

"Hey!" Tyler yelled, catapulting from the water, Eric sploshing right behind him. They shoved their wet feet into their shoes, grabbed their phones and T-shirts from the deck, and took off for the fence. "Gotta go! They're home."

Dakota watched as Tyler and Eric and two other older boys she barely knew scaled the pickets as swift as gazelles. They hoisted Hannah over and waited for her. But she couldn't move.

"Come on!" Hannah urged, waving her hand so wildly it appeared not to belong to her at all. It flapped like a bird's broken wing. Like one of the pom-poms Hannah wielded on the sidelines during football season.

Dakota almost laughed at her until Tyler pounded his fist against the fence, cursing, and she finally took his hand. He lifted her without effort it seemed, and her feet hit the ground running.

****

Dakota felt sick. She curled onto her side and glanced at her phone on the nightstand. It had been silent, the screen dark for hours now. She almost believed it hadn't happened. That she hadn't done it. But that was stupid. Of course, she had. She couldn't blame Hannah. Not really. Though Hannah had encouraged her—*C'mon. He's seventeen. He's got expectations. Plus, everybody's done it. It's no biggie*—and coached her through it as they'd swigged from a bottle of wine Hannah had pilfered from her parents' liquor cabinet.

Hannah had redone Dakota's hair and makeup, which had been washed away by the pool water, and told her how to pose—*Let your hair down. Soften your eyes. Think of something sexy. Like Channing Tatum reading you poetry. Don't laugh. Lean forward a little and tuck your elbows in. It makes your boobs look bigger*—and snapped the pics. She'd even helped her choose the best one. The one where Dakota's lacy red bra, which really belonged to Hannah, fell down from her shoulders, just revealing her breasts. But Dakota had been the one to hit Send. And now she'd give anything to take it back.

Grown-ups were always saying how you'd regret the choices you didn't make. But Dakota thought that was a load of crap. You'd always regret the stupid choices you made much more. Like sending Tyler the half-naked photo he'd been asking for. A stupid choice if ever there was one. There are no choices without consequences. Didn't her mom always tell her patients that? Consequences like the brutal churning in her gut. Like horndog Tyler texting her back:

finaly u show me sum skin damn ur hot wen can i c u like that 4 real

Hannah had typed for her—*soon, sexy*—and they'd giggled about Tyler's atrocious text-spelling before Dakota had deleted the word *sexy* and sent the reply hurtling out into the universe. Like an asteroid meant to destroy her life.

She slipped from the bed where Hannah lay sleeping and padded down the stairs to the Montgomerys' living room. She knew the house was empty. Hannah's parents were away for the night at some ritzy fundraiser sponsored by her dad's law firm, and her older brother, Zach, had stayed on at USC for the summer semester. But she couldn't shake the feeling someone else was there, watching her. A pair of unblinking eyes just beyond her view.

It's that stupid Bundy book, she thought.

After their phones had finally gone quiet, Hannah had dozed off, and Dakota had snuck the worn paperback from her duffle bag and read for at least an hour about the way Bundy had escaped from jail and crept into the Chi Omega sorority house through the door with a broken lock and bludgeoned to death two girls not much older than her and Hannah. It made her skin crawl in a way that wasn't entirely unpleasant, and she reread whole paragraphs, imagining herself in that house, lying perfectly still under the covers while Bundy made quick work of Hannah. Of the two of them, Hannah would definitely be the first to go.

Dakota shook her head at her own morbid freakdom. No wonder her parents were skeeved out by her lately. Well, at least her dad. Her mom understood, being a morbid freak herself. She worked with murderers every day. Crazy ones too. As if there were any other kind.

Dakota tiptoed toward the sofa where Snowball, Hannah's enormous Persian, had already staked claim to the middle cushion. Without lifting his head, he eyeballed her warily, and Dakota wondered if he could smell Gus on her T-shirt. Or if he was thinking about it too. The last night she'd spent here. Prom night. He'd been perched on the counter, amid the red plastic cups and half-empty party trays, casually licking his paw while Dakota's whole world plummeted from beneath her.

"It's just me, big guy."

She scratched the top of his head until he purred with contentment. Then she left him to his throne, taking the pauper's seat on the beanbag instead. She flipped on the television and turned the sound down low, scrolling through the channels numbly. The screen's silvery white light cast shadows around her, conjuring ghosts of the past that flashed and flickered at the edges of her vision.

There. Her eyes darted to the basement door. It looked innocent enough, painted the same eggshell white as the Montgomerys' kitchen and affixed with an antique brass doorknob. When they were little, Hannah had declared it their secret fortress, with its long, creaky staircase, its washing machine treasure chest to store the jewels they'd pilfered, and its grumbling beast that would stop intruders in their tracks. *Don't tell Mom,* Hannah had whispered. *But I think the beast eats socks.*

The door was closed now. But on prom night, it had been left ajar, beckoning to Dakota like an open book. She'd peered down into the dimly lit cavern trying to make sense of the two familiar shapes moving in the dark below her.

She could still see it. Hadn't stopped seeing it. Even though she desperately wanted to. Hannah's mother moaning like a wounded creature with her back pressed against the beast. Which had long ago lost its fascination and revealed itself as nothing more than an unremarkable Whirlpool dryer. Fingers curled like talons, head flung back. A man too, unrecognizable at first. His mouth latched to her pale neck like a vampire. A regular Edward Cullen, her father. His favorite blue flannel shirt had given him away.

Dakota had been petrified. Like the redwood trees in that ancient forest they'd visited a few years back. A volcano had erupted smack-dab in the middle of her life, fixing her there forever on that step at the top of that staircase behind that wretched door.

Snowball jumped from the sofa, meandered toward her, and rubbed his face against her knee with vigor, reminding her that life had gone on. That she wasn't a petrified tree after all. Though she felt like one sometimes, the way she stood mute in front of her dad when he said good morning. When he said good night. When he said all the things in-between. But especially when he asked her what was wrong. What could she say to him that wouldn't sound like a total lie?

It was going to be a long summer. Endless. Dakota sighed, letting her eyes wander back to the TV screen, where she resumed her aimless clicking. Until—

She sat up straight and pushed Snowball aside, turning up the volume. The spooky intro music belonged to one of those true-crime news shows she liked—the kind she planned to work for someday— and she recognized the setting even before the camera panned wide, revealing an elderly woman walking the hilly shoreline of Lake Berryessa. Her white hair whipped across her face as she stooped to place a teddy bear at the foot of a wooden cross.

> **Today marks forty years since Glenda Donnelly's only daughter, thirteen-year-old Susanna, left her family's home in Allendale on a walk with her best friend, her beagle, Hank. Neither she nor Hank ever returned. Susanna's charred remains were discovered weeks later, here at Lake Berryessa in Napa, California. It took four more years before detectives realized she had been preyed upon by a serial killer, an enigma dubbed the Shadow Man. Today, the police are no closer to solving Susanna's decades-old murder or the murders of the fifteen young women who came after her, falling victim to the same tragic fate. The Shadow Man has proven elusive, evading all attempts by law enforcement to shine a light on his face. Recently, a group of online sleuths has set out to . . .**

Better than Bundy, Dakota admitted to herself. Because it had happened here, practically in her backyard. The idea of Shadow Man worked like the swimming pool trick, blurring all her bad decisions. The nude pic that lived on Tyler's phone now, like patient zero with a virus waiting to spread. The basement door and her father and Mrs. Montgomery too. Until it all felt like something she'd seen in a movie. Something that didn't belong to her at all and never had.

Dakota leaned in, riveted. It turned out murder could be a useful distraction.

AFTER

CHAPTER EIGHT

(MONDAY, OCTOBER 1, 2018)

A fierce little ray of midday sun sneaks through the blinds I'd pulled tight. I tug at the blanket, shielding my face from its callous persistence, but the jerking leaves my feet cold, my legs exposed. The bed feels oddly shaped and hard beneath me.

I roll onto my side with effort and force my eyes open despite the vague throbbing in my skull. The night—the last few nights, if I'm being honest—comes back to me with the sudden brutality of a gut punch. A sandbag shot delivered by Dakota's buoyant smile. Because the yearbook photo I'd snatched from Dad's bunk bed is right there next to me. On the floor.

I'm on the floor. In the office. Beneath the suspect wall.

The ray of light I'd cursed doesn't belong to the sun after all—there are no windows in here—but the desk lamp I must've carted in from the other room after it got dark, possibly several nights ago. It had toppled over at my feet next to an empty bottle of Russian Standard, its small bright bulb drilling me with judgment.

I close my eyes again—sweet relief—too tired and achy to reach the five feet to shut it off. My mind is a jumble of tangled threads, a smattering of breadcrumbs, each one leading me back to last Tuesday. To Mol's Junkyard and my father. To the photograph and its inscription. To what came after I'd fled from Glory Hole with the past nipping like a wolf at my heels.

The days since then collapse like a house of cards into one long, dark night of pounding vodka and staring at the faces on my wall and falling under the spell of a heavy, dreamless sleep. Rinse and repeat. I realize I can't even be certain how many days have passed.

I stand slowly, wary as a newborn fawn, Dakota's 49ers sweatshirt falling in a heap at my bare feet. No wonder I'd been cold. I take a few uncertain steps, testing my legs, and survey the damage.

I count four bottles in total, all drained dry. A half-eaten bowl of mac and cheese, and whatever I'd eaten it with—*spoon? fork? soup ladle?*—God knows where. An empty gallon of chocolate-fudge-brownie ice cream, Dakota's favorite flavor. No coincidence, I'm sure. Because when I wallow, I go full-bore. And the sight of it comes with a flash of memory. Me, in the self-checkout at the grocery, catching a frightening glimpse of myself in the little camera aimed at my face. The scanner's beep punctuating my descent down every rung of the dignity ladder. Vodka. Vodka. Vodka. Ice cream. At least I'd eaten something.

In the corner, Gus lifts his head and whines. And a breath I didn't know I'd been holding rushes out of me in a sudden, dizzying gust. I hadn't gone so far off the rails that I'd forgotten him again.

So.

It's not that bad then.

Nothing two aspirin and a little hair of the dog won't fix.

But as soon as I think it, I hear myself, my former respectable doctor self, laughing with derision at what she would've described as gross minimization. *Call it what it is, Mollie.* An all-out drinking binge. Apparently, the apple doesn't fall far because since Dakota disappeared, I've had more than a few of them. But hell, I feel entitled. What did my old self know about life anyway? Sure, she'd been through a few rough patches. But nothing like this. Nothing like *orbity*, the long-forgotten word for the loss of a child I'd discovered online. At first, I'd thought it sounded too pretty, too fantastical, but after I imagined my soul severed, disconnected, and careening off without me, I deemed it a decent fit.

I spot my phone balanced at the edge of the Napa State box, its battery dangerously low. I approach it with caution, like it's a coiled snake, as if it could strike at any moment, as if it could bite. Already, I'm panicked. Because I remember just enough. I'd texted Sawyer. Maybe more than once. But not enough to have a clue what I'd said or when.

The screen casually informs me of the date: Monday, October 1. The only time I'd done worse had been just after Cole left. When I couldn't decide who was more pathetic. Him leaving me the way he had or me letting him stay for as long I did. And I'd downed his leftover case of Stella before he'd made it to Seattle, answered his call with a slurred *hullooo*. The Sawyer texts are cringeworthy. But not as bad as drunk me pleading with Cole—*why?*—the only word I'd seemed capable of back then.

r u awake?

wanna come over?

i miss u.

hellllloooooo? sawyerrrrrrrr?

I grimace through the string of desperate messages I'd spewed at 3 a.m. this morning. *Is that a winking emoji?*

Sawyer hadn't responded, not right away. Because any reasonable person our age would be asleep at 3 a.m., not playing detective while downing cheap liquor straight from the bottle. But he'd called a few times this morning. And there was this:

Damn. Four hours too late.

Hey—should I be flattered or worried?

For bonus humiliation, there are several where-are-you texts from Luci and a voicemail from Detective Sharpe that I delete without playing. I know exactly why he's calling. That part I remember. I'd left him a message detailing a half-baked conspiracy I'd concocted involving my father and the yearbook photo and Boyd Blackburn. I'd blathered on about it for so long I'd been mercifully cut off by the beep. Even if the news of my parking lot escapade hadn't reached him yet, I'd be living down that voicemail forever. Which is precisely how long I expect to be doing this. This in-between life.

As I slog around the room cleaning up my mess, Gus trailing long-faced behind me, the thrumming in my head takes a brutal turn, growing sharper and more insistent. The *rat-tat-tat* of a snare drum quickening the beat. But I deserve it. I'd broken the worst kind of promise. The promise I'd made to myself the last time I'd said never again, again. Which only reminds me of my dad and the lyrics to one of his favorite country tunes and the wet vowels of his plastered singing. I've got five hours to turn *this*—the shell-shocked face I catch in the dark screen of my computer—back into Dr. Mollie Roark. Because childless, divorced pariah is still one step up from fall-down drunk.

****

I circle the lot outside Napa Valley College, watching the familiar cars fill the spaces like pieces on a chess board. Luci and Boludo, apparently still alive and kicking, in a spot near the front, alongside Jane's slick BMW. Sawyer's pickup truck nearest the exit for a quick getaway. *This is progress*, he'd joked. *I used to leave her running.* And Boyd's vintage VW bug, a faded yellow, parked in the middle of it all, chameleonlike.

I'm not fooled. I spot him on my fifth pass around, ignoring the honking behind me to get a good look as Boyd stoops from the car and lumbers inside. Last week, I hadn't realized his height, but his legs unfold from the miniature interior, thin and spindly as a spider's.

I do another loop, ignoring the predictable buzz of Cole's weekly call, his regular reminder of our shared regrets. And then one more, waiting until the last possible minute. Because I don't want to be late, but I can't bear to be early. To face Luci's steely-eyed glare. *Teatrera*, she'd say, branding me a drama queen. Or Sawyer's pitying hand on my back. Mostly, I don't trust myself around Boyd. Not with the remnants of firewater still simmering my blood. My father had called it that, and I couldn't disagree. Alcohol could burn your whole life down if you let it. No different than the wildfires that razed the Napa hillside.

I position the Jeep directly across from Boyd's bug in a stare down. Hardly satisfying with its innocent eyes. Its jolly face, the color of a dying daffodil. I don't even enjoy kicking the tire as I pass or bumping the side panel with my hip. But I hope it leaves a mark.

A blazing hot shower, a swipe of mascara, and a long swig of black coffee had brought me back to the land of the living. Still, my brain lags two steps behind me as I open the door to the student break room and blink into the fluorescent lights, stunned. The pleasant hum of small talk grates like a buzz saw, but I prefer it to the sudden silence. In the dead space, I feel their eyes on me.

"Hello, everyone." There's only one seat left—sandwiched between Jane and Boyd, and I fill it, nodding at him. "I hope you all had a good week."

Luciana laughs—a spurt of scorn—but I dodge her eyes, delivering the group rules mindlessly. I could recite them in my sleep. Boyd is distracting me, running his thumb over his burn like a talisman. His backpack sits at his feet, upright and close to him, like a loyal dog. It's partly unzipped, but, despite my efforts, I can't quite see inside.

"Who would like to begin?" I ask, hoping once somebody starts talking, I can disappear behind the veil of conversation and retreat into myself. Nodding along, making the occasional murmur of agreement. Passing the time until I can do what I came to do. Which I'll admit involves me sneak-attacking Boyd with the yearbook I'd left on my passenger seat.

"I'll go," Luciana says, raising her hand like an overeager student. My stomach curdles, a sloshing pit of leftover booze and ice cream. "For those of you who don't know my story, I've got issues. Trust issues. Which started long before I met Mateo. And when he murdered my Isabella, he killed what was left of my faith in people. *Muerte.*" Of course, she says it right to me. Like our own private joke. Or a hex uttered with graveyard dirt and coffin nails in her pocket.

"It's not easy for me to make friends. But I did make one. And she broke my trust. She made me worry about her for six whole days, wondering if she was lying in a ditch somewhere, dead like my little girl. Then, she shows up acting like nothing happened."

Some doors are meant to stay closed. And I'm nailing a board over this one. The cryptic text I'd sent to Luciana before I'd gone dark. I don't blame her for being pissed. I blame her for expecting things of me. Things I thought we'd both understood the other incapable of giving.

"Maybe your friend didn't know how you were feeling," Jane suggests.

I wince. For her. For what's coming.

"*¿En serio?* Since when am I not clear with my feelings, Jane?"

Jane's head jerks back, eyes wide. But she blinks bravely at Luciana. Stupidly and in awe, as if she's staring directly at the sun.

"Besides, I sent her—*my so-called friend*—fifteen texts."

Nine, actually. Who's the drama queen now? Each one a variation on the *dónde estás, Mollie* theme.

"I think Jane is onto something," Sawyer says, with the kind of practiced neutrality it took me four years of grad school to master. And when he offers me an encouraging smile, I feel overwhelmed with gratitude. And guilt. Because I'm supposed to be the one keeping the basket cases in check. Not him.

"This guy who served in my battalion went to the doctor for a physical when he got home from his third tour overseas. He hadn't been sleeping well, and he dozed off on the doctor's exam table. The doc came in and tapped his shoulder to wake him up. And he totally lost it. Leapt off the table, started cursing at her. Security escorted him out of the building. Of course, they didn't know ten months earlier he'd been sleeping on duty at the front gate of our compound when an enemy mortar round struck the building."

Luciana cocks her head at him, stubborn and still primed for a fight. "*¿Qué importa?* What's your point?"

"My point is that it probably isn't about you. Just like it wasn't about that doctor my buddy cursed out. Sometimes other people's stuff is so big they can't see around it."

It's a kick to the gut, and for a second, I lose my breath. *Is that what he thinks of me?*

"Thank you for sharing, Sawyer." In my therapist voice. I'm such a fraud. And a lousy friend. "What a perfect metaphor for loss. Some days I feel like I was dead asleep when I got ambushed by enemy fire."

When our eyes meet, he winks at me, knocking the rust off my old, tired heart again. Turns out it still works. Even if it cranks and groans like one of my dad's hopeless cases.

"Ain't that the truth," he says.

But Luci huffs at my psychobabble. "Enemy fire should never come from a friend. It's bad enough I let that *pendejo*, Mateo, into my life. That I couldn't see him for the wolf he was."

My chest aches as I force myself to look at her. "We're only human, Luci. We've all made mistakes. I'm sure everyone in this group has regrets, things they'd do differently this time around."

Next to me, Boyd shifts in his seat, and I can feel him working up the nerve to say something. The air between us fizzes; his fingers coil into tight fists. I don't want to look at him, but I can't help myself. I want to show him I know he's a liar.

But when I turn, he's right there, hazel eyes as innocent as his VW's. His backpack is gaping now. He drops his gaze to his lap, but all I see is a gray hoodie crumpled on top, one arm loose and hanging out the side. Dakota had one just like it with Napa Grizzlies Swim Team appliqued on the back. I stick my hands beneath my thighs, so I won't grab for it. Now that would be crazy.

"What would you do differently?" he asks. "If you could."

I know he's talking only to me.

****

As soon as the hour is up, I spring from my seat, a sprinter off the line, my heart firing like a starter's pistol. But before I reach the door, Luciana corners me with a saucy glare, allowing Boyd to duck out behind her. His long legs make quick work of the hallway, the hoodie stowed inside his backpack getting farther from me with every step.

"Well?" Such a harmless word. But not the way she says it, lilting and vicious as a slap, in spite of her wry smile. I deserve it. Because she'd been the one to answer Boyd's question, while I'd gaped, open-mouthed. *I would've never showed up to that house party in Vallejo*, she'd said. *And Mateo de Leon would've been somebody I'd never met. Instead of the man who took everything from me.* I owe her for that one, and I know it. And she knows I know.

"Anything you'd like to say to me? Maybe lo siento? Or perdoname, por favor?"

I give her arm a firm squeeze as she slips into her leather jacket. "I'm sorry, Luci. But Sawyer was right. It's really not about you."

She starts to mount a protest, but I interrupt. "Tacos tomorrow, okay? I've got to—"

I point up ahead to Boyd just as the exit door closes after him. It makes an impossibly loud noise. Crisp and final, like the snap of a twig under a heavy boot. I push past Luciana, leaving her shaking her head and muttering in Spanish.

"Hey," I call out to Boyd, as soon as I clear the door. The wide expanse of the parking lot looms between us. Boyd glides across it effortlessly, head down against the blustery wind that's kicked up out of nowhere, raising goosebumps beneath my thin sweater. "Wait up."

He glances over his shoulder, and I give my best attempt at a friendly wave. I used to be good at that once upon a time. At cracking even the hardest nuts with a smile and a willing ear. But that person feels so far from me now. I regard her with wistfulness and a little embarrassment, the same way I do the love notes Cole and I had exchanged in our first year of dating. *How sweet. How pathetic.*

This new version of me—bitter lunatic—eats love notes for breakfast. My arm feels wild and unhinged as I signal to Boyd, like it might pop from its socket. My face contorts, more Pennywise than Bozo. Because he doesn't stop. He doesn't even slow down.

Any second now he'll be in his car and leaving. And he won't come back. Not ever. He'll take the answers with him. The answers I need in a way I can't explain, as essential as breathing.

A savage panic pierces my chest, splintering behind my breastbone. I stop, doubled over and gasping with the sudden sharpness of it. The way it steals the air from my lungs.

"What's your sister's name?" The wind carries my thin voice back to me. As if I'd asked myself the question. With it, tiny whispers in my head. *Dakota. Dakota. Dakota.* "Because I didn't find any Blackburns in the yearbook."

Boyd fumbles at the door of his VW, the sunny yellow now jaundiced beneath the street lamp, tinged with the green of an overcooked egg. His keys drop from his hand and strike the pavement with a clatter. He stares at them regretfully—we both do—lying there like a dead thing.

I stagger toward him like a dead thing myself. When he finally pries his eyes from the pavement, he takes a step back, bumping up against his car. Next to him—his long limbs, his burn scar, his

74

pockmarked cheeks—it looks cartoonish, ridiculously small and cheerful. I'd like to take a bat to it.

"Who are you really?" I ask. Softer. Coaxing. How my father had murmured to the squirrels through the window. *C'mon. Just a little closer, you rat bastard. Gimme a clean shot.* "You can tell me the truth. Where'd you get Dakota's hoodie?"

"I—I don't have her . . . I am telling the truth."

"I don't believe you. You don't even have a sister. Or a kid. Much less a dead one. You don't belong in this group. Now, tell me who you are and how the fuck you knew my daughter before I call the police."

I hope I'm still drunk. That my frontal lobe—the responsible one—is out to lunch, pickled in Absolut and unable to come to the phone right now. Because I sound wasted even if I've never felt more sober. My brain, burned clean by rage. Not at Boyd. I know that on some level. But at my father. At Cole. Mostly at myself.

"Mollie." I shrug off Sawyer's touch and catch his reflection, his worried frown, in the window of the VW. Further back, some of the group has gathered, watching me warily. "Relax."

Relax? That rankling word I'd always steered the psych interns away from, especially with an agitated patient. The implication behind it, the dismissal, prods like a stick to the ribs.

A laugh scrapes up my throat, a vicious cackle. I'm the agitated patient now. I reach for Boyd's keys, scooping them up before he can stop me. Before he can get away.

"I *am* relaxed."

But I'm brandishing them now, squeezing them so tight, my palm hurts. Sawyer takes my wrist and lowers it gently, gesturing at Boyd.

"The man is trying to say something."

Boyd's cheeks are fire-red, his eyes tearing. "Mandy," he whispers. "Amanda Phillips. She's my half sister. That's why you didn't . . . uh . . . why there are no . . . you know, Blackburns."

He unzips his backpack and holds up a ratty gray sweatshirt in surrender. It's not Dakota's. Of course it's not. Hers is in an evidence room downtown. Her favorite, she'd taken it with her that day when she'd left the house. The police had found the sweatshirt in a ditch a mile from the lake. So it couldn't be this one.

The rage drains from me, a sudden bloodletting, and my legs weaken. I don't have the strength to protest when Sawyer takes Boyd's keys from my hand and returns them. Fast and furtive as a burrowing animal, Boyd opens his door and lowers himself inside. His engine fires, and he speeds out of the parking lot, zipping into the night.

"Damn, Mollie. You hurt yourself."

When I look down, my shaking hand rests in Sawyer's, tiny pricks of red dotting my palm where the key's teeth dug in. I stare at it, at Sawyer's fingers holding mine, stilling them, but only because I'm afraid to put my eyes anywhere else. To look at Luciana. Or Jane. Or Debbie.

It's only her second group and probably her last. Now that she's realized what I am. The Lead Basket Case. But hardly fit to lead anyone.

"And you scared that guy shitless. You really think your Shadow Man bops around town in a yellow bug?"

I pull away from Sawyer, newly indignant. "Do you know who else drove a Beetle?"

"Ren McCormack in *Footloose?*" The corner of his mouth tilts up ever so slightly in a wry smile I'd like to slap—*or kiss*—off him.

"Ted Bundy, smartass. That's who."

****

Sawyer insists on following me home, his headlights blinding me in the rearview every time he gets too close. To my foggy brain, it feels like a metaphor for something. Which is why I'm not letting him in. No matter how much I want to.

I sit in the driveway, unmoving, blasting Metallica until the Jeep trembles and hoping Sawyer will take the hint. The house looks strange—so grandiose and empty—from out here. Especially when I imagine it through Sawyer's eyes. After his divorce, he'd moved into a cottage at the Blue Rose. And though I'd never seen it, I knew the home Cole bought for us would dwarf it like one of those wooly mammoth skeletons presiding over an entire room in a museum. Too big to be believed. Too big for one person. A half a person at that. Maybe I'll sleep in the Jeep tonight.

Sawyer raps forcefully on my window with his prosthetic knuckles, shrugging at me when I jump. I lower the music to a soft throb and crack the door.

"I tried the real thing," he says, fluttering his fingers at me. "But I guess you've probably gone deaf by now. If only I knew sign language."

"Ha. Ha. Ha." I shut off the car, relenting. Sawyer's not the hint-taking kind. "You really didn't have to come all the way out here. I'm fine. Totally fine."

He doesn't argue. Which makes me nervous. Instead, he opens the door the rest of the way and waits for me to step out. Which I don't. "I assume you're using the Aerosmith definition of *fine*. Since you are a heavy metal groupie. You know, *fucked up, insecure*—"

"Neurotic and emotional," I finish for him, punctuating it with a dry twist of my mouth. "Technically, Aerosmith is hard rock. And I meant *fine* fine. The Webster Dictionary definition."

"It's okay if you're not. We all have bad days."

"Do you? Because you always seem so well-adjusted for—" I flip my hand toward him, then draw it back, wincing at my own cruelty. "I'm sorry. I didn't mean it like that."

"It's okay. I guess I am pretty well-adjusted for a guy who left his arm in pieces in the desert. A guy whose only kid died on his watch."

He smiles sadly, and I sink back into my seat with a sigh.

"Aren't you angry?" I ask.

Sawyer says nothing. He moves with purpose, shutting my door and walking around to the other side, sliding into the passenger seat. Definitely not the hint-taking kind then. I flash him a look, equal parts dread and expectation.

"Since you're obviously not coming out . . . and yeah, I'm pissed as hell sometimes. You know, after Noah died, I wanted to reenlist. To be downrange again. I needed to go somewhere. *Anywhere.* Afghanistan, Iraq, Timbuktu—I didn't care. As long as I could blow some motherfuckers up."

I blink against the harshness of it. But it resonates deep down. The need to watch someone else's life go *boom.* "I didn't even know that was possible. With an injury like yours."

"It's rare. But it happens. You have to apply for a waiver that gets reviewed by a bunch of higher-ups. Anyway, some desk jockey said I was too messed up in the head to go back. That I'd be a risk to the other guys. That I wasn't doing it for the right reasons. Hell if I know what those are."

"That's sort of the way I feel about doing therapy again. Like I'd be more harm than good to anybody. But sometimes I wish I could get lost in someone else's problems for a while."

My stomach turns. Because tomorrow is Tuesday. The day Wendall Grady promised he'd come back. He hadn't seemed the sort of man to shirk his promises. Or change his mind. "For what it's worth, I'm glad they wouldn't take you, Lieutenant Sawyer."

My hand makes its way to his thigh. I glare at it like the traitor it's just proven itself to be.

"Me too. I realized it'd be the last thing Noah would want. Me putting my life—and my buddies' lives—on the line out of anger. Because I couldn't just man up and forgive myself."

In the silence, our fingers intertwine, and he side-eyes me, his face brightening. "Wanna know what I do now when I get really hacked off?" He takes his hand away and reaches into his pocket, then scrolls through pictures on his cell phone until he finds the one. "I look at this."

A little blond boy dressed as Spiderman grins at me from the screen. He's carrying a pumpkin so stuffed with candy that a mini

Snickers bar has gone over the edge and tumbled to the sidewalk below. His blue-sky eyes and mischievous grin belong to Sawyer. "This was one week before he died. The last picture I've got. He slept with his costume on that night. I can't be mad at this picture. He was like joy personified, you know?"

My throat tightens as I nod, thinking of Dakota. All her Halloweens. The princess. The penguin. The zombie cheerleader. "I just need some kind of closure. I can't even look at Dakota's pictures without thinking of *him*. Without imagining what he did to her. He's tainted every memory, and I don't even know his name. Sometimes I feel like I'm losing my mind."

Sawyer pulls me to him in an awkward embrace. There's the console between us and the stinging cold metal of his left arm against my side. But it's perfect too, and I inhale him. Earth and pine needles. "Well, you would know," he teases, his voice muffled in my hair.

I laugh, but it feels like a deep breath. A cleansing one. And then, I hear myself say it. "Do you want to come inside?"

Sawyer pulls back to look at me, uncertain, and I turn away. Desire and shame and the whole messed-up night swirl inside me, distilling to one pure emotion. The one I know best even if it makes no sense. Even if it's misdirected.

"Really? You're saying no. After all the times you've begged me to—"

"To go out to dinner with me. And I haven't *begged* you to do anything." He tries to touch me, but I curl against the door suddenly and unreasonably, wishing I had just gotten out of the car ages ago. "You've also made it pretty clear you didn't want anything serious. Or frankly to even lay eyes on me beyond a goddamn parking lot until those—I'm guessing—drunken texts you sent last night. So forgive me if I'm a little confused."

He's right. He's so right. I know he's right. "Whatever."

I have a flash of a petulant Dakota, her tone heavy with sarcasm, and the lump is back in my throat again. Which only confirms how right he is.

"Mollie, c'mon. This isn't a *no*. It's a *not tonight*. It's a *one step at a time*. Are we clear about that?"

I fling open the door and step out, looming down to growl at him. "Crystal clear."

Then I stomp toward the house, me and my lonely shadow, until both of us are swallowed into the belly of the beast.

CHAPTER NINE

(TUESDAY, OCTOBER 2, 2018)

I can't stop looking at Wendall's black Stetson, positioned on the table between us. Me, in my posh ergo chair, channeling my long-lost doctor self. Wendall, all loose skin stretched over bone, contorted on the sofa. One toothpick leg crossed over the other.

The hat is a line in the sand, a point of demarcation. Without it, I might forget who I'm supposed to be. The reason I woke early this morning, sober as a judge. The reason I set the alarm for the first time in months. Put on lipstick and a shirt with buttons, pants without a drawstring. I even flat-ironed my hair.

Because if I'm going to do this again, I want to do it all the way. To prove to myself I'm better than Sawyer. I can be downrange again, taking fire in the trenches. Bring it on.

So far, Wendall has played his part, rolling up early—but not too early—in his spiffy Cadillac. Summoning me with two delicate beeps of the horn. And offering me a gracious smile as he followed me inside and penned his name at the bottom of my treatment form.

But that hat is strangely disquieting. As surely as I try to keep my eyes from it, it draws me in, constantly flitting into my periphery. Like a broken-winged blackbird, unable to take flight. Or one of Luciana's tarot cards, facedown and waiting to reveal my fate.

"I appreciate you seein' me. Wasn't sure if you would, to be honest. I thought maybe I spooked ya good last week."

"It takes a lot to spook me these days," I say. Like guys in VWs, yearbook photos, hood ornaments. Cowboy hats. "Besides, you piqued my curiosity."

He coughs, a dry, relentless hacking that judders his whole body and sends the stench of tobacco wafting. I offer my regrets to the sofa, which has no doubt been sprayed with wintergreen Skoal. "Did I?"

"I don't usually begin this way." Nothing about this seems usual. "With a question pertaining to myself. But, if you don't mind . . ."

"Not at all. I'm a bit unorthodox myself."

I take a quick breath to steady myself. I don't look at the hat. Especially not at the brim. It takes the shape of a sinister smile. "How did you know about my daughter?"

"Well, I'm an old man. I still read the papers. And I remembered you."

"Remembered?" I hope he can't hear the wariness in my voice, the way it creaks and cracks, like ice in a springtime thaw. "Do I know you?" *There.* Better.

"From Napa State Hospital." He tilts his head, waiting. He wants me to ask any one of the hundred questions ripening in my brain. But I wait too. In here, I can outwait anyone. It feels good to be a part of the game again. This chess match of therapy. "I wasn't a patient," he says, finally. "If that's what you were thinkin'. I worked there as an orderly for fifteen years."

I search his face for a hint of recognition. For something familiar in those loose bags under his eyes, the creases in his forehead, the bit of stubble above his thin upper lip. His earnest expression. "I'm sorry. I don't believe we ever met."

He shrugs. Which, of course, is not a yes or a no. "I retired a few years after you started work, I believe. The patients, they always seemed to like you. And when I saw the story in the *Chronicle* about your little girl, I followed it every day, hoping for you. But you must've realized, working with the kinds of people we did, what the outcome would be."

I leave that one alone. It feels dangerous to admit how hope can take hold, how cruel it can be. How merciless. And in its absence, a whirling black vortex not unlike Glory Hole that had sucked me under and spit out my bones.

"So last week you told me you'd come here to unburden yourself. To push some stones off your chest, I believe. Tell me more about that."

He rights himself on the cushions and nods. "I agree. Let's get right down to brass tacks. Neither of us has time to waste. It all started back in Nam. The wretched things I saw over there. The wretched things I did. It's like napalm to the soul. Nobody came out the same way they went in."

My father had always said war was like a blade. It excised the soft parts from him. And he'd come back all teeth and sinew and metal fragments. He'd even let me press on the spot where the doctors had left a small piece of shrapnel in his calf. "How did it change you?"

"Obscenely."

I sit back, contemplating that, his hat fully in view again. I know better than to ask the question my twelve-year-old self hadn't been able to resist. *Did you ever kill anybody over there, Daddy?* Which had gotten me a smack to the side of the head and a slurred diatribe about showing some goddamned respect for a veteran. But that word—*obscenely*—and the way Wendall had said it, with a gratuitous raise of his thinning brows, demands exploration.

"But," he begins before me. "Change might be the wrong word. I prefer reveal. The war revealed me—my true colors—like one of them paint-with-water pictures the kiddies used to like. Before they got suckered into video games and cell phones."

"Revealed in what way?" I ask, trying not to sound too curious. Neutral, always. Neutral and encouraging.

"Before the war, I'd been engaged to marry Clotilda Abbott. A real sweetheart, that one."

"And after?"

He shakes his head. "We married, alright. I pinned that goddamned Purple Heart to my uniform, and we took our vows at Holy Hope Baptist Church. But I kept expectin' God to strike me down 'cause I was somebody different on the inside. Somebody she didn't know. Like old Charlie got inside of me and gobbled up all the good stuff."

I fend off a shiver. Remind myself he's a dying old man. Skin brittle as fish scales. Bones I could crack with one solid kick. A dying old man who said he could help me. "How were you different?"

He waves off the question with a scarecrow hand. "Tilda's been dead going on twenty-five years now. Her kidneys never did work right. And the doctors said she was too sickly to have a baby. I always wanted a son of my own. A little Grady. But let's be honest, I would've messed up a kid somethin' awful."

"What makes you say that?"

He chuckles like he knows what I'm thinking. That my dad had screwed me up royally.

"You know how it is. The apple don't fall far. And this tree is rotten through and through. Anyway, I took care of Tilda the best I could. I tried to make her happy. But a man has needs."

I feel a little silly. *Infidelity*. That's what he's here to confess. Nothing more. But the relief doesn't hit me the way I expect. My hands are still clasped tight in my lap, keeping a death grip on each other.

"Needs?"

"Needs," he repeats. It sounds like a dirty word. Looks like it too, the way his wiry eyebrows arch. "I'd call us dogs, but that would be an insult—to the dogs. Anyway, I don't need to tell you how men are. You've got experience."

He may as well have punched me in the throat. My words stick there like a shard of bone. How could he know *that?*

Wendall happily fills the silence, plugging along as if I'm not reeling. "Yep. Napa State could be a real education on the male gender. Now, those were some sick puppies. Am I right? Oh, shoot. There I go again, disparaging the doggies."

"It sounds as if you have quite a negative view of men." I'm relieved I manage to croak out some therapist mumbo jumbo. But Wendall doesn't seem to notice. He looks off into the corner, as if he's gone somewhere else in his mind.

"We did meet one time, you know. There. At Napa State. There was an incident on the night shift. One of the patients had knocked a nurse unconscious in the day room. They were supposed to keep that door locked after hours, but whoever's job it was had forgotten or not shown up or just been plain lazy. You know how understaffed they were. It's all about money, money, money."

It takes me a second to catch up to him again, to stop chasing my tail. *We did meet one time.* And when I do, there's this: A furtive flash of movement behind the dayroom door. I'd walked a few steps past, too tired to notice. I'd already slogged through an eleven-hour shift. By the time I'd run back, Karen Dalton's eye had swollen shut, and she wasn't moving.

"You looked tired that day. Probably that's why you don't remember me being there."

I wait again, certain he's about to expose his king. Whatever it is that's brought him here. To me, of all people. But he shifts toward the edge of the sofa and reaches for the hat. He's decided without me. It's time to go. Game over.

"It's a good thing I was, though. Poor Nurse Dalton was about to find herself in a very compromising position. She never did thank me properly."

It wasn't the first attack I'd witnessed at the hospital nor the last. So it takes me a while. But after I sift through the years of pummeling fists, broken arms, and blood spatter on linoleum, I find him. A middle-aged orderly about Wendall's height, with bright eyes that had practically glowed in the dark room. He'd been kneeling beside Nurse Dalton when I'd burst in. The patient who'd attacked her had already bolted.

I want to shout, *I remember you!* But instead I ask, "Are you leaving? We've only just started."

"My stamina's not what it used to be. This damn cancer . . . I swear I sleep like a cat. Sixteen hours a day."

"Are you sure that's it? I wouldn't be a very good therapist if I didn't point out that you avoided my question. About your needs. And now you're hightailing it out of my office."

He shakes a long finger at me. "You are a sharp cookie. Turns out unburdening isn't as easy as I thought it would be. Now that I'm here with you. Face-to-face. The stones . . . well, they aren't pretty."

"Would you like to come back again tomorrow?" I stop short of begging him. *Please, you said you could help me.* Because looking at him, I can't imagine how. "We can take it one stone at a time. Start with the little ones first."

"Now you're talkin'. I know it's a tad unorthodox, like you said. But maybe we could bend the rules a little. If that's okay with you, of course, Doc."

"As long as we stick to a schedule." My halfhearted attempt to maintain some kind of professionalism. Some semblance of a therapeutic frame, patched together with matchsticks and Scotch tape.

"A schedule it is then."

He perches the hat on his knee so I can see it clearly now. What had me captivated. "Are those . . ." I point at the edge of the felt, the little indentions in the shape of—*what else?* A sickle. ". . . bite marks?"

He holds it up, squinting to inspect it more closely. "Well, I'll be damn. I reckon they are. I've had this hat for thirty some odd years. Used to bring it on my hunting trips. Some kind of critter must've grabbed ahold of it. You never can tell what a warm body will do when it's fightin' to stay that way."

I imagine tipping my own king in resignation, the sound of Wendall's gravelly voice scratching in my ear. *Checkmate.*

CHAPTER TEN

"¡ÁNDALE!" Luciana whoops and giggles, extending her hands out of the Jeep's sunroof, her ringed fingers splayed in the wind as I pilot us down the freeway toward Allendale. "A girl could get used to a ride like this. Especially compared to a beater like mine."

I shake my head at her with mock disapproval. "Don't bad-mouth Boludo. You've already given him a horrible complex with that nickname. It's no wonder he's always breaking down on you."

She flops back into the seat, scrunching her nose at me. "Don't think you're forgiven. Just because you're bringing me on some crazy Thelma-and-Louise adventure. I was really worried about you, Mollie. I even called the hospitals, thinking you'd had an accident. Or maybe hurt yourself. I know we said we'd never, but . . ."

I squeeze her shoulder, remembering the promise we'd made over tears and margaritas on our first Taco Tuesday. No matter how bad it gets, we stick it out. We don't let them win. *Them* being Mateo, of course. Mateo and Shadow Man. Though somehow, I'd pictured Cole's face, then my father's, when I'd said it. "I'm sorry I let you down. That I gave you a reason not to trust me. You're my closest friend, and I screwed up."

"*¿Grande?*"

"Yes. *Grande.* I screwed up big."

"So . . . am I Thelma or Louise?" she asks.

I can't hide my grin. Because this is why I'd asked Luciana along. Why I'm grateful she'd agreed. I need her to distract me from the hysterical chatter in my head. The chatter that only quiets beneath screaming men with guitars, a pint of vodka, or Sawyer's rough lips.

"Who do you want to be?"

Luciana shrugs. "My mom never let me see that movie. She said it would turn me into a crazy gringa. But one of them gets lucky with Brad Pitt, right? That's me. *Obviamente.*"

I tap my blinker and ease toward the 505 exit, nothing but scorched earth in either direction. Tall grass, long-withered under the summer sun. Even now, in the fall twilight, it's just waiting to catch fire. I'm not sure if it's Boyd or Wendall or my own paranoia. But inside I feel like a struck match. "Of course. Brad's all yours."

"Mi amor, Bradley," she says, exaggerating her accent and clasping her hands to her heart. "Speaking of *amor*, how did it go with Sawyer on Monday night? He said he'd make sure you—"

"Didn't stalk Boyd home?"

I wish I had. It probably would've ended better. For me anyway. Or maybe not. Last time I'd pulled a stunt like that I'd been served with a restraining order. *Mollie Roark is not permitted to contact Tyler Lowry or his parents or go within fifty feet of Napa Preparatory Academy, where Mr. Lowry is a student.* No matter, because by then I'd all but ruled out Tyler anyway. Not that he wasn't capable of murder—

everybody is—but he'd always struck me as way too cocky and way too stupid to get away with it for long. The kind of Neanderthal who'd texted my daughter, *come on baby i like u sooo much pls send me sexy pics so i can dream about u.* The kind of guy who'd off somebody and brag about it to his minions the next day.

"No," Luciana says, coyly. "Got home safely. Which is guy code for . . ." She bats her eyelashes at me. ". . . you know."

"Luci, how many times can I say it? We are *just* friends."

"Right. Friends who suck face."

I sigh at the haughty little purse of her lips and for a singular moment—an awful moment—I almost chide her. I almost call her Dakota. "You sound like a fifteen-year-old girl," I say, blinking back tears.

"Estoy en lo cierto. And you know it. I'm *so* right."

"Sawyer and I may *suck face*, as you put it, from time to time. But we are both undeniably and irrevocably broken. Do you know what happens when two broken people get together?"

"They make passionate love that heals all their broken pieces." With a grand sweep of her arms, her voice swells. I know she's baiting me. But also, deep down, I think she believes it. I don't say it out loud, but it's that kind of sentimental BS that made her a perfect mark for a creep like Mateo in the first place.

"Someone's been watching too many telenovelas. Two broken people are depressing as hell. All they can manage to do is break everything around them." It's not Sawyer I'm thinking of, though. It's me and Cole. How we'd brought this on ourselves. How the hairline fracture between us had splintered and widened and swallowed Dakota whole. Come to think of it, I'd been something of a perfect mark myself. "I'm not sure I'll ever put my own pieces back together, much less somebody else's."

"Alright then. Just friends, it is. But don't think you can change your mind and go after Brad. He's off limits."

I roll my eyes at her, and a curtain of silence falls between us. Both expectant and conclusive, like the end of a Broadway show.

I'm not sure whether I'm the starlet waiting to bow to the audience or the stagehand watching with good-natured envy.

Luciana flips through her phone, reading softly to herself. "¡Ay, Dios mío!" she says, her face stricken. *So stagehand then.* "What kind of place are you taking me to?"

"What do you mean?" I ask. "We're going to Allendale. I told you."

The Jeep rumbles through the final turn and onto the gravel road as she shows me the screen. The Wikipedia page for the great metropolis of Allendale. "You didn't tell me it was in a story about the end of the world. May the goddess protect us."

"Luci, you can't be serious."

But she is apparently, handpicking the worst phrases, her panic gathering strength. "A story by Ray Bradbury. Post-apocalyptic. Incinerated by a nuclear weapon . . ."

All I can hear is my father's voice at the side of my bunk, rumbling like distant thunder, as he'd read the story to me from a yellowed issue of *The Martian Chronicles* by the light of a lantern casting disfigured shapes on the wall. I'd felt a secret thrill, a little zip of horror, when he'd recited, "Today is August 4, 2026 . . . in the city of Allendale, California."

Luciana draws a deep breath as she makes the sign of the cross. "The family incinerated . . . and the dog is the only living creature!"

I don't tell her I'd been to cursed Allendale just last week. I don't mention the squirrels hung like war flags on my father's fence posts or the gaping punji pit where I'd nearly been speared. I sure as hell don't tell her Bradbury's bit about the dog was what I'd liked best, because the dog had lived, at least for a while. That was when we still had Roscoe, the old basset with bad hips. My dad had found him dumped on the side of the road just beyond the junkyard. A lot of dogs turned up that way—Sambo and Rex and Waggles—and my father carted them home and let me name them and dress them up and push them around in an old baby stroller. Until Roscoe. He'd been the last.

I reach for the radio dial. Something fierce and pounding to stamp the memory down, send it back into the boneyard where it belongs.

But just then, I see it. Straight from the pages of my childhood, the part at the end when the story turns dark. When Hansel and Gretel roast in the witch's oven, and Red Riding Hood discovers a wolf in grandma's bed.

I point up ahead. "That's it. Whitetails and Whoppers. The place from the jumping card."

Luciana screams.

I brake hard, the back wheels of the Jeep sliding like a snake across the gravel. In the headlights' glow, a winged creature swoops into the ditch and out again, ensnaring something small and furry in its talons.

Luciana's got my arm in the same sort of death grip. "It's just an owl," I say, surprised at my own voice. How shaky it sounds. Like those cracks in the ice are deeper than I thought and spreading. "It's caught something."

Probably a ground squirrel by the size of it. Dad didn't like them either, the way they'd popped in and out of their burrows before he could get a clean shot. *Assholes in foxholes*, he'd mutter under his breath as he plugged their dens with concrete.

"El búho. An owl," she repeats, releasing me. "Are you serious?"

I nod, feeling uneasy as I listen to the sound of her breathing. She buries her head in her hands.

"Are you okay, Luci?"

"Don't you know anything about mysticism? Symbols in nature? Chica, you really are clueless. You're such a doctor. All science, science, science."

She makes it sound like a bad thing. And look like it too, the way she shakes her head at me.

"My abuela, Cinta, saw an owl the day before she was set to travel to Mexico City. Do you know what happened there the next day? El terremoto. The big one. The whole city was destroyed. But she was safe at home. She always told me, 'Luci, los búhos pueden ver en la oscuridad.' Owls can see in the dark. They see things coming, and if we're blessed, they warn us. She always thought that owl was my grandfather's spirit sent to protect her."

Saying nothing, I park the car and shut the engine. My pulse pounds with a rhythm so frenetic I wonder if Luciana can hear it, can see it throbbing in my neck. I crack the door and peer into the trees that line the storefront, searching for the owl. I need to see it. I don't know why.

"There," Luciana says, softly. "In the tree."

Dangling down from a slim branch and firmly in the owl's clutches, the legs of the ground squirrel scrabble for life. In the twilight, two gleaming eyes meet mine. The owl's head swivels once to its right. Then, it opens its wings, like an archangel, and takes to the sky.

****

Luciana trails behind me as we approach the storefront. At every soft snap of a twig in the underbrush, I hear her suck in a breath. I can't stop thinking about that helpless ground squirrel, doomed but thrashing against its fate. I feel that way sometimes. Like the universe has me by the scruff.

A set of rickety stairs deposits us at the entrance, just beneath the sign. It's the way I remember but different too. Distorted like Mol's had been by the dull lens of adulthood. Smaller and shabbier and less alive. Up close, the store's cheerful green paint peels back from the boards, revealing a second skin, a darker green below. The color of camouflage. A homemade sign taped in the front window proclaims half-off ammo and deer bait now that the season is over. The severed head of a buck, who didn't get so lucky, welcomes us with a glassy stare from just beyond the screen door. *How could I have ever belonged here? In this world. Where killing is sport.*

Dad had told me: *Steady. Steady now. Look 'em in the eyes before you pull that trigger.* But I'd squeezed mine shut instead, sending my first shot into the belly of a sycamore and the six-pointer in my rifle's sights bounding into the thicket, vanished before I'd opened them.

I push the door open, hear the familiar jingle—the set of ancient brass bells—and I'm gone thirty-something years into the past. When that sound had moved me, as enchanted as a dream, and I'd tapped them with my finger until my father snatched my hand away and buried it in his.

"Wow," Luciana whispers. "Miedo." And I'm not sure whether she's referring to the creepy Hall of Horns—the long, dark corridor at the back of the store lined ceiling to floor with antlers of all sizes—or the bear of a man at the counter, his beard thick and wiry as a Brillo Pad.

"Hello?" If my voice sprouted legs, it would be on tiptoe, light-footed and ready to run.

Grizzly Man glances up at me from his tattered copy of *Outdoor Life* and grunts. Since I don't speak bear, I wave meekly in return. The store is cold and empty, not the bustling landmark I remember. The place where men like my father gathered to tell their tall tales to their own kind.

Luciana runs a hand along the shelf nearest the counter where the brightly colored fishing lures hang like ornaments on a Christmas tree. She selects an unnaturally green minnow and turns to me, holding the hook to her ear. "I thought it was an earring," she says.

Grizzly Man clears his throat. Which is probably bear speak for *step away from the merchandise.* My heart somersaults in my chest when he speaks.

"What can I do ya for, ladies? Ya don't look like the huntin'-and-fishin' type."

"I've got a pair of horns hanging on that wall, believe it or not."

"Do ya now?" He nods at me, but his eyes seem unconvinced. "Ya here for the sale then? We got the decoys and deer calls on clearance."

Luciana snorts, disguising her derision with a loud cough. When I give her a look, she slinks away down the clothing aisle, taking up a position between the camo jackets and fishing vests.

"We're not here for the sale. I was hoping you could take a peek at a picture for me."

Grizzly sits up, rolling the magazine tightly between his paws, and swipes the air. "Goddamn. Are you a cop? I don't want no trouble. I just got off parole."

Keeping my face therapist neutral, I slide Dakota's yearbook photo across the counter. She'd been frantic that morning when she'd discovered the tiniest of pimples on her chin. *You can't even see it*, I'd told her as she caked on my concealer in the mirror.

Are you kidding, Mom? School pictures, remember? This zit is going to be immortal. When I'm forty it'll still be there, staring back at me, reminding me how freakin' ugly I was. Do you think they can photoshop it out?

Her yearbook picture. But that's not the way I think of it. Not anymore. It's the photo I gave the detectives the day she never came home. The photo they showed on the news every night for over a month. The one plastered on that godforsaken billboard and shared online. Propped on an easel in front of her coffin. It's ruined forever, a manifestation of my pain. And now it's the photo I tap with my finger, drawing Grizzly's eyes.

"I'm not a cop. This is my daughter, Dakota. Do you recognize her?"

He studies the picture more carefully than I'd expected. My body tenses in the silence under the weight of what he might say. What he might know. "This is that girl that got—that got kidnapped a few years back, right?"

I nod, though it still seems surreal. My girl. Kidnapped. And *murdered*. The word he didn't say. A fresh surge of devastation crashes against my chest—a bone-crushing tidal wave—and it's unbearable. "She had a business card for this place. I only just found it. I was thinking she might've come in here."

Luciana appears next to me, holding a camo T-shirt across her chest.

"Isn't this cute?" she asks.

Grizzly perks up, like he's been kicked in the flank. The slight upturn of his ursine mouth disgusts me. He licks his lips, barely visible beneath his brown scruff.

"It's on sale too," he says. "You can try it on if you like."

Luciana seems not to hear him. She nudges me. "Did you tell him about her hair? That it was pink? Not like the picture."

"Pink hair," Grizzly repeats, and I nod again as he tears his gaze away from Luciana's breasts and back to the photograph.

"She'd dyed it," I explain. And that too comes with a surge. Of regret this time, bitter and twisting and relentless. I hate myself. "The color of bubblegum."

He shakes his head and pushes the photo back to me. I leave it there, not wanting to claim it. The last yearbook photo. Dakota had been right. That picture was a vampire, immortal and life-sucking. "Never seen her. Sorry."

"Are you sure?" Luciana asks. "*Mira*. Look again."

Grizzly smirks. "Español, eh? Just like my old lady, Fernanda. *Ex*-old lady. She was a spicy little Latina too. Always runnin' her mouth. Anyway, I'm sure I ain't seen this girl. I only been workin' here 'bout a year. Before that, that puta, Fernanda, got me a two-year stint down at Folsom Prison."

Luciana's a warrior like me. Her war paint, a lukewarm, lipstick smile—tight and polite and placid. But behind her eyes, I see it. I'm no stranger to fear. Terror either. That icicle dagger that falls in a blink from nowhere, piercing all the soft parts it finds and turning them cold.

"It's okay," I tell him. "Maybe I can leave this here. You can ask around."

The photo sits, untouched, as he frowns at it. Like he's thinking bear thoughts. Instinctual and predatory. I feel it too. The sting of ice at my neck. But it means nothing to me now. I shrug it off, shoo it away. Since I lost Dakota, fear is as inconsequential as a fly.

"You with that other guy?" he asks.

"What other guy?"

"Tall, skinny fella. Had the same picture. Came in here a while back askin' the same kind of questions."

"Did he leave a name?" I try to sound the opposite of how I feel. Desperate. Maniacal. Ready to throttle him if necessary. He has no fucking idea who I am. What I'm capable of. I'm not sure *I* know.

"Nah. He was real jittery. I knew he wasn't no cop. Wouldn't have the stomach for it. But I do remember somethin' about him."

"Well?"

Grizzly leans back, hands on his ample stomach. "What's it worth to ya?"

"*Ladrón*," Luciana mutters, tossing the camo T-shirt at him. "Taking advantage of a mother who's lost her child. You want that on your conscience?"

"Your money's good too, chilosa. Unless you have somethin' else in mind."

I stalk toward the Hall of Horns, rage and fear bubbling up in my blood. What a strange, powerful concoction. There's no way to know if it's still here, affixed to the wall near the horns of the whitetail buck whose life I'd ended with a perfectly placed bullet to the heart. But, if it is, I figure it belongs to me. To my family. And now seems as good a time as any to claim it.

"Do you know my father?" My own voice frightens me. The sharp edge of it, so much like my dad's.

Grizzly's eyes—two dull marbles—open wide in a way that satisfies something clawed and hungry inside me. "They used to call him Crazy Krandel."

At the end of the corridor, in front of the back exit, a small portion of the wall is marked *WAR MEMORABILIA*.

I spot the bayonet right away. The M7 my father had carted back from Vietnam and donated to Whitetails and Whoppers at his

97

shrink's suggestion. Those were the days when he still listened to his doctors.

I smack the display case, popping the cheap lock, and open it, wrapping my fingers around the black plastic handle, strangling it in my grip. "I hated that nickname. Because it was the truth. He's stark raving mad." *And I'm a chip off the old cuckoo block.* But that seems obvious, with the way the words force themselves from my mouth. Plunging like paratroopers into battle, they leave bits of spittle in the corners.

Grizzly curses under his breath and puts his hands in the air, his palms white as ivory. Probably sweaty too. He's human after all, then. "I told you, lady. I don't want no trouble."

"Crazy Krandel used to wake me up with the army's bayonet drill. Want to hear it?"

He shakes his head no. As if I care. "I'll tell you what you wanna know," he says. "All of it. I swear." But even as he makes his pledge, one of those beefy bear paws drops beneath the counter. Like he's pinning a sockeye salmon beneath it, readying himself to take a bite.

"It goes like this. Kill, kill, kill without mercy . . ." No time to waste, I stalk toward him, raising the bayonet. I hear myself laugh, and it sounds as distant and strange as those brass bells on the door.

He raises his hand, slow and measured. Turns out he's caught a pistol. Not a fish. And he waves it at me. "Damn, woman. You are as nutty as a fruitcake. In here, I'm in charge. And there ain't nothin' for free. So, if you wanna make a deal, I'll bite. Otherwise, you can take your old man's knife and stick it where—"

Luci charges from behind a rack of fishing hats, aiming her cell phone right at him. "*Hablas mucho.* You're a big talker, aren't you? Go ahead, keep talking. I'll bet the cops would like to know there's an ex-con working in a store that sells firearms. And I have him on video brandishing a gun at a woman who lost her only child. Whose side do you think they'll be on? What will Fernanda think, seeing you carted back to prison?"

Maybe it's only my imagination. But Grizzly's chin seems to tremble, and along with it, his beard. It reminds me of my father's squirrel pelts shivering in the wind. How something so dead can look alive. He lowers the gun and deposits it on the counter.

"Alright. Alright. That guy with your daughter . . . he had a—" I flinch at him, just to watch him squirm. "A burn mark. A burn mark on his arm."

"Now, was that so hard?" I slide the bayonet into my back pocket and snatch Dakota's photo from the counter, my hands shaking with a life of their own. "If you say anything about this to anyone, I'll send Crazy Krandel up here."

Luci waves the phone in his face, taunting him. "And the video goes viral, *chiloso.*"

"Got it?" I ask.

He opens his mouth, but no sound comes out. Which I figure is as good as a yes.

"Next time, don't be an asshole."

I follow Luciana to the door. But before I leave, I toss the bells onto the concrete and stomp them beneath my heel just because I can. Because it feels good to be the owl swooping down to take what it wants. To be the destroyer. Rather than the bits of gristle and fur left behind.

****

Neither of us speaks. Luciana pulls her feet onto the seat beneath her, leaving the bayonet alone on the floorboard. She rolls down the window and lets the night air buffet through her fingers. Like she's flying. It reminds me of the black bird on Dakota's shoulder, leaving the confines of its cage behind. *Had Dakota felt like that? Had I caged her?*

Every so often, Luciana wipes at a tear trail down her cheek and sniffles. Confused, I do what I always do. Turn on the radio. Slayer is scream-singing about the skin of the dead and what it feels like when they steal your soul. The guitar and the yelling and the beat of the drum blow my mind clean. Banish Grizzly to his steel-barred cage in the corner.

"You were a badass in there, Luci. A total Thelma. What happened? What's wrong?"

"You should've warned me. That was muy loca. You know I don't like violence. We both could've gotten hurt. Or worse. Now I won't sleep for a week."

"Well, you said you wanted to be Thelma," I say, hoping for a half smile at least. "That makes me Louise. She's the one who killed that guy, Harlan."

Luci shakes her head. But at least she stops crying.

"I didn't plan it. It just . . ." There's so much wrong with what I'm about to say. I'd never let a patient get away with it. "It just happened."

"¡No me jodas! Things don't just happen. You've been acting crazy. You pulled a knife on that guy."

"Yeah, and he deserved it. He's a bully with a gun. And he insulted you. You were afraid of him. I could tell. He reminded you of Mateo." She groans, a vocal eye roll. And I know I've gone too far. Therapizing her. Even if it is true.

"That was not about *me*."

"Luci, I had to know. Whatever he was hiding. It was important. I'm glad I did it. Because I was right about Boyd."

"Boyd?"

"Who else do you know with a burn mark on his arm?"

She sighs, still not meeting my eyes. "La coincidencia. Have you ever thought it might be just that?"

"But you don't believe in coincidences. You're the one who told me to go there in the first place. *Never ignore a jumping card.* Remember that?"

"I told you to go see your father. Not to turn into an idiota." Finally, she looks at me, still shell-shocked. "Did your dad really do that? Yell that every morning?"

"Not *every* morning."

"You never said anything. I knew you and him had your differences, but that . . . ay, Dios mío. No child should suffer that way."

"He wasn't always crazy." *Crazy Krandel shoots 'em dead. Smack in the middle of the forehead. Crazy Krandel fries 'em up. Then Mollie eats them squirrels for sup.* The title track of my childhood beats in the back of my brain like a tiny fist. I almost find myself humming along to the tune of my destruction. "Dad turned nineteen in Vietnam. Can you imagine? It figures he came back with severe PTSD. My mom thought it would go away, but it only got worse when they had me. As I got older, he refused to take his meds, and he'd have these episodes of extreme paranoia. After a while, the episodes got longer and longer until he was just full-time Crazy Krandel. He did things then. Bad things."

Luciana lowers her head. Like I'm a poor, pitiful wretch. She can't even bear to look at me. "Did he hurt you?"

Hurt. Such a small word. A word that could've fit in the pocket of my father's corduroy jacket, tucked next to the Swiss army knife he'd carried. A word so small and so sneaky it could seep into the cracks of his mind without him ever knowing. *Hurt people hurt people*, my mom would whisper in the early days, before she'd given up on him. With the sounds of my father's rage clamoring in the background. And then there was the silence. The faraway look in his eyes, as if he existed in another world. His body, just a shell in this one.

"He smacked me around a few times. But mostly, the hurt happened in here." I tap my head with a sad smile. "Psychological warfare."

"And you lived with him? What judge would agree to that? Hombre estúpido."

"My mom tried. Maybe a little too hard. A year or so after they'd split, she helped me make up a lie about my dad to tell the judge. She wanted it to be the worst thing possible, so they'd have no choice but to grant her full custody. But it didn't work. I wasn't a very good liar, and the judge figured it out. Plus, he was partial to my dad anyway, being a Vietnam vet himself."

"Lo siento mucho."

"It's alright. It's over now." As if that could ever be true. Some part of me had gone on living at Mol's long after I'd run away. Some part of me still existed there—a second, secret, shivering heart—buried in the woods among Roscoe's bones. Barely beating in the dark earth beside his basset skull, which would be smooth and perfect by now, save for that single bullet hole.

I'm speeding, hurtling down the freeway, toward home. But mostly away from Allendale, my personal dystopia. Next to me, Luciana clears her throat.

"My grandma always told me to honor the past. That it's our legacy. But, you know what I think? The past is the worst gift I ever got—worse than the time Mateo gave me Jessica Rabbit seat covers for Boludo—and it just keeps right on giving. What's that old saying? *It ain't over till it's over.*"

I nod. "Or until the fat lady sings."

We both laugh, but I know exactly what she means. Some things are never over. Never can be. Never will.

****

I go alone to Cuttings Wharf. To the house tucked at the end of the cul-de-sac with its mint-green siding and its dismal plastic Santa toppled over in the front lawn. In another two months or so, they could stand him up again and no one would be the wiser. But the cracks in his faded red suit tell me he hasn't been upright for a while. That Christmases passed with him lying here. Summers too.

I envy that Santa. Because my stomach curdles at the thought of another Christmas without Dakota. The first had been bad enough. Like I'd been dropped in the middle of an ocean with a cannonball chained around my neck. But last year—the second Christmas—

was the worst. Because by then, I'd learned how to keep my head above water. Still, there was no shore in sight. Only circling shark fins, an infinite horizon, and the burn of salt in my throat.

I pause on the front stoop, swallow a sob, and let my tears distill to fury. Then I step from the shadows into the glow of the porch lamp and rap at the door before I can rethink it. Boyd Blackburn deserves what's coming to him. Just like Grizzly.

From inside, I hear a steady thump that grows louder and clearer until the door cracks open.

"Who is it?" The real-life Martha Blackburn appears, with a voice as sweet and fragile as a candy cane. She inches her walker a bit closer and peers up at me through the gap, smiling. This might be harder than I thought.

I smile back at her, and she lets the gap widen, revealing a hallway. And then a living room. A plastic-covered sofa, a well-worn armchair, and a grandfather clock presided over by a muted, forty-two-inch Judge Judy. "Uh, hi. I'm a friend of Boyd's. Is he home?"

"Oh." She looks me over skeptically. I wish I'd worn the *Trust Me, I'm a Jedi* T-shirt Cole had left behind. Or at least a pressed button-down shirt and my reading glasses. "Do you go to ITT too, dear?"

"Something like that," I say. "He's tutoring me, actually."

"Now that's my Boyd. Always wanting to help a fellow student. And a pretty one at that. What class?"

I freeze in the spotlight of her question, my heart rattling around like a pebble in a steel drum. And for a moment, I see it. The way I'll toss her aside like a bag of bones, her walker clattering against the hardwood.

"Oh, silly me." She ushers me inside, oblivious. "It must be Computer Forensics. He told me he'd made a few friends in there. Am I right?"

I let out a shaky breath and follow her. "Absolutely. Computer Forensics. It's my favorite."

"His too. Goodness, I'll bet he's tickled pink that you two have so much in common." She waves me over to the sofa and hands me a folded stack of T-shirts and underwear. "Take this down to him, will you? I can't climb those stairs like I used to since the knee replacement. And Lord knows he won't relocate the Overbridge for me."

I take the warm stack in one hand, averting my eyes from the Hanes briefs, size L, bleached white and smelling of lavender. "The Overbridge?"

"It's from Star Wars." I recognize her tone. Equal parts exasperation and fondness. Standard mother-ese, the language that's lost to me now. "I'll let him explain it to you, dear."

I don't tell her I already know about the Overbridge. That Cole had insisted on giving me, and then Dakota, a proper Star Wars education, which meant watching all the films in order every May fourth. But then that day became like any other, with me seeing patients at the hospital and Dakota at swim practice and Cole on call after surgery. I couldn't remember when we'd stopped, only that we had. Now it seems crucial. The beginning of the end of our family. The fine cracks that would grow into fissures that would break open the ground beneath me.

Martha points to the door at the end of the hallway. "Right down those steps. Technically, it's the basement, but I play along. Boyd always did have an active imagination. And after his accident . . . well, I really think that's what got him through it. All of his best friends were make-believe."

I march ahead, unflinching, stopping short just before I reach the doorway. I pretend to adjust the picture hanging crooked on the wall. I want a better look at it, and I squint in the dim light to make it out.

"Who is that?" I blurt. "I'm sorry. I just didn't realize Boyd had a—"

"Oh, no, dear. Don't worry. That's not his girlfriend if that's what you are thinking. She'd be a bit young for him anyway." She taps the pretty face behind the plexiglass. "This is Amanda. Boyd's half sister. She goes to some fancy private school."

Martha mistakes the little cave of my open mouth for curiosity. Instead of what it really is. A sudden shock. A tectonic shift of my core. Boyd had been telling the truth. It makes me question everything. Maybe Cole was right about me. Maybe I am paranoid.

"My ex remarried a woman half his age with quadruple his bank account. Some high falutin' lawyer. He decided he wanted to be a daddy again. Can you imagine? A brand-new baby at age fifty?" There's something familiar in her sigh too. She's a scorned woman. A woman left behind. Not unlike myself. "Listen to me. Talking your ear off. I'm sure you want to get to your studies. Boyd will be so happy to see you."

She calls out to him, "Boyd, honey. You've got company," squashing the element of surprise beneath her orthopedic loafers.

I descend into the Overbridge one creaky wooden stair at a time, anticipating the humming swipe of Boyd's light saber cutting through the darkness. But what little I can see in the glow of a lava lamp is more craft-store than Death Star lair. Martha's a champion scrapbooker, it seems, with a mountainous tower of storage containers marked SCRAPBOOK SUPPLIES. At the base of the steps, I pass a tangled jungle of Christmas lights and cautiously traverse the plains of broken-down cardboard boxes.

I set the stack of laundry on a card table and approach Boyd from behind, his neck slim and pale as a swan's. I tap his shoulder.

A quick glance back, and he scrambles up from his recliner. Noise-canceling headphones tossed aside. "Whoa. What the—" He stumbles toward the bookcase in the corner, steadying himself with one hand and clutching his chest with the other, breathing audibly in the dank quiet. "What the hell are you doing here? How you'd get in?"

I put a finger to my lips. "Your mother thinks we're studying computer forensics. And she's very happy you have a *real* friend. So let's not disappoint her."

Keeping his eyes on me, Boyd grasps at the floor to retrieve his headphones. They've tumbled partway under the computer console, and the sleeves of his ill-fitting bathrobe don't quite cover the burn on his arm. It's worse than I'd thought. Near the crook of his elbow, his arm is disfigured. Like the fire took a great big bite. Twig-legs protrude from the bottom of his robe. One look at the Wookiee slippers on his feet makes me certain.

Boyd didn't kill Dakota.

But I push the thought away. I don't trust my eyes anymore. Napa State taught me that, at least. I've seen too many baby-faced men with mile-long rap sheets. Too many sheep with wolves' teeth.

"I know you lied to me," I say.

"I told you. My sister has a different last name. I can show you if you don't—"

"Not about your sister. Your mother was kind enough to explain all that."

"What then?" Boyd paces from one end of the room to the other, and I follow him with my eyes. He stops in front of the wall and stares up at *A New Hope* movie poster, Darth Vader's face looming in the background.

"For one thing, you don't have a dead kid. And two, you know my daughter better than you let on. *Knew* her, I mean." That word sinks like a barb into my chest and sticks there. "You went looking for her at Whitetails and Whoppers."

Boyd shakes his head so fast I can't tell if he's denying it still. Or if the truth has possessed him like a spirit, rattling his brain and demanding its way out. I walk to him, slipping my father's bayonet from my back pocket, where I'd concealed it beneath my sweater.

In that moment, I understand better than I ever did how easy it is to become someone else. Someone who'd bare her teeth and brandish a knife twice in one day. I remember what one of my patients at Napa had told me once, something I'd branded as a cognitive distortion. A way to minimize the forty-three knife wounds he'd cut into his mother's body. *It wasn't me that stabbed her. But it was. That's the part I can't get over.*

Knife in hand, I get it now. My soul rolls end over end like a tossed quarter—dark to light and back again. Who knows where it'll land?

Boyd's high-pitched scream startles us both. But I silence it fast, clamping my hand across his mouth. His lips squirm beneath my fingers.

"Everything alright down there?" Martha calls from the top of the stairs.

Tell her it's fine, I mouth to him, holding the knife where he can see it. Apparently, the quarter landed. Shadow side up.

"It's fine." But his voice squeaks out, and I narrow my eyes at him, taking a step closer. A step that compels him to try again. "I just tripped over Yoda."

"Didn't I tell you to turn on some lights down there? And keep her in the cage. You'll break your neck one day. Or hers."

"C'mon, Ma. We covered this already. Technically, she doesn't have a neck. She's not like other vertebrates."

After another of Martha's drawn-out sighs, the door shuts, leaving us alone. With Yoda. Who I've spotted coiled next to the recliner. Her spotted skin a perfect camouflage against the brown carpet.

"A snake? Really?"

He murmurs against my hand before I lower it, allowing him to speak. "She's a ball python. They're really shy, so she won't hurt you. Even if I wanted her to."

"That's comforting."

"About as comforting as the knife you've got pointed at me. Aren't you a doctor? A psychologist? You're supposed to help people."

"Not anymore." Still, I bring the knife to my side, thinking of my promise to help Wendall. And the part of me that still lives, barely, buried miles under the stinking refuse of grief and rage. "I need to know the truth about what happened to my daughter. And I'll do whatever I need to do to get it. Understand?"

107

He nods and scoots away from the wall, scooping up Yoda. She curls around herself, forming a twisted ball on the crook of his elbow, her skin pulsing.

"What happened to you?" I ask him. "To your arm?"

He deposits Yoda into a large terrarium, partially hidden by life-size cutouts of Luke Skywalker and C-3PO, and runs his hand down the length of her. "I fell into a fiery pool like Darth Vader. Only the power of the dark side kept me alive. Isn't that right, girl?"

Watching his shoulders slump over the tank, I feel the hot pinprick of pity at the center of my cold heart. Slowly, slowly, it starts to thaw. "I don't think Yoda would approve of you cavorting with the dark side. Besides, from the way you're dressed, I thought you were part Wookiee."

He laughs sharply. As if my humor caught him off guard. And why wouldn't it? I'd been wielding a knife moments ago.

"Dakota said you used to watch Star Wars together."

"What? What did you say?"

My half-thawed heart clunks to a stop. I hear a soft splash as Yoda slinks into a basin of water. Boyd spins around to face me, his eyes wide. And then my whole world catches fire.

"Don't freak out. Don't freak out. Don't freak out." He stares at my hands, repeating the words like a mantra. I realize I'm pointing the bayonet again. Right at him.

"You have exactly ten seconds to explain to me why you—*a thirty-two-year-old man*—were talking to my daughter about anything. And it better be convincing. Or you'll get a taste of the real dark side from somebody's who's been there and back."

Boyd slips away from Yoda's enclosure, muttering under his breath, and I stalk him as he scurries toward the back wall.

"Wait—how do you know how old I—"

"Nine . . . eight . . . seven . . ."

"Okay, okay. We only talked online. In a chat room. I didn't know she was a kid. Not at first."

"What kind of chat room?" I demand, waving the knife like a deranged conductor, commanding my own maniacal orchestra. With wrath pounding the bass drum in time to my pulse, fear piping merrily on the flute, and despair on the sax, wailing away like John Coltrane.

Boyd raises his hands in defense against all of it. Against me. "Not the kind you're thinking. The site was all about finding Shadow Man. A bunch of us true-crime buffs trying to piece the evidence together. Dakota was good at it. We worked together sometimes."

I flash back to Dakota, flopped on her bed with her cell or her laptop. She'd turn it over or snap it shut every time I walked in. When had that started? That blatant secrecy I'd attributed to normal adolescent development. Identity versus role confusion, according to Erikson's stages. No one ever told me the line between normal and not could be razor thin, practically indiscernible. "The detectives never found anything like that on her computer. What was it called?"

"Shadow Seekers. And they wouldn't find it there. She always used the computer at the public library, because—"

"Because?"

"Because she thought you'd overreact. You and her dad." A villainous laugh claws up the back of my throat, and Boyd backpedals blindly, bumping into a movie poster. The tape at the corners loosens, and it droops down from the wall, revealing a white board behind it.

"She didn't want to be at home anyway. She never really said why. Just that things were messed up. And she thought . . ."

Boyd goes on without me. Because I'm stuck, gaping. Trying to make sense of what I see. But he flinches when I reach behind him and rip the first poster free. Then, the others. They fall to the ground unceremoniously.

Boyd has his own suspect wall, as familiar to me as my own hand. With Tyler. Cole. And the same hodgepodge of copied newspaper clippings of the elusive Shadow Man and his reign of terror. But I'm drawn elsewhere. To the one face absent from my wall. Though

I recognize the woman in the photocopy, she's alien to me now. Clad in a stark white button-down, her sleek brown hair shining. She's clearly a professional. She's certainly happy. She must be. Only I know otherwise.

Because that woman is me. I'd taken the headshot at Cole's insistence. For the website he'd set up to promote my nonexistent private practice. In the office I'd never used until Wendall. Now, it's practically a mug shot. Looking at her—*me*—from here, she's guilty as hell.

My legs shake beneath me, and I slump down to the floor, letting the bayonet fall. "You think I killed my daughter? You think I burned her body and dumped it in the middle of nowhere like a sack of trash?"

Boyd gulps and points to the little red *X* on the edge of photocopy. "Not anymore. But I had to follow the breadcrumbs. That's why I came to your group. I needed to see for myself what you were like."

"And? Was my grief convincing enough for you?"

"It sounds bad, I know. But what do you expect? You and your husband were the last ones to see Dakota alive. And she said . . ."

He looks at me the way I look at myself sometimes. The way the judge had looked at me too as a little girl. Like he can see down to the rotten core. Where the secrets and the half-truths writhe like worms. Suddenly Boyd doesn't seem so powerless.

"She told me you hit her."

I pull my knees to my aching chest and open my mouth to speak. To protest. But my lungs squeeze shut, trapping the words in my throat. They burn like poison. I can't quite figure out what hurts the most—what she'd said or who she'd said it to. Either way, I don't want Boyd to watch me lose it.

"I think I should leave now." But when I don't move—I'm not sure I can—he extends his hand, his scars silvery in the lamplight.

I'm too proud. Too shaken. Too indignant. He lets it drop, useless at his side.

"Dakota was nice to me," he says, looking down at his slippers. "And smart too. She told me, *Chewie*—that's my username—*just go where the clues lead you.* So that's what I did."

I'm halfway up the stairs when Boyd calls out to me. "Are you gonna tell the police about me? I mean, it's not like I have anything to hide."

The doorknob feels as cold as death in my hot palm. I imagine Martha on the other side, pressing her ear to the door.

"Hey, you left your . . . uh . . ." He holds the bayonet at arm's length. I can't blame him. Since I'd snatched it from the wall, the few screws holding me together had come unloosed.

"Keep it."

****

Sawyer's truck is parked in my driveway. Not that I'm surprised. I blame Luciana and her big mouth. Because after I'd dropped her off at home—and she'd begged me not to do anything stupid—he'd fired off a string of texts I hadn't bothered to answer.

Luci is pretty shaken up. Did you pull a knife on a guy?
She wants me to check on you.
I'm coming over. OK?
I'll wear my RBA.
That's Ranger Body Armor, FYI.
C'mon, that was funny.

I belt out one last chorus of "Welcome to the Jungle" before I put the Jeep in park and kill the engine. Sawyer waves at me from the front porch, hangdog. I didn't think I could feel any worse, but I do. Because he's still in his groundskeeper's uniform: mud-spattered boots and a well-worn Blue Rose work shirt.

"How long have you been here?"

He shrugs. "Well, I watched your neighbor take his kid to soccer practice and bring him home again. So . . ."

"I didn't ask you to come."

"Luci called me at work. She thinks you're having a breakdown, and I'm the only one who can talk some sense into you."

I leave that last bit alone, ignoring the urge to collapse against him. "A breakdown, huh? That would imply I'm not already broken."

"Yeah, I figured you were *fine*. Like usual. So, if you're all good, I guess I'll just mosey on along."

He stands up and brushes past me, close enough for me to touch. I grab his arm and he freezes, his muscles tensing beneath my hand. I hate how warm his skin feels. But I especially hate how much I like touching him.

"I thought you didn't ask me to come."

"I didn't ask you to leave either."

Frustrated, he sighs, and I let his arm go. In the silence, I hear Gus scratching at the front door. That sound, unabashedly needy, weakens my resolve.

"It's been a rough day," I admit, heading for the door. "I can tell you about it—*I'd like to*—but I need to let the dog out first."

As I unlock the door, Gus pushes it open with his front paws, bounding into the yard with reckless enthusiasm. He stops briefly to sniff Sawyer's boots, then dives into the grass, rolling like a worm. Sawyer laughs, and I do too. It's like releasing a breath I've been holding.

"He'll be at this for a while," I say. "Do you want to come inside?" And just like that, I'm right back to not breathing. I'd made a total fool of myself last night with those very same words. "For coffee, I mean."

"Coffee sounds great." He pauses for a beat and smiles. "Just give me a sec to grab my RBA."

In spite of everything, I smile back. "Safety first."

****

Coffee cup in hand, Sawyer follows me down the hallway to Dakota's room, an exhausted Gus trailing behind him. I stop when I reach the door and take a quick, scalding sip. Thanks to the caffeine, I feel halfway normal again. Thanks to Sawyer too. So maybe Luciana had a point.

I turn the knob and brace myself for it. Whatever it is that sucks me in here and won't let me go.

"So you didn't know anything about the website? Or this guy, Boyd?" Sawyer asks, lingering in the threshold.

He lets me go in alone, though I don't ask him to. I wonder how he does that. How he reads my mind. Like he already knows this place doesn't belong to anyone but me.

"She was into serial killers. She'd been reading a bunch of books. Thriller and true crime. That sort of thing. Cole didn't like it. I thought it was just a weird phase. Maybe something to do with my work at the hospital. But she never said anything about the Shadow Man. And she definitely did not mention Boyd. I'm not even sure she knew his real name."

I walk to Dakota's desk and unplug her laptop, feeling ridiculous for leaving it plugged in. Since the detectives had returned it, I'd opened it twice and then only to listen to her music. But when I look to Sawyer—shame reddening my face—there's no need to explain.

"Do you think it's possible that Dakota . . ." He steps aside to let me out, laughing a little under his breath. Like he can't quite believe what he's about to say.

"Do I think my teenage daughter solved a twenty-year-old cold case? No."

Still shaking my head, I cart the computer and my coffee cup to the living room and take a seat on the sofa. I run my hand along the laptop's cover and across the SpongeBob stickers Dakota had affixed there before she became too cool for cartoons.

"So it's just a coincidence? What does Boyd think?"

That I murdered my daughter. "I didn't ask him."

The exasperated way Sawyer flops onto the couch next to me qualifies as sarcasm. "Right. Because what the heck would he know?"

"He wasn't exactly cooperative." I picture Boyd hunkering down in the basement, staring at his own suspect wall and flinging the bayonet at my photo. Bullseye.

"I'm guessing you had something to do with that. Where is that knife you stole anyway?"

"I didn't steal it. It belonged to my dad. I just reclaimed it."

I ignore Sawyer's frustrated muttering and turn my attention to Dakota's computer. With a few clicks on the keyboard, I find it.

Shadow Seekers: *Join the Hunt for Shadow Man.*

"I think I've heard of this site before," I say, scrolling through the links to articles I've read and reread. At the bottom of the web page is a timeline and with each hatch mark, a different face. The faces of Shadow Man's every known victim.

Sawyer clears his throat, points to the screen. "What's Shadow Snoops?"

But I don't look. He's only trying to distract me. Dread crawls up my neck and stands my hairs on end as I follow the timeline. The long stretch of unmarked line between 1996 and 2016. I can barely stand the anticipation. Though I already know how it ends.

There it is. That goddamned yearbook shot. "She hated this photo. It seems wrong, you know? To use it. I should've picked a different one for the detectives."

Sawyer shuffles to the other side of me so he can lay his good hand on my back, rubbing small circles between my shoulder blades that don't solve a godforsaken thing. But somehow, they make it so I can keep going.

I click on the link for Shadow Snoops and a log-in box appears. Registered users only.

"She probably used her email address for her username, right?" I ask, hopeful.

Sawyer nods, so I key it in. *DRoar18@qmail.net.*

"It's the year she would've graduated. 2018."

"What about the password?" he asks. "Any guesses?"

I try all the usual suspects, sucking in a breath each time I hit Enter. Variations of her name, Gus, Grizzlies, Tyler. 123456. And even *password*. Each time, the same dispassionate message: *You have entered an invalid username and/or password combination.*

Finally, I admit defeat and select the link to recover her username and password. The shadow of a running man appears on the screen. He stops in the middle like he's mocking us, and words take form:

To begin, please complete your verification phrase.

His wings are clipped . . .

The cursor winks at me, waiting. "We're screwed."

I sit back against the sofa and close my eyes. "I didn't know her at all. How is that possible?"

"She was fifteen. That's how. You knew more than most parents, so don't beat yourself up. When I was fifteen, my mom thought I busted my jaw playing football."

"And? How'd you really do it?"

"Wouldn't you like to know?" He smirks, taking the computer onto his lap. "I have an idea. We'll set up a new account. At least we can get inside and take a look around. But, Mollie, you're gonna have to go to the police about this. They need to talk to Boyd."

I shrug, noncommittal. Because I'm not sure I want them talking to Boyd about me.

"Promise me," he says.

If it comes to that, I've broken worse. "I promise."

Five minutes later, *One-Armed Jack* is a card-carrying member of the Shadow Snoops.

"Keep scrolling," I tell him. "All the way back. I want to see her last message." But also, I can't bear to see the newest ones. They rush by in a blur. Heartrending phrases. Mindless speculation. And the blame game. Step right up if you want to play.

Was it really Shadow?

After twenty years?

I don't buy it.

What about the boyfriend?

The parents?

The mom looks guilty as hell.

Okay. No one wrote that. At least not that I see. But I'm sure it's there somewhere. An accusatory finger waiting to be pointed.

"What's with these names?" he asks, pointing to the screen, his wry smile threatening to break my concentration. "DocSherlock. Jojo666. DevilDragon, Wishbone3? Wishbone1 and 2 were already taken, I guess."

"Hurry." I tap my fingers against Sawyer's leg, and he scrolls ahead, faster, spinning the wheel of the mouse like we're playing roulette. "Wait. Stop."

The wheel grinds to a halt on a winner.

"Chewie?" Sawyer asks. "As in Chewbacca?"

"Yeah. That's Boyd. And look, August 16, 2016. That's one day before she went missing." One day. I'd had an entire day left with her and hadn't even known it. The thought of that day—how I'd spent it—makes me sick.

"I don't remember seeing Chewie in the most recent posts. He must've dropped out after Dakota disappeared. It seems like he was the only one who knew she had been a member of the site. If that had gotten out, the media would've been all over it. I mean, what a story. Don't you think?"

I nod, sickened by the thought, and take the mouse from Sawyer's hand, scrolling a bit further, my heart stuttering. I don't know why I'm afraid. The worst thing has already happened. So many worst things. "There it is. That's got to be her."

Cagedbird18: *There will come soft rains.*

Chewie: *Cryptic, Birdie.*

Cagedbird18: *I'll DM you.*

"Oh my God, Dakota." I let the mouse rest on the table. Set my shaky hand in my lap. And turn to Sawyer.

"Translate, please," he says.

"It's a story by Ray Bradbury." I hear Luciana's panicked breath. But it's coming from my own mouth this time. "It's set in Allendale.

That's where Shadow Man's first victim lived. My dad lives there too."

Sawyer takes a long swig of coffee. Then he says exactly what I'm thinking.

"We need to get into Dakota's direct messages."

CHAPTER ELEVEN

(SATURDAY, JULY 11, 2016)

DAKOTA studied the computer screen through blurry eyes, dabbing beneath them with a tissue. According to Faces by Hannah, vigorous rubbing of the delicate under-eye area could cause premature wrinkles. Dakota had her doubts about Hannah's advice and for good reason. After she'd brushed her teeth with charcoal—for a "Kardashian white smile"—staining her mouth a dead-man's gray, Tyler's crew had called her *Zombie Tongue* for an entire month. But what harm could there be in blotting? She didn't have a good reason for crying anyway. Only the usual one.

Her parents' shrill bickering had jolted her awake that morning, and even Gus's nuzzling didn't ease the ache in her stomach. They'd kept it up while she showered and hadn't even noticed when she'd slipped out the front door, her hair still wet, and sped away on her bicycle.

"I'm going to Hannah's," she'd announced to Gus, in an otherwise empty kitchen. He'd slumped down on the linoleum with a forlorn whimper channeled straight from her soul. She'd written the same words on a Post-it she stuck to the fridge as she listened to the war rage on.

Upstairs, her mother had half-yelled, half-sobbed, "I can't do this anymore, Cole."

"Then don't."

Cue slamming door. Cue Dakota making a run for it.

As Dakota had pedaled down Ridgecrest, the wind whipped at her face, burning her eyes until she'd teared up and nearly crashed into the curb in front of the library.

B.W.C., she'd thought, humorlessly, trudging up the steps. *Biking while crying.* Pathetic.

But then she'd crossed through the doors and into her oasis. A place where order could be catalogued, chaos bound and contained between pieces of binder's board. A place where answers could be found if you knew where to look for them.

Dakota's favorite computer waited unoccupied in the cubicle near Storybook Corner, and she'd slid into the heavy wooden chair with a sigh. In under sixty seconds, she'd texted Hannah another flimsy excuse and logged on to Shadow Snoops, dabbing away the evidence of her mess of a morning.

Welcome, Cagedbird18.

Your last login was July 10, 2016 1:37 p.m.

Dakota studied her profile picture with satisfaction. She'd doodled it herself in English Lit last year, not knowing then that it would become the story of her life. A girl's face in silhouette. In her head, a tiny cage with a tiny bird inside. That Maya Angelou had it right. Dakota's wings were clipped. In her throat, a song that wasn't hers to sing. No matter how badly she wanted to sing it. Because she knew if she said it out loud—*Dad is having an affair with Mrs. Montgomery*—it would break her mother. It would break everything.

Dakota took out her pocket notepad and placed it beside her on the desk. She scrolled through what she'd missed since yesterday afternoon. Which was not much. Just a rules reminder from the admin to be respectful to other users and refrain from slander and absurd conspiracy theories. This, after someone had actually suggested Pat Benatar had unmasked Shadow Man in 1982, leading her to pen "Shadows of the Night."

Admin: *Remember the rules, Shadow Snoops. Play nice out there. There's another human being behind that screen. Please, take your conspiracy theories somewhere else. May we suggest Roswell, New Mexico.*

Dakota smiled. If only life had rules like that.

She consulted the list of questions she'd jotted down last night after finishing the Bundy book. Better that than tossing and turning and listening for the sounds of a serial killer's muted footsteps.

Cagedbird18: *Does anybody know anything about Todd Akers, the Donnelly's neighbor? He graduated from high school with Mary Ann Strauss, mother of third victim, Emily.*

Chewie: *Ruled him out years ago.*

Dakota rolled her eyes at the screen.

Cagedbird18: *Why?*

Chewie: *Do your homework, noob.*

What a prick. This Chewie guy—and Dakota had no doubt he was a guy even though his profile pic was the default gender-neutral smiley face—had apparently anointed himself king of the Snoops, declaring her a lowly peasant. Yesterday, he'd shot down DocSherlock's theory that Shadow Man was a cop and Jojo666's suggestion that some of the crimes were the work of a copycat.

Cagedbird18: *Meaning?*

Chewie: *Meaning don't be a moof-milker.*

It had been a while since Dakota laughed, and she didn't want to. The sound sputtered from her mouth without her permission like the backfire of an old engine. So she'd been right about the name *Chewie*. The king of the Snoops was a Star Wars geek. Dakota vaguely remembered the moof-milker scene. She'd biked to the cineplex over Christmas break three days in a row to see *The Force Awakens*, feeling guilt-ridden when her mom had asked if she wanted to catch the film on Christmas Day since Dad was on call.

While Chewie stewed, Dakota opened a new window and googled *moof-milker*. She lowered the sound and watched as Harrison Ford, her mother's favorite, appeared in the Millennium Falcon.

Chewie: *Akers is old news. Some of us take this investigation seriously.*

DocSherlock: *Back off, Chewie. Cagedbird, Akers was paralyzed in an industrial accident in 1995.*

Chewie: *See. Some of us actually do our homework. Unless Cagedbird is saying Shadow Man's a quadriplegic . . .*

Cagedbird18: *Listen, fur bag. I did my homework. According to the last Shadow Man article in the Chronicle, the accident happened in 1996. AFTER the last vic disappeared. The reporter called Akers the best possible suspect.*

Chewie: *Fur bag?*

Cagedbird18: *Chewie is short for Chewbacca, is it not? BTW I am not a moof-milker. I'd never put a compressor on the ignition line.*

Dakota sat back in her chair, smug. "What do you say to that?" she muttered under her breath, waving off the librarian who apparently thought she'd been summoned.

Chewie has gone offline.

Coward.

DocSherlock: *Don't let Chewie get you down. He's a bit of a purist. A lot of folks joined the site after that news show last month. Chewie calls them CSI wannabes.*

That stung. Dakota didn't feel like a wannabe. She'd been listening to her mom's stories about her crazy patients for years. Like the guy with the shoe fetish who'd cut off his victim's foot and kept it in his closet wearing a red high heel. Dad didn't know Mom had told her that one. And now that she'd finished *The Stranger Beside Me*, she planned to beg her mom for her copy of *Mindhunter*.

DocSherlock: *The date in the Chronicle was a mistake. They did a correction on the story the following day, but Akers sued for libel and won. You'll find all that on the main webpage in the folder marked EXTRAS. Happy hunting!*

Of course. The one folder she hadn't bothered with. Chewie had probably named it himself. To throw off the noobs.

Cagedbird18: *Thanks, Doc! I'll check it out.*

But even as she typed, Dakota had already opened the link and saved the folder to the desktop. She'd delete it before she left like she always did. Not that anyone cared. But she relished the ritual of it, the guarding of her precious secret. She wondered if her dad felt that way too, locking their little family in a box for safekeeping while he banged her best friend's mother.

An alert flashed on her screen.

Chewie has sent you a direct message.

Dakota's heart raced like a rabbit as she opened her inbox, which had been empty until now. She scanned the two lines of text, uncertain how to feel.

Hi Cagedbird. I'm sorry for being a jerk. Not many girls can quote Han Solo. I'm assuming you're a girl because of your profile pic. I'm not a girl, btw.

Her fingers poised over the keyboard, ready to strike. Her answer seemed essential, life-changing even, like picking between Robert Frost's diverging roads in the woods. All her choices felt that way lately. Monumental. A day at the mall with Hannah or the public library? Avoid Tyler or break it off with him? Tell her mother or keep her mouth shut? Panic rose up in her chest, and she reached for the mouse, hurriedly closing the message before she lost it right there in Storybook Corner.

She took a few deep breaths and then a few more, focusing on the construction paper rainbow taped to the wall near the Babbling Book Brook. In her head, she said it five times fast, laughing silently at her own gibberish. Then she opened the folder marked EXTRAS and started to scroll.

Near the top, she spotted the 2006 *Chronicle* retraction. The original article had been penned by a gumshoe reporter who fingered Akers in a Shadow Man ten-year anniversary piece. To be fair, Akers looked guilty in all the ways that counted. He'd been convicted of child molestation in 1992 and locked up in San Quentin for two years. All that time, Shadow Man had stayed quiet.

Dakota eyed her suspect list. She still couldn't rule Akers out. Mostly because his name was the only one on her list, and to cross it out would've felt like touching the pool wall a millisecond outside of gold medal time. Besides, there were only two murders after Akers was paroled. Both could've been copycats.

She clicked through the articles one by one, reading each twice and taking better notes than she had in AP Bio. She wouldn't let Chewie get the best of her again.

With the last article opened on her screen—a 1992 story from the now defunct *Allendale Gazette*—she turned her phone over to check the time.

Hannah had responded to her lame excuse hours ago, calling her exactly that.

Lame. But you can redeem yourself. Party at Tyler's tonight. Get ready at Liv's house at 5?

Dakota sighed and texted back one unenthusiastic letter—*K*—as she read the headline in front of her.

Allendale Community Unites In Search For Missing Girl Feared To Be Fourteenth Shadow Man Victim

The tight-knit community of Allendale came together this weekend to aid police in their search for Jessica Guzman. The fourteen-year-old has been missing since Thursday evening when she

went jogging with her Golden Retriever, Blondie, and never returned. Friday morning, a road crew discovered the dog's collar discarded in a ditch off Sweeney Road, several miles from Putah Creek Road where Jessica was last seen running. Blondie returned home on Saturday morning, unharmed. The discovery of the dog's collar has intensified investigators' fears that Jessica was kidnapped by the elusive Shadow Man, who is suspected in the murders of no less than thirteen other young girls, many of whom resided in the Napa area.

Dakota scribbled a note—*Blondie's collar in ditch off Sweeney*—even as her eyes were drawn to the photographs at the center of the page. Jessica Guzman's broad smile revealed twin dimples in her cheeks, which gave her face a spunky cuteness. But the long waves of her hair down her shoulders and her fierce bone structure—that's what Hannah would've called it—hinted at her future as a drop-dead stunner. A future that would never be.

The camera loves her, Dakota thought, recalling her disgust when she'd seen her own freshman yearbook photo. That stupid pimple she'd tried to cover glaring at her like a third eye. For a split-stupefying-second, jealousy gnashed its teeth against her insides. Until she shook her head at her sheer lunacy. Jealous of a dead girl. *Seriously?*

Dakota already knew how Jessica's story ended. Like all the others. With a cold, hard stop in Shadow Man's graveyard. Only this time, three years went by before her remains had been recovered in the woods at Lake Berryessa. The teeth were hers, bones too. But she'd aged. She'd grown. In captivity, presumably. Shadow Man had evolved.

But then he'd stopped entirely. Or had he? Dakota wondered about that more than anything else. So did all the Shadow Snoops. There was an entire folder dedicated to it. *The Desistance Problem,* they called it, and she was partial to the *Captive Theory* herself. The idea that Shadow Man hadn't died or had kids or been locked up or found God but rather had decided to hold on to his victims. To keep them alive a little longer.

Dakota nearly overlooked the other photos, unremarkable by comparison. Four dark figures with hats and walking sticks—she couldn't tell if they were men or women—trudging through a field in their safety vests. The caption read *Volunteers comb a field near Putah Creek Road.* But what came next stopped her heart.

An unsmiling man. His eyes squinted, not meeting the camera. Behind him, a chain-link fence and a sign for Mol's Junkyard, and when she looked harder, a dog with long ears like a basset hound. Her mother had told her she had one once. Roscoe, she'd called him. Dakota read the caption in a whisper, "Local small business owner, Victor Krandel, offers water to volunteers during the search."

Victor Krandel.

Dakota sat still as a stone, letting the name sink into her. Then she printed a word in her notebook, barely feeling her fingers as she wrote. *Grandpa?*

****

Sweat stung Dakota's eyes as she pedaled up the drive in the uneasy quiet. The gravel crunched beneath her tires like the snap of small bones, and her stomach twisted. She tossed her bike in the front yard and surveyed the scene for clues. Better to know what sort of ambush awaited her. For starters, the Mercedes was gone. Which meant her dad was too. In some ways, that was better. She didn't have to dodge his eyes. Or listen to them go at it like a pair of cranky tomcats. But in other ways, it was worse. Her mom would be mopey, drifting through the house as gray as a ghost.

"Mom?"

Gus barreled around the corner, wagging his tail at her. He followed her into the kitchen, eyeing his empty food dish with anticipation. Weekends, Mom always fed him around noon. It was after two now, and Gus's silver bowl gleamed like a whistle. He whined softly, nudging her hand with his wet nose.

"Alright, alright," she told him, scooping a cup of King Canine, the ninety-five-bucks-a-bag kibble Gus's vet had recommended when he'd started packing on the pounds last year.

As Gus dove in nose first, Dakota scanned the kitchen. Her Post-it was gone. Mom's fancy purse rested on the counter, the keys to the Range Rover tucked into the side pocket. In the sink, a single glass that smelled worse than Hannah's bottle of pretend Gatorade. She rinsed it clean, dried it carefully, and returned it to the cabinet. She felt certain her mother wouldn't want anyone to see it. Especially not her father.

The knot in Dakota's stomach tangled tighter and tighter until it ached. It reminded her of standing on the starter's block at the pool's edge waiting for the signal. But now, there was only silence and nowhere to go but up the stairs.

Dakota went to her room first, slipping her pocket notepad beneath the mattress. Then she called out again for her mother. At the end of the hallway, her parents' bedroom door loomed—closed and shadowy—like something out of a horror flick. The kind her dad completely forbade, but that she and her mom watched when he was on call, both of them shielding their eyes at the worst parts.

Dakota knocked first, pressing her ear to the door. She waited and listened.

Ever since she'd walked in on her father in Hannah's basement last month, she'd been acutely aware of one thing. Obvious but shocking all the same. Her parents, both of them, had a life apart from her. A life where they behaved like people she didn't know, people who didn't belong to her. Mollie and Cole, not Mom and Dad. It felt dangerous to be so close to it. The door, the knob in her hand, too flimsy to protect her from their other lives, their other selves.

Finally, she opened it.

Dakota didn't recognize her mother at first. Not because she looked any different. Brown hair tucked in a loose bun. Weekend sweats. The freckle on her neck Dakota would know anywhere. But *her* mother didn't nap. Ever. Yet, there she was, lying on the bed with her back to Dakota, the curtains drawn.

"Mom?" she asked, tapping her shoulder the way she would rouse a sleeping dragon.

Startled, her mother faced her with a gasp. "What time is it? Where's your father?"

"Uh . . ."

There it was, plain as day. Her mother's *other* self. Peeking from behind her red-rimmed eyes, seeping out from her breath. Dakota debated whether to face it head-on or pretend not to see it. "It's 2:30. Dad's not here."

"Of course he is. He went to Hannah's to pick you up. And by the way, young lady, no one gave you permission to leave this morning."

Her mother sat up and frowned, Mom-mask shifting back into place.

Dakota swallowed a lump and repeated herself more firmly this time. "Dad is not here. His car is gone."

"But he left . . ." The mask slipped again as her mother searched out the clock on the nightstand. As if it had something vital to tell her. As if it could explain the inexplicable. "He left hours ago. How did you get home?"

Hours ago. Dakota's thoughts whirled round and round and round like a board game spinner, landing finally, firmly at the top of the Montgomerys' basement stairs. Do not pass go. Do not collect $200. You lose.

"Dakota." Her mother's voice was sharp.

"I rode my bike."

"From Hannah's house?"

She couldn't answer. She didn't want to lie. Lying made her no better than her father. But the truth was a domino line. Once she'd tipped the first domino, the whole thing would come down eventually, bit by gory bit, so she shrugged instead.

Her mother reached for the phone. "I'm calling the Montgomerys."

"No, Mom. You don't have to do that. I wasn't there. I was at Tyler's, and I asked Hannah to cover for me. Dad's probably driving around looking for me right now, and he didn't want to worry you."

Dakota hated her mom then, with a fierceness that licked up her chest like a flame. Her mother returned the phone to its cradle without further protest. She didn't bother to suggest the obvious—calling her dad's cell, which was practically welded to his hand at all times. That meant her mother didn't want to know the truth. Or worse, she already knew and had decided to live with it.

"You're grounded." Even that didn't sound convincing.

Dakota nodded her head, though it felt heavy, loaded as a powder keg. It was bound to explode eventually. With an unceremonious, passive-aggressive boom. "Grandpa still lives in Allendale, right? Why can't I see him?"

Her mother flinched. And Dakota felt satisfied as she watched her walk to the dresser mirror and dot concealer under eyes. Her skillful dabbing would've made Hannah proud. "You know why."

"Because he's crazy, and you don't like him."

She was on a roll now. Her mother's jaw tightened; her forehead tensed in her best attempt at a frown despite the Botox. Hannah's mother was five years younger with perfect skin and probably didn't need Botox yet. So the affair made sense, evolutionarily speaking. Her father was no less advanced than an ape. No more, either, apparently.

"We've talked about this. Grandpa is mentally ill and has a drinking problem. It's not safe for you to be around him. He's unpredictable. Anyway, what's brought all this on?"

"Do you and Dad think I'm like Grandpa? *Mentally ill?*"

"What?"

Her mother met her eyes in the mirror, and Dakota looked away. She hadn't meant to ask that question. She'd meant to say something snotty. Something like—*just wondering who I'd live with if you and Dad kill each other*. But now she couldn't take it back.

"I heard you tell Dad you thought I was depressed. And Dad is always asking how I'm feeling and if I want to talk about it."

"Are you? Depressed? Is that why you're wondering about Grandpa?"

"I didn't realize I needed a reason to ask about him. Maybe I'm curious why everyone in this family is freakin' crazy. Or maybe I'm just wondering who I'm going to live with when you and Dad finally kill each other."

That's more like it, she thought. Until she felt the hot wallop of her mother's hand across her cheek. It stung worse than the last time.

****

Dakota lay in bed, studying her cell, her feet tucked under Gus's warm belly. According to Google, Mol's Junkyard had been closed for fifteen years, and the lone Yelp review declared it a one-star eyesore that should've been condemned by the county. There was no picture, no telephone number, and no sign of Grandpa Krandel. Dakota knew her mother would definitely not approve, which only made her more certain she had to go there to see it—to see him—for herself.

A predictable text bubble from Hannah appeared on her screen, and Dakota's stomach knotted.

Where r u?

Grounded.

She hoped Hannah would let her leave it at that, so she wouldn't have to lie. It was hard enough avoiding her dad, but lately skirting Hannah's texts and calls had become as impossible as shaking her own shadow. Still, what choice did she have? Her father had handed her a ticking bomb and left it for her to decide where to toss it. The trouble was that any which way she threw it, lives would implode. That included Hannah's.

WTF. You never get grounded.

Dakota tugged the covers over her head, wishing she was a little girl again, believing she could disappear beneath them.

Got caught on Snapchat with Ty.

The lie came easy off her fingers. Thank God she didn't have to say it out loud. Because surely her guilt, sticking like a pebble in her throat, would give her away.

OMG. Were you fully clothed?

Dakota burrowed further under, raising her knees to make a blanket fort above her. She knew now, there was no disappearing. Whatever disaster your life became, you had to stay there. Stand there. Face it.

I asked him to delete that pic.

Begged was more like it. But he'd responded with an emoji wink—which reminded her of the wink he gave Mrs. McCarthy when she'd chided him for talking in class—as well as two poorly punctuated sentences: *i won't show anybody babe i swear.*

Of course, Hannah wouldn't understand. Her next text served as concrete evidence.

Why? It was hot.

Dakota didn't know how to answer. Because she partly felt proud Hannah would say that. About *her*. When Hannah was clearly the hot one. On the other hand, it served as further confirmation. That picture lied. It told Tyler things about her that weren't true. Not even close. He'd already been pressuring her to wear the lacy red bra that didn't even belong to her. And worse, to live up to its expectations.

"Dakota? Honey?"

When she heard her mother's voice on the other side of her door, she steeled herself against it, tucking her phone beneath the pillow.

"Can I come in?"

But her mom didn't wait for an answer. She just barged right in like always, ignoring the KEEP OUT sign she'd bought Dakota at that fancy home-interior store in downtown Napa. She'd cringed when Dakota had slapped a few glittery pink skulls on it to make it her own. That was her mother's problem. She couldn't let Dakota have anything for herself. It had to belong to her too.

She felt her mother's weight on the bed next to her, heard her mother's weary sigh, but she stayed buried.

"I shouldn't have done that, sweetie. Mom and Dad aren't getting along right now, but I was wrong to take it out on you. If you want to talk about Grandpa, we can. Anytime you want. Just say the word."

Dakota held so still. She hoped her mother would wonder if she'd stopped breathing.

"Okay. I understand you're angry with me. You're entitled to your feelings."

When all else failed, her mother went into full-therapist mode.

"Maybe you should talk with someone. I can ask the school counselor if she'll see—"

"No, Mom." Dakota emerged, hot and red-faced, from beneath the covers. She didn't know how her mother did it exactly, but she managed to win every time. "I don't need to talk to anyone. I just want to be alone."

Her mother patted her leg, and Dakota stared at her hand, wondering how it could be so gentle one moment and so cruel the next. She must've known what Dakota was thinking, because she pulled it back quickly and tucked it beneath the other hand crossed at her waist.

"I left that book you wanted on your desk."

Dakota merely nodded at the worn copy of *Mindhunter* she'd coveted, denying her mother the smile she so clearly wanted.

"When you finish that one, maybe it's time for *Silence of the Lambs*. What do you say?"

Another nod. This one even flatter than the last.

"Just don't tell Dad, okay?"

"Okay," Dakota answered, halfway agreeable. But in her mind, she scoffed at her mother and sliced her with her smart mouth. *Keeping secrets runs in the family.*

AFTER

CHAPTER TWELVE

(WEDNESDAY, OCTOBER 3, 2018)

WENDALL tells me he's having a good day. Which means he didn't have to pull the car to the side of the road to vomit on the drive over. Already, he's been talking for longer than the twenty minutes he'd managed yesterday.

I'm better too, even with the fog of exhaustion muddling my thoughts. Sawyer and I hadn't given up on hacking into Dakota's Shadows Snoops account until the early hours of the morning. But at least I had a lead now. It had been so long since I'd had anything beyond the familiar faces on my suspect wall and my own suspicions scratching my mind raw.

Wendall's cowboy hat rests on his spindly knee like a crow on a telephone line, and every now and then, he reaches for it, touching it gently as if to remind himself it's still there. I start to wonder if he's siphoning his strength from its smooth black felt.

"So what have the doctors said about your prognosis?" I ask him. He'd already told me he'd had the standard treatment. A lobectomy where the doctors had *sliced and diced* him, followed by chemo to *fry that devil inside.*

He chuckles and offers a droll smile. "Not much of anything useful. Doctors are a lot like cops. They know more than what they say. And they never give you a straight answer."

I cock my head, ready to challenge him. I have to push him while I can. Who knows how long this vigor will last? Although, when I think of Cole—all the half-truths, the non-answers—I have to admit he's right. "You realize I'm a doctor. Is that how you feel about me?"

"Nah. Head doctors are a different breed. You folks can't hook me up to an X-ray machine and see what's shakin' up in here." He taps the side of his head. "And thank the bejesus for that. There's a lot of dark places between these ears."

"What would I find—if I could look inside?"

"Well, let me map it out for you. You already know some about Vietnam. I'll call that the scorched jungle. Then there's this great big sinkhole. That's my whole goddamned childhood. Barely got outta that one alive."

"Would you like to tell me about it?"

"Ain't much to tell. My momma was a whore, and my daddy was a good for nothin' piece of shit. They say Momma left me in a phone booth when I was just a baby. So I grew up in Holy Pines. That's an orphanage near Sacramento. Nowadays, they don't call 'em that. It was a huge redbrick building with its own pine forest. Pretty as can be. But you know what I picture when I think about it now? A massive hole in the ground, like a gigantic mouth that swallowed everything that came near it. Especially little boys. I talked funny as a kid, and I got teased somethin' awful. Joinin' up with old Uncle Sam was the only thing that saved me."

"So the army was your escape?"

"Yeah. Ain't that a hoot? I'm still not sure which was worse, the Viet Cong or those little shits at Holy Pines." I wait for him to laugh, but his eyes darken with indignation. "I was good at it though. Good at killin' the enemy and gettin' other men to do the same. Ain't that a damn awful thing to realize? You come back and you try to act normal. But normal won't claim you no more. That's why I took the orderly job at the loony bin. I wanted to be around somebody less normal than me."

"You're painting quite a desolate picture. A scorched jungle. A sinkhole. What else is up there?"

Wendall strokes his hat. "I'm gettin' to that. First, I gotta ask you somethin' about a legal matter. Purely hypothetical, mind you."

I nod, already uneasy.

"If a person was to tell you about somethin' bad they did in the past—somethin' real bad that they never got caught for—would you be obliged to report that matter to the authorities?"

After working at Napa State, the question isn't a surprise, though spontaneous confessions were rare there. The drive for self-protection is so strong that even full-on psychosis is no match. "It depends. Remember, we spoke about the limitations of confidentiality. If you tell me about an imminent plan to hurt yourself or someone else, then all bets are off. But confessing to something in the past would typically be kept between us."

He leans back against the sofa, which seems to have accepted him now, albeit reluctantly, the cushions giving way under his weight. "Alright then. You want to know what else is up there? It's a field as far as the eye can see. Lush green grass beneath your toes. The smell of the earth. And all the deer you'd ever want to hunt, just grazing."

"A field? That doesn't sound so bad."

"Just wait," he says, with a strike of his finger to the air. "It's only a field at first glance. But when you get up close, that's when you see them. The stones. A helluva lot of stones. You catch my drift?"

The room feels colder as he sets his eyes on me. They're brighter today. Clearer. Sharp as tacks.

"I may need you to spell it out for me."

He doesn't look away when he answers. "Under every one of them stones is a body. It's the biggest damn graveyard you ever did see."

****

After Wendall leaves, I lock the door and wheel the ergo chair back to the other room, to the suspect wall. I rub my arms, not for the first time, to stop my skin from crawling and focus on Dakota's picture, pushpinned at the center, until my breathing is slow and measured again.

Wendall is a murderer.

It shouldn't bother me. I'd spent years with murderers at Napa State. Counseled them, joked with them, even pitied them sometimes. At least three times a week, I'd sat in a circle in a closed room where I'd been the only non-murderer, armed with only a small plastic alarm. So small any one of them could've crushed it under his boot. Still, I hadn't minded.

But Wendall feels different. Or I feel different. Or both.

Because he's never been caught, for one. And for two, he's not just a murderer. Like one of those paranoid schizophrenics who gets hyped up on coke and the voices in his own head and stabs his mother. Wendall had said *stones*—as in more than one. Wendall had said *graveyard*—as in more than two or three. Wendall had said *I'm getting tired now, Doc* but not much else, depositing his hat on his head with a courteous nod.

Before he'd stood to go, I'd managed to ask him one question. A necessary one. "Are you planning on hurting anyone else?"

To which he'd held out his hands, palms down, both of them shaky. His skin so pale, I'd seen the ice blue rivers of his veins beneath it. "I couldn't hurt a fly. Even if I wanted to."

I'd left the unspoken question—*Do you want to?*—between us, which filled the room with a sickly dread.

Wendall is a serial murderer.

That's why he'd come here, to me, to unburden himself. That's why he'd told me we could help each other. I'm supposed to offer absolution. In return, he'll grant me a peek behind the curtain.

I reach for my cell and start to dial Sawyer. But I hang up fast, before it rings. It feels too familiar and too dangerous. My need to be rescued. If I'm honest, it's the reason I'd ended up married to Cole in the first place. And look how well that turned out. He'd said it himself the night before he left. *I can't take care of you anymore, Mol. You have to do that for yourself. Sink or swim.*

I'd bit back the urge to spit in his face. *Take care of me?* I'd heard my voice crack. *Is that what you were doing? Because you did a shitty job of it.*

Seeing Sawyer last night sitting on my sofa, drinking from my coffee cup, grinning his perfectly imperfect grin, I'd realized. No man had set foot in the house since Cole, and his ghost lingers there still in the caverns of my own bitter, cobwebbed heart. I'm neither sinking nor swimming without him. Just treading water.

I scroll through my contacts until I find the number for Detective Sharpe. Each shrill ring buzzes my nerves, reminding me I don't exactly have a plan aside from the usual one: Find the bastard who killed my daughter. Vague, sure, but no less profound.

The last ring goes to voicemail, and I disconnect. Probably for the best. Until I get my bearings. Until I figure out what to say.

I shut off the lights and close up the office, trudging back toward the house where a dog and two ghosts wait for me. The in-between person.

On any other Wednesday, before all this, I would've been taking my lunch break, leaving the cold, dank corridors of the hospital to cop a squat in the sunshine somewhere on the sprawling grounds and eat something unnecessarily healthy, like a kale salad. Napa State Hospital could be drudgerous and depressing as hell, but it had its moments.

Gus's barking whacks through the memory with the urgency of an axe. I move faster than I have in months, skirting around the house to the unmarked police car parked in the driveway.

Luciana must be rubbing off on me, because it's no coincidence. It can't be. Detective Clifton Sharpe leans against the front hood looking like Morgan Freeman as Alex Cross. Tall and grizzled and obviously a much better detective than I'd ever given him credit for. Dakota would be so jealous. When she'd stayed home from school with the flu freshman year, I'd played hooky from work, and we'd watched *Kiss the Girls* and *Along Came a Spider* in our pajamas. Looking back at us now, shoveling popcorn without a care, I wonder if I'd missed something. A sign that our lives would become a film noir. Improbably dark, impossibly sad, and with no real ending in sight.

"Are you a mind reader now?" I ask.

His face is a blank. I know this trick. I've used this trick. But I fall for it anyway, launching my explanation.

"I literally just called you. I know things have stalled a bit with the investigation, so I've been doing some poking around, and we need to talk."

He stands up, hands on his hips, towering over me, and I see my father in the unforgiving lines on his face. "You're right. We do need to talk. Unfortunately, it's a conversation we've had before. Several times."

"If this is about Boyd, I can explain. I—"

"*Boyd?* The guy you left me a message about the other day? Something about a yearbook photo and your father."

Inwardly, I groan at the drunken conspiracy theory that I knew would come back to haunt me at the most inopportune time.

He removes a small notepad from his pocket and scrutinizes the last page, shaking his head. "This fellow told me his name was Lyle Mitchum. He's the assistant manager over at Whitetails and Whoppers. Anyway, you scared him real good, ripping that bayonet off the wall like you did. He didn't even want to call us. But apparently his boss was pretty adamant about his reporting it since the knife is a relic and all. Lucky for him, he took down your license plate, you know. Petty theft. Criminal threats. Assault with a deadly weapon. C'mon, Mollie, what were you thinking?"

"Well, I—" He doesn't give me a chance to answer. Bulldozes right through me like my father always did. It's just as well. How could I explain the burned circuit in my brain? Frayed and fried from the relentless surge of torment and fury.

"I thought you'd learned your lesson after the incident with the Lowry kid. The restraining order, remember that?"

"Yeah, I remember it well. And I'm not sorry. C'mon, Cliff. He sent half-naked pictures of my daughter to the entire lacrosse team. If you ask me, he should've been arrested for distributing child pornography."

But, of course, he didn't ask me. A weary raising of his brows is a not-so-subtle reminder. We've discussed this before. Many times. Tyler had been kicked off the team and suspended from school. These things were apparently considered sufficient punishment for a dumb jock with a dead ex-girlfriend. End of discussion.

"Lucky for you, the bait-and-tackle shop is in Solano County. Sheriff Guffield and I go way back. We bowl on the same team every Thursday night. He's an understanding guy, that Guffy. I explained the whole situation to him, and he agreed not to press charges, so long as you don't go back there. And you return that stolen bayonet."

I nod. Because it's probably not the right time to mention I'd left the bayonet in the basement of the other man I'd threatened that night.

"You need to back off. Let us do our jobs."

I scoff. "I have been. For two whole years now."

"There's a lot happening behind the scenes, I can promise you that. You heard about Joe DeAngelo, right? The Golden State Killer.

The Feds are trying some of the same fancy genealogy stuff with the trace DNA we got off that collar back in '92."

"But I think Dakota went up there. To Whitetails and Whoppers. I found a card in her book, and I think she was—"

"I know you want to help. But we've been through this before. Sometimes, when these kinds of things happen to us, we start to see connections that aren't really there."

"What about Lyle Mitchum's criminal history? I'll bet Sheriff Guffield doesn't know about that. He's on parole. He shouldn't be working around guns. He pulled one on me, you know."

Detective Sharpe sighs so loudly that it seems to require all his effort. "Mr. Mitchum's boss happens to be Guffy's brother-in-law, so I don't think you'll get very far with that one, but I'll mention it when I see him. Look, I know how hard this must be. I really do. I understand what you're going through."

He pats my arm with the kind of practiced sincerity I know all too well. So well that I instantly distrust it. How many times had I done that? Looked at a man facing a lifetime commitment in a state psychiatric hospital and told him I understood? When really, I'd been clueless.

"You don't understand. You couldn't possibly. Your kids are alive, right? Monica and James. Your wife, she still tolerates you. So until your life gets blown up like mine, don't give me that bullshit. Save it for the next dead girl's mother."

I'm glad he doesn't argue. He respects me that much, at least. "Just don't get into any trouble I can't talk you out of, okay?"

I give him a halfhearted wave as he heads back toward his car. We both know it's not an answer or a promise. Because I respect him too. Enough not to lie to his face.

****

"You owe me for this, muchacha." Those are Luciana's last words before she knocks on the door, summoning poor Martha Blackburn.

She'd had a few things to say on the drive over to Boyd's house too. But I'd promised her a full tune-up for Boludo if she went along with another of *mis planes absurdos.* Given the life-sized Princess Leia poster I'd spotted above Boyd's bed in the basement, I suspected he would be more agreeable with a sexy Latina who had done her hair up into those two iconic side buns. Especially a sexy Latina who hadn't threatened his life. She'd have Boyd on his knees in no time.

"No one's home," Luciana says, standing on her tiptoes to peer through the small grid of windows at the top of the door. "It's dark in there."

I shake my head at her and motion to the yellow VW parked in the driveway. "Boyd's home. Knock again."

"¡Eres imposible!" She groans and rolls her eyes at me, then raps again, a little harder this time.

"C'mon, Luci. Put some muscle into it. Boludo's life depends on it."

"Fine." She pounds the door with the side of her fist, making a hollow thud that I imagine will rouse Boyd even in the confines of the Overbridge. "But not for Boludo. For Dakota."

I don't deserve her. Luciana's the kind of friend who doesn't mind that I'm an in-between person. Dakota would've liked her.

Finally, Boyd flings the door open. Whatever he'd planned to say gets lost between brain and mouth, and he gapes at the both of us, stuttering, until he finds his voice. "You again? You're lucky I didn't call the cops last night."

"Why didn't you?" I demand, stepping in front of Luciana, my own plans—for Boyd's seduction or, at the very least, an apology— lost too in the wake of his judgmental frown. "Is it because you've got something to hide?"

"I felt sorry for you. That's why. And frankly, you scare me."

"Good."

Luciana clears her throat and bats her eyelashes, drawing Boyd's attention. "I apologize for my friend's behavior. She's very rude.

What she meant to say is she's sorry about what happened, and she hopes you can forgive her. Isn't that right, Mollie?"

I mutter something like a halfhearted yes, but Boyd's not really listening. His neck reddens as he shuffles from one Chewie slipper to the other.

"You were at the group the other night, weren't you?" he asks Luciana.

She nods, coyly turning her head to the side to reveal one of her perfectly rounded buns.

"I like your hair." So predictable. He touches the haywire ends of his own.

"So, anyway, Luci's right. I was out of line last night. And I was hoping you'd be willing to talk more about Shadow Snoops."

"What else do you want to know?" Even as he asks, he takes a step back from the doorway, back from me, and I resist the urge to grab him by his T-shirt and pin him to the wall.

"I saw Dakota's last public post to you about going back to where it all began. Allendale, I presume. She told you to check your direct messages. What did she say? Do you know where she went? Why she went there? Have you seen her other messages?"

Every question is more desperate than the last. And then, there are the questions I leave unspoken. *What did she tell you about me? Did she hate me? Is all of this my fault?*

"I think what Mollie means to say is, aren't you going to invite us in?"

Boyd doesn't answer. Instead, he holds up a finger. "Wait here," he says, before he disappears back down the hallway. I hear the basement door creak open.

"Se bueno," Luciana whispers. "Be nice."

"I'm trying."

"Try harder."

When he returns, bayonet in hand, Luciana gasps. I can feel her eyes on me, burning. As far as she'd known—what I'd told her—I'd tossed the knife out the window on the freeway after dropping her off last night and had only yelled at poor Boyd. "You should take it back. It's a relic. Vietnam era. It might be worth something."

I recoil, disgusted with it and with myself. The thing probably is cursed. I can only imagine what it's done in my father's hands. Still, I take it from him. "I'll return it to the store," I say, mostly for Luciana's benefit.

Boyd nods at me, stoically, as if I've managed to convince him I'm a sensible person. "As for your questions, I wish I could help. But Dakota never sent me that message. I didn't hear from her again. I can only guess why she went to Allendale, same as you."

When I reach out, he jumps back. "Boyd, please. You went to that bait shop. You've got a suspect wall just like mine. I know you cared about Dakota. There must be something you can tell me."

Luciana shifts in the silence that follows, and I catch her staring at Boyd's arm, studying it like a tarot card. "How did Dakota get to Allendale?" she asks. "She didn't have a driver's permit or a car she could use without being caught."

Boyd swallows, and his neck writhes with the effort. "Uber? Taxi? I don't know. Maybe you should ask her grandfather. He lives up there, doesn't he?"

I grip tight to the bayonet's handle and take a few slow, deep breaths. I feel sick. "Did Dakota tell you that? Was she in contact with him?"

Boyd looks down when he answers. Like my eyes might be dangerous. Might turn as yellow as a Sith's. Since I've obviously embraced the dark side of the force. "He took her to get a tattoo, so . . ."

I stumble back from the door, head spinning, and stagger across the yard. This morning's oatmeal pushes its way back up and onto the Blackburns' Santa. Hands on knees, I stare at his black plastic boots, desecrated now. The longer I stare, the more I see something else.

My father's duffel bag of secrets. And the only time I'd ever peeked inside.

Goddamn it, he'd muttered, browsing the ammo inside Whitetails and Whoppers on the first day of deer season. *I forgot to lock the truck.* I'd gone scurrying back with the keys like a dutiful daughter before he started in about Charlie robbing us blind. He'd warned me not to look, but the bag had beckoned me from the truck bed. I'd helped him load it that morning, felt the weight of it. A quick glance back to the store, and I'd tugged on the zipper, its teeth opening to me, willingly. Complicit in my betrayal.

I never did make sense of what I'd seen there. Though for years it woke me in a cold sweat, my heart racing like a runaway freight train. Roscoe's long brown ear—he'd been missing for three days. Blood on the white patch above his nose. No collar, but there was no mistaking him. I'd shut the bag and stuffed my scream so far down my gullet, it came rushing back up, and I'd puked right there under the tailgate.

Back at the trailer that night, I'd lain stiff as a board in my bunk while Dad had pounded down can after can of his Olde English. Until finally, he'd leaned down over me, his breath stale and sour, and whispered, *Be careful, Mol. Them Charlie bastards shot Roscoe.* Then he'd tapped my forehead with his finger. *Right between the eyes.*

"¿Estas bien, chica?" Luciana's voice brings me back. "Are you okay?"

If I open my mouth, I'm sure I'll throw up again, so I just nod and surrender the bayonet to her. She takes me by the arm and leads me back to the Jeep. She doesn't even protest when I crank up the heavy metal so loud the whole car vibrates.

"What else did Boyd say?" I shout at her, my head throbbing with the past. That ancient drum that beats louder than Megadeth.

She scowls at the house, the door shut now. "Mentiroso."

"You think he's lying?"

"I know he is."

"About what?"

I turn down the music and wait for her to speak. "When I asked him how Dakota got to Allendale, his eyes went right to it. I read his face. Didn't you see it?"

I shrug helplessly.

"His little yellow bug. That's what he looked at. That's how she got there."

****

I need a drink. I need two drinks. Three. Maybe four.

Gus leads the way into the kitchen, his tail wagging as I retrieve a glass from the cabinet. It's the best thing about dogs. Not a trace of judgment.

"Just one," I tell him. Which is why I need a glass. If I drink straight from the bottle, I won't stop until it's empty. The prick of his ears tells me he understands.

I leave the glass on the counter, waiting.

Gus follows me into the bedroom and watches with curiosity as I drag the step stool into the closet. I got rid of all my cheap booze after the last episode, the last *never again*. But I still have my secret stash. The Macallan 18 I'd hidden in a shoe box when things went from bad to worse with Cole.

The bottle is half empty, and the amber liquid sloshes up the sides as I walk. The last time I'd poured myself a glass of scotch from this bottle, Dakota had vanished. I try not to think about the things I'd said to her. The things I'd done.

On my way out, I catch my face in the dresser mirror and shudder at what I find there. Hollow eyes. Sallow skin. Desperation. I look away before I frighten myself.

I'm just like him. Just like my father.

I push the thought away, but there's another, even worse, at its heels.

What if my father killed Dakota?

It's so ludicrous, so vile, I can hardly bear it, and I stop and steady myself with a hand to the wall.

"Just one," I tell Gus again. Because the urge to swig it down, all of it, threatens to bowl me over.

When I move again, Gus trots along behind me, back to the kitchen, where my hand shakes as it pours one generous glass. I take a sip and let it burn in my mouth before I swallow. The voice in my head, the relentless chatter, grows further away, as if I've muffled it with a pillow. Still, it's there.

This is why he drank.

I'm just like him.

Gus cowers when I let out a half groan, half roar, and spill out the rest of the glass. I upturn the bottle and watch it stream down the sink. Every last drop.

****

Roscoe never could run fast. His legs were too stubby, his ears too long. His hips too achy and arthritic. But he had the spirit of a horse, and he'd do his best to gallop alongside me, jowls flapping. I spot him in my dream, up ahead this time, galloping as nimbly as I'd ever seen him. I have to jog, then sprint, to keep up, and I keep slipping, the earth soft and muddy under my bare feet.

I call out to him, but my voice doesn't work, and my chest aches with the effort of trying. He vanishes into the grove of sycamore trees, and I slow down, knowing I shouldn't go any further. Dad always told me to steer clear of the sycamores. *Charlie's in there*, he'd warned. And I'd believed him. Because the trees seemed to move their limbs like people, reaching their gnarled hands down to snatch me up.

Roscoe's faint bark urges me to press on until the sky above turns as dark as the ground below. A person can run forever in a dream.

When I find him, Roscoe is nose down, digging, spotlighted by the moon. I walk toward him. Even though my blood is whooshing through my veins and every strike of my heart is a death knell, urging me to turn back.

The hole is massive by now. Who knows how long he's been digging? A dog can dig forever in a dream too.

When I peer into it, I feel dizzy. But I see what Roscoe's looking for. What I'm looking for. My father's black duffel bag.

Stretching my hand out into the infinite blackness, I reach toward it, already knowing what's inside.

When I reach, I fall.

****

I startle awake and quickly turn over, searching for the clock.

Then I remember where I am. On the sofa, where I'd fallen asleep scouring Shadow Snoops for traces of my daughter. Until I'd found myself in the grove of sycamores watching Roscoe dig a hole.

Dreams are roads to the unconscious. Freud had gotten that right at least. And my roads are especially screwed up.

Shivering, I tuck my hands into the arms of my sweatshirt—Dakota's 49ers sweatshirt, if I'm being honest—and sit up. It doesn't smell like her anymore, but I can't bring myself to wash it.

Somewhere, Gus growls, a low rumble of thunder from his chest. A warning of a storm. I shush him, mostly because the sound goes straight through me, leaving fear in its wake.

I find him at the door, scratching. With a desperation I recognize as my own.

When he growls again, I fling it open recklessly, certain someone, something will be on the other side.

The night is clear and cold. There's no one.

No one and nothing.

BEFORE

CHAPTER THIRTEEN

(MONDAY, JULY 18, 2016)

DAKOTA uncapped her highlighter, holding the top between her teeth as she underscored two more lines in bright yellow, the exact color of crime-scene tape. It turned out *Mindhunter* was a treasure trove. Or rather, a treasure map, leading her straight to Shadow Man. Each clue inked onto her notepad like a set of coordinates to chart her path.

It had been nine days since her mother had laid the book on her desk, and Dakota regarded it with reverence, a veritable bible of criminal profiling right there in her lap. So far, she'd classified Shadow Man as the organized type of serial killer, which meant his crimes were planned like Bundy or BTK or John Wayne Gacy. His victims, specially selected and hunted. He'd be intelligent, articulate. A con man, possibly using a ruse to draw his victims to him. Probably arrogant too, thinking he could outsmart the cops. He wouldn't ever be careless enough to leave a weapon behind. Preoccupied with control, he might've been a military man or even tried his hand at law enforcement, so DocSherlock's theory hadn't been far off the mark.

She couldn't wait to throw that in Chewie's face. *Boyd's face.* Whatever his face actually looked like, she pictured the fur and kind eyes of a Wookiee. He'd told her his real first name yesterday afternoon. Typed it, actually, at the bottom of a message he'd sent.

> *Birdie,*
>
> *Here's the link to The Phil Donahue Show, circa 1985, that I promised. This is vintage Shadow Man. The real deal. So don't go sharing it around.*
>
> *May the Force be with you,*
>
> *Boyd (aka Chewie)*

Swelling with pride—Chewie trusted her!—she'd put the sound on low and hunkered over the library computer, straining to hear every word of the twenty-minute video clip from Donahue's episode on unsolved crimes. But she hadn't written back yet. Mainly because she couldn't decide whether to go with her standard *Birdie* or the riskier *Dakota.*

You don't know this guy at all.
He could be an axe murderer, a rapist. A real sicko.
Heck, he could be Shadow Man.

Her thoughts came in her mother's voice. Stern but anxious, they bit at her brain.

"Are you seriously studying right now, genius?" Tyler side-eyed her as he drove, steering his little black Jetta toward the Lake Berryessa exit. "You do remember it's summer, right?"

She hated the way her laugh came out, all flirty and self-deprecating. "This book is just for fun."

Tyler's laugh, the cackle of a demented hyena, grated worse than her own. She couldn't remember the last time they'd been totally alone—a couple of weeks after prom, maybe—and she felt awkward next to him. "Your definition of fun needs a major readjustment. C'mon, loosen up a little."

"I'm plenty loose." She stared at his hand, which had wandered to her bare leg, and her face warmed. When he laughed again, she bristled, annoyed. Not with him—well, not entirely. Tyler Lowry couldn't help being who he was any more than Ted Bundy or Shadow Man. But with herself, or who she used to be, because that clueless girl somehow believed she'd needed to impress him. "This whole lake trip was my idea, wasn't it?"

He nodded, pushing a sun-bleached lock of hair from his forehead. "I still can't believe Dakota Roark lied to her mom."

Frankly, neither could Dakota. But she'd gotten good at that lately. It had been an easy sell—*Hannah's mom is taking us shopping in the city*—with Hannah eagerly agreeing to cover for her, thinking Dakota had plans to spend the day making out with Tyler lakeside. Tyler thought so too, judging by the sly grin on his face.

"I guess Little Miss Perfect has a dark side," he added, squeezing her knee.

She shrugged, suddenly emboldened by her secret plan. "There's a lot you don't know about me."

He raised one eyebrow, impossibly cool. "Let's hope so."

****

"Keep going straight on Highway 28 East," Dakota said, studying the hand-drawn map she'd printed from the Shadow Snoops' EXTRAS folder and tucked inside her book, where it was hidden from Tyler's view.

He frowned at her, slowing the car to a crawl. "Shouldn't I turn off here? Eric said Pleasure Cove is a great spot."

She would've laughed, but she felt a tiny pang of sympathy for him, realizing exactly the type of pleasure he had in mind. He wouldn't be visiting Pleasure Cove today, literally or figuratively. "I know a better place. It's more secluded."

"Alright."

Tyler revved the engine and sped down the highway, passing the turn just as she'd asked him to. Just as Shadow Man had done twenty years ago for the last time. And many times before that. Thirteen of the sixteen victims had been found near the southeast corner of the lake. He must have been familiar with the area. Maybe he lived or worked nearby. According to *Mindhunter*, most serial killers had a comfort zone, a home base, where they stalked and killed their prey.

Dakota watched the wind blow through the sycamores in the distance. Even as the sun streamed in through the window, warming her, she shivered.

"Hey, how come you weren't at my party last weekend?"

It took her a moment to remember where she was. Who she was talking to. Tyler with his chiseled jaw and tanned skin. Tyler who'd already committed to playing lacrosse at Duke. Tyler who'd practically seen her naked. "I told you. I got grounded."

"Puh-lease. You never get grounded."

"Yeah. Hannah said the same thing."

"Well, I was bummed when you didn't show." For a moment that lasted as long as a lightning strike, Dakota wondered if she'd misjudged him. "I thought for sure you'd be there. Maybe in that sexy red bra."

"Speaking of the red bra, did you delete that picture yet?"

"Are you kidding? It's my wallpaper." He chuckled softly, patting the outline of his phone in his shorts pocket. If he'd had it anywhere else, she would've grabbed for it herself. Tossed it out the window. Watched it crack like an egg against the highway. "I'm joking, Dakota. *God.*"

"So you deleted it, then?"

"I can't. Not until I see the real thing."

"Take this road here," she said, her stomach making the same hairpin turn as Tyler's Jetta. Dakota cracked the window and took a breath, her whole body jostling as the wheels met gravel. "Keep going. It's just a little further."

"You weren't lying. This spot is way out in the boonies. You're not gonna kill me, are you? Toss me in the lake?"

Dakota resisted her good-girl impulse. The prim voice in her head always telling her how to act, how to be, how to seem. Where had that voice gotten her lately, anyway?

"Why do you think I'm reading a book about serial killers?"

Tyler did a double take, and she laughed dryly.

"But I'm not dumb enough to toss you in the lake. The decomposing gases under your skin would float you right up. Or with my luck, you'd get tangled up in a fishing net and dragged to the surface."

He thought about it for a while, his face darkening.

"You're so weird lately."

She didn't disagree. Just pointed up ahead, where the road came to a shadowy end.

"This is the place."

Tyler parked the car and looked at her expectantly. But she reached for her backpack, cracked the door, and hopped out fast, avoiding his blue eyes. Just in case. It wouldn't be the first time she'd fallen victim to their spell. On prom night—before the incident—she'd let him slip his hand inside the top of her strapless dress. *No.* She'd more than let him. She'd wanted him to.

"C'mon," she said, knocking on the window of the driver's side where Tyler sat, sullen. "I'll race you to the water."

Dakota knew Tyler would sprint after her. She also knew he'd run out of steam. They both would. Because the path to the lake, long grown over, appeared as a scramble of hatched lines on the map, the words *less than a mile but feels like twenty* printed by whoever had drawn it.

"How'd you find this spot anyway?" Tyler asked, stopping to wipe the sweat from his forehead. He'd already tugged off his T-shirt, those hard-earned lacrosse muscles on full display, and Dakota thought of her old self. How she'd drooled over him like Gus at his food bowl.

She listened to the push and pull of her breath until it slowed, imagining herself as one of Shadow Man's victims, running for her life through these woods with the devil himself behind her. It hadn't happened that way, of course. By the time those dead girls made it here, their legs were useless. Just flesh and bone getting cold and going nowhere.

"I read about it." Which was true enough. A 1980 article in the *Napa Valley Register*, published after a fox trapper had discovered the remains of victims number four and five, Miriam Woodbury and Jacqueline Pierce, within a half-mile radius of where they'd found Susanna Donnelly. A grid search had uncovered two more victims, who'd disappeared in the late seventies, giving the police no choice but to utter those two fateful words: *serial killer*. "Some people say it's haunted."

It was the best she could do without telling him the whole sordid story that he'd probably blab to everybody at Napa Prep.

"Cool," he said, trudging ahead, oblivious to the graveyard beneath his feet. And the dark thoughts, sunk like headstones, in Dakota's mind.

This is a long way to carry a body. Shadow Man must have been strong and fit.

When Dakota spotted the shoreline through the trees, she pulled up short, letting Tyler go without her. A lone fisherman stood on the small patch of beach, his line cast into the water. She couldn't make him out, not with the midday sun glaring off the water. Just past him, Glenda Donnelly's wooden cross, the one Dakota had first seen on *True Crime Confidential.*

"I guess you're not the only one who knows about this place."

Tyler sounded disappointed, but he waved to the man, and the man waved back, a gesture that eased Dakota, though she couldn't say why. Surely, even Shadow Man could be polite when he needed to be. *Especially* when he needed to be.

She turned her eyes from him and quickly caught up to Tyler.

"Wanna swim?" he asked, already peeling off his socks and heading for the water, his sneakers discarded carelessly in the grass.

"You go ahead. I'll be there in a minute."

She ignored Tyler's frustrated groan and retrieved the map from her bag, glancing back at the fisherman. He recast his line, and it dropped into the water without a sound, sending ripples back to the shore. Somewhere in the woods, she heard the cry of a bird, as sudden and shocking as a scream. But Tyler swam on, arm over arm, and the fisherman waited for fate to take a bite. So Dakota walked back in the direction from where they'd come, purposefully meandering so she could tell Tyler, if he asked, that she was just wandering.

Really, she knew exactly where she needed to go. The map told her the way. West from the giant tree with the face of a grumpy old man. Straight ahead to the clearing between the sycamores. This was Shadow Man's burial ground. She had to see it for herself. How better to know him?

Dakota stood at its center, weeds tickling her legs, and spun around to take it in. The grainy newspaper photo had told her nothing of the black heart of this place. As the strong summer wind kicked up, it felt ironically alive, smelling of hot, dry grass and dust. The sycamores moved gracefully above her like angels spreading their wings. Their leaves murmuring to her in a language she couldn't understand.

Near one of the big, mossy rocks, the trapper had found Miriam's skull. It had been bashed with a blunt object, possibly the butt of a rifle, and burned. Dakota serpentined through the rocks, surveying the ground, half-expecting to see it there, its empty eyeholes fixed on her. Or to feel the bony fingertips of Jacqueline's scorched hand latching onto her ankle, still red hot.

As she peered into the deep crevice between two of the larger boulders, the earth there began to move, to pulse. Almost imperceptibly. Until the brown and gold of the grass at her feet writhed in a slow, easy rhythm.

A snake!

The realization knocked the wind from her, and Dakota clasped her hand to her chest. She lifted her foot to inch backwards, but the snake moved too. She heard herself cry out.

"Gopher snake. It won't hurt you."

The voice came from the path behind her. Deep and unfamiliar. But she turned toward it, already knowing who she'd find.

Up close, the fisherman looked her father's age. What she could see of him anyway. His wide-brimmed hat shadowed his eyes, partially obscuring the rest of his face.

"Are you sure? It looks exactly like a rattlesnake."

What she could see of the fisherman's mouth turned upward into a gash of a smile, revealing a top row of jagged teeth. "Yep. You wouldn't be the first to be fooled. Sometimes, he'll even act like a rattler, shaking his tail back and forth at you. But he's not venomous."

Dakota nodded, only half-convinced. It unnerved her the way the fisherman said *he* like the snake was his good buddy.

"He's probably more scared than you are. Just come toward me."

The fisherman extended his hand toward her, the other still latched tight to his cooler and reel. She looked at his stubby fingers, black hair on pale knuckles. Then back to the snake. And she thought—of all things—about Ted Bundy and the fake crutches he'd hobbled around on, searching for his next victim.

Dakota stepped back, and the fisherman let his hand fall to his side with an embarrassed shrug. So what if he wasn't Shadow Man?

Surely, he'd hidden some dark part of himself from the world, from her. No different than her father. Than Tyler. Probably Boyd too. All of them shadow men.

"Did you catch anything?" she asked as the long tail of the snake disappeared between the rocks.

"The bass weren't really biting today, but I hooked a couple of catfish." He opened the lid of the cooler and offered her a glimpse of wide mouths and slimy whiskers. The eyes filmy with death. The slick, black bodies piled like casualties in a mass grave, one of them still flopping.

"What about you?" he asked. "Find what you were looking for?"

The snake might as well have slithered right across her shoe. Because she turned cold again, fixed to the spot. Until the fisherman pointed to the map in her hand.

She opened her mouth to answer him, but he spoke first.

"Be careful around here. If you can't tell the gophers from the rattlers, you might get yourself in trouble."

****

"I want to leave." Dakota hadn't intended to say it quite like that, but as soon as Tyler waded out of the water, his broad shoulders already pinked from the sun, she expelled the words in one fast breath.

"Now? Why? We just got here." Tyler stretched out onto the oversized beach towel he'd arranged on the shore, leaving her perched on the corner, her feet tucked beneath her. His bare chest rose and fell with each breath, and she turned away before he caught her looking. "Where'd you go, anyway?"

"I saw a snake." She held out her phone to Tyler, showing him the image of a gopher snake she'd located on Wikipedia. She'd still been buzzing, high on adrenaline, when she'd read the description. *The gopher snake, a constrictor, kills its prey by suffocating it or pressing it against the wall of its burrow.*

160

"Okay." He thought she was a big baby. His voice gave it away. "That's why you want to leave?"

"Not exactly." How could she explain it to him when she didn't understand it herself? This place felt all wrong. She felt stupid for begging Tyler to bring her here. "I think I'm just tired. I swam laps this morning and . . ."

Dakota couldn't think what to say next. She hadn't swum laps in nearly a month. Her mom still dropped her off at the Napa Valley Swim Club three times a week, but she avoided the sleek, black-capped swimmers in the lap lanes and stayed in the shallow end, practicing her underwater breath-holding technique. She'd managed to increase her personal best to seventy-five seconds.

"I know," he said. "You're super competitive like me. You probably pushed yourself too hard."

"Probably. Coach wants me to swim the fifty free this season, so I've been working on my sprints."

Dakota's phone beeped in her pocket, and she startled. As if the phone gods had struck her down and branded her a liar.

"You sure are jumpy," Tyler said. He rolled over on his side toward her and plucked her book from her backpack with a grin. "Maybe you should stop reading this stuff, *Mindhunter*." He made it sound like a dirty word.

"You looked in my bag?"

"It fell out when I got the towel. I didn't know it was top secret."

"It's not. I just—"

Another beep of her phone, and Dakota slid it out, averting her eyes from Tyler's face, somehow handsome even when it was scrunched in confusion.

Three missed calls from her mother, two messages. And two texts, both from Hannah, sprinkled with all caps and exclamation points.

911!

GO HOME NOW!!! Mom got called into the hospital this morning and ran into your dad. They know we're not shopping in San Fran!!!

Dakota's stomach lurched. Not only because she'd been caught in a lie. But also because she'd caught her father in one. That morning her dad had left the house before she and her mother had even finished breakfast. Golf bag in tow, he'd been headed for a round at Silverado Country Club. *Maybe I'll get a hole in one*, he'd teased, ruffling Dakota's hair. Apparently, that had been code for banging Mrs. Montgomery.

"Now we really have to go," she said, springing to her feet and tugging at the towel beneath Tyler. It didn't budge and neither did he. She stood over him, panic gathering strength in her chest.

"My parents know I'm not with Hannah."

Tyler grabbed her leg, stilling her. "You're already in trouble. What's a couple more hours? I haven't even seen your bathing suit yet."

Suddenly Tyler's horndog logic sounded perfectly reasonable. Why should she rush home to get grounded? Why did she have to tell the truth when no one else did? Why shouldn't she have fun with her totally smokin' boyfriend? Or whatever he was.

She tugged off her T-shirt and her cutoff shorts, pretending to ignore Tyler's gawking at the white bikini she'd let Hannah talk her into buying.

"There," she told him. "Happy now?" Then she ran toward the cool, mossy water like her whole life depended on it. Like Shadow Man himself was on her heels.

****

Dakota pushed Tyler's hand away from the place it kept wandering— the bright silver button on her shorts—grateful for the console between them. Not that it had waylaid Tyler. He'd still managed to untie her bikini top beneath her T-shirt. Next stop, Pleasure Cove. She felt ridiculous for telling herself the day wouldn't end this way.

"I think we should go," she told him as he kissed her neck. "It's almost five. My parents are gonna be so pissed."

"C'mon, D. I want you so bad." His hand again, more insistent this time. Why couldn't he just stick to kissing? She liked kissing.

"Tyler. Stop."

He pulled away from her and flopped back against his seat, breathless. Like he'd played a full four quarters. "God, you're such a tease sending me that picture."

"I didn't want to send it. You kept asking me."

"Well, I'm not fifteen anymore. And making out is getting old. I get that you're not ready to put me on varsity, but at least let me try out for the JV team."

"What are you talking about? You haven't even asked me to be your girlfriend yet and you want me to . . ." She widened her eyes at him. She couldn't say it out loud. Surely that was reason enough not to do it.

"So if I ask you to be my girlfriend . . ."

Dakota sighed and shook her head. "Just take me home."

"Whatever." He put the Jetta in gear but stopped mid-reverse. "You know, Hannah was right about you. You're totally immature."

"Then don't hang out with me anymore. There you go. Problem solved."

"Fine. I won't."

"And delete that picture. *Now*. I want to see you do it."

"Here," he said, tossing his phone at her. "Do it yourself. No big loss. It's not like you're Kylie Jenner or something."

****

Half a mile from her house, Dakota spoke, breaking the silence between them only because she had to. "Let me out here."

Tyler stopped the car without a word, staring ahead smugly. He'd won, and his tires gloated on his behalf, squealing as he sped away.

Dakota jogged on the shoulder until she reached the corner and the Pedersons' mailbox, a plain silver container atop a battered fence post. It had been run over more than once. She opened her backpack and removed the large white envelope she'd addressed that morning, still uncertain whether she would send it at all.

Now, anticipating what was to come, it seemed necessary, like a lifeline.

No. Not a lifeline. A whip. A way to lash back at the universe. At Tyler—what a prick. At Hannah—who was supposed to *have* Dakota's back, not *stab* her in it. At her father, of course. But mostly at her mother. Dakota listened to her mother's voicemail again— the fifth one she'd left in the last five hours—to remind herself, like pressing a bruise.

In this message, unlike most of the others, Mom was done crying. The wetness in her voice had hardened into ice. She spit it back at Dakota like only she could, aiming her icicle darts at all the soft places.

You think you're grown up now?

You think you can handle things on your own?

That you can just go where you want to when you want to and lie to me and your father and not answer my calls? Make me leave work early because I was so worried sick?

Well, I've got news for you, missy. You can't. At your age, I was practically raising myself. What have you done besides get some bird-brained boy to like you? Congratulations. We'll see how long that lasts when you don't give him the only thing he wants.

Dakota clenched her fist tight before she realized she'd crumpled the envelope's edge.

Inside it, the school picture she despised. Not because of the pimple that had cruelly showed up on her chin that morning, but because she looked like a little girl. A plain one at that. Nothing like Hannah with her expertly made-up face.

But no matter, it was the kind of picture a grandparent would cherish. She'd inscribed it on the back and tacked a note to the front, written in tiny print on two of her mother's Post-its.

Dear Grandpa,

I don't know you, but I'd like to. I've asked Mom about you, but she won't say much. She doesn't know I'm reaching out. She'd be really mad, so don't tell her. Could I come to visit you at Mol's? If you want to meet me too, come to the Napa Public Library this Sunday at 1 p.m. If you're not there, I'll be disappointed, but I'll understand.

Your granddaughter,

Dakota

P.S. Mom said you named me. Thanks!

Dakota smoothed the envelope's bent edge, stuck it between the Pedersons' outgoing bills, and closed it tight. The small red flag was already raised, and she pondered it for a moment.

Red for stop.

Red for danger.

Red for blood.

Then she turned away and began to walk home.

AFTER

CHAPTER FOURTEEN

(THURSDAY, OCTOBER 4, 2018)

I wake, still on the sofa and oddly contorted. Head pounding. Back aching. Face smushed into one of the throw pillows that's no doubt made the sort of red lines that will take hours to fade from my cheeks. I find the bayonet on the floor. It must've slipped from my hand during the night. Some guard I am. I'm not even certain when I fell back asleep, only that I'd stared at the ceiling for what seemed like hours, listening for the faintest noise and gripping the bayonet's handle, my nerves frayed down to the bare ends.

"What was out there last night, buddy? Tell me."

Gus cocks his head. It's not the first time I've asked him a question like that. When he'd wandered back onto the front lawn, the day after Dakota went missing, fur wet and tongue hanging, his collar missing, I'd dropped to my knees and begged him to take me to her. Until Cole had pulled me away, guided me upstairs, and put me to bed with two Valium while the police scurried around our home like mice.

At first, I'd been relieved when Gus came back. Because those chestnut brown eyes had borne witness, and as long as Gus was alive, a part of me had hope of knowing, however miniscule. My girl's final moments locked away inside his canine brain. It reminded me of a joke Cole told Dakota the day we brought Gus home. *What do you call a blonde with a brain?* Dakota had twittered, still giddy, as she'd waited for the punchline. *A golden retriever.*

But then relief turned to disgust. Disgust to resentment. Resentment to hate. I'd needed a scapegoat. A place to lay blame. *Why didn't you protect her?* I'd asked Gus that too, demanded it until he'd cowered, afraid of me. When really, I'd been asking myself. That was my question to answer. Because what is a mother if not a protector? My own mother had taught me that, even if her plan blew up like one of Dad's homemade bombs, right in her face.

As soon as I stand, Gus whines and trots to the door. I crack it open, and he's through my legs and pushing his way out, nose first. He darts across the grass, paying no mind to the squirrel scrambling up the fence post or his favorite oak tree, the one he usually takes his time marking. I stuff my bare feet into sneakers and run after him, down the path to my office.

"Show me," I call after him as he disappears behind the trees. "What did you see?"

I sound crazy. I feel crazy. But maybe this time, finally, he'll answer me.

When I round the corner, I skid to a panicked stop, my brain a slate wiped clean. On it, writ large, two words. A name. *Wendall Grady.* He's propped up against the Cadillac, one hand on the hood. The other lifts in a slow wave.

I curse myself for not checking the clock before I'd sprinted from the house braless, in sweats and a ponytail, still half-asleep.

Gus stops too, in the center of the driveway. His tail drops low, only the end wagging. I wait for his throaty bark, but it never comes. Instead, like that old wind-up cowboy, Wendall takes a knee and coaxes Gus to him. When he runs his bony hand over Gus's head, smoothing the fur on his neck, my own hair prickles.

"Get back here!"

But Gus is smitten with Wendall's cowboy hat, sniffing it in earnest the way he'd done at the dog park in another life. A past life when Dakota and I would load him into the Jeep and drive to Canine Commons for another butt-sniffing session. That's what Dakota had called it. And after she'd googled the question *Why do dogs sniff other dogs' butts*, we'd laughed until our stomachs hurt. Then we'd marveled at our Gus, with his nose 100,000 times more sensitive than ours.

"It's alright," Wendall says. He dodges Gus's snout and reaches into his pants pocket, revealing a small pack of saltine crackers. "The nausea gets so bad these days, I don't go far without them."

I'm grateful he doesn't seem to notice my bedhead or my thin T-shirt, but I wrap my arms across my chest anyway.

"May I?" he asks.

I nod as Gus prances with excitement. Never one to delay gratification, he gobbles the whole pack of crackers in a single chomp and stares up at Wendall waiting for round two, cowboy hat forgotten.

"I've always been fond of doggies," Wendall says, tottering a little as he stands. "Before this damn cancer devil came to collect his due, I volunteered down at the shelter on Jackson. Never did have a dog of my own. Tilda was allergic. But way back when, the sisters at Holy Pines let me feed this stray mutt for a while. Until he hauled off and bit Sister Frances. Can't say I blame him. But he had to go. They took him straight to the pound, and I lost the best buddy a boy ever had. Nowadays, I'm just a sick puppy myself. Ready to be put down."

I swallow hard at the image. If Wendall was a dog, he'd be a hound, long jowls and droopy eyes. The sort that spends half the day snoozing in a spot of sunshine and can't be bothered to walk on a leash. But there's something unpredictable about him. Now that he's back on his feet, at eye level, I shift uncomfortably under the weight of his gaze.

"Am I running very late or are you very early?" I ask.

Wendall glances at his watch, loose on his skeleton arm. "Didn't we say eight o'clock? Or did my old brain have a thinko again?"

I search his face for evidence of untruth, but all I find is a faint blush of embarrassment over his usual yellowed pallor. He looks away and reaches to stroke Gus's head again. Eight hundred days ago, I would've sent him away, told him to come back at his scheduled time, and then grilled him at said time like it was the Spanish Inquisition. A violation of the therapeutic frame, however small, was worth exploring back then. Now, I only care about one thing. Wendall said he could help me.

"I believe we'd decided on ten as our regular time. You told me your home health care nurse stops by around nine. And you usually have your chemo appointments in the early afternoon. But it's alright. If you just give me a moment to . . ." With a sheepish smile, I gesture to the whole mess of me. ". . . look a bit more presentable. I can be with you in about fifteen minutes."

"Shall I wait inside?"

I'm grateful I didn't bring the key. It means I don't have to lie or invent a thin excuse. "Would you mind waiting outside? I've left the key up at the house."

I take a few steps, then pat my leg, summoning Gus. He's busy licking the saltine crumbs from Wendall's hand. Apparently murderers taste no different than the rest of us.

****

I fill Gus's bowl, pocket my office key, and make myself presentable in seven minutes flat. An impossible feat for the Dr. Roark of olden days who'd been a bona-fide member of the frequent-buyer Botox club and a master of the flat iron. That woman had never readied herself in under one hour. But then, she'd had Cole to impress. Along with the other doctors' wives, most of whom bought their boobs and counted carbs and gluten among their worst enemies. Frankly, I'm glad the former me bit the dust. Her loss is no loss at all. To prove it, I stuff a store-bought mini-muffin—twenty-five delectable grams of carbs—in my mouth as I truck it back down the path to Wendall.

He's still there, sitting sideways in the front seat of the Cadillac, door open and humming along to the radio, his snakeskin boots keeping time against the quarry stones. I recognize the song's melody well before the swing of the chorus.

"I'm a 'Girl Watcher' by The O'Kaysons," I say. "Now that's an oldie."

"Indeed. But not as old as this codger. That song came out in 1968, the year after I joined up. I'm surprised you know it."

"It was one of my father's favorites. I'm not as young as I look." I chide myself for being too casual. Wendall's showing up here early and unannounced has me off my game. Maybe that's the whole point.

"Well, your father has good taste." One eye disappears behind the veined skin of his lid, and I can't tell if he's winking at me or squinting against the sun. He hums a little of the song, the part about watching girls go by, snapping his fingers to the rhythm.

"Shall we?" I ask, gesturing to the door. I need to get back on my turf. Where I set the pace. Where I make the rules.

Wendall kills the engine, silencing the song, and follows me, laboring with each step.

A turn of the key, and here we are again. In this place that feels like a tomb. Cold and inky and reeking of the past. I flip the switch, and the ghosts retreat to the shadows. For now. My gaze flits to the place where they gather, dark and hungry, at the door to my real office. Thankfully, I'd remembered to close it. I take up my spot at the edge of the ergo chair, relieved.

Wendall slinks in behind me and assumes his usual position beneath the lamp, black hat resting safely on his knee. "I've got a confession to make, Doc."

I wait for him to tell me what I've already figured out. It's not the first time. Most of therapy is simply waiting for the patient to tell you what you already know. What you've known all along.

"I told a fib. A little white lie." I lean in, encouraging, and brace for it. "I didn't forget our session time. I got here early on purpose, hopin' you'd be around. You see, I want to clear somethin' up. Somethin' you might've misunderstood."

His eyes are a cool blue, but his knee jiggles with a mind of its own. His hat moves atop it as if there's a frantic animal trapped underneath. I want to reach for it, but I don't.

"Go on. I'm listening."

"I've killed people. A whole heap of them. But not like you think."

In my mind, I see the field stretch before me, the gravestones he'd described sprouting there like dead flowers. Nearby, a heap of bodies—all shapes and sizes and states of decay—waiting for the proper interment in Wendall's boneyard. But mostly, I think of Dakota. How I'd railed against burying her. Against putting my baby in the ground and turning my back as they'd shoveled dirt on the pale-pink casket someone had picked out for her—probably Cole—because I couldn't do it myself. *What other choice is there?* Cole had asked, his voice breaking.

The muffin I'd scarfed starts to push its way back up. I swallow it down again, its acidic sweetness burning my throat.

"What is it that you believe I think of you?" A dangerous question for a therapist. To invite the transference into the room, prop it up on a chair, and give it a voice. At Napa State, I might spend months working up to a question like that, especially with the sort of patients I had there. With moods that could turn like the weather and sanity as fragile as a Fabergé egg.

"Well, to put it bluntly, you probably have me figured for some sicko. Like Bundy or BTK or Zodiac. Hell, like that Shadow Man who killed your little girl."

I flinch at the last bit, but I don't deny it. "Have you often felt misunderstood?"

"My whole cotton pickin' life, Doc. Starting way back at that godforsaken Holy Pines when I stabbed this big ole bully—Tony Berlucci—with a pencil for callin' my momma a streetwalker. Tony had a thing for pickin' on the underdog. Heck, I'd say I was a bit of an antihero for a while. But Sister Frances didn't think so. She made me take off my shoe, and she beat me with it somethin' awful. In front of everybody. The holier the woman, the harder she'd hit. I spent the entire night in the naughty room."

He lowers his head, looking every bit a scolded hound dog now. Tail between his legs. "That's the way you made me feel, Doc. Looking at me the way you did yesterday, the way you did when you saw me this morning. Like I'm right back in the naughty room."

"To be fair, you did mention a graveyard filled with bodies. Might some part of you be invested in being misunderstood? Asking for it, even? Like a self-fulfilling prophecy."

His eyes light up, and he smacks the poor sofa with his hand. The thwack of flesh on leather pistol-starts my heart.

"You hit the damn nail right on the head. Why else would I have volunteered for Nam? The most misunderstood war in history, I tell ya, and I was on the frontline. Nobody knows what it was really like over there. Not unless you lived it yourself."

"I'm here to listen, if you'd like." I don't push. Wendall's leading me in circles. But at the center of it all is whatever he's holding back. The bone he's got buried. I'm hoping—there's that godforsaken word again—it's the very thing that can help me.

"It started in bootcamp. The brainwashing. They never called 'em Vietnamese. Always Charlie, Viet Cong, other things too.

Words I won't say in front of a lady. By the end of it, the enemy were animals to me. But worse. Animals that didn't deserve mercy. Once I got there, it was like a dream. The worst dream you ever had that you couldn't wake up from. Did you know Uncle Sam started passing out amphetamines—pep pills they called 'em back then—to keep us awake? I was twenty-one years old. Can you imagine? *Twenty-one!* High as a kite, crazy as a loon, and so goddamned angry. No wonder I had the highest body count in my unit. That's how I made Lieutenant. How I became a regular ole war hero."

Body count. Those words take me back to Mol's in an instant, twelve years old and watching my father etch another line on that rusted-out barrel. I dig my fingers into the plush arms of the ergo chair and breathe until the memory passes.

"Are those the bodies in the graveyard you spoke of?"

"Some," he says. "Truth be told, I couldn't even tell ya how many I killed over there."

"And the others?"

Wendall leans back against the sofa and lets out a long sigh. His black hat stills on his knee, the animal I'd imagined beneath it long gone now. "I suppose I should just come right out with it. Like ripping off a Band-Aid."

"That's usually the best way to say a hard thing." Don't I know it. I thought Cole had too. He was a cancer doctor after all, supposedly trained in the empathic and skillful delivery of the worst news of your life. But when I'd returned empty-handed from the grocery store, drained from dread, he'd tried to pussyfoot around it. *Sit down, Mollie,* he'd said. As if that mattered. As if sitting down made it easier to bear the loss of your only child.

I study Wendall's face. The veined valleys beneath his eyes, the furrows that frame his mouth as it moves. Who is he really? What has he done? Questions I've been asking myself about every man since my father.

"The other bodies belong to the Shadow Man."

****

I don't shock easily. As a shrink, especially a shrink at Napa State, shock is a job hazard. It tells the bad patients too much about you. What makes you tick. What twists your stomach. And the good ones clam up like oysters if you gasp or look at them funny. So, like every good therapist, my reactions happen underground. I choose what stays buried and what rises to the surface.

But when I hear Wendall speak those words, my underground is upended. Everything from down below—panic, fear, confusion, rage—winds up written on my face, on my body. But not just written, scrawled in red ink. I know because my neck gets hot, my hands go numb, and my ribs turn into a vise, squeezing the air from my lungs.

"Now, don't you go faintin' on me, Doc."

That's when I realize I'm standing, shaking. Wendall's hand is on my shoulder, patting it the same way he'd tapped Gus's head, his voice nearer than I'd like. I can smell him too, the sickly-sweet odor of tobacco. That muffin may be destined to come up after all.

"I'm okay," I say, stutter-stepping backwards until I feel my chair behind my thighs. I collapse into it, my legs useless stumps. I search the room for something, anything I can use as a weapon— the lamp maybe—though I'd hardly need it as weak as Wendall is now. "It's just . . . you . . . you surprised me."

"It's my fault. I stuck my foot in my big ole mouth again." He retreats toward the sofa—still regal in its calm—and I wish I'd been nicer to it, admired its buttery leather like it deserved. Maybe it would swallow him now, suck him down beneath the cushions and spit out his bones.

"Are you sure you're alright? You look whiter than Clotilda's bedsheets. And let me tell you, she used to bleach 'em within an inch of their lives."

I nod at Wendall. It's all I can do. His face blurs in and out of focus.

"I'm not him, if that's what you're thinkin'. Lord, no. Killin' in war is something altogether different than killin' just 'cause you want to. Cause it feels good. I ain't that far gone."

His hat is a black cat curled on the table. His hat is an asp ready to strike. There are words on my tongue, precious words. Words I've waited so long to say.

They don't come out.

"But I am complicit. I thought he'd stopped. I should've said somethin' to somebody. If I had, your pretty little girl would still be alive. I'm sure of it. That's why I'm here. That's why I found you." When I don't speak, can't speak still, he shrugs his shoulders, thin as a wire hanger beneath his button-down. "There you go. That's the heaviest stone I've got."

Now it's resting on *my* chest, pinning me to the chair, until a single word escapes in a tearful gasp. "Who?"

"You're not gonna tell the police, are you? I swear I didn't know what that loon was capable of."

"Wendall, who is it?"

He coughs, pounds at his chest, his voice coming out raspy. "That's just it. I ain't one hundred percent certain. He goes by a moniker, MQKlinger—like the character in *M.A.S.H.*—on the World Wide Web and claims to know me. I'm guessing it could be one of my old military buddies."

"So you've chatted with him online?"

"He messaged me about five years back, after I started the Shadow Seekers website. Well, I didn't build it myself, of course. I ain't into all the newfangled technology . . . that Book of Faces or the Tweeter. But after Clotilda died, I got bored and turned into an amateur sleuth. A real Sherlock myself, if I dare say so. Like a lot of folks, I went down the Shadow Man rabbit hole. Thought I could catch that rascal."

My head is spinning, spinning, spinning, the way five-year-old Dakota had spun with Cole, hands clasped together, laughing. Until they'd both fallen into the grass. "What did he tell you?"

"A whole lotta crazy, that's what. I didn't take him seriously. Rantin' about conspiracy theories and spy games. Some real James Bond–type shenanigans. Then he told me he was Shadow Man. And he'd killed those girls 'cause they were secret government agents sent to destroy him."

The single clawed finger of a memory tries to pry its way out of the lockbox in my brain. I grind my teeth, clamping down the lid even tighter. *There.* It's gone. "You think you know this guy? From Vietnam?"

"Just a hunch." He coughs again, harder this time, his face straining with the effort. "His username and all. Plus, we did a lot of burnin' over there. Practically burned that whole damn country to the ground. Crispy critters. That's all we left behind. Reminded me of Shadow Man, ya know?"

Of course, I knew. I'd committed Dakota's autopsy to memory, even the unbearable parts.

Reconstruction of the remains revealed the deceased was a moderately built young adult female. The jaw was completely burnt with charring of the bone underneath. Gum tissue was partly cooked with a heat hematoma present in the region.

"I'm sorry, Doc. I dropped a regular ole A-bomb on you, didn't I?"

Other bones also showed evidence of charring, which likely occurred after death. Dakota's backpack had been there too. What was left of it.

I swallow, forcing the lump in my throat back down. "What do you expect me to do now? Why haven't you gone to the police?"

Another vicious cough and Wendall doubles over, sputtering. "That one hurt like hell."

Still hacking, he reaches for a tissue, wiping a smear of scarlet across his lips. At the center of his palm, a spot of blood so shocking and bright, I can't look away. The last time I'd seen blood like that, it marked the back of my own hand. That blood had belonged to Dakota.

****

Wendall was right. A-bomb on target, delivered right to the center of my universe. As he drives away—he'd stubbornly refused an ambulance—I take inventory. My internal landscape a pile of rubble. In the middle of it all, the twisted wreckage of my devastated heart. But my brain remains somehow unscathed, a still-ticking clock in Hiroshima the day after. With every tick I think of MQKlinger and the website. It makes perfect sense. Shadow Man was a Shadow Snoop. Same as Dakota, Boyd, and apparently, Wendall, king of all the Snoops.

With Wendall's treatment folder in my hand, I lock the office and sprint back to the house, faster than I've run in years. Even faster than the Dr. Roark of olden days, racing on a road to nowhere, hoofing it on the best treadmill money could buy till I'd burned the requisite five hundred calories per day.

I fling open the door and head straight for the sofa, where Gus has been keeping my seat warm. He eyes me guiltily and slinks from the center cushion, leaving a set of dirty pawprints behind. I don't have time to care. I fire up Dakota's computer, logging into Shadow Snoops as One-Armed Jack, the user ID Sawyer had created. As I scroll through the comments, I send a text to One-Armed Jack himself.

Can you pick a lock?

His reply comes seconds later, and I let out the breath I'd been holding. Because old habits die hard. Even though I already know Sawyer is nothing like Cole, leaving my *just checking in, love you* texts unanswered for an entire hospital shift. Sawyer is dependable. And after Hurricane Cole, dependable is sexy. Dependable is downright irresistible.

Good morning to you too. And it depends who's asking.

Impossible as a daisy sprouting on this radioactive morning, I feel the corners of my mouth turn up into a smile.

I'll take that as a yes. Pick me up in twenty minutes?

The phone stays quiet. Glaring at it doesn't seem to help, so I distract myself with an Easter egg hunt, my eagle-eyed search amid the Shadow Snoops for MQKlinger.

Did you ever watch the show? Wendall had asked. *I always felt bad for ole Klinger. Pulling all those crazy stunts to earn himself a Section 8. Can't say I blame him. By the end of Nam, we'd all earned one.* He'd leaned out the window of the Cadillac and grinned. I probably had grimaced back, seeing his top row of teeth still coated by a thin sheen of blood.

Promise me you'll go straight to the hospital. And he'd promised. Which is why I need Sawyer to hurry.

I text him again, a string of question marks. Nothing. I call him, and it goes straight to voicemail. C'mon, Mr. Dependable. Don't let me down now.

I open the folder I'd carted back from the office and find the home address Wendall had penned on the top portion of Dr. Mollie Roark's fancy-schmancy treatment agreement. 1910 Meadowlark Way. I carefully type it into my phone's maps app for later. Wendall lives in Alta Heights, one of the older, quieter neighborhoods in town, near Napa State Hospital. I zoom in on the quaint ranch-style one story with its two-car garage and redbrick face. Hardly the house of a man who can't be trusted. But like faces, houses lie too.

I close the app and return to my mindless scrolling. Since we'd opened the account on Tuesday, I'd already poured over most of Dakota's public comments, the majority of them between her and Chewie. With Jojo666 providing comic relief and DocSherlock lurking in the background, piping up to defend her when Chewie got overzealous. Not that she'd needed it. This was my girl. Smart and spunky and funny too. The girl I remembered. Before everything went to hell. I read through them again, but there's no sign of

MQKlinger in Summer 2016, so I keep moving down, down, down the screen until the beep of my phone interrupts.

At ease, soldier. I had to check my lock-picking schedule. Some of us common folk do work, ya know.

Though I'm alone, my face gets hot. I'd forgotten the day, forgotten Sawyer works. Forgotten all of it but myself. What I need. That says a lot about me. What level of crazy I've reached. Forget MQKlinger. I need a Section 8 myself.

Sorry. I wouldn't ask if it wasn't important.

Yeah, lock-picking usually is. Took an early lunch. I'll be outside in five.

I close the laptop and tuck it under my arm. It's coming with me. As I hurry past Gus, asleep on his bed in the foyer, he lifts his head to consider me.

"Stay off the sofa," I tell him. "And keep an eye out." But he's already got both of them shut again, dead to the world.

****

Sawyer's truck smells like the freshly cut grass that's stuck to his work boots and stained the legs of his jeans. It takes me back to Mol's. Not to the junkyard itself, but to the nearby county road all grown up with weeds almost as tall as me. A few times every summer the farmers would come through with their tractors, mowing it down and baling it into hay. In the evenings, after the dust had settled, Dad would send me into the ditches to look for treasure visible in the choppy leftovers. Tires, tools, and fast-food bags, poking up from the hacked-off grass that reminded me of a bad haircut. But the smell, that made it all worth it. Too bad Cole had ruined it for me years ago, when he'd told me that fresh-cut scent was the grass's response to trauma. *It's fighting for its life*, he'd said.

"So just to recap . . ." Sawyer takes his eyes from the road to give me a sideways glance. "We're breaking into the home of a dying old man—your patient, by the way—for no particular reason other than your therapist's intuition." He says that last bit with the kind of skepticism I reserve for Luciana's fortune-telling. "The same intuition that had you chasing poor Boyd out of the parking lot on Monday."

"When you put it like that, it sounds bad." I gesture up ahead to the street sign on the corner. "This one. Take a left."

"You're totally right. My fault. I was a disaster at P.R. Probably why they kept passing me over for that promotion to Captain."

I shake my head at him, laughing. Already I feel better, lighter. A little less radioactive. "There's just something creepy about the guy. He shows up at my house, uninvited. Basically confesses to murder. And then takes it all back. Says it was a big misunderstanding. That he was so obsessed with a serial killer, he paid somebody to make a website, and then lo and behold, Shadow Man confesses to him. Doesn't that seem odd?"

Half-grinning, Sawyer shrugs, and I steel myself for a barrage of sarcasm. "About as odd as a person signing up to work with murderers. Oh wait. I mean, psychotic murderers. Are you even supposed to be telling me all this? Don't they have rules for that?"

He guides the truck to the curb as I give his shoulder a firm shove. Even though he's technically right. "They might've passed you over because you're too much of a smartass." My voice softens when he looks at me, brown eyes dancing. "But seriously, thank you. For doing this."

"Don't thank me yet. The last time I picked a lock I still had two hands."

****

You can learn a lot in five minutes. Five minutes with Cole at Bistro Jeanty, and I'd decided he was way too good for me and, therefore, had to win him over to prove to myself I could. I never met a game I didn't play to win. Five minutes at Napa State and I'd been in over my head. But it felt familiar too. The kind of overwhelming chaos I'd grown used to at Mol's. Five minutes with Sawyer, my first Grieving Parents group, felt like more than five minutes. Like I'd known him my whole life. And five minutes with Dakota, sweet little face swaddled in a pink hospital blanket, her tiny fingers wrapped around one of mine, and I'd realized I could be a mother after all. That I wanted to. No matter what I'd grown up with. Or without.

But five minutes can also tell you nothing at all. The house across the street is holding its cards close to the vest. There are no signs of life, except for the well-manicured lawn, the neatly trimmed bushes. Windows curtained, doors shut. Driveway empty. The whole street is Ray Bradburyesque, and I half-expect the mangy dog from the story to come round the corner and collapse in the street. Just a bag of bones waiting to be carted off by mechanical mice and deposited in the incinerator.

"Let's go," Sawyer says. "If you still want to."

Despite my shaky breath, I nod. "I just need to see inside." As if a house is a mind is a heart is a soul. Not just a lifeless container filled with things.

"You wait here and be my lookout. I'll ring the bell first. If nobody answers, then I'll go around back. If I get in, I'll come to the front door. Keep your head on a swivel and call me if you see anybody headed my way."

I agree. What else can I do? The only real breaking-and-entering experience I can claim comes from my former patients. And let's face it, they were lousy criminals who'd been caught for much worse.

Sawyer cuts the engine and opens his door, but I grab him by the arm, pulling him back. "Wait. Do you have everything you need?"

"Two paper clips, credit card, and a tension wrench." He tosses me the truck keys and hops down into the street. "Oh yeah, and this stupid need to impress you. Yep, got it all."

I watch Sawyer trek across the street and up the drive to ring the bell. When no one answers, he waits and rings it again. Satisfied, he walks around the side of the house to the wooden fence and reaches over, probably unlatching the gate. Then he casually disappears behind it without so much as a nervous glance. I guess that's what three tours of duty will do to a man.

Meanwhile, my heart is a ricocheting pinball, and I haven't even set foot outside the truck. A lone car rolls past, and I duck down like I'm dodging sniper fire. A bicyclist whizzes down the sidewalk, and I clutch my chest like I'm cage-diving with sharks. By the time Sawyer cracks the front door, I'm exhausted and wired at the same time.

My tingling legs want to sprint—jog at the very least—but I force myself to walk across the street as if I belong here. I slip inside the door and press my back to the wall, just breathing. Hard.

"You work fast," I say, finally.

"Sliding glass door. Easiest lock I ever picked. The only lock, if we're being honest."

"I thought you said—"

"I was a Ranger, Mollie. Not a spy." He shrugs, sheepish. "But we're in regardless. So . . ."

"Right. What now?" A laugh bubbles over, nothing but nerves fizzing like a shook-up soda. But it's a release too. When I stop, I scan the living room, focused. From the Philips television set with the built-in VCR to the lace doilies on the coffee table, it's been left in time. The décor, circa 1994. Circa Clotilda, I'm guessing. There's an odor—faintly chemical but not unpleasant. "You take the bedrooms. I'll look around out here."

Sawyer takes a step toward the dark hallway that leads past the kitchen and into the bowels of the house. "It would help if I knew what I was looking for."

"I'm not sure," I say, rifling through the drawer of the entry way table. Nothing to see here but keys and a flashlight. "But I'll know it when I see it. Anything creepy or suspicious."

"Got it. Bodies, weapons, souvenirs. Your standard serial-killer starter kit."

With Sawyer rummaging in the next room, I tackle the bookcase next. Apparently, Wendall reads. A lot. Practical

Homicide Investigation, The Big Book of Serial Killers, and a whole alphabetized section devoted to Vietnam. I can't help but think of Dakota. Like eyes, books are the windows to the soul. And Wendall's soul is not so different than mine or my daughter's, intrigued by the dark.

The bottom shelf interests me most. Two large boxes squat atop it, busting at the seams. The cardboard pliable, softened with age. I slide one of the boxes out and open it. It's the least organized of anything in this room, just haphazard stacks of magazines. *Life, Reader's Digest, National Geographic.* I sift through them until I reach the bottom.

A single copy of *Dime Store Detective*, dated September 1979. On the cover, a young, scantily clad woman gagged and bound at the wrists and ankles. I mouth the titillating headline to myself—*The Blonde Who Caught a Ride to Rape and Murder*—and toss it back in the box before the image gets stuck in my head.

That definitely qualifies as creepy. But it's no smoking gun. My father had read the same sort of magazines. Before they'd split, I'd overheard him and my mother arguing about it. Later that night, I'd snuck out of my room and dug the magazine from the trash where Mom had tossed it with an authoritative slam of the garbage-can lid. The picture on the front—a woman in a silky black dress with the blade of a knife at her throat, her mouth open in a silent scream—had scared me so badly, I'd thrown it right back. At Mol's, he hadn't bothered hiding them. There'd been a small stack of *Dime Store Detective* in the bathroom under my issues of *Teen Beat.* No wonder I turned out the way I did, helper of sick men.

"Got anything good yet?" Sawyer calls out.

"I wouldn't call it good per se. But I did find a creepy true-crime magazine from the seventies. You?"

"There's a BB gun in the closet. Otherwise, nada. I have to hand it to him. For a one-and-done military man, the guy is neater than me. You could bounce a quarter off these bedsheets. The bathroom floor is clean enough to eat from. But I'll check out the other room."

As soon as he says it, I realize the source of the house's lemony odor. *Pine-Sol.*

I pad across the hardwood, practically on tiptoe, toward the coffee table, where the remote control rests beside a box of toothpicks and an oversized plastic bag of medications. Beneath it, there's a collection of photo albums ordered by decade. Sawyer wasn't kidding.

1971. The handwriting on the back proclaims it so. A dignified Wendall, in uniform, standing at the altar with a sturdy young woman. His Clotilda. Neither had smiled, their faces grave. As if they already knew marriage would be no picnic. What expression would I have offered the camera—what strange contortions of the brow, what pained twist of the mouth—had I known the abysmal fate of the union of Cole Roark and Mollie Krandel? I should've worn black on my wedding day.

Two pages later, their expressions hadn't changed, but the background had shifted. They posed on either side of a FOR SALE sign outside the very house I had weaseled my way into.

I open the 1980s album to the middle and work my way back. In 1985, a bare-chested Wendall holds a stringer of catfish. His catch, at least, had garnered a wide grin. Life had honed him, turned his body lean and ropy. Clotilda had changed too. She'd grown softer, beefier. Dimpled thighs like ham hocks, exposed beneath a caftan. Fleshy, ruddy cheeks under a floppy hat.

The next turn of the page comes with a kick to the gut. A hard kick that leaves me breathless. The photograph is professional, the title embossed in black at the top: 1981 VIETNAM VETERAN'S ASSOCIATION, CHAPTER 702. In the sea of stern-faced men, I don't recognize Wendall right away. I have to hunt for him. But it doesn't take long, because there's someone I do know. Wendall is standing at my father's side, arm draped over his shoulder like an old friend.

I flip through the rest of the album. All of it devoted to War Hero Wendall. He'd even been president of Chapter 702 for a while, posing with then-governor Deukmejian.

From outside the window, an engine purrs, soft at first. A car passing on the street, perhaps. Then louder and louder until it's a full-on growl. There's no denying we're in trouble. Through a gap in the thick curtains, I see the nose of the Cadillac in the driveway, those dueling sickles mocking me.

My mouth goes bone dry, panic roaring in my ears. Or maybe that's just the sound of my blood rushing through my head, pushing its way into all those tiny blood vessels the way water charges through an opened floodgate. I shut the album fast and return it to its resting place.

"Mollie!" Sawyer's heard it too. He grabs me by the arm, jerks me to my feet, and I cling to the metal of his hand. "We gotta go!"

He pulls me past the kitchen and into a smaller room I haven't seen yet. Just beyond the desk with its ancient PC is the sliding glass door, the backyard. Freedom. Sawyer slips out first, grimacing as he bumps against the sharp edge of the desk, and reaches for me. But the computer comes to life and I'm transfixed by the words on the screen, even as the front door yawns open.

Welcome, DocSherlock. Your session has been idle for over ten minutes. Please reenter your password to log on.

Frozen, I listen to the jingle of Wendall's keys as he sets them atop the table in the entry, the click of the light switch. But it's the heavy clunk of his snakeskin boots that finally spurs me into action.

I'm like a cat, swift and damn lucky, as I follow Sawyer's path around the desk and out. He points ahead to the back fence, to the one missing plank, as he gently guides the door shut. "That way," he whispers. "We'll sneak out the neighbor's yard. I'm pretty sure the house is vacant."

I fast-walk across the plush carpet grass, dodging Wendall's collection of garden gnomes. Until my foot catches the water hose coiled between them and my luck runs out.

A gnome perched atop an impossibly tall, improbably red mushroom tumbles over, knocking into another. His matching pointy red hat cracks, and he falls to the ground, headless.

"Just leave it," Sawyer tells me. As if there's anything else to be done. I crouch low and slide through the opening, joining him on the other side in a yard nothing like Wendall's. What grass I can see is burnt by the sun. Dead leaves blanket the rest. The house's rotting foundation sags at the middle of it all, threatening to sink into the earth, and a world-weary tabby cat lies stretched in a sun spot, regarding us with disinterest. "He probably won't even notice it's broken."

"He's DocSherlock." I'm relieved to say it out loud. Even if I'm not sure what it means. "I saw his computer before we ran. His username was still on the screen."

Sawyer frowns but doesn't answer. When I start to move toward the neighbor's gate, he holds me in place, low and flush against him by the fence line. He puts a finger to my mouth, making the ragged push and pull of my breathing seem dangerously loud. Loud as a steam engine.

"Hey, neighbor!" I know it's Wendall. But the easy twang of his therapy voice is gone, something hard and vicious in its place. I'd disappear into Sawyer's pocket if I could. "I told you to keep your goddamned furball out of my yard."

Wendall curses under his breath, and though I can't see him, I imagine him cradling the gnome like a baby in his arms, scowling in disgust. The cat perks its ears and vanishes beneath the porch. I wish I could do the same.

"You owe me for this! If that damn cat so much as pisses over the fence line again, he's gonna get an ass full of lead, you hear me?"

In the tense silence that follows, I flinch, ready to run. But Sawyer won't let me.

"Don't test me!" The gnome's body catapults over the fence, smashing against the side of the house. Next comes the head, its pieces showering into the dirt. Then the *thwack* of the sliding glass door as it closes.

188

Sawyer releases me, and I trail him on trembling legs through the neighbor's gate. It's marked with a bright yellow CONDEMNED notice that matches the one on the door.

We don't speak again until we're locked in the truck and two blocks away with Sawyer driving like he stole it. He turns to me, his hands surprisingly steady on the wheel.

"I guess he noticed."

****

Sawyer leans back in his seat while I fiddle with the radio, searching for something head-splitting to drown out Wendall's voice and my own. Because right now, they're dueling it out like a battle of the bands. But Sawyer shuts the engine, leaving us in silence in my driveway.

"Well that was intense for a Thursday afternoon in the suburbs." He covers my hand with his as he speaks. It's kind of a miracle, the way it grounds me to the present.

"Yeah. I don't know how you do it. *Did it*, I mean. All those tours of duty. People trying to kill you, blow you up. I can't even handle a grumpy old man."

Sawyer shakes his head at me, unsmiling. "First off, *grumpy*? I'd say foaming at the mouth. You were spot on. The guy's got issues. And second, it's no harder than what you do, listening to people's worst moments. Bearing witness to the horrible things they've barely lived through. How do you do *that*?"

I shrug. "Compartmentalization, I guess."

"Exactly. The only difference is when you're in combat, you're just one big empty compartment. You leave all the other stuff behind. At home. For safekeeping. The problem is when you come back, it's not so easy to find. It's not always where you left it." He taps his chest with his prosthetic. "A part of me, in here, is still as lifeless as my arm."

I unbuckle my seat belt and slide across the bench seat toward him. He opens his arm to me and wraps it around my shoulders. "I don't believe that. Not for one second." But I know what he means. He's talking about the in-between people we are. How impossible it feels to get back to the other side. The land of the living.

I reach into my pocket and unfold the picture I'd stolen from Wendall's album, pointing Sawyer's eyes to the second row. "Wendall knows my father."

"Your dad? I thought you said he lived out in the middle of nowhere. That he was . . ." He doesn't want to repeat what I said. Which only makes me more certain. Sawyer is less in-between than me.

"Batshit crazy? He is. But this photo was taken in the early 80s. He was still on his meds then."

Sawyer studies the photo, but he has the look of a man who's just pretending. Whose mind is elsewhere. "Mollie, I think you should steer clear of this guy. I know we didn't find anything to prove he's Shadow Man, but maybe stay with Luci for a while. He knows where you live."

He's absolutely right. No doubt about that. "I can't."

"No. You *won't*."

"Fine. I won't. Because I can't. He knows something about what happened to Dakota. More than what he's saying. I'm sure of it. And I'm so close. I can get it out of him."

"I assume there's a completely legitimate reason why this is not a job for the police."

"The detective thinks I'm just like my father. *Cuckoo*."

Sawyer pulls me closer and laughs into my hair. I want to turn my face to him and let him kiss me hard, make me forget. At least for a while.

"And Sawyer, he's not wrong. I am like my father in a way. In every way. Obsessive, paranoid, a binge drinker . . ."

"Of course you are. You lost a child."

"Impulsive, irresponsible . . ." I risk a glance up at him. "Hard to love . . ."

It's not a question. I must be. Cole had left no doubt about that. But he answers me anyway. With his fingers on the back of my

190

neck, he brings my lips to his. Not in the blatant statement of a kiss I'd imagined, more of a gentle promise, and it's perfect. Because it coaxes me from beneath my hard shell.

"I wasn't done," I say, launching into the rest of my loser list. "Stubborn. Unemployed. A total—"

"Neither was I."

He kisses me again, this one as tender as the last. Proving he's not a shadow man at all. He's the real deal.

"There's something I want to show you. Can you spare a few more minutes?"

He pulls his phone from his pocket and types out a text, holding it up for me to see.

Stopped to help a lady change a flat tire. I'll be back a few minutes late.

"I'm all yours," he says. "At least for the next fifteen minutes."

"So chivalrous of you," I tease. "But just to be clear, I'm perfectly capable of changing my own tires. It's the only non-dysfunctional thing my dad taught me."

****

Sawyer follows me down the path to my office. Where I plan to lay myself bare. To fling open the door and show him just how crazy I've become. I focus on the stones beneath my feet. The breeze tickling the back of my neck where Sawyer's hand had been minutes ago. Anything to distract me from myself. I can't believe I'm doing this sober.

I pause on the steps, key in hand, considering. It's my last chance to chicken out.

"I've never been back here," Sawyer says. "What is this place?"

"The guesthouse my ex-husband turned into an office. He thought working would help me feel normal again." My laugh is a knife strike, sudden and sharp. "Guess the joke's on him, though. Since I was never all that normal to begin with."

Sawyer sighs. "Hey, Mollie, just in case I wasn't clear before. You're the exact opposite of hard to love. Okay?"

I turn the key and crack the door. The sun spotlights the sofa, illuminating the rich brown leather. Finally, it gets its due. But smack-dab in the middle sits the tissue Wendall must've left behind, stained red with his blood and sullying the entire scene. Luciana would probably call it an omen. I wrinkle my nose in disgust as I toss it into the wastebasket.

"Nice sofa," Sawyer says, perching on the oversized arm. "A little fancy for my tastes, but . . ."

If I wasn't so nervous, I'd kiss him. Just for saying that. "Cole picked it out. He picked out everything. I think he hoped all this stuff would make me right again. Would make us right again."

I walk toward the other door, feeling Sawyer's eyes on my back. "So this is what I wanted to show you. My real office." It feels as if I've slipped my skin, showing him the ruined parts beneath.

Sawyer goes right for the suspect wall, examining it up close. Who wouldn't? He looks it up and down, then takes a step back and looks again. "Damn. This is impressive."

"And crazy, right? I mean, what kind of person does this?" I think of Boyd and his wall. *A lonely person.* So that too.

"I wouldn't call it crazy. More like determined. Steadfast. A single-minded focus. You'd make a good sniper."

I think he's right. Because I can barely hear him over the roar of the past. The day Gus had returned, mangy and thin, and the police had photographed him.

Did he usually wear a collar? Detective Sharpe had asked me, scribbling in his notepad though I hadn't even answered yet. I'd imagined he was writing about me. That he knew the mistakes I'd made. That this was all my fault. Because then, I hadn't even noticed Gus's collar was missing. More evidence of what an awful mother I was.

Yes. A blue one. With his name in white letters and our phone number printed on the inside. Dakota had insisted on it. *It's gone.*

Sawyer touches my arm. I feel it, but my sights are set beyond him—I'm a regular Chris Kyle, the legendary SEAL sniper—and I can't turn away. There, resting atop the box of things I'd carted back from Napa State, is a blue collar. It reads *Gus.*

BEFORE

CHAPTER
FIFTEEN

(SATURDAY, JULY 23, 2016)

DAKOTA'S porcelain pedestal sink was the scene of an arduous ritual sacrifice, splattered with the newly let blood of a unicorn. That's how it looked anyway. An inch of standing pink water, pink droplets everywhere. Boxes of hair color—pink and bleach—discarded on the tile. Two of her mother's white towels, stained. And Dakota's hair, pink too.

"It's not *pink*," Hannah insisted, smoothing the ends as she blow-dried. "It's rose gold. And it's sophisticated. Trust me."

Dakota turned her head right to left, left to right and shrugged, not wanting to give her the satisfaction of agreement. With some things, Hannah could be trusted. Eyeliner, sunless tanning lotion, hair dye. With others, like the basic rules of friendship, not so much.

"C'mon, admit it. You look hot. Dickface—oh, sorry, I mean, *Tyler*—eat your heart out."

Dakota winced at the mention of his name. She hadn't heard from Tyler since Monday when he'd left her at the Pedersons' mailbox. Not that she'd expected to. Senior boys don't apologize. And they certainly don't obsess. They move on. "It's okay, I guess."

"*Okay?* It looks just like Kylie Jenner's. Maybe even better. *I knew it.* You're still mad at me."

Yes. Very. "No, I'm not."

Hannah groaned as she wielded a can of hairspray, leaving a plume of metallic sweetness in the air. And—*bleh*—in Dakota's mouth.

"I've told you a thousand times, I didn't mean it like that. Dickface twisted my words. I said you were inexperienced, and he needed to take it slow."

"I don't understand why you were talking about me in the first place."

"Look, Tyler was my friend first. I'm the one who set you guys up. It's only natural he would come to me for advice. I was looking out for you, *biatch*."

"Alright, alright. I get it." Even though she didn't.

Hannah ran two hands through Dakota's hair and stepped back, admiring her work.

"Your mom's gonna freak, you know."

Dakota nodded, her face cracking into a smile that wasn't meant for Hannah at all but for herself. Because even more than getting Tyler's attention, ticking off her mom was the whole point. She'd be back from Saturday errands any minute now with her two reusable bags of organic groceries and her fresh gel manicure.

"Speaking of which, you've gotta go. I'm supposed to be grounded, remember?"

Hannah shook her head, pitying, and headed down the stairs. "Twice in one month, you rebel. That's got to be your lifetime record. Let me just get a quick pic for the vlog. My viewers are going to love it."

She aimed the lens of her phone and Dakota relented, hoping she didn't look as silly as she felt, posing in one of her dad's old, stretched-out T-shirts, barefoot in her bathroom. Not exactly high fashion.

"Wait until Dickface sees this," Hannah said. "You look like a rose petal."

Dakota felt more like the stem. Lanky and full of thorns. "I doubt he'll care."

"So let's make him." She tugged down one side of the shirt, baring Dakota's collarbone, and mussed her hair. Out came the lip gloss. Just a dab. "Gorgeous. Now, look over your shoulder at me."

As Hannah snapped another photo, Dakota caught a glimpse of herself in the mirror and sighed. "I look like I just woke up."

"But in who's bed? That's the question."

"You're such a perv. Don't post that."

Hannah said nothing, giggling like Dakota had meant it as a compliment. Then she took off down the stairs, giving Gus a cursory pat on the head and Dakota the wave of a pageant queen. Her loyal subjects. Gus had no shame. And neither did she.

Dakota looked on from the window as Hannah pedaled away on her bike. She returned to the bathroom sink and opened the stopper, watching the unicorn blood swirl down the drain into nothing.

****

When Dakota heard the Range Rover round the drive, she positioned herself at the kitchen counter, an apple in her hand, and waited. "Get ready," she warned Gus.

The door opened, and her mother gaped at her, holding the two reusable bags of organic groceries in her newly manicured fingers. Predictability was her mother's weakness. Well, one of them anyway.

198

"What the hell did you do to yourself?"

"Chill, Mom. It's summer. It'll wash out before school starts." She took a casual bite of the apple, chewing slowly. As if she had all the time in the world.

"Chill? *Seriously?* I think you've been spending too much time with Hannah. Did she do this to you? This ridiculous pink hair?"

Dakota shook her head, wondering why she felt insulted. She could misbehave perfectly well on her own. She didn't need Hannah's help. "It's not pink. It's rose gold."

"You're supposed to be grounded. That means no friends, no phone, and definitely no . . . whatever this is. I'm calling her mother."

"Go ahead. Or maybe you should just ask Dad to talk to her. Since they're obviously so close."

She hadn't planned to say that. Of all things. She knew she'd pushed too far. But sometimes too far was the only way. Because it had been days since she'd logged on to Shadow Snoops, and she was supposed to meet Grandpa Krandel tomorrow. And as of this moment, she was still a caged bird with her wings clipped.

"What did you say?" Her mom spun her around by the arm, those manicured nails—shiny red, of course—digging into her flesh.

"Ouch, Mom. You're hurting me. I just meant Dad's always at the hospital, always working. He's barely even home anymore."

Her mom let go, tears already glossing her eyes.

They both stared at Dakota's arm, at the little red marks there. Those half-moons that might turn into fingertip bruises. Or not. Only time would tell.

"I . . . I'm sorry." Her mother delivered the apology to a head of kale. She'd already turned away, wiping at her cheeks and busying herself with the groceries.

Wordlessly, Dakota helped. Almond milk in the fridge. Bananas in the wooden bowl on the counter. Paper towels on the rack.

Finally, with the bags emptied, she sat on a bar stool, sniffling herself, and said it. The words she hoped would get her *un-*

grounded. But more than that, words to get her mom back on her team. Because lately, she'd never felt more alone.

"Tyler broke up with me."

****

Hours later, the spots on Dakota's arm had faded, but she had her phone back and her mother's permission to bike to the library tomorrow. Still, it wasn't a real victory. Because her mom had felt so guilty, she hadn't even mounted a proper protest, retrieving the phone from the master bedroom and passing it to her, not meeting her eyes. They'd barely talked about Tyler at all. Dakota had tried, but her mom seemed distracted. Not like she used to, when they could chat for hours about nothing.

After, her mother just stayed in the bedroom with the door closed. If Dakota pressed her ear to the place where the wood panel met the side jamb, she could hear her crying, so she retreated to her own bedroom. Her usual hideout, beneath the covers, headphones stuck in her ears.

It only got worse when Hannah texted.

Check this out. Dickface liked ur photo.

Dakota clicked the link, and her face appeared on the screen. Well, it was sort of her face, the raw materials anyway. But Hannah had photoshopped her into someone she hardly recognized. Her lips, fuller and redder than they'd ever been in real life. Her skin, smooth and dewy. Even her nose looked different, more regal somehow. And her boobs, *her boobs*, well, she actually had boobs. No pushup bra required. The caption: *Sugar and spice and all things . . . naughty. Who says pink is the color of innocence?*

Dakota studied the picture, cataloguing all the things she wasn't. A flame of rage licked up to the center of her chest and burned. Of course, Tyler had liked it.

What is this? she finally texted back. *I told you not to post that one.*

Come on, D. I made you beautiful. Ur already up to 1,000 likes.

Disgusted with herself, she balled her hands into tight fists and slammed them into the mattress, but it didn't help. She felt stupid for ever listening to Hannah.

Abandoning the phone on her nightstand, she padded down the hallway to her parents' bedroom and knocked softly. When the door cracked open and her father's beleaguered face appeared, she nearly gasped. She couldn't remember the last time she'd seen him. Behind him, her mother sat on the bed, head buried in her knees.

"I didn't hear you get home," she said. "Is Mom okay?"

"Jeez, Dakota. You really did dye it pink. What's going on with you lately? It's like we don't even know you."

Spontaneous human combustion. That's what Dakota thought of. Charles Dickens had written about it in *Bleak House,* one of the books she'd read for freshman AP English last fall. And she'd googled it, fascinated. She knew now there was no such thing. Because if a body could auto-ignite, hers would've caught fire right then and blown up, leaving a pile of ashes at her father's feet.

Instead, she stood there, intact, until her mother whimpered, and her father closed the door in her face.

CHAPTER SIXTEEN

(SUNDAY, JULY 24, 2016)

DAKOTA leaned her head against the Jeep's warm window and closed her eyes as her mother piloted the streets of downtown Napa. Every few seconds, Gus popped up from the backseat and stuck his snout between them, wet against Dakota's arm. Her mom had insisted on driving her to the library—*it's too hot to ride your bike*, she'd said—which Dakota concluded meant one of three things in a twisted multiple-choice test. Either her mother didn't trust her, or she wanted to talk. Or worse, all of the above.

"Are you sure you don't want to come with me to the dog park? Gus and I would love to have you. Wouldn't you, boy?"

At the mention of his name, Gus pranced forward and zeroed in on her mom's face, his long tongue like a heat-seeking missile. Dakota grabbed him by the collar and tugged him off.

"I already told you." Her voice sounded hard as nails, so she started again. "It's just that I want to get a head start on my summer reading list. I heard Mr. Ryan's no joke." That part was true, at least. Mr. Ryan, sophomore AP English, had the reputation of being a GPA crusher.

"Well, it's good to hear you're still a smarty pants."

"Mom, I dyed my hair. I didn't get a lobotomy."

Unexpected as a summer rainstorm, her mom's laughter surprised her, and Dakota found herself laughing too. It had been too long since they'd had fun together. "It's really not that bad, I guess," her mom said, tugging at a strand of Dakota's hair.

"Gee, thanks."

"You know what I mean."

The giggling between them slowly died, leaving a strange void. A dreary silence, the exact opposite of laughter. Even Gus slumped to the seat, laying his chin to his paws.

"Are you and Dad getting a divorce?"

Her mom pulled alongside the library's entrance and sighed deeply. Which didn't mean no. And probably meant yes. At best, a maybe. Another multiple choice for which she had no answer.

"Why would you ask that? Is this about Tyler? Are you still upset?" She fired off the questions so fast, Dakota hardly had a chance to be properly outraged. "You're better off without that boy. He was too old for you anyway."

"No. It's not about Tyler. It's about you and Dad. The two of you are always fighting. And you seem sad all the time."

Dakota felt her own eyes well with tears, and she looked away, down the sidewalk where a little girl skipped with a book in one arm and her mother beside her. Dakota wanted to feel that buoyant. To feel so happy that skipping seemed like a reasonable thing to do.

"Honey, you know Dad's been working hard lately. Doctor Samuels retires next year, and your father thinks he's got a shot at being the next chief oncologist. It's really important to him."

"More important than you and me?"

"Of course not. Relationships are complicated. They ebb and flow. But no matter what happens between your father and me, we both love you very much. I'm sorry I haven't told you that lately. I've been so . . ."

Dakota cracked the passenger door, suddenly eager to escape. As much as she wanted her mom to feel bad—so, so bad—she also couldn't bear it when she did. "Biatchy? That's what Hannah would say."

"I was going to say distracted." Another sudden shower of laughter, and it helped a little. Even if it wasn't exactly skip-worthy. "But, yes. *Biatchy*."

****

Dakota wasted no time securing her computer and logging in. In exactly thirty minutes, Grandpa Krandel might show his face. And in one hour, her mom would be back from the dog park to pick her up, and she'd expect her to be holding a book from the summer reading list. Which left little time for Shadow Snoops and Chewie. *Boyd.* She thought of him as Boyd now.

Chewie: *Long time, no talk, Birdie.*

DocSherlock: *It hasn't been the same around here without you, Cagedbird. Chewie's been sulking.*

Chewie: *Have not.*

DocSherlock: *Have so.*

Chewie: *Okay. Maybe a little. Where've you been?*

Cagedbird18: *Sleuthing, of course. I went to Lake Berryessa to see it for myself.*

Jojo666: *It's hella freaky, right?*

Cagedbird18: *A little. The gopher snake didn't help.*

Jojo666: *Yikes. I'd have probably dropped dead right there. The coppers would've thought I was #17.*

Chewie: *Gopher snakes are harmless, Jojo. They get a bad rap.*

Jojo666: *Seriously, Chewie? Are you gonna start defending Shadow Man too?*

Chewie: *Anyhoo . . . Birdie, I've been to Lake B a few times myself. I'm a local.*

Dakota ignored the little zap of excitement at the base of her spine. So Boyd lived near the lake. Maybe in Napa. Maybe he even attended Napa Prep. She planned to scour her yearbook as soon as she got a chance.

DocSherlock: *So did you find any clues, Cagedbird? Any bones left behind?*

Dakota shuddered and rubbed her arms, chasing away her goosebumps.

Chewie: *Yeah, have you shed any light on Shadow Man yet?*

Chewie: **winks*

Chewie: *See what I did there.*

Cagedbird18: *No clues at the lake. Unless a creepy fisherman counts. But I watched the Donahue episode you sent. And yes, a master of puns you are.*

Chewie: *What'd you think?*

Cagedbird18: **yawn*

Cagedbird18: *The 80s were so civilized.*

Chewie: *Hey, don't hate. The 1980s only gave us the most epic film of all time . . .*

Cagedbird18: *E.T.?*

Cagedbird18: *Sixteen Candles?*

Cagedbird18: *Back to the Future?*

She wondered, a little too late, if this counted as flirting.

Jojo666: *Get a room, you two.*

Apparently, it did.

Chewie has sent you a direct message.

Dakota opened her inbox and guffawed—then ducked to avoid the librarian's glare—as *The Empire Strikes Back* movie poster loaded onto her screen. Boyd captioned it: *The only sequel that's ever outdone the original.*

Beneath the picture, he'd written to her again.

Birdie,

Do you live in Napa too? I've been working on something—something big—and I'm dying to show someone. Well, not just anyone. You. Are you in?

Boyd (aka Chewie)

P.S. I'm not a serial killer. LOL.

Dakota logged off in a hurry, imagining her mother peering over her shoulder. She sat there, breathless, staring at her image reflected in the screen. Against the white background of the Shadow Seekers homepage, she was only a profile. A shadow herself. Behind her, the clock's silhouette.

Frantic she'd missed it, she spun around. The hands reassured her. It was exactly one o'clock. Right on time.

Dakota left Storybook Corner and walked toward the sliding glass doors. They parted for her as she neared, and the warm air streamed in, thick and smelling of summer. It invited her, but she stepped back, and the doors closed again, sealing her inside the cold tomb of the library. She repeated the dance again, wondering why she felt so skittish. She'd wanted this, after all. Asked for it. Did her father feel this way too? One foot in one life, one foot in another.

As she stood there trying to decide—*in or out, in or out*—she spotted a pickup truck rumbling down the street. It didn't belong there, with its rusted-out hood, its bald tires, and its two-tone shell, spattered with bird droppings. As if its parts had been salvaged like transplanted organs, pieced together and then left to die anyway. On the back window, someone had painted **4 SALE $500.** Which seemed foolishly optimistic.

The truck slowed in front of the entrance but didn't turn in. Even before she saw the driver—a blur of unruly gray hair and mottled skin—Dakota just knew. It had to be him.

206

She followed the truck with her eyes as it lumbered on, and then her feet, stumbling across the threshold and into the lot, where she stood motionless, with the heat of the asphalt radiating through the soles of her sandals. The truck and its old-man driver U-turned at the end of the street and parked one block down.

Dakota inched out further into the lot, ducking behind an SUV. The truck's front window regarded her like the eye of a beast, grimy and cracked down the middle. In its belly, the old man. He hunkered down in his seat, watchful, his head pointed toward the library doors.

She took another step forward, revealing herself, and then another, until she came to a stop on the sidewalk and lifted her hand to wave. Still as a scarecrow, he made no moves, no sign he'd spotted her. And then, she had an awful thought.

My pink hair. What if he doesn't recognize me?

Dakota waved again, more enthusiastically this time. Big and bold and smiling, the way she had every morning when her mom dropped her off at her kindergarten classroom. But he responded like her too-cool, high-school self, averting his eyes and ignoring her.

She approached the truck with caution, as if the sidewalk cracks were trip wires blocking the path. Her heart thumped, impossibly loud, in her ears. Like the bang of war drums. Still, it couldn't muffle the drone of the radio announcer, his sharp voice carrying out of the truck's open window. Her grandfather's arm hung there too, bare fist balled tight. The rest of it, clad in the sleeve of a camouflage jacket.

> In other military news around the world, thousands of Japanese citizens are protesting the presence of the United States military on the island of Okinawa, in the wake of allegations that an American contractor and former Marine raped and murdered a local woman . . .

The old man pounded the side of the truck, and Dakota startled.

"Goddamn Japs," he muttered. "Ain't no better than Charlie. They been on our asses since we dropped the A-bomb."

She winced at the raw hate in his words. It contorted his face, shaped his mouth into an animal's.

"Are you Victor Krandel?" Though who else could this be? This man who sounded as unhinged as her mother had promised. In his voice, wild and alien, she heard something familiar, and it scared her more than she wanted to admit.

"Hirohito didn't know what hit him, did he, Mol?"

Mol? Is this a test? But his eyes were somewhere else. Far, far away.

"Grandpa? It's me. Dakota."

He looked at her, then. Intently. As if seeing her for the first time.

"*Dakota.* Well, hot damn. It is you. And right on time. You look just like your mama. But she never had pink hair. I can't believe she let you get away with that."

"She doesn't like it."

"I ain't surprised. She can get a real stick up her ass sometimes, can't she?"

Dakota laughed, but it didn't quite reach her insides.

"I always told your mama that Dakota would be a pretty name for a little girl. Thought it might be too hippy-dippy for her though. We used to go up to Badlands every summer. And I'd take your mama and grandma fossil hunting. One time, over in Cedar Pass, we found a thirty-million-year-old skull with these teeny tiny teeth."

When he told her, he bared his own, as mucky and cracked as his windshield, and she steadied herself to not shrink away.

"That sounds neat." She couldn't imagine her mother anywhere near this man. But it must be true. Because her mom had told her the same story when they'd visited the Petrified Forest. "So I was hoping we could—"

"Who the hell is that?"

She followed Victor's panicked gaze back to the parking lot. To the black sedan with tinted windows that idled near the entrance.

"I don't know. Probably somebody going to the library." *Duh.* That's what she would've said if it hadn't been him asking, spittle on his lips, each word hard as a nail. If he hadn't clutched at the waist of his camo pants, where he wore a gun affixed to his belt. Dakota ate her sarcasm in one sour lump.

"Son of a bitch. I knew he'd find me. He's gonna make me pay for what I did. He'll take me back there."

Dakota gaped at her grandfather as he jerked the truck into gear.

"Back where?" Her voice, half-squeak, half-whisper.

"To Nam." He backed up so fast, he rammed the front bumper of the car behind him, setting off the alarm.

"Wait," she pleaded. "It's okay. It's no one."

But he'd already pulled out, tires squealing. A plume of white smoke erupting from his tailpipe.

Across the street, the sedan's passenger door opened, and Dakota waited. She wondered if she'd ever held her breath that long. Maybe she'd set a new record right here on the sidewalk.

Finally, a boy stepped from inside and slung a backpack over one shoulder. He adjusted his glasses and kicked the door shut with his sneaker. Dakota recognized him from freshman algebra.

"I'll be done by three, Mom," he called out, halfway down the sidewalk.

The sedan glided away, like a black swan, parting the smoke her grandfather had left behind.

****

Dakota listened to the rhythmic huff of Gus's panting as she flipped the pages of her library book, pretending to read. Her mom hadn't said much on the drive home, just hummed along to the radio and sipped her anti-aging wheatgrass smoothie—the one all the Napa Prep moms drank, Hannah's included, after a famous TV doctor endorsed it on his morning show—its unnatural green seeping up the straw and turning Dakota's stomach. *The adult version of peer pressure,* Dakota thought sadly. Instead of pink hair and booze and sex, Mom had health food and two-thousand-dollar handbags. Although the Louis—or just *Louie*—was elegant, she had to admit.

"Hey, mom?" she began, without knowing exactly what she'd say next.

Her mother glanced at her, eyebrows slightly raised. Like she'd only just remembered Dakota was there. Her space face, Dakota called it, and she'd seen it a lot lately.

"What did you say was wrong with grandpa? Like his official diagnosis?"

Dakota hoped she sounded casual. Not the way she felt, like a frayed wire, exposed and sparking. Grandpa Krandel's darting eyes still visible when she closed her own. Her mother answered with a heavy sigh, telling Dakota she suspected nothing out of the ordinary. Only the typical annoying teenager needling her mom's soft spots whenever she could.

"This again? What's going on?"

Dakota turned the cover of her book toward her mother, glad she'd thought to pick it.

"*The Bell Jar?* That's the book you chose from the reading list? Do you know what it's about?"

Dakota nodded gravely. "Mental illness."

Her mother sighed again. "No one really knows exactly what's wrong with your grandfather because he usually refuses treatment. But he's managed to rack up a few diagnoses over the years. PTSD. Schizophrenia. Schizotypal Personality Disorder. And Schizoaffective Disorder. That's the most likely one."

"Schizo . . . schizo-what?"

That part—the signs and symptoms and prognosis—rolled off her mother's tongue like a second language. Thanks to Dakota's father, she had a copy of every version of the DSM ever printed.

So romantic, her mother had teased, but Dakota knew she secretly cherished her collection.

"It means he has some of the symptoms of schizophrenia. Like paranoia. Sometimes he gets so paranoid, he even hears voices. And he also has some of the symptoms of depression. His alcohol binges didn't help with that. When I was growing up, he'd feel so sad that he had trouble doing normal dad things."

"That sounds really bad."

"It is." Two words heavy as millstones. Dakota wished her mom hadn't agreed so easily.

"So he's a lot like the patients you work with?"

"In some ways, yes." Dakota thought of the stories her mom had told her. The senior at Sycamore Community College who'd stabbed his own sister with a screwdriver because he thought she was the devil. The lonely mechanic who'd shot up a restaurant, believing they'd poisoned him. The voices and the visions. The illusions that seemed so real that there was no convincing otherwise.

"Did Grandpa ever hurt you?" she asked.

Her mother's eyes welled as she sucked up another gulp of wheatgrass. Gus stuck his head between them and snuffed at her mother's shoulder. The profound silence had a voice of its own. *Yes*, it whispered. *Yes*.

CHAPTER SEVENTEEN

(SATURDAY, JULY 30, 2016)

DAKOTA'S wet feet smacked against the locker room tile as she ran. She skidded to a stop, nearly slipping, when the Hot Tub Harpies— that's what she called them, but not to their faces, of course—glared at her from their perch. The mosaiced edge of the whirlpool where they parked themselves, chitchatting, until their thick legs reddened and their feet wrinkled, waterlogged.

Screw you, Harpies. She had to hurry. Because Boyd would be outside the Y to pick her up in ten minutes. Her stomach flip-flopped at the idea of it. The promise it held. That something might actually go right this summer. That Boyd Blackburn would be the perfect combination of Zac Efron, Steve Carrell, and Channing Tatum, and he'd scoop her up and away from the drain she'd been circling since prom night.

Dakota wrapped herself in a towel and twisted her body like a pretzel, peeling off her suit beneath it, careful to keep herself covered. Unlike the Harpies who flaunted their saggy breasts like badges of honor. She grabbed a change of clothes from her duffel bag and darted for the stalls. Nine minutes and counting.

She cursed herself for not coming in sooner, but she'd wanted one more shot at her personal best. So she'd floated for a while in the shallow end, letting the water swaddle her like a baby. Relaxation of the muscles, the mind, and the breath. Always the first step. Then, the final three breaths, a check of the pace clock, and the descent to the bottom. When she'd broken the surface, she already knew. *Eighty seconds.*

Afterward, she swam a few lengths of the pool, gliding and gloating. But at least she wouldn't have to lie later when her mom asked if she'd done her laps. Even if it wasn't the thirty she'd promised her coach. Still, her not-so-stalwart commitment to swim would mean less than nothing to her mother if she knew where Dakota was headed. And who she was headed there with.

As Dakota rushed around the corner, Mrs. Troupe, head of the Harpies, cleared her throat with a dramatic rattle, her eyes firmly locked on the posted NO RUNNING sign.

Dakota shrugged at her without slowing down, her insides fizzing. Ready to explode like a shook-up soda. She'd been bubbling like this since Tuesday, when she'd written Boyd back. *Correction.* When she'd flirted back. Even her father had noticed. *You're in a good mood,* he'd told her just yesterday, before leaving for the hospital where he'd no doubt be sneaking off to the on-call room with her best friend's mother while some sick kid lay dying down the hall. But she'd nodded at him, revealing nothing.

Dear Chewie,

Thanks for reassuring me you're not a serial killer. You really know how to make a girl feel comfortable. But what about a one-off? That's what my mom calls the guys with a single victim. I should probably explain she's a shrink who works with people like that. Not just some weirdo who likes to talk about murderers.

As for your question, I'm in. But I don't drive. Can you pick me up at the Napa Valley Swim Club downtown? And bring me back after? Saturday at 3:30 p.m. I'll be wearing your namesake.

Birdie

P.S. I'm not a serial killer either. LOL.

Dakota spared ten seconds to rub off the steam for a final check in the mirror. Her hair was still damp at the crown. She'd only had time for a partial blow dry. And her cheeks flushed in the humid locker room. She didn't have Hannah's bone structure or her ample chest or the patience to paint the flawless cat eye. But the pink hair lent an air of mystery. A bit of an edge she'd never had before. Not to mention the oversized T-shirt—her father's—she'd knotted at the back, exposing a thin line of skin above her jean shorts. The perfect touch. Sexy, even. As sexy as a giant Chewbacca face could be.

She burst through the double doors, smiling, and stood out front, surveying the parking lot. The after-work crowd, loosened ties and smudged mascara, flocked by her and inside, dead-eyed. Like hypnotized lemmings, incapable of breaking free. None of them seemed like a Zac-Steve-Channing. Not even close. She drifted toward the benches where she sat and waited, the sun drying her hair.

With each passing car, every pair of trousered legs, her heart skipped, her breath stopped. She distracted herself with her phone—Hannah's photo of her, up to ten thousand likes now. Though she knew better, she scrolled through the comments anyway, the words like razors slicing her skin. A million little cuts.

Slut.

Hot bod. I'd do her.

Damn. Nice rack.

Photoshop fail.

Probably a hag IRL.

IRL. In real life. Whatever that was. Lately, she felt like her real life had been hijacked. A runaway train on a collision course. An airplane aimed at the side of a high-rise. A caged bird, songless and trapped behind bars of iron. It all ended the same. With a big freakin' boom.

She hit the tiny *X* on the side of the screen escaping as fast as she could, like the jump from a burning building, and pretended it all disappeared. Then she texted Hannah again.

Please take it down. The 'rents are gonna freak if they see it.

Time dragged, the seconds limping along behind her like an old dog. She thought of the hound in the photo and her grandfather. Their brief meeting seemed like a dream now, looking back. Like something she'd seen in a movie. Maybe one of the far-fetched spy thrillers Hannah had dragged her to in the spring before prom. When she'd happily allowed Hannah and Eric to bookend her and Tyler. When she'd shared his popcorn, stupidly grinning when his fingers brushed her own. And had jumped, clutching his arm, when the grizzled hero got blown up for the third time.

But that was before everything. Or rather, before *the* thing. The incident.

And still, somehow, the clock on her phone read only 3:35.

"Birdie?"

A VW bug idled in her periphery. She stared at her shoes, afraid to look up. Hope surged through her, light-saber electric.

"I like your shirt," he said. "*Wookiee of the Year.* Classic."

She laughed then. He did too. A squirmy sort of laugh that turned her stomach. Because the laugh, the voice, belonged to a man, not a boy. His face, when she finally looked at it, a man's too. With shadowy stubble like her father. A crooked, slightly yellowed smile. Sweat at his hairline. A red flush on his neck. She took it all in, horrified, but she smiled back, small and polite.

"Boyd?" she asked, still hoping he'd say no. That Zac-Steve-Channing would swoop in and rescue her. Not that she needed rescuing. Boyd seemed harmless.

Like Ted Bundy, her mother's voice prodded.

A middle-aged dork, she argued back.

Oblivious, Boyd nodded and extended a hand across the passenger seat toward the open window. She took a step forward and reached inside, nearly jerking away when she saw the thick scar there, snaking out from beneath his long sleeve. His palm felt slightly moist against her own, and she held it longer than she wanted, to prove to him she wasn't rude. To prove to her mother she wasn't afraid.

"It's nice to finally meet you," he said. "Weird but nice."

"Same."

Dakota stood there, frozen, with the heat of the day rising from the asphalt, the car door hot to the touch.

A VW bug.

Boyd's eyes flitted across her face to her midriff. It felt the exact opposite of how she'd thought it would.

The unassuming car of a serial killer.

Her mom was in her head again, and she banished her the only way she knew how. With action.

She clasped the handle beneath her fingers and tugged it toward her. The door opened with a satisfying pop.

"Do I know you?" Boyd said as she ducked her head, pink hair falling like a curtain around her face. "I mean, in real life."

IRL. The universe mocked her. Poked her in the ribs, stuck out its tongue.

She slid onto the seat, lifting her bare thighs above the hot surface, and turned to him. "Uh . . . I don't think so."

"It's Dakota, right? Your real name? You go to school with my sister, Amanda. Mandy Phillips. Actually, she's my half sister, but—"

"Do you have AC in this thing?" She needed him to stop talking. Needed to think. That old dog had suddenly picked up speed—the seconds buzzing by in a blur, too fast—and she couldn't catch him.

Amanda Phillips had sat three desks behind her in AP English class. Tyler and Eric made fun of her sometimes, *moo*ing as she hurried down the hall, head down. Admittedly, Dakota had laughed. Once, she'd even *moo*ed along, giggling with Hannah.

"Sorry. It went out a year ago. And I don't have the cash to get it fixed. It's vintage."

"It's okay," she said, her shirt already sticking to the skin between her shoulder blades. "I'll just leave the window down. Does the door handle work at least?"

She was only half-joking, testing it, before pulling it to her, the sound sharp and final.

"You know Ted Bundy drove a Beetle, right?"

The flush on Boyd's neck crept higher. He tucked his scarred hand inside his sleeve and rested it on his lap, piloting the wheel with his left.

Dakota watched as the library grew smaller and smaller in the side mirror. But not as small as she felt. Whatever happened now, death by heatstroke or Star Wars–obsessed serial killer, she deserved it.

****

Fear dried Dakota's mouth, and it took effort to swallow. She squeezed her eyes shut—she couldn't look—and held out her hands. It felt warmer than she'd expected, and she flinched. Its pure muscle writhed beneath her grip.

"Careful," Boyd said. "Don't drop her. Sensitive she is."

Dakota opened her eyes, laughing at his silly joke with pure relief. Because she was holding a snake—a ball python, she'd been told—in a dark basement with an odd stranger, and she wasn't dead yet. She'd even made it past Boyd's mother, who'd barely pried her eyes from the television after he'd mumbled something to her about lending a Star Wars costume to a friend from ITT Tech. Dakota doubted she looked old enough for college, but Boyd's mom waved them on without a second look. As if he could've told her anything. Even the truth. *Hunting serial killers with your underage friend? That's nice, dear.*

"You know Yoda is a boy's name, right?"

"Not my Yoda. Look at her eyes. The same green-gold as the Jedi Master himself. And she's both wise and powerful."

Dakota pretended to examine the small head protruding from the snake-ball in her hands. *Green-gold eyes.* She'd take Boyd's word for it.

"The Force is strong with this one," Dakota teased as Boyd nodded, serious as a heart attack.

He took Yoda from her hands, depositing her in a glass terrarium, where she stayed tightly balled. "Yoda likes you," he said, stroking the snake's scales with his finger. "She trusts you."

Dakota stayed quiet. Because she most definitely did not like Yoda. Or Boyd's Overbridge that smelled of feet and old pizza and required her to descend a set of stairs not unlike those which led to the Montgomerys' basement.

"Now, I'd like you to meet Leia."

"I think I already have." She grinned, pointing up at the Princess Leia poster taped above his bed.

Boyd motioned her over to the computer at his desk, trying to hide his blush. He pressed a few keys, bringing the screen to life. She watched over his shoulder as an animated Princess Leia appeared with her blaster raised and ready to fire.

"So Leia is a PC?"

"Not exactly. Leia is an artificial intelligence engine I programmed to hunt Shadow Man. Do you want to give it a spin?"

Dakota nodded, dragging a folding chair from the cluttered corner of the basement and parking it next to Boyd's recliner.

"How does it work?" she asked.

"Well, I taught it how to think like a detective. A really smart detective. I already inputted all the information we have about each of Shadow Man's sixteen known victims. Age. Race. Hair color. Parents' jobs. Location of the body and in what condition it was found. Everything. Then Leia digests it all and makes sense of it. Tells me the commonalities. I tested her for the first time last weekend."

"And?" Dakota leaned forward, barely able to contain her excitement. "How long have you been working on this?"

"Two years maybe. Since I joined Shadow Snoops. I know I'm pathetic."

"Are you kidding? This is so cool. It's like that supercomputer they used to decipher the Zodiac's messages, right?"

With a modest grin, Boyd shrugged. "That's the idea anyway. I've been dying to show you. Go ahead. Hover on the blaster."

She moved the cursor across the screen and a button appeared with another line she recognized: *I've got a bad feeling about this.*

"Do you dream in Star Wars quotes too?"

"Wookiees don't dream," he deadpanned.

"I suppose I should click the button then."

"Only if you want to unmask Shadow Man. With Leia's help, of course."

Dakota's finger hovered over the mouse. She wanted to enjoy this feeling a little longer. The anticipation of something good for a change.

"I've got a bad feeling about this," she said, exaggerating each word. As if the fate of the galaxy was at stake.

****

Boyd's VW sure could move. It zipped along the highway like a little yellow butterfly. But Dakota was still worried they'd be late. That her mom would be waiting.

She'd see her with Boyd.

And she'd completely lose her mind. Total freak-out. Even worse than when she'd gone to the lake with Tyler. Or dyed her hair pink.

Dakota fidgeted with the printed page on her lap. Formulated in Leia's brain and spit out from Boyd's printer, it contained an analysis of two hundred variables, the most common rank ordered by percentage match among victims. She ran her finger down the column to the one that interested her most: *Miscellaneous*. They'd both agreed the dog-walking meant something. But what?

Category		Percentage Match
Age	Adolescent (13–18)	100
Gender	Female	100
Race	Caucasian	100
Location of Remains	Solano County	100
Condition of Body	Burned	100
Parents' Marital Status	Married	90
Eye Color	Brown	80
Hair Color	Brunette	75
Parent Occupation	Professional	69
Abducted From	Solano County	63
	Napa County	37
School Attended	Willis High School	50
Miscellaneous	Abducted with dog	50
Hobbies	Cheerleading	15
	Basketball team	20

"Don't worry. Chewie will get you there by five," Boyd said, smirking. "He's faster than he looks, and his serial-killer mobile has a sweet, souped-up engine."

Dakota giggled. "You know, your fascination with the dark side is really more Darth Vader than Chewbacca."

"I'll give you that. But c'mon, I'm a total Chewie, right?"

"Why?"

"Isn't it obvious?"

Dakota shook her head.

"Well, he's big and awkward and goofy. Like me." Boyd sighed, keeping his eyes fixed to the road. "And he's sort of ugly."

"You're not ugly."

"Well, I have four years of high school experience to contradict that."

"High school sucks."

Boyd said nothing, just twisted his mouth. Like he'd tasted something sour.

"What?" she asked. "Why are you making that face?"

"You don't have to humor me. Amanda plays tuba in the band, and I went to a few football games last fall, so I know high school doesn't suck for you. Weren't you nominated for some homecoming thing?"

"Homecoming Court? Like that means anything. People only voted for me because I'm best friends with the hottest girl in school. But she's not very nice anymore. This guy I used to like is a complete asshole. And my parents . . . *God.* They're the worst. My dad is totally checked out. And my mom's a nutcase—and a shrink. I mean, my screen name is Cagedbird, and that's not just because I worship Maya Angelou."

Dakota tried to stop herself from rambling, but she couldn't. The same way she couldn't paperweight herself to the bottom of the pool forever. Eventually, she had to come up for air. Spilling her guts like this, it felt like breathing. A big, refreshing gulp.

"I'd give anything to be your age," she told him. "What are you . . . like twenty-five? Twenty-six?"

"Something like that."

"And you've got a job and your own money."

"Yeah. Minimum wage at Reptiles 'R' Us."

She rolled her eyes at his doom and gloom. "When I'm twenty-five, high school will be nothing more than a distant memory. Just an itsy-bitsy speed bump in award-winning investigative journalist Dakota Roark's rearview."

"On your way to superstardom?"

"On *our* way as the dynamic duo who cracked Shadow Man's case wide open. This caged bird is ready to fly."

"I like it." Even so, Boyd's smile, when it came, strained his face, so that she couldn't distinguish it from a wince or a grimace. "But I've gotta tell ya, in my rearview, high school is more of a pothole."

****

Dakota folded the AI print out again and again and again until it fit in the palm of her hand. She tucked it inside the back of her Shadow Man notebook and checked her phone.

Her mom was late. One hour late. Without a text or call. The parking lot at the Napa Valley Swim Club had begun to resemble the ocean at night—vast and gray, without another person in sight. She stood in the middle of it as she dialed her mom's cell again, each shrill ring a jellyfish sting to her soul. In the deep-down bottom of her stomach, the sharks began circling.

"Hello, you have reached Doctor Mollie Roark. Please leave a—"

Dakota hung up and wandered back to the sidewalk. She took a seat on the bench.

Distracted. Her mom had said it herself days ago. But this took it to another level. Dr. Mollie Roark was never late. Not for work. Not for Dakota's swim meets. Not even for the dentist. *Perpetual punctuality. A hazard of growing up with an army vet*, she'd told Dakota once. Now, Dakota understood there must've been many hazards, the least of which was being on time.

She scrolled through her phone, worrying. For a moment, she considered calling her dad at the hospital. But that seemed like a betrayal since her mom's distractibility was most definitely his fault. Also, because she couldn't imagine enduring an entire car ride home with him.

Instead, she texted Hannah.

Did you get my message about the pic? Are you ignoring me?

The response came in an instant. And those circling sharks began to nibble.

Ignoring you? Seriously? WTF.

Dakota blinked at the screen. Pecked out a response. Held her breath.

Did I do something wrong?

She obviously had. As if Hannah had overheard Dakota dissing her to Boyd. But that was impossible.

Like you don't know.

Dakota replied with a string of question marks and waited. Seconds later, a link appeared. And so did her mother, piloting the Range Rover toward her like it was any other Friday. Her eyes, though, told a different story, once Dakota could see them. The dark circles, the puffy lids, the red rims.

Dakota tugged the door open, and they both spoke at once.

"Where were you, Mom?"

"I'm so sorry I'm late."

"Well," Dakota demanded, tossing her bag into the backseat. "Are you going to explain?"

"Something came up, honey."

"And you couldn't call or text? Did your phone explode? Is that what happened?"

Her mom's lower lip trembled. "I . . . I just forgot."

"Right. You forgot."

"Traffic was—"

"It's Saturday."

"There was an accident, and—"

"Just don't, Mom. Don't bother."

Dakota huffed as she secured her seat belt. She reached for the door, slamming it louder than she needed to.

They drove for a while before her mom extended an olive branch. A shaky little twig Dakota longed to snap.

"Since when do you wear your dad's clothes? His *Wookiee in Training* shirt at that."

"Since when are you late?"

Peace offering sufficiently obliterated, her mom didn't try again.

Dakota held back her tears, even as they burned her throat. Below, the sharks fed in a frenzy. Because she knew the truth. She'd clicked the link, read the headline. Seen it for herself.

Renowned Pediatric Oncologist At Napa Children's Hospital Accused Of Sexual Harassment

AFTER

CHAPTER EIGHTEEN

(THURSDAY, OCTOBER 4, 2018)

THE police are in my house again, running their gloved hands over my things. But this time, I can't retreat to my room and hide under the covers in a Valium-induced stupor, letting Cole take the brunt of their bad news, deflecting the barrage of their questions. He's a free fish now, rid of me. And Sawyer went back to the Blue Rose hours ago, under protest. No way would I let him bear witness to Detective Sharpe's pity—that hangdog headshake—the moment he laid eyes on my suspect wall. And the overflowing trash can in the corner of my real office, the one I hadn't bothered to take out since last weekend's binge. I should've gotten rid of it before the cops got here, but I'd been too shaken to notice.

Too bad Detective Sharpe notices everything. Now, it's too late. The judgment train has left the station. Its lone passenger stands in the doorway, fielding calls and directing traffic as the officers scuttle by. I avoid his scrutinous gaze, hunkering on the leather sofa that's much too good for me, wishing it would let me squirm beneath its cushions and stay there. Like a worn penny, lost from someone's pocket.

The office is dusted for prints.

The collar, photographed and collected. It leaves in a plastic bag, marked EVIDENCE. They'll probably cart away my empty vodka bottles too. Unequivocal evidence of my breakdown. Of just how far Dr. Mollie Roark has fallen.

Finally, when there's nothing left to be done save for my utter humiliation, Detective Sharpe fires the first shot at my dignity. It lands with the subtlety of a cannonball.

"Alright, Mollie. Let's go over your story one more time. You said you and Mr. Sawyer—"

"It's not a story, Cliff. A story sounds made up."

He breathes hard, both nostrils flaring. "I didn't say you made anything up. I just want to be sure I understand what happened. From your perspective."

"Sawyer was here with me when I found it. He told you exactly what happened."

Detective Sharpe joins me on the sofa. He looks like he belongs there, a sharp-dressed detective on his throne. "Mr. Sawyer confirmed you brought him here and got upset when you saw the collar."

"Of course I got upset." My voice starts to tremble, and I sink my nails into the sofa's soft flesh. "That collar has been missing since . . . well, you know. That means someone broke into this office and put it here."

"We didn't find any signs of forced entry, and the only prints on that collar are yours. I had them put a rush on it at the lab. I'm not saying it's not possible, and we'll have to wait on the DNA, but I want to rule everything else out before the media gets wind of this and starts a shit storm. Puts the Feds on my ass."

I remember when they'd taken our prints, Cole's and mine. *To cover all the bases*, Detective Sharpe had assured us, his voice warm and buttery smooth back then. That was before I'd gone rogue. Before I'd wielded a bayonet. Before the restraining order. Before they'd even found Dakota's charred remains. Cole had resisted. I'd merely gone along, wondering what he had to hide. Now, I understand his outrage.

"But I already told you that I touched the collar. I didn't mean to . . . I just . . . I was so shocked I couldn't help it."

I look at my hands, then bring them to my lap. These are the hands that held Dakota, that soothed her when she cried. That made puppet shadows and Christmas cookies and braided her hair for swim meets. I hate these hands. Because they'd done harm too. Irreparable harm. These hands didn't kill Dakota, but they might as well have.

"Mollie, have you been drinking today?"

Neither of us can see the trash can from here, and for that, I'm grateful.

"No. Those bottles were from a long time ago." *Four days.* But Detective Sharpe doesn't need to know that. "I never got around to tossing them out."

"So you haven't been out here in a while?" He gives me a look intended to bring the toughest suspects to their knees. But I hold his stare without breaking. After all, I'm a shrink. And a mother. I've seen worse.

"Go ahead," I tell him. "Don't hold back. Say whatever it is you're thinking."

"Is it possible the collar was here all along? Maybe inside that box? You got a little tipsy and pulled it out not realizing."

"Absolutely not. Gus wore that collar all the time. He ran off once at the dog park chasing a squirrel, and we thought we'd lost him. Dakota was inconsolable. So we had that made, and we never took it off. The bastard is messing with me. That's what I think."

"Who?"

"Who do you think? The goddamned Shadow Man. Or whoever it is that killed her."

Detective Sharpe hoists himself to his feet, meandering toward the other room. As if he's just a wandering Columbo and not a steely-eyed detective aiming right for it with the speed and precision of an arrow.

"That wall you've got in here. It's impressive." What he really means to say is wackadoodle. The technical term for what he thinks I am. "But it worries me. You've got the Lowry boy on there. And your own husband."

"*Ex.* Ex-husband."

"I won't even ask how you ended up with a confidential FBI profile. You're the head doctor, Mollie, so it's probably not my place to say this, but I think you need help. Maybe a professional to talk to, to help you figure this all out."

I join him at the door, stare straight ahead with him at the suspect wall. As many times as I'd studied it, it looks different somehow. "With all due respect, that is what I'm doing. I'm figuring this out. Because somebody has to."

His laugh is one note, dissonant. He pushes the door shut, my wall disappearing behind it.

"I never could figure out why folks always say that. *With all due respect.* Right before they throw a great big turd pie in your face."

"That's not how I meant it."

He flips his hand, as if to say don't bother. "Listen, I don't know exactly what happened here today, but if this is indeed some kind of message from our guy, you should probably get a hotel. Don't ya think?"

I nod. Because that's what is expected of me.

Detective Sharpe leaves me with a promise to arrange an unmarked patrol and to call with any updates. Because that's what is expected of him. We're both professionals.

When he reaches his car, he doesn't turn to wave like usual. He only glances over his shoulder with a cursory nod, a tight purse of his lips, that can only mean my pie hit its target.

I force myself to wait until he's gone. Then I'm off to the races, nearly tripping over the awful wool rug in a hurry to get back inside to my suspect wall. In the silence, it's obvious to me now what's changed.

A few of the Shadow Man articles are rearranged and tacked at the bottom with pushpins.

Shadow Man Continues To Elude Authorities

Was Missing Napa Teen A Victim Of The Shadow Man?

Here Without You: Family Grieves As Search For Missing Allendale Teen Reaches 200th Day

The headlines overlap each other, forming a message. Though I doubt anyone would believe me. Which is probably the point. It's a message meant for a wackadoodle like me. As the typed words blur together, I barely stay upright.

Shadow Man Was Here.

****

I sit on the floor for hours, thinking of Dakota. Wondering what to do next. I feel drunk, though I'm stone-cold sober. Not for lack of trying. At some point, I'd crawled to the trash can and taken out the bottles, one by one, turning them upside down over my mouth, desperate for one more drop of vodka. The one fat and perfect drop that would finally erase it all. But I'd already drained them dry. I think of the bottle I'd tossed in the kitchen, but the house seems so far away.

I should be frantic. Excited even. This is what I've waited for. To be certain Shadow Man killed my daughter. To have a chance to draw him out, to meet him face-to-face. One monster to another. To give him what he deserves. But I'm paralyzed, tied to the stake, by all I did and didn't do.

What kind of mother hits their child? I finally let myself think it, and now it's all I can think. I didn't deserve Dakota, and that's why she isn't mine anymore. Another darker thought crawls up from the slimy recesses where I'd banished it. *I don't deserve to live.*

The sudden buzz of my phone in my pocket sends the thought scurrying from the light like the earthworms that buried themselves under my dad's kill-count barrel. I read the text from Sawyer, wondering at his timing.

Are you okay? Do you want me to stop by after work?

I don't deserve him either, and I'd told him as much before he'd left. Before I'd made him leave. *Go back to work,* I'd said, after he'd given his statement to Detective Sharpe. *You shouldn't have to deal with my mess. You've got your own stuff to worry about.*

I'm durable, Mollie. That's what he'd said, chuckling as he'd tapped a finger to his prosthetic. He meant inside though, where I'm damaged beyond repair, the exact opposite of durable.

I'm alright. No need to come over.

I regret it the moment I hit Send. Because the last time I'd started spiraling, I'd gone on a six-day bender.

Are you sure? Have you seen the news?

While I rush to open my phone's web browser, two more texts come in. Luciana and her insistent *CALL ME!* And Jane, who I'm fairly certain has never texted me before: *I'm here for you.*

I type *Shadow Man news* into the search bar and await my fate. The first result is dated today. Breaking news from the online *Napa Valley Register.*

Potential New Lead In Shadow Man Case

Forty-two years after his first-known crime, the serial murderer known as the Shadow Man may have just taken a step out of the proverbial

shadows. According to an anonymous source close to the Napa Police Department, the family of one of Shadow Man's seventeen victims discovered an item believed to have been left by the enigmatic killer, possibly as an attempt to taunt police. The spokeswoman for Napa PD, Helen Yi, declined to comment on the incident and would not confirm speculation that the item discovered was associated with fifteen-year-old Dakota Roark, whose remains were discovered at Lake Berryessa in September 2016.

Peter Jacoby, Chief Psychologist at Napa State Hospital, explained that these kinds of messages are not uncommon in serial-murder cases. "These communications serve a psychological purpose for the serial killer. He believes he is smarter than the police and takes joy in playing a cat-and-mouse game. Take the Zodiac, for example. He purported to leave clues to his identity in several ciphers, three of which remain unsolved to this day. Imagine the immense pride he feels— the narcissistic delight—as the police, the FBI, and the world's most-famous cryptologists try and fail to solve his puzzles, which very likely do not reveal his identity. Other killers, like BTK, planted evidence taken from murder scenes in locations where they knew it would be found. Though these sorts of messages are typical of a serial killer's psyche, they are less commonly sent directly to the families of victims."

When asked why Shadow Man may have decided to direct his clue to the family member of a prior victim, Dr. Jacoby replied, "That is the million-dollar question. It's certainly brazen. Because he hasn't communicated before, his motives are unclear. But I wonder if for Shadow Man, for whatever reason, that particular victim was personal."

Media whore, Dr. Jackass again. He must be on the *Napa Valley Register*'s speed dial. That or he's sleeping with the editor. I feel like he's speaking right to me. Now and then, my last day at the hospital.

It's not personal, Mollie, believe me. I asked the Board to reconsider. But you're losing your shit. You've been crying in your therapy groups. You cursed at a patient. Given the nature of our work, we have to be pillars of mental health. You know that.

I still wish I'd kneed him in his own tiny pillar. But he's not wrong. It does feel personal. As personal as being axed by the guy you're screwing.

Later, I'll have to thank Peter. He's the reason I get up off the ground, drag my leaden feet out of the guesthouse, and plod back home. Because I won't give him the satisfaction of being right about me. I repeat the words aloud. It's not a mantra. It's not an affirmation. This is a fucking battle cry.

"I am a pillar. And I am most definitely not losing my shit."

****

Boyd's yellow VW is parked in my driveway. I see it through the trees as I round the path. He taps the horn before he spots me, then holds up two sheepish hands. Like this is a stick-up, and I've got a muzzle pressed between his shoulder blades.

I follow his lead, act tough, but I'm grateful to see him. He's my last human connection to Dakota. Even if he does know what no one else does—what an awful mother I'd been when it counted most.

"What do you want?" I ask as he cranks the window down. From inside the house, Gus barks once, twice. The sharp, staccato bursts, his version of warning shots fired over the bow.

"Is it true? Shadow Man left a clue?" He drops his voice, lowers his eyes. *"Here?"*

"How do you know that?"

"I've got an alert set up. Anytime there's a mention of Shadow Man online, I get an email. So I read the story. Shadow Snoops is blowing up. I logged on as soon as I heard."

"What are they saying?"

"That the cops found a dog collar at your house."

Right on cue, Gus mounts his onslaught, and Boyd's eyes dart to the house and back to me. The kinder version of myself, long dead now, would tell Boyd how harmless Gus is. That he hadn't stopped Shadow Man. The worst he'd do amounted to death by licking. Wendall was proof of that.

"I'm going to ask you one more time. What. Do. You. Want?"

"I want to help." He looks at me so earnestly I almost turn away, ashamed. "As long as you promise not to hurt me. No more bayonets."

I smirk, because I think he's making a joke.

"Or weapons of any kind." Apparently, he isn't.

"What makes you think you can help me? And why do you even want to? I understand you knew Dakota a little, but—" He raises his eyebrows in expectation. "Alright, alright. I promise."

Boyd reaches for his phone on the passenger seat. He taps the screen a few times and holds it out to me. "This is why."

It's a photograph of a newspaper clipping from December 1980. **Remains Discovered At Lake Berryessa Match Those Of Missing Napa Teen, Miriam Woodbury.** I zoom in on the tiny print, finding all I need to know in the first paragraph.

> **Since their daughter and the family dog, Bucky, went missing in the spring of 1980, Joe and**

Alice Woodbury knew this day would come. Yet, they were still unprepared for the loss of one of their twin girls, Miriam, whose partial remains were discovered this week by a fox trapper at Lake Berryessa. "As painful as it's been for us, it's been worse for Martha, losing her twin," the Woodburys explained.

A small photo in the corner shows the twin girls in matching dresses.

"Miriam and Martha," I say aloud. "Miriam was your aunt."

He nods. "I know it was a lifetime ago, but for my mom, it's like yesterday. That's why I found the Shadow Seekers website and joined Shadow Snoops. With all she's done for me, I thought maybe someday I'd be able to give her some peace. A long shot, but I had to try."

"Did Dakota know?" Her knowing feels essential to me. That we both saw this picture. That we both felt Boyd's hand-me-down pain.

"Not right away. I didn't go sharing it around on the site. But I trusted Dakota."

"She must've trusted you too." I wince as I imagine her telling him. *My mom slaps me sometimes.* I hope she was angry when she'd said it, not crying. That I couldn't bear.

"She did trust me. That's why I'm here. You asked about Dakota's last post, the one we'd exchanged the day before she went missing—when she told me she was going to Allendale."

"Right. *There will come soft rains* . . . You said you didn't know how she got there or exactly where she went."

He sets his eyes on mine, words waiting to be chosen and spoken, but he falters at the pivot point. Which words? Truth or lie? It's a look I've seen before. On my mother's face when she testified before the judge: *Mollie told me her daddy has been touching her privates.* On Cole's, every time he denied it: *I'm not cheating on you. You're paranoid.* Dakota's too: *Everything's fine, Mom.*

Even though I expect it—*mentiroso*, Luciana had called him—it stings like the first time, the last time, and every time in-between. Because it's true what they say. The truth hurts. And it rises. Undeniable as a smoke signal in a clear blue sky.

"I lied."

****

The inside of Boyd's VW smells like a pine forest, the odor emitting from a small green tree dangling from his rearview mirror alongside a plastic Yoda.

"You know who else drove a bug?" I ask him, buckling my seat belt. In more ways than one. Because Boyd has something to show me at his house. The reason they'd gone to Allendale.

"Ted Bundy," he answers, humorlessly. "Dakota said the same thing. She tested the door handle too."

The tears are there in an instant, but I laugh in spite of them. "That's my girl."

I close my eyes and lean my head back, trying to conjure her here, in this seat with Boyd on her left, driving her to Allendale. Trying to feel what she felt. To think her thoughts. But it's a blank, a void. It's unknowable. "So you met her a few times then? In real life?"

"I'm sorry I didn't tell you right away. I figured it would look bad. Me being older and the way I am and all."

"What do you mean?"

He takes his right hand from the steering wheel, displaying his burn scar. "I got picked on a lot in school. Freddie Krueger. Bernie Blackburn. They were relentless. Needless to say, I've never had much luck with the ladies."

I open my mouth, ready to give my two cents. That the living at home in Mom's basement or the Chewbacca slippers or the python might be to blame. But I think better of it. Maybe my heart hasn't hardened to stone after all.

"I know what you're about to ask. You still want to know wha happened, don't you? How I got this thing."

"So it wasn't the fiery pool after all, huh?" I'm ashamed of how curious I am. My unrelenting need to know. About other people. Because when it came to the important stuff, *my stuff*, I'd been clueless, indifferent. As content in my ignorance as a pig in slop.

"An answer for an answer." Hands at ten and two, he lays down the gauntlet without taking his eyes from the road.

"Alright. I suppose that's fair."

"Okay. Picture this. Boyd Blackburn, eleven years old, at a Halloween party. He's the new kid in school again, and he's desperate to impress. He likes comic books, but his mom can't afford to buy a costume, so she sews him one herself. The Human Torch from the Fantastic Four. He's a sight to behold. Everybody says so. And what does he do when he gets dared to stick his hand in the fire pit? I mean, he is the Human Torch, after all."

"Geez, Boyd. That's awful."

"Yep. The third-degree-skin-graft kind of awful." He shrugs, with the kind of grin-and-bear-it smile I know well. "I suppose it could've been worse."

"It could always be worse," I say. Though I don't believe that. Sometimes, the thing that happens to you is the worst. The loss of Dakota is all I am some days. Her absence is my substance. Which makes me even less than an in-between person. It means I'm nothing at all.

"Your turn," Boyd says.

I look out the window at the Napa River—we must be close to Cuttings Wharf—grounding myself again. Because I am a pillar. *Of salt.*

"I don't know if you remember, but you never answered my question that night at the Grieving Parents group. What would you do differently?"

Of course, I remember. The question meant for me. But I don't tell Boyd. It's bad enough he's asking again, forcing me back there, to that last day. To the last time I saw Dakota. If there is something worse than losing a child, it's this: With my last words, I'd cursed at her, called her a sneak and a liar.

"I'd listen better," I say. "And whatever she told me, I'd believe her."

Boyd nods, apparently satisfied, and leaves me to suffocate in silence beneath the mountain of my regrets.

"My mom's home," he tells me, easing the VW into the driveway. In the glow of his headlights, I spot Santa. Someone must've taken pity on him since my last visit, cleaned him and stood him upright. His boots, once defiled by my vomit, are a faded shade of black.

Boyd catches me looking. "It's already October. Mom thought it'd be easier to leave him out."

"Did she have to—?"

"Don't sweat it. I sprayed him off with a garden hose before she got home."

I follow Boyd inside and wave at Martha, grateful her eyes are fixed on the giant screen. "She never misses *Wheel of Fortune*."

"It's true," she says. "That Pat Sajak. Golly, now there's a man."

His cheeks reddening beneath patchy stubble, Boyd motions me over to the basement. He leads me down the stairs, past the scrapbook supplies to the heart of the Overbridge, where Yoda rules from her terrarium throne. From beneath his desk, he produces a plastic crate stacked top to bottom with newspaper clippings and file folders.

"My Shadow Man research," he says, sifting through the pile. He offers me a thin folder near the top. "This is why we went to Allendale. It's where the clues led us. And it seems spot-on with that dog collar you found."

I run my hand across the smooth brown paper, where Boyd wrote DOGS in black marker. That word is a lightning rod. A witch's finger, stirring my memories in a poison brew. They bubble to the surface, undying and grotesque. I open the folder anyway.

238

Five pages in total, each titled SOLANO COUNTY DOG LICENSE APPLICATION. I scan the first, my eyes drawn to the names I recognize as well as my own.

Owner: Glenda and Mark Donnelly
Dog Name: Hank
Breed: Beagle
Adopted from Solano County SPCA: May 21, 1976

Boyd perches at the edge of his recliner, his fingers drumming against his thighs until he can't keep quiet anymore. "Eight of Shadow Man's Allendale victims, including my Aunt Miriam, had dogs. Dakota and I thought it might be important. Some of the dogs might not have been registered, and the records from the seventies had already been destroyed. But the eighties were still being stored in an old warehouse off the 505."

I flip the pages, my stomach knotting itself like a hanging rope. Jennifer Dooley, the youngest of Shadow Man's victims, vanished from a carnival with her bulldog, Duke.

Owner: Scott and Lisa Dooley
Dog Name: Duke
Breed: Bulldog
Adopted from Solano County SPCA: June 5, 1981

Victim number eleven, Stacey Johannsen, had run away from home with Trixie after a fight with her mother. Her badly burned body turned up three months later at the Lake Berryessa site. The coroner ruled the cause of death as blunt force trauma to the head. Trixie was never found.

Owner: Marta Johannsen
Dog Name: Trixie
Breed: Mixed

Adopted from Solano County SPCA: April 1, 1983

Carrie Munroe, victim thirteen. She'd never returned from sunbathing at the park with her dog, Buster. Her skull was found in a field two miles from Lake Berryessa. Buster never came home.

> **Owner: George Monroe**
> **Dog Name: Buster**
> **Breed: Basset Hound**
> **Adopted from Solano County SPCA: December 24, 1985**

And finally, Jessica Guzman, victim fourteen, snatched while jogging with Blondie. The dog's collar turned up in a field in Allendale. With skin cells left behind on the nylon, DNA unknown.

> **Owner: Raul Guzman**
> **Dog Name: Blondie**
> **Breed: Golden Retriever**
> **Adopted from Solano County SPCA: May 15, 1990**

"See anything in common?" he asks.

"Yeah, obviously. All adopted at the SPCA. Just like Gus." But there's something else nagging me, pieces forming in the back of my mind, disfigured and misshapen. Like Frankenstein's monster. I can't say it out loud. Not to Boyd. Not to anyone. When he continues on, oblivious, so do I.

"My mom told me that my grandparents adopted Bucky too. She remembered how excited she and Miriam were to pick him out. But Miriam cried the whole way home. She wanted to adopt them all."

"Dakota was the same," I say, remembering how she'd lifted Gus's ear to whisper to him on the ride home—*We'll rescue your friends soon*—as Cole and I turned to each other with the same panicked face.

I push the memory aside and flip to the first page, to the Donnellys' license. "You said the seventies records were destroyed. Where'd this one come from?"

Boyd lifts his eyes, puffs his chest. "Glenda Donnelly. I called her a few months after Dakota went missing, and she mailed me a copy. It turns out they'd adopted Hank just a few weeks before Susanna disappeared. She held on to the form, not knowing if it might be important one day."

The same way I'd held on to everything Dakota touched that summer—movie stubs, books, Post-its. I hadn't even returned *The Bell Jar* to the library. When they'd mailed the year-overdue notice last summer, I'd mailed it right back after sobbing for a good hour. Return to sender.

"Did anyone else know what you were working on?" I ask, closing the folder and returning it to Boyd's outstretched hand. "Any of the other Shadow Snoops?"

Shaking his head, Boyd tosses the folder on his desk. He walks to the terrarium and lifts Yoda, her granite skin pulsing as she coils herself into a ball. "I certainly didn't tell anyone. I was a bit of a Shadow Man elitist. It got too crowded on the site for me, too much morbid curiosity. I left completely after Dakota went missing. But she might have exchanged intel with some of the other users."

"Like who? I joined the site, so . . ."

If Boyd is surprised, he doesn't show it. He gently strokes Yoda's head with his finger. It's barely visible between the folds of her skin. "Maybe Jojo666 or DocSherlock. They were online a lot."

"Do you know anything about DocSherlock or Jojo?"

He shrugs. "Not really. Why?"

"That is exactly why. Dakota was talking to these people. And *you.* You were all complete strangers. Just names on a screen."

"Welcome to the internet," Boyd deadpans. But then he looks at me, sees my face, and his tone softens. "If it helps, they were both already on the site when I joined back in 2014."

"So what are you planning to do with that?" I ask, gesturing to the **DOGS** folder.

"It's yours if you want it. Just keep my name out of it, okay?" He clutches Yoda to him like a security blanket, and my therapist's antennae prick.

"What are you so worried about?"

"Aside from your proclivity for weapons? The cops. They don't take too kindly to guys like me meeting pretty teenage girls. Haven't you ever seen *To Catch a Predator*?"

"Girls? Or girl?"

"Girl. Singular. Jeez. Are you sure you're a shrink, not a lawyer?"

"When it comes to my kid, I'm both."

I wait for him to tell me I'm too late. But he only hands me the folder, cradling Yoda in the crook of his arm and nodding. "Fair enough. Hey, I want to show you something."

Boyd cracks the basement door, and I shuffle out behind him. Now that *Jeopardy!* is on, Martha dozes, her head lolled to one side.

"I'm glad she's asleep," Boyd whispers. "She doesn't like it when I bring Yoda upstairs."

He pads down the hall, stopping short of the living room, and I nearly ram him from behind. I stifle a laugh, imagining Yoda, still coiled in a tight ball, flying through the air and landing squarely on Martha's lap.

"This is Miriam," he says, pointing to a framed photograph hanging on the wall. In it, two girls pose in front of a picnic table. "And my mom."

I move in closer, peering over his shoulder, and follow his finger as he speaks.

"And Bucky. The dog."

Boyd's mouth keeps moving, Martha's snore rattling in the background. Yoda pushes her head out from between her coils and considers me. But I take it all in from somewhere else. Somewhere far away and long ago.

In a place where I had a basset hound named Roscoe.

A mutt I called Waggles.

A bulldog, Rex.

And before them all, my very first dog, a collie my father had named Rambo before I'd even arrived at Mol's. I'd called him Sambo instead. A collie that looked just like Bucky.

****

"One more question," I tell Boyd, his VW idling in my driveway, his headlights glowing like cat eyes against the dark house. "Do you know Dakota's password?"

He frowns. "You don't believe me? About the message?"

"I just . . . I'd like to read what she wrote to you. To everyone. It may sound silly, but it makes me feel like she's not so far gone."

"The site requires a password change every ninety days, so the old one—whatever it was—would be disabled by now."

"What about her password recovery phrase? *His wings are clipped . . .*"

Boyd takes his cell phone from his pocket. "You really don't know?"

"Could you make me feel any worse?"

"Sorry. It's just that it was Dakota's favorite poem, and she got the caged-bird on her shoulder." He types a few words into the search bar and holds the screen out to me. "The next two lines of the poem. That should do it. But—"

He takes a big breath.

"You already tried it, didn't you?"

"Yeah. I had to. After she disappeared, I . . . I guess I missed her. I wanted to see if there was anything important. A clue maybe."

The car suddenly feels way too small. Like there's not enough oxygen for the both of us. I crack the door and half-gasp. "Tell me."

"Everything had been deleted. All of it. There was nothing left."

****

After Boyd leaves, I let Gus out and sit beneath the porch light, watching him make the rounds to all his favorite spots. The oak tree. The big rock in the corner of the yard. Each of the Jeep's four tires. The clearing where the squirrels congregate in the daytime. Finally, exhausted, he slumps next to me.

"What am I going to do, buddy? I'm so confused."

Gus rolls onto to his side, lifting his paws. Because his answer clearly involves a belly rub. The solution to most of Gus's life problems. I halfheartedly oblige, holding my phone in one hand and scratching with the other.

I delete the three new messages from Cole that I'm certain are a more insistent and annoying variation of the first. *I saw the news. Mollie, what the hell is going on there? Call me. Please.*

Then I enter the number from the business card I'd kept in my Jeep since the infamous marijuana makeout. When the voicemail prompts me, I take a breath and speak. Gus cocks his head at me, making me feel guiltier than I already do. But Boyd had said *girls*. The therapist in me knows words are important. The mother in me can't let that go.

"Hi, Officer McGinnis. This is Mollie Roark. You gave me your card about two weeks ago and told me to call if I needed anything. And, well, I do need something. Just a little favor, between you and me. There's this guy—Boyd Blackburn. I checked him out myself online. No official criminal record. But, should I be worried that he had been hanging with my daughter? Please don't tell anyone I called . . ."

Gus and I sit side by side, watching the headlights pass in the distance. In some other life, Gus didn't come home that day. A jogger or a hunter or a group of kids playing in the woods found his body, by then just bits of matted fur and bone. His blue collar, the only tangible thing left.

In some other life, Dakota didn't know Boyd. Or my father. Or DocSherlock. She didn't break her wrist when I let her roller-skate in the kitchen. She didn't wander off for ten whole minutes at the fairgrounds when I'd stopped to check my phone. She didn't send half-naked pictures of herself to an asshole jock. She didn't die. Because, in that life, I did it better. Which is to say I did the very least a mother should do.

CHAPTER NINETEEN

(FRIDAY, OCTOBER 5, 2018)

I'M sitting in my ergo chair, logged on to Shadow Snoops, hunting for back-posts from MQKlinger and ignoring Cole's fourth what-the-hell-is-going-there phone call when Wendall's Cadillac rumbles up the quarry stone drive.

Not today, DocSherlock. Today, I will not be surprised. That's because I've been up all night trying to answer one question. I've got the undereye luggage to prove it. The pounding headache, pungent breath, and yesterday's clothes too. But none of that matters. Nothing matters but this.

Is my father Shadow Man?

Wait—no. That's one question but not *the* question.

Did my father murder Dakota?

I hope the man rapping at my office door can lead me to the answer. Today. Because it's Friday, and my sanity—*my sobriety*—won't last the weekend without knowing.

"Come in," I say. "It's open."

The door yawns wide. Then Wendall hobbles across the threshold, two hands gripping a metal walker. "I'm a bona fide cripple now. The doc says this thing will ease some of the strain on my lungs."

"I'm glad you were able to make it at all."

He grunts and totters to the sofa, waving me off when I slide the coffee table toward me to widen his path. Instead, he leaves the walker beside it and goes it alone, leaning like a felled tree before he drops to the cushions in a heap. Nothing but a sack of bones under a black Stetson. "On the plus side, I'd say I move a lot faster on six legs."

I hear myself laugh. But inside, it's all mechanized. Input and output. Soulless as a robot, inhuman as Sawyer's IED, I'm programmed for one mission. One question to which all others will lead.

"How are you feeling?" *Pleasantries first.*

"Well, they loaded me up with some new meds that are supposed to stop me from hacking up a lung."

"And the coughing up blood?" That bright red spot. I look at his hands, my hands, still expecting to see it there.

"Apparently normal for a dead man walking."

Wendall's gray face cracks into a dry smile. I return the gesture. Input and output.

"Speaking of the dead, you certainly gave me a lot to think about yesterday."

He nods gravely, removing his hat and setting it atop his lap. "MQKlinger, huh? That dinky dau's been livin' in my head for years. I sure am grateful to share the burden for a while. I'm just sorry I had to trouble you after all you've been through. I hope like heck I haven't put us in harm's way."

Dinky dau. That's straight from Vietnam. Straight from my father's mouth too. As in, *I don't need to see a goddamn shrink. I ain't no dinky dau.*

"What do you mean harm's way?"

"Well, you already know I read the papers. And I reckon somebody snuck into my house yesterday too. After I told you about Shadow Man. Mighty big coinkydink, ain't it?"

I arrange my face into a proper expression of surprise and sympathy. Widened eyes for one thousand one, one thousand two. Then, pursed lips. A head shake. "That's awful. Did you call the police?"

"Nah. They'd probably laugh at me and brand me an old coot. Nothin' was missin'. Not that I could see. But the sliding glass door was unlocked. And they decapitated my best garden gnome. The bastards."

"They?"

I search Wendall's face, even as he's searching mine. But the monster I'd heard raging across the fence is well-hidden beneath the stagnant blue of his eyes.

"They," he repeats with no explanation.

The sinking feeling in my stomach reminds me just how lost I am. A few days ago, I'd been convinced Boyd was Shadow Man. And yesterday, Wendall. I'd been certain. Certain enough I'd broken into his house looking for—what? A body? A confession? And now, it's my own father I suspect. But I'm only doing what Dakota said. Following the clues. Even if they are all made up in my head. *Who's the craziest Krandel now?*

"Well, at first I thought the neighbor's cat had done it. That damn rascal is always sneakin' into my yard, using my flower beds as his own litter box au naturel. Then I got to thinkin' about the door being open, and somethin' don't add up. You didn't tell anybody about Klinger being Shadow Man, did ya?"

"Of course not. But, Wendall, you told me you came here to help me. That you needed to help me. There must be something else you can tell me about MQKlinger."

So far, I'd found only a handful of posts from the screen name.

Anybody think Shadow Man is made up by the government? Just like those so-called mass shootings. They want us to be afraid. Always afraid.

A few cards short of a full deck, that was certain. Still, I couldn't imagine my father typing those messages. Or even using a computer. When I'd brought home a Walkman in the fifth grade, he'd smashed it with a hammer and stayed up all night waiting for Charlie to trace the radio signal.

"Did you save any of the messages he sent you? The police can track those."

I can't tell if the eager bob of his head is playful or patronizing. "Already done, Doc. I'm one step ahead of ya. I had my IT guy look into it back then. He researched those . . . oh, what do you call those long-number thingies?"

"An IP address?"

"Bingo. Traced it to the public library up in Allendale. But it's a dead end. The place closed down last year anyway. None of these kiddies read actual books anymore. Hell, don't they want to dog-ear the pages? Riffle them, so they make that fluttery sound?"

I can still picture the library's quaint redbrick face, the open mouth of the book drop. The chip at the top of the first stair where rumor had it that the mayor's son had crashed his motorcycle. Nothing like the sleek Napa Public Library where Dakota spent her time.

"Not your girl though. Am I right? I remember readin' in the paper she was real smart. Top of her class."

I blink at him, momentarily stunned. But I won't lose focus. I won't compromise the mission. "Let's stay on track. You said MQKlinger might've served with you in Vietnam. What unit were you in?"

With a grimace, Wendall straightens up, his back rigid as a board, and salutes. "Bravo Company, the Fourth Battalion of the Tenth Infantry, Ground Assault Division, reporting for duty, ma'am."

It's not the way he says it—the cadence of his voice, like boots on the ground, marching in unison—but what he says that makes me flinch. Unforgettable as my own name. Mumbled and whispered and shouted by my father to no one but the squirrels and the sky. And sometimes—on a very, very bad day—to me. *Private First Class Victor Krandel of Bravo Company, the Fourth Battalion of the Tenth Infantry, Ground Assault Division.*

I breathe slow and controlled, like I'd taught myself years ago, and the memory retreats again. Input and output. One mission. All questions lead here. To this.

"Did you know my father? Is that why you came here? To tell me he's Shadow Man?"

Wendall looks down and rubs his head, smoothing the few strands of white that remain. I wish I could see inside it, past the mottled flesh, through the gray matter, down to the synapses. "Your father was a good soldier."

"Are you protecting him?"

"Victor Krandel was a good soldier and a good boy. *A boy.* That's what he was. Eighteen years old and barely shavin' when he got called up. War wounds us all. But some wounds you can't see. They're in here." He taps his forehead, somber. "Like a broken bone that ain't set, they don't heal right. Not ever."

"So what are you saying? Just spit it out."

"If you're askin' if I think your daddy is MQKlinger . . . if I think your daddy is Shadow Man . . . if I think he'd be capable of murderin' his own grandchild—"

"Yes. Yes! That's what I'm asking."

"Then I'd have to say you're askin' the wrong man."

"Have you talked to him? Are you still in touch?"

"The last time I saw Victor? Well, I'd say that was back in 1981. At the Vietnam Veterans Association picnic. I do believe we even had our picture taken." He chuckles softly, and I shiver.

"Fine. I'll ask him myself." I stand up, suddenly feeling exposed and icky. As if he's the one who can see straight through to my synapses, firing in all directions now. I can't wait to be rid of him. "I think we're done here."

Wendall moves with no urgency. His long fingers secure the top of his hat, like one of those claw game machines. It moves toward his head as certain as death.

"Right after mass at Holy Pines, Sister Frances would go out to the chicken house. Every single Sunday like clockwork, she'd come back with a big ole covered basket. One day I followed her out there, asked her what she was doin'. She told me if I wanted to know so bad, I could watch. I remember it clear as day. Me standing there, practically catchin' flies in my mouth as she broke those chickens' necks easy as pie. One right after the other, like it was nothin'. When she was done, she made me carry the basket. Made me pluck them feathers off too. And you know what that bitch said? 'Young man, next time, before you ask the question, be sure you're ready for the answer.'"

The word *bitch* rings in my ears long after the rumble of Wendall's Cadillac fades.

CHAPTER TWENTY

(SUNDAY, JULY 31, 2016)

DAKOTA smelled pancakes. And the syrupy sweetness—what it meant—turned her stomach. Because her mom only made pancakes on Sundays, the ones when her dad wasn't on call. So she would have to face him. Both of them.

Once upon a time, she looked forward to Pancake Sundays. To her parents' easy banter. To the fat weekend newspaper. To the stacks of blueberry pancakes she piled higher than her dad's just to see his eyes pop. To Gus, under the table, licking his chops and waiting patiently to make his move. Which usually involved him making his poor-hungry-doggie face at her until she gave in.

Dakota snagged her laptop from the desk and slipped under the covers, going straight to Google. The article Hannah had texted her last night came up first. She'd already read it. Only once.

Because once had been enough to burn the words on her brain like a regrettable tattoo.

Renowned Pediatric Oncologist At Napa Children's Hospital Accused Of Sexual Harassment

Dr. Cole Roark, a pediatric oncologist at Napa Children's Hospital, has been placed on paid administrative leave following accusations of sexual harassment by an unnamed female staff member. Mara Levy, attorney for the complainant, provided the Napa Valley Register with a summary of the allegations against Dr. Roark, which included fondling the staff member's buttocks, referring to her as a whore, and staring down the front of her loose-fitting scrubs. The staff member also alleged Dr. Roark displayed predatory behavior, attempting to isolate her from her colleagues and initiate a sexual relationship, implying her job would be at risk if she did not cooperate with his advances. According to Caroline Crews, Public Relations Director, "The safety and well-being of the staff at Napa Children's Hospital is our utmost priority. We take all allegations of harassment seriously and will take appropriate action following a full investigation." Dr. Roark could not be reached for comment.

Welcome to the new Pancake Sunday.

Dakota slogged through her morning routine. Her teeth had never been this minty clean, her face never scrubbed so pink. Though a part of her wanted to get it over with, another part sickened with dread. She even braided her hair. Then she descended the stairs in her bare feet. One. Step. At. A. Time. Like walking to the guillotine.

Her mother spotted her first, turning back to the griddle as she wiped a dish towel beneath her eyes. Then, her father, plastic smile in place.

"Hey, sleepyhead."

This could be worse than she thought.

"Hungry?" he asked.

She shrugged, her mother's sniffling punctuating the silence.

"Sit down, kiddo."

So she did, pouring herself a glass of orange juice and taking a swig. She suddenly wished it was Hannah's pretend Gatorade.

"Your mom and I need to talk to you about something."

But her mom looked out the kitchen window and beyond. Full-on space face. She might as well have been in another country.

"We don't want to worry you, but some kids might ask you about it. And we—"

"I get it, Dad. Just tell me. Tell me what you want me to say when my friends ask me if you're a perv."

"Dakota!" That brought her mom back to Earth. Straight through the upper atmosphere and plummeting. "Apologize to your father."

Instead, Dakota crossed her arms and pouted. She felt small again. She wished she were. That she could sink to the floor and wail, kicking her feet and smacking her fists against the linoleum.

"It's okay, Mol. She's upset. She's entitled to her feelings. Isn't that what you always say?"

Dakota hated that she'd somehow won her father a point in this secret game her parents played.

"Sometimes we forget you're a big girl now, sweetie. A smart girl. You're practically a grown-up. Fourteen, almost fifteen—two more weeks—going on thirty-five. So I'm going to talk to you like a grown-up. You know I've had my eyes on the chief onc spot. Well, I'm not the only one. And competition brings out the worst in people. They try to take you down any way they can. If they can't beat you, they destroy you."

Beneath the table, Gus rubbed himself against her leg. She found his fur and sunk her hand in it. Instantly better.

"Some people at the hospital don't want me to have that job. And they're willing to do just about anything to make sure of it. Including making up lies about me."

"So it's not true, then?"

Gus licked her fingers. She concentrated on that, on his smooth tongue, while her mother glared at her. "Of course it's not true. Your dad would never do something like that."

"It's a reasonable question. Your mother is right. I would never. I respect women. Always have. Hell, I'm raising one."

"It's Hannah's mom, isn't it? She's the unnamed female staff member in the article."

Her father nodded; her mother whimpered. Between them, Dakota felt the tension tighten like a noose. The rope around her own neck. In her mind, the old, tired scene played out. The basement stairs, the moaning, the Whirlpool dryer, her father's faded flannel.

"Hannah's mad at me," she said, disgusted at the sound of herself. That same small voice, the voice of a child. She cleared her throat.

"That's something we wanted to talk to you about." Her mother suddenly had opinions. "Your father and I think it would be best if you didn't spend time with Hannah right now. It's a delicate situation, and we don't want either of you caught in the middle."

Dakota reached onto her father's plate, breaking off the corner of a half-eaten pancake. She slipped it beneath the table, and it disappeared into Gus's mouth.

"Dakota? Are you listening to me?"

"Mol, jeez. Cut her some slack."

"Really, Cole? Cut *her* some slack? What about me? What about—"

"It's fine, Mom. I heard you. Hannah and I haven't really hung out much this summer anyway. She's got cheerleading, and I've got . . ." *Serial killers.* ". . . other stuff."

Her parents put down their swords, stopped moving, speaking, bickering for a precious moment, and she seized it. "Is that it? Can I go now?"

She didn't wait for an answer. Gus followed her up the stairs and into her room, onto her bed where she covered her face with a pillow and screamed. Her lungs ached. Though it didn't count, inside she knew. She'd just broken the world record for holding her breath.

****

Dakota listened to the sounds of her parents' war. The clipped voices, snide remarks, muffled inside her blanket cocoon. The slam of a door, sharp as a gunshot. Then, an engine outside. Her father's Mercedes revved, growled, and charged out the drive like a hungry beast in pursuit of its next meal. The rumble grew faint and disappeared entirely. Still, she waited for a while to be sure before she emerged into the pin-drop quiet, a droopy butterfly.

Dakota thought of calling for her mother, but she didn't. She'd rather see her first, so she could assess the damage. The emotional fallout.

But Gus gave her away, bounding down the stairs and into the kitchen like an oaf.

"Dakota? Is that you?"

Just a skirmish then, Dakota thought, hearing her mother's voice. *Nothing serious. No casualties.* But then came the clinking, the fumbling. When she reached the bottom stair, she realized she'd been fooled.

Her mother had already downed most of a bottle of red wine. Dakota saw it on the counter, already corked and tucked away. The glass probably quickly rinsed and returned to the cabinet. Her mother too, carefully arranged at the table with three plates of soggy pancakes. As if nothing had happened. As if this wasn't a thing she did now. Ever since . . . well, Dakota couldn't remember exactly when the drinking started. It had crept up on her. Like puberty. One day, she'd awakened to dark hair on her legs, and her mom tossing drinks back like a frat boy.

"Yeah. It's me. Can I ride my bike to the library?"

"Sit down first. Just for a minute. Talk to me."

Her mother patted the seat next to her, her limbs loose and wavy. But her eyes had a dangerous sheen, glinting like broken glass. Dakota had to look away.

"Let me help with the dishes," she said, scraping the pancakes onto one plate. Somehow, her fingers were already sticky.

"So when did you find out?" her mother asked. "About Dad."

Dakota deposited the stack in the sink and ran the water, sending the mushy mess straight down the disposal. When her mother jolted at the grating noise, pressed her fingers to her temples, Dakota hid her satisfaction. "Hannah texted me last night. She sent me the link to the article."

"That girl has never been a good friend to you."

"It's not about Hannah." Dakota let the water get scalding hot, her hands already reddening. "She's just sticking up for her mom. You can't blame her for that."

But Dakota did begrudge Hannah one thing—she'd believed her mom's story.

"Do you think Dad is telling the truth?" she asked as her mother joined her at the sink with the rest of the breakfast dishes. Forks, knives. Metal on metal, they landed with a clatter in the soapy water.

"Of course, sweetie." Her mother put an arm around her shoulders and tugged her in close. Dakota wriggled away, her mother's breath, sick and fruity, wafting after her. "Do you?"

"I want to, but . . ." The stairs again, the basement below. Pale neck. Lips. The moaning. Her father's flannel.

"But what?"

Dakota turned off the water and shook the suds from her hands. Her eyes kept flitting to the bottle of wine lingering in the background like an annoying party guest. "Do you really think Mrs. Montgomery would just make the whole thing up?"

"Honestly, Dakota, I do. The woman is histrionic. She always has to be the center of attention. You know she was raped in college."

Dakota didn't know, of course. The words scraped her raw. The way her mother said it. Like Mrs. Montgomery was to blame. But the alcohol was talking now, and there was no way to stop it.

"Or at least she claimed she was. Announced it in front of the entire PTA. When we were supposed to be talking about school safety. Who does that?"

"If you believe Dad, why are you so upset?"

Dakota opened the cabinet. As she suspected, a single wine glass was out of place and still wet. Water streaked down the sides as she held it out to her mother.

"If you believe him, why are you drinking?"

She set the glass on the counter and left her mother standing there. When she reached the door, she heard it smash against the linoleum, but she didn't turn back.

****

Dakota arrived fifteen minutes before the library's noon opening. She circled the parking lot once, twice, three times, jumping her bike on the curb the way her dad taught her when she'd first learned to ride. He'd been different then. But she couldn't say how or when or why he'd changed. She only knew the terrain between then and now was vast and uncharted.

Coasting past the entrance, the bicycle picked up speed, and she lifted her hands from the bars. Her dad taught her that too. If she concentrated hard enough, she could still hear him, his voice carrying behind her, keeping her upright. *Sit up in the saddle. Relax. Keep your eyes on the road. The bike will go where you're looking.*

At the edge of her vision, a two-tone pickup truck rumbled past the lot. She knew better than to turn her head. But it happened so fast, as automatic as blinking. As unavoidable as a sneeze and just as jarring. Her front wheel skidded off the sidewalk. She braked hard, overcorrected, and rammed her tire into the curb. The bike toppled over, throwing her to the ground.

Stunned, Dakota sat on the hard, hot cement surveying the damage. Her bike appeared intact, just a slipped chain and a scrape to the frame. Same for her own points of contact. Road rash on her elbow and knee and a serious ego bruise. When she gathered herself, she realized the truck had pulled into the empty lot. It idled in the back row of spots, as far from the door as possible. As she suspected, Grandpa Krandel hunkered down behind the wheel, peering out at her.

Dakota stood up and brushed herself off, grateful no one but her grandpa had seen her bite it. She waved to him, righted her bike, and began to wheel it in his direction, the chain hanging loose and clunking.

"I didn't know you were coming." She spoke to a closed window. "I'm sorry about last week. I hope you're feeling better." By better, she meant slightly less crazy.

He held up a prescription bottle. Dakota leaned in to read the label through the grimy glass.

Aripiprazole. 30 mg. Take one tablet one time daily.

She jumped when he shook it wildly, a maniacal grin on his face. He cranked the window down part way, stopping when it got stuck. "Doctor Patty says this stuff will keep me safe. She calls 'em my anti-Nam pills. And hot.damn, she's right. That SOB hasn't followed me in days."

Dakota tried not to look confused. Or skeptical. Certainly not afraid. He'd come all this way, presumably for her. She owed him a second chance. Maybe he'd remember something about the Shadow

Man investigation. After all, he'd been right in the middle of it, handing out water to search volunteers as they combed the grass for Jessica Guzman's remains.

"But what about you? You took a tumble there on your bicycle."

"I'm okay," she said. "But my bike . . ."

"Yep. You slipped the chain. Did your mom tell you I'm a mechanic? I can fix just about anything."

"She said you used to build cars from parts."

"That's right. I built this truck, and ain't she a beauty?"

Dakota averted her eyes from the dent in the door frame, the spare tire on the rear. The five in 4 SALE $500 had a white line through it. It now read 4 SALE $400. "Wow. Impressive. Any buyers?"

"Not yet. You interested?"

"I can't drive yet." She gestured to the shiny red Schwinn—with its fresh scratch—her parents had put a bow on for her thirteenth birthday. "Hence, the bike."

"Hell, don't let that stop you. I had your mama drivin' into town by the time she started junior high school."

Dakota covered her laugh with a cough when she realized he wasn't kidding.

"How did you know I would be here?" she asked.

"Didn't. Just figured if you're anything like your mama, the library is your favorite place."

"I love the library. But I'm not like her."

Saying it out loud didn't make it true. But Grandpa Krandel played along. He held up his hands, his palms as grimy as the window. "Alright, alright. I gotcha. You two couldn't be more different. The pink hair gave that away."

Dakota smiled, grateful for his lip service. "So . . . can you help me fix my bike?"

"I'll do ya one better." The door squeaked as he forced it open. He stepped out of the truck and into her universe. A gangly giant.

He tossed the bike into the truck bed, surprising Dakota with his strength. "You take the driver's seat."

****

"There you go! Now shift down to first. Atta girl!" Grandpa Krandel pumped his fist as Dakota piloted the old truck around the outskirts of the library parking lot. "It took your mama a whole week to learn how to drive a stick. Look at you, an hour later and you're a natural."

Dakota braked, and the truck juddered to a standstill, sending Grandpa Krandel's dash collection of papers and candy wrappers tumbling. Not the smoothest landing, but good enough. As stuffy as it was in that beat-up cab, the dust thick on the floorboard, the air felt light. She could breathe in here. Best of all, she hadn't thought of her parents once. Not the basement incident. Not the humiliating headline. Not even her mother and the shattered wine glass that was probably long swept up and gone by now.

"What is this?" Dakota asked, stretching her hand down to gather a trinket that had fallen at her feet.

"Don't touch that." Hard as armor, that voice. "It's a talisman. Lucky, ya know? Keeps me safe."

He snatched it up and held it in his fist, breathing hard. Sucking up all the air she'd relished. Eyes wild, his fingers trembled.

"Safe from what?"

He opened his hand one finger at a time, revealing the tiny soapstone four-leaf clover. "Doc Patty gave it to me. I had one in Nam just like it. Found it in the MASH tent after the ole punji pit gobbled me up. And my luck turned around. Four days later I hopped a Freedom Bird and headed back stateside. But somehow, somewhere, some way, I'd lost the damn thing. That's why my whole life went to shit."

"I'm sorry."

"Me too. I didn't mean to snap like that, to scare ya. Sometimes I forget I'm not over there anymore huntin' Charlie. Being hunted myself. I'm safe now."

He said it again. "I'm safe now."

And again. "I'm safe now."

Until she finally understood how to help, realized she wanted to. "You're safe now, Grandpa."

****

Dakota pedaled for home, her bike freshly oiled from a leaky can in the back of the pickup. The chain zipped along the sprocket without effort. An easy fix for Grandpa Krandel.

She leaned her bike against Gus's favorite oak tree, relieved to see the Mercedes still gone.

As she climbed the front steps, her knee ached a little. The scrape had already started to scab over. Around it, the skin a deep purple. After her grandpa's story about the punji pit, she couldn't complain, though. He'd rendered her injury small potatoes when he'd shown her the scar on his foot where the bamboo went straight through. But that hadn't been the worst of it.

"We studied Vietnam in my U.S. history class," she'd said later, after he'd removed the bike from the bed of the truck and dropped to his knee to examine the chain.

He'd chuckled, seemingly calm again. "That's your first mistake. Can't learn about Nam from a book."

"What was it like?" As she'd spoken the question aloud, her mouth had dried. Her stomach twisted. Maybe it was wrong to ask. She didn't want to set him off again.

"Those books of yours say anything about My Lai?"

"You mean the massacre?"

He'd nodded, lifting the bike chain and slipping it back on the ring. He'd coated it with oil and turned the pedals with his hand, the noise filling the uneasy silence.

264

"The whole damn war was a massacre. That's what them books don't tell ya. What constant fear will do to a man who's really still a boy. Fear and rage and testosterone. Young men shouldn't be soldiers."

"Mom told me you were eighteen when you got drafted."

"Sure was. Too young to drink but not too young for killin', apparently. I ain't to blame for what I did over there. Doc Patty told me that. She says I was right to set the record straight. Tell the truth and let the chips fall. Even if it means I got to keep lookin' over my shoulder."

The chain had kept spinning and spinning, louder and louder. Like a helicopter, she'd thought. His Freedom Bird. When her phone had buzzed in her pocket, Grandpa Krandel's hand stopped on a dime.

"What's that?" he'd asked. "Are you recording me? Did he put you up to this?" Then he'd smacked his own head, hard, and Dakota felt her eyes well. "Get a grip, PFC Krandel. Get a goddamned grip."

Dakota couldn't remember exactly what she'd said. How she'd soothed him. Only her grandpa's dark eyes glaring at her like she was the enemy.

AFTER

CHAPTER TWENTY-ONE

(FRIDAY, OCTOBER 5, 2018)

I drive to Mol's Junkyard with the mid-afternoon sun blaring through my windshield, as indisputable and painful as the truth. Whatever it is, it always hurts. I park the Jeep at a truck stop in Allendale and douse my nerves with stale coffee and heavy metal while I wait for the dark. When the sun sinks below the horizon and the truckers pull in and bed down for the night, I hit the road. Dad is sure to be passed out drunk by now. Or well on his way.

In the glow of my flashlight, Mol's is straight out of a cheesy horror flick. The kind where you know what's coming, but you jump and clutch your chest anyway, heart racing. A soft light streams from the trailer, muted by the years-old grime on the windows. The only sounds come from the woods. The hypnotic buzz of the crickets. The animals, darting unseen through the brush. The soft rustle of the wind.

I walk past the old pickup, down the fence line, covering my mouth to block the smell and counting squirrel pelts as I go. I can't help it. The breeze blows their tails, makes them twitch at the edge of my vision. At least counting gives my mind something to do. By the time I reach the tattered American flag at the perimeter, I'm at thirty.

I skirt under the fence and scan the ground, sweeping my flashlight left to right, until I find a good walking stick. Without it, I'm as vulnerable as a soldier in the thickest thick of the jungle, lost and alone. Because where I'm going—my father's hunting shed in the forbidden grove of sycamores—there are bound to be traps.

My pace is turtle-slow, cautious. I lead with a tap of the stick, making my way through the knee-high grass, across the field that reminds me of Wendall's mindscape, toward the tree line. I pass one sycamore, then another. It grows impossibly dark; the space beyond my flashlight, a black hole of nothingness. In that inky stillness, finally, the memory breaks free, casting off its chains like silly string and bowling me over with its strength. Its vividness.

I hadn't meant to break my father's rules, the last time I'd come out here, to the sycamore grove. But Roscoe had been missing for two days. At first, I'd only stood at the boundary, whistling and calling into the wind. Then I'd heard something—*a dog's whimper?*—and I'd followed it without thinking, the trees complicit in my betrayal. Or had they been against me all along? Soldiers of the wandering ghosts my father warned me about, trapped in limbo between this life and the next. Hapless victims of a bad death.

The trees haven't changed. They swallow me in their cover, shielding me with their pale bodies as I move. I still remember the way, though the path is grown over. My father had built the shed himself. Before he'd lost his mind, we'd come here together to scout for deer or rabbits, laughing and eating marshmallows straight from the bag.

I duck under a spindly branch, my shoulder brushing against tree bark. The first sign of Crazy Krandel is nailed to the trunk, long dead. I shine my light on the snake, its skin dried out like a raisin. Only the rattle at the end of its tail gives it away. Knowing my father and his traps, it had most certainly been alive and very, very angry when he'd staked it here. Another sweep of the flashlight reveals a large nail in the low-hanging limb up ahead. No sign of a snake though. It had probably rotted and dropped to the ground where it turned to dust like all dead things.

Fifty yards away, I spot the shed. Its silvery gray wood and sheet-metal roof the color of Wendall's tombstones. It's leaning a bit but otherwise intact. I feel inexplicable relief and dread, both.

I'd been nearly this close when my father had caught me last time. One hand had whipped me around by the shoulder, the other struck my cheek hard. My father's eyes, wild as I'd ever seen them. He'd dragged me behind him, inside, muttering about Charlie and how he'd finally realized exactly what I was.

A goddamned spy.

You've been working for Charlie all this time, recording me.

Where is it? The wire you're wearing?

The memory is a drug. It goes straight to my head. I slow my pace even further, taking my time, tapping the ground with my walking stick.

A few steps to the shed and the earth gives way under the stick's pressure, collapsing onto itself. *Good ole punji pit*, as my father had said, and I lean over it, peering down inside. But the hole is empty. No finely sharpened bamboo to cripple an intruder.

I study it with awe and horror, poking the dirt-and-leaf cover with the stick. *A two-step Charlie, maybe.* That would make sense. My father and I had never made one, but he'd told me about the Viet Cong traps where a venomous snake awaited an unlucky soldier. One step. Two steps. Dead. Whatever snake he'd doomed down here had died years ago.

I crouch lower, shining my light into the muck. And lower still. Until a pair of yellow eyes flash at me and I scream, jumping over the pit and landing safely on the other side, my walking stick tumbling from my hand.

I grip my flashlight tighter and let out a shaky breath, a hysterical laugh, as my thoughts race—skunk? raccoon? possum?—but a thwack to my head silences everything.

Shit. Trip wire.

Left ear ringing, I hit the dirt, hard as concrete in the summer drought. I roll onto my back with a groan and watch the pendulum swing above me among the stars. On the end of the rope, a bowling ball my dad had probably plucked out of a dumpster.

The world dims, but before it goes black, I see my father's face. Not now but then. His mouth frothing with anger as he'd pushed me inside the shed.

The wire! he'd yelled, grabbing at my T-shirt. He began to sob. *Where is it? Tell me now or I'll have no choice.*

I'd opened my mouth but found I couldn't speak.

Tears and snot streaming down his face, he'd held up the rifle and pointed it at my chest. Its barrel, a mouth that couldn't be satisfied. *Strip*, he'd told me. *All of it.*

My eyes roll back as the sky fades in and out. Somewhere, somehow, I hear Dakota's laughter.

"I'm not a spy." As if my voice can reach into the past. As if it can carry that far. As if I can still save myself.

****

Fire. My feet are on fire.

From out of shadowy blankness, the thought rushes in with urgency. I open my eyes. Sit up, head throbbing. World whirling like a demented merry-go-round.

Fire.

I look at my feet, shine my flashlight there. Sneakers, intact. No stakes or spikes or rabid animals.

Fire.

Pull up a pants leg. Now I'm dancing.

Ants. Fire ants. Just like the ones that marched in formation to and from the kitchen window every time Dad left a half-eaten can of Beanee Weenees on the counter.

I brush at my legs with desperation, skirting past the dropped bowling ball. I see now how close I'd come. The thick tree cover had broken the ball's descent, slowing it just enough to stop me from being a strike. A single pin knocked down for good.

I run all-out toward the shed. Foolish, I know. But a part of me would like to die out here, impaled by one of my father's booby traps. Because he'd be the one to find me. He'd have to live with that.

The door to the shed sticks a bit, but I muscle it with my shoulder, and it gives way to the darkness, dank and absolute. I stumble inside, breaking through a spider's web and tripping over a few empty beer cans as I swat my legs and gulp in the musty air. On the shelf across from me, I find a half-full water bottle. I uncap it and splash it onto my lower half. Then I cup the rest in my hand and splash my face too, hoping it will ease the dull pounding. Clear the blurry spots from my field of vision.

The fire finally doused, I scan the small room, trying to collect myself. I've been trying to do that forever, it seems. Retrieve my scattered pieces. With foolish hope, I pull the tattered cord attached to the end of a bare lightbulb. It flickers briefly, illuminating the dirt floor, the spiderwebbed corners—I delight in its warm glow—before dying with a ceremonious pop. *Figures.* Flashlight it is, then.

This place is not what I expected. I'd expected evidence, proof of a dichotomy. Innocence or guilt. Good or evil. Father or monster. I thought for certain I'd find it here, the answer I'd been looking for. Instead, I get Olde English, rusted tools, and a cluster of spiders.

But there is one thing I recognize. My father's footlocker. I'd helped him lug it here. Again, his shrink's idea. To put some distance between him and the war. *As if.*

I examine its face, shut tight and sealed with an old padlock. Surely this must be the reason he'd forbade me from coming here. I prop the flashlight on the shelf and take the shovel from its hook. Then I swing it like an axe at the lock, flinching with every strike. I imagine the sound traveling through the cool night air and back to the trailer like a will-o'-the-wisp, sneaking in through the keyhole and rousing my father from his fitful sleep. He'd come lumbering through the grove like a giant, with his rifle at the ready. And I'd have to prove—again—I'm not a spy after all. Only his unlucky daughter.

I stop noticing the strikes and just swing, harder and faster. Until I'm lost in the rhythm of it. Until sweat drips from my nose. Until the grinding metal sends up sparks. Until finally, finally, the lock snaps.

Kneeling beside it, I lift the lid. The underside is plastered with old-fashioned pinup girls. Dad had a thing for buxom blondes. Not unlike my ex-husband, apparently. I lift the first item with care, holding it up to the light and setting it beside me. A slightly moist set of army fatigues, with a large tear in one of the legs. It's been repaired, haphazardly stitched together with white thread. A helmet, slightly dented. A large tarp and a rucksack, caked with mud that flakes off in my hand as I examine it. As if my father had only just returned from the battlefield.

Further down, I find his medal—the Purple Heart—resting on his neatly folded dress blues. As a girl, I'd coveted it, pinning it to my doll's dress when my father wasn't looking. Until I'd learned what it meant and left it quarantined in its box, set in the drawer. The ribbon, once vibrant, is now the drab color of a day-old bruise.

His uniform too has seen better days. I spot one of the missing gold buttons in the corner of the trunk and roll it between my fingers, feeling like I might cry. The last time I'd seen my father in his uniform, we'd buried my mother at Roseview Cemetery. I hadn't expected him to show. Not after the things he'd done, the way I'd run from him and never gone back. I remember him cresting the grassy hill and taking a place at the back of the small crowd, his face stoic. Not unlike the toy soldiers my mother had hung on our Christmas tree.

I peer down into the empty footlocker. Judging by the length of this thing, there should be at least six more inches of space. I run my hand along the bottom, then rap at it, listening to the hollow thump of my knuckles.

I spring to my feet and search the shelf, retrieving a screwdriver and my flashlight. The beam of light reveals a thin opening at the inner edges of the locker, and I work the flat end of the tool inside, prying up the bottom.

Strip! All of it! Down to your skivvies. My father's voice comes back to me, and I spin around expecting him to be there, looming over my shoulder. Instead, there's only the half-open door, drooping from its top hinge and swaying slightly, governed by the wind. And the shadow of a sycamore made menacing by a trick of the light.

Shaking off a shiver, I turn back and reach into the hidden compartment and withdraw a stack of papers, stamped with a red CONFIDENTIAL and bearing the seal of the United States Army. I lean back against the footlocker and begin to read.

Sworn testimony of Private First Class Victor Krandel of Bravo Company, the 4th Battalion of the 10th Infantry, Ground Assault Division

Agent Cooley: Good morning, Private First Class Krandel. My name is Mark Cooley. I am an officer with the United States Army Criminal Investigation Command. Do you understand why you are here today?

Private First Class Krandel: To testify about possible incidents of criminal misconduct during the time of my service in Vietnam.

Agent Cooley: That's correct. As I understand it, you recently contacted C.I.D. to clarify or retract sworn statements you provided to the Vietnam War Crimes Working Group. Is that correct?

Private First Class Krandel: Yes, sir.

Agent Cooley: And you now allege you have knowledge of misconduct by your superior officer?

Private First Class Krandel: I believe so.

Agent Cooley: Is that an affirmative?

Private First Class Krandel: Yes, sir, I do. Cam Chi was the worst of it.

Agent Cooley: Cam Chi village in Vietnam?

Private First Class Krandel; Yes, sir.

Agent Cooley: Tell us what you recall.

Private First Class Krandel: That night we had orders for a planned operation there. At Cam Chi.

Agent Cooley: When was this?

Private First Class Krandel: December 30, 1969. My friend, John, had been hurt real bad by a booby trap just outside of the village. Damn punji pit. A lot worse than the one that got me a few months later.

Agent Cooley: You are referring to Private John Bailey of Bravo Company, correct?

Private First Class Krandel: Yes, sir.

Agent Cooley: Let the record reflect Private Bailey was impaled by a Vietnamese tiger trap one mile south of the Cam Chi village on December 29, 1969. He was airlifted by MedEvac and succumbed to his injuries that same night.

Agent Cooley: You say there was a planned operation. What were your orders?

Private First Class Krandel: To search and destroy.

Agent Cooley: What did you understand that to mean?

Private First Class Krandel: Officially or unofficially? Officially it meant to kill any enemy combatants—the VC. Unofficially, we understood that meant everybody. Men, women, children. All of 'em.

Agent Cooley: Who gave you those orders?

Private First Class Krandel: We got 'em secondhand. But I figure they came from Pugh down to Grady.

Agent Cooley: For clarification, do you mean Captain Gerald Pugh and Lieutenant Wendall Grady?

Private First Class Krandel: Yes, sir.

Agent Cooley: What happened when you arrived at Cam Chi?

Private First Class Krandel: When we first made our approach, the place looked deserted, so we set up camp and waited a while. We were comin' off a long trek through some real swampy jungle. I'm talkin' knee-deep in slime. I was glad for the break. My skin had literally started peelin' off my feet. That night, Lieutenant Grady handed out pep pills to help us stay awake. Just in case Charlie showed up. At daybreak, one of my buddies saw some mama-sans walking back to the village with water, a few little kids right behind 'em. We asked Lieutenant Grady what to do.

Agent Cooley: Did Lieutenant Grady give any orders at that time?

Private First Class Krandel: Yes, sir. He told me to fire upon them.

Agent Cooley: You specifically?

Private First Class Krandel: Yes, sir.

Agent Cooley: Do you know why?

Private First Class Krandel: I never asked him. That would have been insubordination. But he'd done it before. I was the baby of our platoon. I guess I figured he wanted to toughen me up.

Agent Cooley: What did you do?

Private First Class Krandel: Right off, I tried to finagle out of it. I told him they were just little kids. And he said something like, "Tough petunias, Krandel. In ten years, they'll be full-sized VC." I did as I was told. I fired on the group of 'em. Killed two women and five kids. Lieutenant Grady told me I'd done a real fine job. That I'd bumped up his kill count. Our unit's kill count. Back then, the units with the highest numbers were earnin' five days R and R at the beach in Vung Tau.

Agent Cooley: What happened next?

Private First Class Krandel: Grady ordered us to set fire to the whole village. If anything moved, we were supposed to kill it.

Agent Cooley: Is that what he said?

Private First Class Krandel: I don't remember his exact words. It's been forty somethin' years. But yeah, basically, smoke 'em out and kill anything that moves. A few of the unit started setting fire to the huts.

Agent Cooley: Did you set fire to anything?

Private First Class Krandel: Not right then. Grady told me to follow him. He'd seen some VC run into a hootch at the edge of the village. So we went in together with our weapons drawn. There were three young gals inside.

Agent Cooley: How old were they?

Private First Class Krandel: Hard to say. Maybe fifteen, sixteen.

Agent Cooley: Were they armed?

Private First Class Krandel: Not that I saw. One of them was hurt real bad. Her leg was all mangled. Grady shot her point blank in the head.

Agent Cooley: Did he say anything to you?

Private First Class Krandel: Not a word. But he ordered me to have my way with one of the girls.

Agent Cooley: He ordered you?

Private First Class Krandel: Well, he sliced off her top with his bayonet and said, "Have a little fun, Krandel. You've gotta loosen up." I told him no, that I wouldn't do it. He said, "Suit yourself," and he shot her too.

Agent Cooley: Where did he shoot her?

Private First Class Krandel: In the head.

Agent Cooley: What happened after that?

Private First Class Krandel: He told me I had one more chance to show him I wasn't a pussy. This time, I attempted to . . . I tried, but I couldn't perform.

Agent Cooley: What do you mean *perform*?

Private First Class Krandel: Jesus Christ. I couldn't get it up. Is that clear enough?

Agent Cooley: Yes, thank you. I want to be sure we have all the facts on record. Then, what did Lieutenant Grady do?

Private First Class Krandel: He shoved me aside and said, "This is how a real man does it." He raped her while I watched. After he was done, he put the bayonet in my hand and told me to finish her and Zippo the whole place, so I did.

Agent Cooley: Please explain what you mean by *finish her*.

Private First Class Krandel: I slashed her throat, and then I set her on fire.

There's more—pages and pages more—but my eyes can't look away from that sentence. I read it again and again and again, the words taking their gruesome shapes in my imagination. But it's not a young and frightened Vietnamese girl in a remote village some fifty years ago but my Dakota. Here and now.

I flip the page, look and look away. The kind of one-second, side-eyed glance I'd give my dad on one of his bad days. A how-bad-

is-it-really glance. I catch words like *napalm, ordered, kill, girl, rape.*
Another flip of the page, more words. *Paranoid, PTSD, therapist,
meds.*

My stomach bottoms out, dropping like a trap door. But I keep
turning, my need to know the unknown outweighing the horror of
knowing.

Sworn Statement of Dr. Patty Frank, Psychologist, Veteran's Administration

August 1, 2016

Victor Krandel first sought treatment at the
Veteran's Administration after he returned from
Vietnam in 1971. At that time, he was diagnosed
with amphetamine-induced psychosis and post-
Vietnam syndrome, which we know today as
Posttraumatic Stress Disorder. Mr. Krandel was
prescribed chlorpromazine, an antipsychotic,
but he stopped taking the medication after a few
years due to the reported side effects, including
drowsiness and impotence. Shortly thereafter, his
marriage ended because of his wife's reported
concerns about his level of aggression toward
her and their daughter, Mollie. She also made
allegations of sexual abuse against Mr. Krandel,
including marital rape and the inappropriate
touching of Mollie, who was approximately six
years old at that time. Those allegations were
never substantiated.

After being granted full custody of his daughter,
Mr. Krandel enjoyed a period of stability,
maintaining compliance with a new medication

regime and participating regularly in treatment. Treatment records suggest Mr. Krandel's symptoms of paranoia remained present but were well-controlled with medication. Though his experiences in Vietnam were tangentially addressed in therapy, Mr. Krandel was typically described as reluctant to disclose any information and resistant to change. Diagnoses from that period are consistent with my own: Schizoaffective Disorder (possibly amphetamine-induced) and Alcohol Dependence, though some clinicians suspected Schizotypal Personality Disorder.

In the mid-1980s, Mr. Krandel dropped out of treatment with the Veteran's Administration. According to Mr. Krandel, he believed the government was controlling him through the use of psychotropic medication, a belief he continues to profess on an intermittent basis. As a result, his compliance with his medication regime has remained inconsistent. Mr. Krandel began treatment with me in the early 2000s, after he was hospitalized on a 5150 psychiatric hold due to his being a danger to others. At the time, Mr. Krandel had threatened a motorist who was stranded outside his compound. Though he was ambivalent about treatment, Mr. Krandel was motivated by the possibility of renewed contact with his estranged daughter and his young granddaughter. As a part of trauma-focused cognitive behavioral therapy, I encouraged Mr. Krandel to provide a detailed account of the severe trauma he sustained during his service in Vietnam, which included serious misconduct on the part of his commanding officer that he had reportedly denied during prior interviews with the Vietnam War Crimes Working Group. Based on my knowledge of Mr. Krandel, I believe his account of events to be true and accurate to—

"What in the Sam Hill are you doing in here? I damn near blew your head off. Ain't nobody been in this shed for years. I thought you were a wanderin' ghost."

I expel a loud breath and toss the papers into the trunk. They scatter like doves against a dark sky. He hasn't told me to, but I put my hands in the air anyway. *Better safe than dead*, he'd say every night when we checked the booby traps outside the trailer.

"You happy now?" he asks.

"Happy?" It comes out in a sob. A sob directed at his shadow on the wall, because I can't turn to look at him. I'm still fifteen, standing before him naked and ashamed.

"You can fit me in one of your neat little boxes like the rest of 'em. Shoot me up with enough meds to kill a horse, ship me off to the loony bin, and call it a day."

"How could I be happy about this?" I flap my hands, desperately. Like the hooked fish I am. "What did you do, Dad? What did you do?"

The silence is absolute. The crickets go mute. Even the wind holds its breath. I face him, then. Him and his lantern and his trusty rifle. His face, so much like my own. So worn down with shock, incapable of it now. Like a toy that's been wounded too many times.

"What did you do?" I clench my teeth to dam the rage. It surges up my throat, unstoppable. "To. My. Daughter." *To me. To Roscoe.* But that stays unspoken.

"She wanted to get to know her grandpa. I met up with her a few times at the library. What's the harm in that? I knew you'd blow a damn gasket."

I see it unfold in a kind of fast slow-motion, spastic as a spliced film reel. *Kill, kill, kill.* I'll bash his head in with the flashlight. Hit him till he stops breathing. *Kill without mercy!* Better yet, the shovel. Then I'll dig a hole with it and bury him in it. The same way he buried Roscoe. *That's the spirit of the bayonet!* No, no. I'll set a fire and let it devour him. Lick by lick. The same way he—

I stand so fast my head spins. My blood rushing, an electric current. I'm at the wall in one stride, shovel in my hand in a death grip. I rear back, ready to swing.

I go cold, when I see it, the freeze coming from deep inside me.

Strands of hair in the flashlight's glow cling to a protruding nail just below the shelf. I have to know they're real. So I reach for them, touch them. They tickle my palm. Real as real could be. I'd know that color anywhere.

It's not pink, Mom. It's rose gold.

****

I am drunk. So drunk I probably won't be able to stand. Yet, here I am driving. Doing a mighty fine job of keeping it between the lines, if I do say so myself. *Atta girl, Mollie.* A chip off the old—

The thought bobs up and down in my head, a persistent little bugger, until I drown it.

Thank God for all-night truck stops and cheap vodka.

I make the turn into the drive, a little wide, but that's alright. I never liked that rose bush anyway.

"Holy shit." That's how it sounds in my head. But it probably comes out different, soaked in vodka. What else should I say when I see two men sitting on my porch? Side by side and not speaking. I wonder how long they've been there, stalemated.

I open the door, and Sawyer moves first. I'm not sure if that makes him the winner or the loser. I was wrong, though. I can stand. Sort of.

"Sawyer," I say, collapsing against his chest, my body suddenly sandbag heavy. He touches the swollen spot on my temple, and I wince a little.

284

"What happened to your head?"

That Sawyer. Ever the optimist. As if getting clocked with a bowling ball is the worst of it. I giggle. I can't help it.

Over his shoulder, I hear a voice. "For God's sakes, Mol, you're plastered."

"Thank you, Captain Obvious." I'm feeling proud of myself for my clever retort. But I push my luck. "Lieutenant Grant Sawyer, meet my sorry excuse for a Cole. I mean, ex-husband meet my Sawyer. Oh, screw it."

CHAPTER TWENTY-TWO

(SATURDAY, OCTOBER 6, 2018)

"JUST let her sleep it off."

"*Seriously?* Sleep it off? It's been twelve fucking hours. I need to know what happened last night. I have a right to know."

I close my eyes again, certain I'm dreaming. Because that's Cole's voice. Angry and entitled as ever. But Cole is a free fish, happily swimming eight hundred miles and the entire state of Oregon away. He's certainly not outside my bedroom door arguing with Sawyer.

Then there's the matter of my head. Even with them shut, my eyeballs grate in their sockets like stones on an anvil. Behind them, a dull, throbbing ache that won't let up. I feel as if I've been pummeled in the head with a bowling ball.

Oh. Wait.

The images come in waves, one after another. Each more punishing than the last.

Sawyer and Cole. Cole and Sawyer. Side by side on my porch.

Truck-stop vodka. *It's still sloshing in my stomach.*

The sticking door of my father's hunting shed.

His footlocker. *Getting seasick now.*

A gold button.

Pink hair.

The wave crests, knocks me over. The urge to vomit, its sudden brutality, catches me by surprise. I stumble out of bed and trip over Gus's squeaky chew toy. Now everyone, Gus included, knows I'm awake. And I haul ass to the bathroom, where I hug the toilet like a long-lost friend.

I'm still sitting there when the first knock hits the bedroom door. "Mol? We need to talk."

The second. "I know you're awake."

And the third. "Goddammit, Mollie. Let me in."

Cole tries the door, which I must've had the good sense to lock. Score one for drunk me.

"Give her a minute, man. She's probably sick as a dog. No offense, Gus."

So I'm not dreaming then. Sawyer's here too. Has been since last night. That was twelve hours ago. The realization hits me—another violent wave—and I panic. Sawyer and Cole have been here, alone together, all night. I think of the things Cole knows about me. It's enough to make me upchuck again.

"Coming," I say, into the toilet. My words echo back to me, and my head thrums.

"It's about damn time."

But when I try to stand, the room spins a little. This might take longer than I thought. "Ten minutes."

Behind the door, Cole grunts, and stalks away. I hear his footsteps.

I brace myself, one hand on the seat, and struggle to the sink. I brush my teeth and wash my face in a meager attempt to restore order. But I don't look in the mirror. I'm afraid to. Not of the sickly green cast to my skin or my bloodshot eyes or my hair, which I'm sure has gone haywire. But of the parts of myself that belong to my father. I can't look at me without seeing him. And I can't look at him. Not ever again.

I change out of the clothes that smell like his sycamore grove. Toss them in the bathroom wastebasket. Then I beeline for my purse on the dresser and start rummaging. Now that I remember—most of it, anyway—I need to be certain I took it with me. A fifty-fifty proposition at best.

With all the contents spread before me, my heart sinks.

It's not here.

But then, neither is my cell.

Or my car key, which must be here somewhere, since I drove home. Regrettably. I scan the room. Night stand, floor, bed. No sign of any of it.

Was I that wasted?

I answer my own question, shame rising thick and hot in my throat. There's nothing left in my stomach, so I wait it out. One dry heave, then another.

Hand on the knob, I brace myself. Nothing can be worse than last night. Nothing can be worse than what I know.

I move quietly down the hallway to the stairs. Below me, my two worlds collide. Sawyer sits at the edge of the sofa, elbows on his knees. Head in his hands, his shoulders drooping. Cole paces behind him, a tiger in a cage. I stare in wonder at the strangeness of it. The wrongness. Like the puzzles Dakota loved as a little girl: *Which one of these things doesn't belong?*

Sawyer spots me first. He doesn't speak, just meets my eyes and returns my sad smile. I clear my throat, then, announcing myself. Not yet trusting my voice. When I swallow, it feels as if I'd chugged a fifth of broken glass instead.

"I see you've finally decided to grace us with your presence." Cole pounces, claws unsheathed. I'm the wounded antelope, lagging behind the pack. All I can do is lie down, expose my own jugular, and hope for a speedy death.

"I'm so sorry. I had no idea you were coming."

"You're sorry? *Now* you're sorry? Do you know how worried I've been? First, I find out—on the news, mind you—that my daughter's killer was here, at this house, leaving some kind of sick clue. You don't answer any of my calls or texts. Then, you disappear for half a fucking day. And I haven't even mentioned the drunk driving. The drinking, which you told me you'd stopped. The crazy shit you were saying last night."

What was I saying? I think it, but I don't speak it. Because I'm not sure I'm ready to lay it all out. To admit it to myself sober.

"Coffee?" Sawyer asks as I descend the stairs on wobbly legs, measuring each step twice.

I nod, grateful.

"Did either of you see my cell phone or my car key?"

"That's what you're worried about?" Cole asks, shaking his head. As if I'm the most disgusting mutation he's ever encountered.

Worse than acute lymphocytic leukemia. Worse than astrocystomas and gangioglimas and all the other tongue-twisting killers. He used to make that same face after work when he'd lost a patient. It's his I-fucking-hate-cancer look. And right now, I'm the cancer.

"You were pretty out of it," Sawyer says. The smell of coffee starts to work its magic, sweeping the cobwebs from my head as he pours. "Cole thought it would be best if . . ."

"One-Armed Jack here is putting it mildly. You were a raving lunatic. I didn't want you doing something stupid."

"Like making a phone call?" It surprises me how easily we slip back to it. This contemptuous dance. "And don't call him that."

Sawyer appears unbothered. He passes me a steaming mug and watches us warily.

"Like getting back behind the wheel and killing someone. *Jeez.* Do you ever think about anybody but yourself?"

I take a sip too fast and let it burn my tongue. Better than saying what I really think. "Fine. Fair enough. But I had something else in my purse. Something important."

Cole rolls his eyes at me. "Not that again."

So I *had* told them.

"What did I say, exactly?" No use avoiding the question now. But I set my eyes on Sawyer. Whatever it is, I'd rather hear it from him. "I don't remember telling you."

Sawyer looks to Cole, and that hurts. Like they're doing their best to co-parent me, the problem child. Thankfully, he speaks first. Or maybe—I'm horrified to think it—they'd planned it that way.

"You said that your dad is Shadow Man. That he killed Dakota."

Leave it to the military man to get right to the point.

I release a long breath I didn't know I'd been holding. "Yes. He is. And he did."

Cole sneers, the way only he can. "Your dad is Shadow Man? So he planted Gus's collar for you to find?"

"Look, I can't explain all of it. But, Dakota's hair—*her pink hair*—was in his shed. And I found these military documents. He did really bad things over there. Horrifying things."

I want to cry, to convince them, but now, of all times, I've no tears left. Luckily, I have something else.

"You don't have to believe me. I got his DNA."

Cole stalks over to the coffee table and reaches beneath it, holding up a familiar paper bag. The kind you might get if you bought a bottle of Absolut in the middle of the night at a truck stop. He sticks his hand inside and produces my cell phone, my car key, and an empty beer can, half-crushed in the center. The kind you might take from your father's junkyard if you needed his saliva.

"This is your DNA sample? A can of Olde English in a paper bag stuffed in your purse? I'm sure the FBI will be really impressed with your immaculate collection methods."

Cole places the items—bag, cell, key—one by one onto the table. But not the can. He tosses it onto the floor, and I steady myself against the countertop, waiting for the rest of his soliloquy. He walks toward me as he talks, pointing his finger like a weapon. "You've lost your goddamned mind. This is what you've been doing? How you've been solving our daughter's murder? What you've been rubbing in my face?"

"Hey, man," Sawyer says, stepping between us. "You're not helping."

I step around Sawyer and brush past Cole, daring him to stop me. "I'm calling Detective Sharpe. Let him decide if he wants to test the can."

"Mollie," Sawyer calls after me, following me into the living room, Cole at his heels.

"Go ahead. Tell her, Grant. She stopped listening to me years ago. Right around the time she screwed her boss. But hey, we all deal with grief differently. Don't we, Mol?"

I snatch the phone from the table like a lifeline and hold it in a death grip, deciding whether to dial it or hurl it at Cole's face.

Sawyer touches my arm, his eyes tender. My hands unclench. "You already called Detective Sharpe last night. Several times. You left messages."

I stand there and let it sink in. All of it. Cole's smug look. The beer can, its cheap shade of gold. And my outgoing calls. Four of them to Detective Sharpe's cell number. Sawyer is my only saving grace.

He sets his prosthetic hand on Cole's shoulder. He probably can't bear to touch him with the real thing. "Wasn't that also around the time you almost got canned for sexual harassment?"

****

"Do you agree with him?" I ask Sawyer, nodding toward the front door. The same one Cole just slammed behind him. Gus sits on his haunches, disappointed. It's well past his time for a walk. "It's okay if you do."

I walk to the door and open it, watching as Gus rushes past. Sawyer joins me at the threshold, but I keep my eyes on Gus.

"Well, that depends. Agree about what exactly?"

"That I've lost my mind."

"Well, you were absolutely wrong to drive in that condition. That was reckless. And irresponsible. And—" I sigh, and he stops short. "You're not crazy. If you say your dad is Shadow Man, I believe you've got good reason to think so."

Gus laps the yard and joins Cole at the far side of it. I squint into the sun, head pounding, and watch them. It's like a window to another life. "Is there a *but* coming?"

"Not a *but*, per se. More of an *and*. As in Boyd *and* Wendall. And the other names on your wall. You suspected them too, remember?"

"I know. And I still do, in a way. But I saw her hair, Sawyer. How did it get there?" The thought of it, the images it conjures—Dakota's precious head knocked back against the wall from a fierce blow; her hair coiled around the nail, ripped from her head—is enough to bowl me over. To break me. I fall against Sawyer's chest and let him hold me together.

"We'll figure it out," he whispers. "It'll be okay." But he must know it won't be. Not really. Still, his words are a salve, and I pretend for a while.

"I never told you about Cole," I say, finally, pulling away to look at him. "How did you know about the sexual harassment thing?"

Sawyer's eyes wander to the yard where Cole leans against Gus's favorite oak, and then back to me. He grins. "You're not the only one who can use Google, Detective Roark."

"But you never mentioned it."

"I knew you'd tell me in your own time. I figured there had to be a reason you kept refusing my dinner offers."

I smile back. Because he still likes me. For now. "Maybe you're not as charming as you think."

"Hmm . . ." He taps his chin, rubs his day-old stubble. "My brothers in arms would probably agree with you on that one.

Although they did call me Galant Grant for a while in bootcamp, after I lugged my battle buddy's pack when he got sick during PT."

"Such a gentleman. How did I ever resist?"

"Hooah."

I start to laugh, but it doesn't last long. At the tree, Cole removes something from his pants pocket, smacks it against his hand. My mouth hangs open as he lights a cigarette and takes a long drag. Cole, renowned oncologist, who'd once referred to smokers as walking carcinogens, is sucking on a cancer stick.

Sawyer follows my gaze. "Didn't know he smoked, huh?"

I shake my head. "I'd call it a surprising new development."

"He told me he picked up the habit a few months before Dakota died. A stress reliever. But he kept it a secret. He thought you'd be disappointed in him."

I try to picture that conversation. Cole baring his soul. It gets under my skin. Makes me nervous. And most of all, angry. Because he didn't say the other thing. The essential thing. That Joanna Montgomery smoked too.

"Jeez. What else did he tell you?"

Sawyer shrugs. "It was a long night."

The smoke plumes around Cole's mouth until the breeze picks up and blows it away. Disappears it. Like it never existed at all. Cole tosses the cigarette to the ground and stamps it out with the toe of his sneaker. "That stuff he said about me and my boss . . ."

"You don't have to explain," Sawyer says. "I get it. There are two sides to every marriage. And then there's the truth."

"I know I don't have to, but I want to." Even so, the words dematerialize. Gone just like that cigarette smoke. How to explain I was drowning. That I'd clung to Dr. Jackass like the last lifeboat. Like a piece of debris in a swollen river. That he could've been anyone. "It was a really hard time."

Gus hops up the steps, flashes his canine smile, and pauses to lick Sawyer's hand. I steal a glance at Cole. Not because I can't believe he's smoking. Or that he lied to me. Or even that he confided in Sawyer. No, what's impossible to fathom is meticulous Cole leaving his crushed cigarette to sully the lawn.

But the gold butt-end in the grass is as undeniable as Cole's indifference as he drifts back toward the house. He mounts the stairs and pushes past me, his eyes daring me to say something. I don't give him the satisfaction.

"So, what now?" I ask Sawyer, once Cole retreats into the kitchen. "I can't just stand here and do nothing. I have to talk to Sharpe. If he won't take my beer-can DNA, then—"

My phone buzzes in my pocket, electrifying my blood. "Restricted," I say, reading the screen. Sawyer raises his eyebrows. Cole races back to the entryway. Even Gus's ears perk.

"Hello." Dread sloshes like swamp water in my stomach.

"Hi, Mollie. It's Officer McGinnis. I wanted to follow up on that message you left for me on Thursday. About Boyd Blackburn. Is this a good time?"

I give the irony what it deserves. A derisive bark. "As good as any."

"Well, you were right. Blackburn's rap sheet is clean as a whistle. Not even a speeding ticket."

Swamp water receding, I let out a breath. "Alright. I guess that's a relief. Anyway, I really appreciate you—"

"Hold up a sec. There was something."

"Oh. Okay."

Cole waves his hand at me: "Put it on speaker." I figure I owe him that much just for showing up here, so I tap the button and Officer McGinnis's voice fills the room.

"Back in 2015, patrol picked up a Boyd Blackburn prowling in a backyard over in Cuttings Wharf. Apparently, a girl heard him rustling around outside her window. Her parents weren't home, and she got scared and called the police. They took him in for questioning."

"Like a Peeping Tom?" I ask, reconsidering everything again.

"That's what they suspected, but they cut him loose. I guess his story checked out."

"His story?"

Officer McGinnis laughs dryly. "Yeah. Of all things, he said he'd lost his snake. I mean, you can't make this shit up."

"And they believed him?"

"Seems like it. I checked with one of the cops, asked if he'd remembered the name Boyd Blackburn. He said the guy gave him the heebie-jeebies. They'd had a slew of prowler reports in the neighborhood that summer. They had him figured for the guy."

"So why didn't they arrest him?"

"Simple. They found the snake in the yard, coiled up under a bush. His mom confirmed his story. The girl couldn't identify him. She'd only seen a shadow. So no probable cause to make an arrest."

Cole's eyes are on me, the questions behind them poised like darts aimed at a bullseye.

"But if you wanted to know whether this guy could've posed a threat to your daughter, I'd say hell yes. Not to mention, he was what, thirty at the time? What would he want with a fourteen- or fifteen-year-old?"

Cole's nostrils flare. I half-expect him to throw something, to punch the wall. To find Boyd and strangle him with a *Star Wars* T-shirt. What I don't expect is the unbearable silence that comes when I hang up the phone. I bear it anyway, because I need time to think. And thinking too hard hurts.

Cole paces to the kitchen and back again. His footfalls come and go, come and go. Then, he clears his throat. "Grant, could you give us a minute?"

I want to cling to Sawyer, to beg him not to leave me alone. Because that's how I feel with Cole. How I'd felt that whole summer before Dakota disappeared. *Alone.* But I nod at him instead.

The front door yawns open and Sawyer steps out onto the porch. I wait for Cole to ask his questions, to make his demands—*Who is*

Boyd? And why didn't you tell me about him? I have a right to know these things—to say all that, with a sprinkling of expletives.

He collapses onto the sofa, drops his head back, and closes his eyes. When he opens them again, they're brimming with sadness. It shocks me. Mainly because I'd waited so long to see it. He'd hardly ever cried, not even at her funeral.

"Come sit," he says.

I take the place across from Cole, in the oversized leather chair he'd always loved. Its color, an exact match for my office sofa. No wonder I'd hated the damn thing. He looks at me like I'm brand new to him, which I suppose I am, and rubs the hollow of his throat. A place I'm sure I'd kissed once upon a time. Another time, another Mollie. "You stopped wearing the necklace," he says, softly.

I know what he means, but my hand goes to my breastbone anyway and comes back empty. Once, a sterling silver heart hung there, MOM engraved at its center. Cole and Dakota had presented it to me in a Tiffany blue box on the last Mother's Day I remember. All the others since, I'd drunk straight through.

"I had to. It was too hard. People would notice it and ask me about it. I'd have to go through the whole tragic story. Or lie." I don't tell him I'd done both. That the lies came easier than the truth.

"You could've told me, Mol."

"Told you what?"

"That you were still struggling."

"And listen to you rub it in? No, thank you. You said yourself I need to let her go. To move on. To bounce back like you. Cole, the amazing rubber ball. Besides, I'm not your problem anymore."

"Is that what you think? That I bounced back?"

I give a halfhearted shrug, ignoring the undeniable. The tears on his cheeks. The pain in his voice. Now that he's here in front of me, it's obvious this fish is not as free as I thought, and it unnerves me.

"I couldn't be here. In this house. In this town. Sleeping in a bedroom just down the hall from hers. I didn't bounce back. I ran away. I thought you, of all people, knew that. Hell, I'm a cancer doctor who smokes. What does that say?"

When I don't answer, he does it for me. "It says I'm messed up. I'm a wreck. And I want to know who killed our girl as bad as you do."

"What about Joanna? Is she still puffin' on the ole cancer sticks?"

I haven't said her name out loud in so long it sounds strange. Like a made-up word. But it still has the same bitter sound, the same cruel meaning: utter betrayal. Cole wipes his cheeks with the back of his hand.

"You didn't think I'd figure it out?" What I don't tell him: He'd paid for the information himself. Two thousand dollars of his alimony to the chief nurse at Napa Children's, a small price to pay to keep tabs on Joanna Montgomery. She'd told me when the Montgomerys finalized their divorce; when Joanna moved into an apartment downtown, leaving Hannah with her dad; and when she'd given her two weeks' notice this spring and made a solo pilgrimage to the land of coffee and grunge rock. Rainy days and my ex-husband.

"We're not . . . we're just . . . we didn't plan it."

"So she just happened to get a nursing job in Seattle?"

"We only reconnected a few months ago, I swear. I really wanted to put things back together with us. It was just too broken, Mol. We were unfixable."

I can't argue with that, but it's never stopped me before. "And what *she* did? That's *fixable*? She must be a helluva handywoman. What does Little Miss Bob Vila think about you coming back here now?"

"This is not about you and me. It's about Dakota. She knows that. I'll always be Dakota's dad." His voice softening, Cole gestures to the window. It frames Sawyer's back, his broad shoulders, as he sits on the front step, patiently waiting. "It looks like you've moved on too. Seems like a nice guy."

"He is. Very nice. But don't pretend it's the same thing."

"C'mon. Let's not do this again."

"How can you trust her? After—"

The honk of a horn blasts me to a stop. I'm grateful to see Detective Sharpe waving at Sawyer from the driver's seat. I let my question die. Because I'm just doing this mindless dance we do. I don't really care about the answer. Cole's a sadder sack than I am. But he's not my sad sack anymore. Thank God for that.

I stand up and head for the door, newly determined. When Cole calls after me to issue his predictable diatribe, I smile a little to myself.

"We're not done here, Mol. Who is Boyd fucking Blackburn? Why didn't you tell me about him? I have a goddamned right to know these things."

****

Detective Sharpe has one heck of a poker face. He doesn't even blink when Cole walks out behind me and positions himself alongside Sawyer. Just shakes his hand and says it's good to see him again. He takes my whole story down, repeating the same monotone lines— *Okay. And then what happened?*—until it's all out, immortalized in ink on the notepad he slips into his jacket pocket.

"What's next?" I ask, anxious to keep talking. Because I already know what's next, and I'm dreading it. The waiting.

"Well, to be honest, the whole thing sounds pretty far-fetched. But I've been around long enough to know that far-fetched can happen. More often than you'd think. Unfortunately, your beer can doesn't exactly satisfy the chain of custody. Does your father own a vehicle?"

"A broken-down old truck, last I saw. He parks it outside the gate."

Detective Sharpe nods. "Any other reason to believe your dad would be capable of this kind of thing? Was he ever abusive to you? To your mother?"

298

There are pictures in my mind. My father's mouth frothed with anger. His hands hard as a ruler against my face. Words too. *Strip! All of it! Down to your skivvies.* But some things are unspeakable. Even for a shrink. "He killed our dog."

Cole frowns at me as he chalks another one up to *Things He Didn't Know About Mollie.* The tally is growing higher than my dad's kill count.

"When?" Detective Sharpe asks.

"Just before I ran away. I was fifteen." The same age Dakota will always be. "1992, I think."

He jots another tragic note into his little book filled with them.

"There's something else too," I add, holding up a finger. "Give me a sec."

I jog toward the house, my pickled brain jostling against my skull before I think better of it and slow to a fast walk. I grab Boyd's DOGS folder from the fireplace, where I'd tucked it for safekeeping, and head back the way I came, toward three pairs of waiting eyes. It's time to lay down all my cards.

Detective Sharpe flips through the pages, frowning.

"How'd you get this—" He stops himself. "Let me guess. Part of your rogue investigation?"

"Dakota's rogue investigation actually. It turns out she was interested in Shadow Man. She'd joined this website, Shadow Seekers."

"The armchair detectives?"

I nod.

"So what am I looking at here?"

"These dogs belonged to Shadow Man's victims. It looks like they were all adopted from the Solano County SPCA. Gus was as well."

I take a breath, trying to keep my focus on Sawyer. Because Cole's already judging me, and I haven't even gotten to the crazy part.

"This is going to sound nuts."

"When has that ever stopped you?" Detective Sharpe deadpans, earning a hearty guffaw from Cole.

"My dad brought dogs home when I was a kid. He always told me he'd found them on the side of the road. That somebody dropped them off. But they match up almost exactly. We had a mutt and a bulldog and a collie like Bucky. The last dog was Roscoe, the basset hound. The one my dad killed."

"What the hell, Mol? How long have you known about this?"

I shrug at Cole as Detective Sharpe studies the folder.

"Alright," he says, giving away nothing. "I'll be in touch when I have news."

He backpedals toward his car, then raises a finger, as if he's just thought of something important.

"I know, I know. Stay in my lane."

"That too." He smiles, megawatt, but it fades fast. "Actually, I was going to ask what happens if you're right. Are you prepared for that? For what it means?"

He doesn't wait for an answer, doesn't say goodbye. No matter, because all I hear are echoes of Wendall. *Young man, next time, before you ask the question, be sure you're ready for the answer.*

BEFORE

CHAPTER TWENTY-THREE

(SATURDAY, AUGUST 6, 2016)

DAKOTA regretted coming the moment she arrived, chauffeured in the passenger seat of Liv's Hummer. Well, Liv's dad's Hummer. Liv already had her driving permit. Along with the type of parents who'd let her drink wine coolers with her friends at her fifteenth birthday party and stock condoms in her bathroom.

"You know Tyler's going to be here, right?"

Dakota nodded. "Obviously. It's his house."

But it wasn't Tyler she worried about. Since Hannah had posted that photo of her, he'd been back on his best behavior, texting her just to say hi like he had in the beginning. It disappointed her how simple he was. Hannah had been right when she'd said boys were not calculus. Not even algebra.

Hannah. She would be here too. That had Dakota's stomach in knots. But she needed to escape the war zone, if only for one night. Besides, if she was being honest, she wanted to see Hannah. She needed to see her.

On Monday, Dakota's dad had been placed on paid administrative leave, pending the outcome of the investigation. *What's to investigate?* she'd overheard him on the phone that night, talking to his attorney. Dad had lawyered up. Just like an innocent man. *A goddamned he-said, she-said. That's what this will turn into.*

That night, battle lines had been drawn. Dakota and her mom, upstairs, hunkered in their bedrooms. Her dad camped out on the sofa, subsisting on rations of PB & J and potato chips. Between them, a minefield of unspoken accusations. A trip wire of silence that felt more dangerous than any of their screaming matches. Only Gus had crossed into enemy territory.

"I heard he wants a second chance at love."

Dakota stared slack-jawed at Liv, before she'd remembered what they'd been talking about. "Tyler wouldn't know love from a lacrosse stick. He's just after a hookup."

From inside the house, the music blasted. So loud, the doorknob shook in her hand. She didn't bother to knock or ring the bell. No one would hear it. Good thing there were at least two miles between the Lowry compound and the nearest neighbors.

"And?" Liv asked as they made their way through the crowd gathered near the keg in the kitchen. "Do you know how many girls would be all over that? Tyler is the whole enchilada. You owe it to womankind to take a big bite."

Rolling her eyes, Dakota took up a position in the hallway. "If the fate of womankind depends on me hooking up with Tyler, we're probably doomed."

"Probably? So you're saying I have a chance."

Dakota heard the beer sloshing in Tyler's voice before she turned around and saw the telltale red cup in his hand. He slung his arm around her carelessly, nearly spilling its contents. She quickly wriggled free, embarrassed for them both. Certain the whole house had gotten quieter, Dakota glanced around. But only Liv watched. And only for a moment, before she backpedaled into the kitchen, fist raised and mouthing "For womankind!"

"How long were you standing there?" Dakota asked, her cheeks on fire.

Tyler wiggled his eyebrows. "Te gustan las enchiladas?"

"Impressive. Eric must've been lying when he said you slept through Spanish I."

"Want a beer? A little cerveza to go with your enchilada?" He cocked his head at her, flashing a grin. The old Dakota would've swooned, considered herself lucky to be the target of Tyler's sexual innuendo.

"Maybe later. Have you seen Hannah?"

"Forget her. She's pissed at you anyway." So he knew, then. Which meant everyone did.

"I really need to talk to her. That's sort of why I came."

"Ouch." Tyler pouted, waiting for her to give in. But when she didn't, he quickly turned his back, scanning the crowd.

"There," he said, finally. Dakota spotted her too, in the middle of a group of girls, barefoot and dancing. One look and she knew. Hannah was wasted. "Be careful. You know how nasty she can be when she's drunk."

"Thanks for the warning."

As she tried to sidestep Tyler, he bumped into her, and she stumbled into the wall. His body pressed against hers, radiating heat, and she sucked in the stench of alcohol and the body spray she'd seen him douse himself in after practice. He grabbed her arm and held her in place, smiling as he grinded against her. "But seriously, you and me. Later."

"Get off me!" she yelled, shoving him in the chest. His beer went flying, splattering onto the floor and halfway up his legs. Now, the whole house *was* watching. Liv and Hannah and Eric and half the lacrosse team and kids she barely knew.

Dakota pushed past a stunned Tyler and headed in the other direction, searching for the quickest escape route. But not before he recovered, just in time to take the last shot. As expected, a game-winner.

"That's not what you said when you sent me those naked pics."

"I wasn't *naked.*"

Tyler guffawed, the loudest hyena in the pack. She covered her mouth, wishing for a takeback. For invisibility. For a time machine to take her far, far away from here. But she had no superpowers, and she remained alarmingly earthbound. So she did the next best thing when faced with complete mortification.

She ran.

****

Dakota sat on the floor of the Lowrys' hall bathroom, licking her wounds. She'd been holed up there for at least thirty minutes, ignoring the intermittent pounding on the door. The occasional but frantic *Hurry up in there! I gotta go!*

Eventually, they all gave up. The Lowrys had at least five bathrooms—one for every member of the family, Tyler had joked with her the first time he'd invited her there—and this was the least interesting of them all. With an empty medicine cabinet, a stark granite countertop, and one of those fancy bowl sinks her mom liked. Pretentious and pretty. But so boring. *Tyler's, then.*

She leaned back against the wall, listening to the drone of the party. Floating above it all, snippets of imagined conversation crept up the pipes, drifted in through the air vent.

Dakota Roark.

The door knob jiggled.

Naked pics.

Someone knocked.

Dakota Roark.

And knocked again.

Naked pics.

"I really need to use the bathroom."

Dakota recognized the voice. She left the cold tile and walked to open it. Hannah rushed inside, straight for the toilet, pulling up her blue jean skirt, without even noticing her. Dakota shut the door, locked it again, and spoke to her own reflection in the mirror.

"Hannah, I wanted to talk to you."

"Jeez. Really, Dakota? Have you ever heard of privacy?"

The irony burned and bubbled under Dakota's skin. She stepped nearer to the mirror, half-expecting her face to be blistered. An outbreak of indignation.

"*Privacy?* You mean like taking that photo down when I asked you to?"

"Oh, whatevs. That photo is the least of your problems. You're just mad because now everybody knows you're not the total goody-goody you pretend to be."

"I wasn't naked," she repeated. It sounded even worse this time.

"Close enough," Hannah muttered. "You know, I don't think we even should be talking. My mom said—"

"Since when do you listen to your parents?"

Hannah stood and fixed her skirt. She joined Dakota at the sink.

"Since my mom told me your dad is a dirty old man."

"And you believe her."

"Is that a question?"

"I just—I'm not saying she's lying . . ."

Hannah froze, her tube of cotton-candy pink lipstick poised at the center of her mouth. Their eyes met in the mirror.

"*But?* It sounds like there's a *but.*"

"But I saw something. On prom night, at your after-party."

Dakota watched that tube of lipstick. It seemed critical to her fate. Hannah swiped it across her top lip and smacked. The *pop* so loud and obnoxious it might as well have been her middle finger. "What is it that you think you saw?"

306

"Remember how your dad was out of town and my mom had an early morning work thing and my dad said he'd come over and help your mom chaperone?"

"Uh, *okay*. I guess. Prom was, like, forever ago."

That they could agree on. Because it felt like forever that she'd been keeping this secret. "Well, the party was kind of wrapping up, and everybody was outside sitting around the fire pit. I came inside to use the bathroom, and I noticed the basement door was open."

Hannah stirs the air with her hand, impatient. "And? Just tell me already."

"I saw your mom and my dad making out."

A sudden burst of laughter escaped Hannah's newly pinked mouth, but the rest of her face appeared unmoved. "Is that why you've been acting weird?"

Dakota shrugged. "Do you believe me?"

"I believe you believe that's what you saw. But Mom says your dad forced himself on her that night. It's all in the complaint she filed at the hospital."

Hannah tucked the tube of lipstick into the back pocket of her skirt and turned away from the mirror. End of conversation.

"I wasn't supposed to tell you that," she said, scooting around Dakota to the door. "So don't repeat it."

"Then why did you?"

"Because I think it's sad. You thinking that. You should know the truth. We're best friends, you know?"

Dakota felt a familiar tug in the center of her chest, remembering fifth-grade Hannah, presenting her with one of those cheesy BFF necklaces. Two halves of a heart cracked down the middle. They'd worn them until the chains turned their necks green. "*Were*. We were best friends."

****

On the drive back home, Dakota listened as Liv filled the silence. Talking took energy, and she felt bone tired. Waterlogged. Like she'd spent the night in the ocean, swimming against the current, and not hiding out in the Hummer, waiting for Liv. And her endless stream of questions.

"Did you know Tyler's dad represented Jay-Z?"

"Do you think Kristin wears too much makeup?"

"Are you going to try out for cross-country this year?"

"Were you, like, birthday-suit naked?"

Dakota gave her answers one word at a time, holding back the rest.

"Yes." *Tyler's dad tells everyone that story, because he's desperate to be cool.*

"Yes." *She takes all her advice from Hannah's vlog, so . . .*

"No." *I'm not even sure I want to swim this year. Much less run three miles on a Saturday morning.*

"No." *But close enough, apparently.*

Finally, Liv turned off Ridgecrest and stopped short of Dakota's driveway—just in case her parents were watching—idling on the shoulder of the road. She'd saved a question. Dakota could tell.

"So is it true about your dad?"

"What do you think?" She meant it sarcastically. But literally too. Because she had no idea. Not anymore. She didn't trust her own memory.

Liv shrugged. "I guess I don't really know your dad that well. Not as well as your mom. Do you think your parents will get a divorce?"

"Maybe."

"Well, it's not the end of the world. Mine are way happier."

Dakota climbed down from the Hummer and waved goodbye. She trudged up the driveway and mounted the steps slowly, carefully, listening for the sounds of angry voices and contemplating the end of life as she knew it.

When it seemed safe, she went inside, heading straight for the stairs, where Gus waited at the top.

"How was the movie? *Suicide Squad*, right?"

Dakota stopped halfway and turned to her father, half-asleep on the sofa. She wanted to lie to his face. She almost hoped he knew.

"It was a little dark and angsty, but Liv and I liked it. Harley Quinn has pink hair. Pink and blue."

"Does she?" He studied her, skeptically. "And Liv's mom drove you home?"

Dakota charged ahead, unconcerned. No way he'd seen Liv in the Hummer. And she'd had the whole night to memorize the entire movie synopsis. To watch and rewatch the trailer. To read the spoilers online.

"Yeah. There's kind of a twist at the end. Because you think the Joker died, but he really didn't."

"I'm guessing you didn't fall for it."

"Not for a second. C'mon, Dad. I'm no amateur."

The subtle raise of his eyebrows told Dakota her father understood they weren't just talking about the movie. Especially when her eyes fixed on a pack of cigarettes protruding from his pocket. For the first time in months, she didn't have to force herself to smile at him when she said goodnight.

CHAPTER TWENTY-FOUR

(SUNDAY, AUGUST 7, 2016)

DAKOTA didn't think of it as lying. Not if she had a good reason. And she did. Several good reasons, actually.

One, she'd never been to Mol's Junkyard, the place named for her mother. Which she supposed might've been a nice gesture if it had been a hotel or a deli or a bookstore. It said something about Grandpa Krandel that he'd name a junkyard after his only child.

Two, the unfortunately named Mol's Junkyard happened to be near Putah Creek Road, where victims fourteen and fifteen had gone missing.

And three, if her parents happened to find out, they'd definitely be riled.

So maybe they weren't the best reasons. But still, there she was, riding shotgun in that dilapidated hunk of steel her grandfather thought he could sell for the newly discounted price of $350. She'd biked to the library, typical Sunday routine, telling her mom she'd planned to spend the whole afternoon finishing *Mindhunter*. In truth, she'd finished it weeks ago and reread it for good measure. She'd even decided on a favorite line: *To understand the "artist," you must study his "art."* Kinda creepy when blood and bones are your go-to medium.

"So whaddya do for fun up there in Napa?" Grandpa Krandel made it sound like a foreign country.

"I'm on the swim team."

"You any good?"

"I won district last year in the 200 free. The first freshman in school history."

He smacked the steering wheel. "Well, hot damn. We got a regular Michael Phelps in the family."

"The thing is, I don't know if I'm even gonna swim this year." She hadn't said that out loud before. Not to anyone. It sounded strange. Like an alien had invaded her body. She didn't quit things. But the thought of it—the grueling early morning practices, the weekend meets, the impossible expectations—seemed exhausting.

"What do your parents think about that?"

She shrugged. "They don't know yet. But they probably won't let me. They like that I'm good at it. Mom thinks I could get a scholarship."

"Well, it's gotta blow your hair back. Like hunting. Give me a gun and a critter to stalk. That's all I need."

Even if the thought of a gun-toting Grandpa Krandel unnerved her, Dakota understood. She was a hunter too. She thought of telling him. *I'm hunting Shadow Man.* But it sounded silly.

Just then, he swerved off the road, his breath quicker than before. He waited until the car behind them rumbled past, his Adam's apple jumping in his throat like a bouncing ball.

"Did you know that car?" she whispered, afraid the sound of her voice would spook him.

He stared after it. "Yes. No. Oh hell if I know. I just had a bad feelin' about it. That ever happen to you?"

Dakota watched his dark eyes dart like squirrels across a highway. "Whenever I freak out, Mom always says I can trace it back to a thought. A thought always comes first. Next, a feeling. Then finally, an action."

"A thought, huh?"

She nodded.

"I suppose I was thinkin' about hunting. That made me think about guns. And about Nam. And him."

"Who?"

A car whizzed by them, the air whooshing in through the window, shaking the truck, and rattling Dakota's nerves, hard as a slap from her mother. She turned to Grandpa Krandel, certain he'd be wide-eyed and white-faced with fear. But he looked off into the ditch and beyond, to a place Dakota couldn't see, had never been. His own space face.

Minutes later, he eased the truck back onto the highway. "You mind if we make a quick stop? I'm runnin' low on ammo. Can't let them damn squirrels think they got the best of me."

****

Dakota craned her neck, gaping at the sign hanging above them. Deer horns sprouted from the head of a giant fish. It should've been funny, but the paint peeled strangely around the fish's gills, drawing its mouth into a devilish grin.

"Welcome to Whitetails and Whoppers." Grandpa Krandel held the door open, ushering her inside. At least he was smiling again. "This used to be your mama's favorite place."

"Mom hunted?"

"Sure did." Dakota couldn't picture it. Not the mom she knew. The mom who got squeamish at the meat counter at Whole

Foods. "In fact, her horns are hangin' in the Hall right next to mine."

He pointed toward a long corridor at the back of the store, its walls covered floor to ceiling in horns of various shapes and sizes, displayed as proudly as a serial-killer's trophies. At its end, a dilapidated screen door, mottled with tears and holes. Like something had clawed its way in. Or out. Beyond it, a lonely card table, where a few men her grandfather's age played dominoes and guzzled from their longneck bottles.

"Go have a look-see."

Dakota didn't want to look or see. But she channeled her inner Lisa Ling and felt her legs move beneath her. She plucked a Whitetails and Whoppers business card from beside the register and stuck it in her pocket. Then she made her way past the aisle of fishing line and lures and beyond two racks of camouflage. She imagined herself years in the future. As a hotshot investigative journalist in pursuit of a lead, a camera crew in tow.

She planted herself in the middle of THE HALL OF HORNS—a sign on the wall proclaimed it so—and listened to the men chattering on the porch outside.

"Hey man, ain't that Crazy Krandel?"

The name stopped her breath.

"Nah. He ain't showed his face since he—"

Dakota pushed the screen door open, its tinny squeak announcing her before she stepped across the threshold. The men stopped speaking, their mouths shut tight as clamshells. The only sound the soft clink of the dominoes against the tabletop.

Finally, one of them looked up at her. He rubbed his bald head like a wishing lamp and frowned. "You lost?"

Dakota shook her head and smiled. "I'm here with my grandpa. I'm working on a school project about an unsolved murder—well, a bunch of murders—that took place around here a long time ago."

She studied their grizzled faces, any one of them old enough to be Shadow Man.

"You got one of us figured for it?" Baldie asked, smirking.

The men twittered, exchanged glances, gulped their beers. Each laid another domino down.

"Should I?"

Dakota surprised herself with that one. And not in a good way. It felt more Nancy Grace than Lisa Ling. She backtracked toward the door, plotting her escape.

"I didn't mean it like that. I just thought—"

"It's a fair question. You gentlemen are playin' with bones there." The voice came from the man at the end of the porch. Dakota wondered how she'd missed him there, leaning against the porch railing. Like he could hold it up with the strength of one shoulder. When she looked at him, he tipped his black cowboy hat. She couldn't decide whether to be flattered or offended.

"Yep. Got our very own boneyard." Baldie's friends guffawed as he gestured to the pile of unused dominoes.

"I just thought maybe one of you remembered the Jessica Guzman case. She disappeared around here in 1992."

Their laughter petered out, and Baldie shrugged at her. The others avoided her eyes, and she couldn't even bear to look at the man in the black hat. Instead, she slunk inside, defeated, and returned her attention to the Hall of Horns.

She found her mother's contribution easily enough—a small set of whitish gray antlers belonging to Mollie Krandel of Allendale, who'd made the kill at Putah Creek. It hung adjacent to a war memorabilia display case, tagged with her grandfather's name. Inside it, an old military-style knife, its handle so worn the plastic cracked at the base.

M7 BAYONET, VIETNAM ERA

DONATED BY PRIVATE FIRST CLASS VICTOR
KRANDEL

BRAVO COMPANY, THE 4th BATTALION OF
THE 10th INFANTRY, GROUND ASSAULT
DIVISION

Dakota imagined her grandfather gripping that handle, his knuckles blanched with fear and desperation as he plunged it into flesh. Human flesh. No wonder he was the way he was, chained to a place on the other side of the world. How could you ever come home after you did something like that? How could you be anyone but Crazy Krandel?

At the front of the store, her grandfather hunched over the front counter, oblivious, studying a box of ammunition. She felt a surge of fresh anger at Baldie and his merry band of old-timers, smack-talking behind his back. But mostly at her mother for abandoning him, for holding the war against him. Her mother, the supposed bastion of empathy, turned out to be a heartless . . . *bitch*.

With that word stuck on repeat, Dakota rifled through the front pocket of her backpack until she found the black Sharpie marker Hannah had used to graffiti Taylor Roland's locker last spring, after she'd called Hannah's vlog *amateur*. At the time, Dakota thought Hannah was being petty. But now, it made complete sense. The desire to immortalize a single word, to hurl an insult she couldn't say out loud.

She uncapped the marker, its smell as potent as her outrage, and extended her hand toward the wooden base.

"Ya know why they're different colors?"

Dakota jumped and the marker tumbled from her hand, making a small black mark on the baseboard. It laid there, a silent accomplice, until she nudged it aside with her shoe. Next to her sneakers, a pair of long legs that ended in snakeskin cowboy boots. She lifted her eyes to the man they belonged to, certain he'd seen the whole thing.

Certain he'd deduced the secret badness of her heart. But she could barely make out his face beneath the shadow of that cowboy hat.

"Uh, I'm sorry," she muttered. "I was just—"

"The horns," he said, stepping in closer. He tapped a long finger against the tip of an antler. "Did you notice the colors? Some dark, some light."

"Oh. Well, now that you mention it . . ."

"Amazin', ain't it? Every year these fellas get a new set. Pretty soon, they'll be going through the velvet shedding just in time to impress the ladies."

Dakota frowned, suddenly and inexplicably self-conscious. She wished Grandpa Krandel would call to her. Or at least hurry. But when she glanced over her shoulder, he had his back to her, stacking his ammunition box by box beside the register like a child's unsteady block tower.

"The velvet is somethin' like a skin." As he spoke, he touched his sun-spotted hand, and Dakota withdrew her own, shoving them down in her pockets. "It helps the horns grow big as they do. But the blood left over mixes with all kinds of plant juices and gives 'em a darker color. It stains the antlers."

The man craned his neck and pointed at the wall, to a large set of horns hanging near the top. "That old buck is mine," he said. "See how dark they are?"

Dakota nodded without looking too close. The Hall of Horns was bad enough. But the Hall of Bloody Horns? *No thank you.* "I don't know much about deer. But these horns are my mother's."

"Are they now?"

While the man leaned in to read her mother's name, Dakota thought, too late, of reaching for the marker. At the front of the store, bells jingled softly as the door opened. A camo-clad family made their way inside, waving to the clerk and dispersing. The kids to the tank of minnows, the mom to the racks of clothing, and the dad to the gun counter, positioning himself right beside Grandpa Krandel.

316

Dakota watched her grandfather's head swivel. First, a hurried spin toward the door, the family. Then, to the Hall of Horns, where his eyes skidded to a stop on the man who stood beside her.

Like a robot, Grandpa Krandel raised a stiff hand. A wave or a salute, Dakota couldn't tell. But he made no movement toward them or away. He stood frozen, watching. Was this what it meant to be a hunter? To size up your catch, to look him in his eyes, to let him look back in yours, both of you understanding the truth of the situation?

"You know my grandpa."

"Indeedy-doody," he said, extending his hand to her. "Wendall Grady. Pleased to make your acquaintance."

"Dakota Roark."

His hand remained suspended between them. After Grandpa Krandel's tower of ammunition toppled, and he beelined for the door. After the bells jingled with maniacal glee. After Dakota rushed down the aisle, carelessly bumping a turkey decoy from its perch atop a display.

When the plastic bird clattered to the ground, the whole store went pin-drop quiet.

Then, finally, Wendall Grady lowered his hand. He took a long step forward and stooped to the ground, scooping something into his clutches.

"You forgot your marker," he called to her.

****

"C'mon, Mol, keep up. We've got traps to check."

Dakota quickened her pace, ignoring his slip. She didn't dare correct Grandpa Krandel. Not now. Not here. In the middle of the woods with his rifle at the ready and five dead squirrels swinging from a carrier over his shoulder.

Since they'd torn out of the Whitetails and Whoppers lot, pushing the old pickup to its limits and spraying up a cloud of dirt and gravel behind them, Grandpa Krandel hadn't said much. But what he had said, he'd said more than a few times. With a kind of intensity that scared her.

I knew that son of a bitch would find me.

I won't be taken alive.

Are you spyin' on me, you rat bastard?

That last one he'd said exactly five times, punctuating it each time with the blast of his rifle. Grandpa Krandel didn't miss. Never mind that the so-called spies had long, furry tails and brains the size of a walnut.

A few steps ahead of her, Grandpa Krandel held up a fist, and Dakota stopped, wiping the sweat from her face with her T-shirt. She caught her breath and looked around. Nothing but trees in every direction.

"Ever heard of a glue trap?" he asked.

Dakota shook her head. A quiet answer seemed the safest. Since she couldn't tell whether the question was meant for her or someone she couldn't see. Someone who lived only in Grandpa Krandel's haunted mind.

"Real clever but a little dangerous. So stay back."

He didn't have to tell her twice. When he leaned his gun against a tree trunk and disappeared behind it, she retreated a few more steps. She thought of running—but where to? Of calling her mother—but what would she say? And what would happen to Grandpa Krandel if she did?

"Got a live one," he yelled, cackling. "And hot damn, it's a rattler. Let's see how you handle that, Grady."

Dakota tightened her arms across her chest and waited, listening to his boots snap the backs of twigs on his way back to her.

"Dakota! Looky what I got."

At least he remembered her name now, but she wished he didn't. She wished he'd forgotten her altogether. Completely and forever. He motioned to her with one hand. In the other, he held out a sheet of cardboard coated with something sticky. She stared at it—mostly at the rattlesnake pinned to its center—her mouth dry as the grass beneath her feet.

"Don't worry. He ain't goin' nowhere. He's stuck. And he's about to be stucker."

More stuck, she thought. But she thought better of criticizing Grandpa Krandel's grammar. Who knew what would set him off?

"So that's a glue trap?" she asked. "And a rattlesnake?"

"Yep. And he's fightin' mad. But he won't be able to move a muscle until I douse him with oil."

Grandpa Krandel tossed the trap to the ground at the base of the sycamore, grabbed his gun, and pointed up ahead, through the trees, where the sunlight glinted off the metal roof of a small shed.

"C'mon," he said. "I'll show ya how to fix it good."

Dread fixed Dakota in place for a moment, same as the snake. She didn't know what was coming. Only that it would be bad. Probably worse than she imagined. But she scrambled along behind her grandfather anyway, more afraid of being out there alone.

"Grady don't like snakes. One time we were creepin' through this tunnel looking for Charlie, and Grady screamed so loud we thought we were dead men. Turns out Charlie left a little surprise hangin' from the ceiling."

Dakota knew what he expected. She should ask: *What? What was hanging there?* But she couldn't look away from the snake and the only two parts that moved—its head and its rattle. Grandpa Krandel kept talking anyway, mumbling really, in a way that reminded her he was only half there.

"A damn rat snake. Can you believe that? One hundred kinds of snakes in Nam. Ninety-eight were deadly; one could crush you like a bug. And then, there was the rat snake. Never hurt nobody . . . but a rat. But that didn't stop Grady from yowlin' like a cat in heat."

She didn't mention the gopher snake she'd seen at Lake Berryessa or the way she'd cried out—okay, *yowled*. Instead, she kept her mouth shut and followed close behind him.

When he spoke, she listened. "Stay right on my six."

Where he stepped, so did she. "Watch out for the ole punji pit."

Where he pointed, she looked. "Careful, bowling ball trip wire."

And when he fixed his finger onto the thick of the sycamores, she heeded his warning. "Don't you go out there without me. I'm pretty sure Charlie still lives at the bottom of that old well. Had to cover it up to keep him away."

When they arrived at the door to the shed, remarkably in one piece, she released a long, shaky breath.

"You know, I never told anybody that story about Grady."

"Not even Mom?"

"Specially not your mama. She didn't like them stories."

Grandpa Krandel lifted the doorknob and leaned against the frame. It creaked open to a musty room, lit only by the meager triangle of sun streaming through the doorway. "It sticks a little. I've been meanin' to fix it."

Dakota waited until he was inside, gathering supplies, his face swallowed by shadows. A hammer. A rusty can of oil. "So . . . Wendall Grady is the guy you thought was following you? In the car at the library? And today?"

He spun suddenly, too fast for his old-man body, and he stumbled a little, righting himself against the wall. "Did he say that? Did he tell you he was followin' me?"

"No. He didn't even mention you . . . not really. He was talking about the horns on the wall. Velvet shedding or something. I didn't really—"

Her grandfather charged past her, hammer and oil in tow. "We gotta hurry and get these traps ready. That SOB is on my tail."

"Why?"

"Because I know who he is. And now the army does too. And it ain't pretty."

"Who is he?" she asked, mostly to herself, since her grandfather had already trucked it back to the tree, where he was about to do God knows what to that snake.

"A goddamn war criminal, that's who." He picked up the trap—stuck rattler and all—and held it at arm's length. "Damn. I knew I was forgettin' somethin'. Could ya grab a couple nails from that old Mason jar on the shelf?"

Dakota nodded, even though her legs felt like rubber. The shed seemed darker now without her grandfather there. It was easy to imagine another rattlesnake coiled silently in the corner, waiting to take his revenge for his doomed buddy outside.

She took out her phone, tapped the flashlight app, and stepped across the threshold, feeling smug as she pointed the beam of light at all the spooky corners and behind the large trunk near the back wall. Seeing no snake, she scanned the shelves for the jar.

Top shelf. Too high for her to reach.

"What're ya doin' in there with that fancy phone? Snitchin' on me to Grady?" She figured Grandpa Krandel meant it as a joke, but the edge in his voice felt like a warning. The lightning before the thunder.

"Coming," she called, already maneuvering the chest across the dirt floor so she could stand atop it.

She climbed up, nearly eye level to the shelf, and slid the jar toward her, leaving a trail in the layer of dust. She plucked three nails from inside—careful to avoid the very fat and very dead horsefly that had met its end there—and tucked them in her pocket. Otherwise, the shelf was bare, except . . .

She aimed her flashlight in the corner where the dust looked more like a snowdrift and the spiders had been building their homes undisturbed, probably for decades. Something metal winked back at her. Her curiosity drew her along, a moth to a flame.

She moved to the edge of the chest and reached her arm out farther, farther, farther, until she snagged it with her finger. Just a little bit more and she'd have it.

Leaning on tiptoe, she managed to grab it—whatever it was—along with a handful of spiderweb she couldn't shake. Which came

321

with the terrible thought of a spider scuttling nearby. Or worse, on her.

She dropped her phone—the shed went dark—and she screamed as she tumbled from the trunk, nearly hitting her head on the wall behind her.

For a few seconds, she laid still as a board, stunned and staring up into nothing. Until her grandfather's voice jolted her into action.

"You alright in there?"

"I think so." She tried to sit up but couldn't. Something had her by the hair and wouldn't let go. With a grunt, she relented, searching the ground for her phone with her fingers. Finally, she flipped it over, the flashlight spotlighting the dim ceiling like a tiny moon. At least it wasn't dark anymore.

"I think I'm stuck," she yelled, her eyes tearing.

"I'm comin'. I'm comin'. These old legs don't move as fast as they used to."

Dakota gave one more effort as Grandpa Krandel lumbered to her side. "Hold on now," he said, his voice softer than she'd ever heard it. "Tiger's got you by the tail."

His hands tugged at her ponytail, jostling, jiggling, unwinding. A little rip. And then, freedom. "You lost a few pink ones," he told her, helping her to her feet.

"Mom would probably say that's karma."

She retrieved the nails from her pocket and held them out to him, still rubbing the sore spot on her head.

"Alright. You ready to fix that ole rattler good?"

Dakota nodded, even though she most definitely was not ready.

As Grandpa Krandel ducked through the doorway, she hung back and scanned the ground for the thing she'd risked life and hair for. The thing that had gone flying from her hand—*there it is!*—landing in the space behind her grandfather's trunk.

She picked it up.

A leather collar, stiff and cracked with age.

She rubbed the grime from the metal tag, aimed her flashlight at it, and read the words inscribed there.

ROSCOE
If lost, please return to
Mol's Junkyard, Allendale.

****

Dakota plucked a grass burr from her shoelace and rolled it gently between her fingers as she reread Boyd's message.

Hi Birdie (aka the next Barbara Walters)! I have news. Big news. I put Leia to work again last night on the dog issue. Nothing. But Obi-Wan says there's more than one way to skin a womp rat. And he's right. Can you meet me this week? I want to tell you in person.

Dakota set the burr beside the keyboard and stared at its prickles. She couldn't focus. Not with Roscoe's collar hidden in her back pocket and visions of Grandpa Krandel and his traps in her head. She'd shut her eyes when he'd oiled up the rattlesnake's tail, partially releasing it from the trap. When he'd fixed the rattle-end to the sycamore, she'd covered her ears. But she couldn't block the hollow thud of the hammer. And she couldn't keep her eyes closed forever. No matter how hard she tried.

Finally, she'd held up Roscoe's collar. Like a crucifix to ward off evil. "What's this?" she'd asked, grateful that the pounding had stopped.

"Where did ya find that ole thing?"

"The shed. It was in the corner on the shelf with the nails. Did it belong to Mom's dog?"

Grandpa Krandel nodded, wiping sweat from his forehead. He stuck the hammer in his back pocket and started toward the house. "Sure did."

"What happened to him?"

Dakota had willed her legs to move, to catch up to him. But she'd felt as rooted as a sycamore. Until the snake whipped into her vision and she'd jogged ahead.

"Somebody shot him. Your mama don't know this. But it was Grady's fault. All of it." When he quickened his pace, she understood the conversation was over. "C'mon. We got more traps to check back at the house."

They'd inspected every last one.

The airhorn trip wire. "First line of defense."

The spiked plyboard. "Your mama made that one with me."

The punji pit. "Already showed you my scar, right? Goddamn Charlie."

And the Altoid-tin alarm. Before he'd driven her back to the library. The whole time, she'd seen only that snake lashing and struggling against its fate.

She shook her head, trying to unsee it even now, and typed her reply.

Hey Chewie!

If we're skinning womp rats, I'm game. How about tomorrow outside the pool at 3:30?

P.S. Who's Barbara Walters?

P.P.S. JK.

Dakota closed her direct messages and scrolled through the posts on the main page. She still had fifteen minutes before the library's 6 p.m. closing time and wanted to be sure she hadn't missed anything important.

She flinched when a new chat bubble popped up on the screen, her heart racing.

DocSherlock: *How ya been, Cagedbird? Haven't seen you or Chewie on the chat in a while.*

Jojo666: *Yeah, it's been pretty boring around here without you two going at it.*

Cagedbird18: *We might have a lead.*

Jojo666: *Ooh la la. Sounds juicy. Spill.*

Cagedbird18: *I will. After we crack the case.*

Jojo666: *We, huh? So are you and the Chewster the first official Shadow Snoops couple?*

Dakota's stomach rolled as she pondered a reply. What if Boyd was out there right now, reading this in his Wookiee slippers? She didn't want to hurt his feelings. Thankfully, she didn't have to.

DocSherlock: *Leave it alone, Jojo. You're just jealous.*

Jojo666 has gone offline.

Her fingers hovered over the keys, still uncertain, when the librarian's voice streamed over the intercom.

"The Napa Public Library will be closing at 6 p.m. Please make your way to the exit shortly."

Dakota logged off the computer and slung her bag over her shoulder. She took one last look back as she headed for the double doors, leaving the grass burr behind for the janitor to wonder about.

****

"Did you finish your book?" her mom asked as Dakota picked at a soggy wonton.

She nodded, stuffing it into her mouth. Anything to get this over with. They hadn't all sat down for dinner since her dad's big scandal broke, and watching her parents pretend they weren't smack-dab in the middle of the Roark apocalypse was too much to bear. She felt the weight of it pressing on her shoulders until she wished she could simply give in, slide from her chair underneath the table, and sit with Gus, gobbling up the eggroll crumbs her dad brushed from his lap.

Dakota wasn't alone in her misery. That much she knew for sure. Her mom had already downed half a bottle of wine. She sucked down the rest of her glass and poured another, ignoring her father's side-eye.

"So, sweetie, we wanted to talk to you—"

"What now?"

"About your birthday," her mom finished, already sounding defeated. "It's next Saturday, you know."

"Um, yeah. I know, Mom. I didn't forget my own freaking birthday."

"Hey, watch the smart mouth, young lady."

Dakota rolled her eyes hard, hoping her dad would send her to her room. "You argue with Mom all the time. What's the difference?"

"The difference is she's your mother, and you need to show her respect."

Dakota snorted. "Like you do?"

Her mother smacked the table, and Gus darted from beneath it, tail tucked between his legs. Dakota watched with envy as he scurried up the stairs. "What has gotten into you?" her mother asked, half plea, half demand.

Dakota stood up and took a step back, out of her mother's firing range. "Wrong question, Mom. Why don't you ask Dad what he's gotten into? He's the one who messed everything up. That's what I want for my birthday. For things to be like they were before."

Huffing, she took the stairs two at a time and slammed the door, relishing an uneasy satisfaction. At least they'd leave her alone now.

She undressed, relieved when she discovered the Whitetails and Whoppers card in the pocket of her jean shorts. If she'd stuck them in the laundry, her mother would've been the one to find it. Disaster averted. She slipped the card between the pages of her yearbook and dropped into bed, exhausted.

Later, when she'd fallen half-asleep her mom came inside and sat beside her, reeking of alcohol. Dakota started to roll away from her, but it hurt too much when her mom whimpered, so she stayed put.

"I'm sorry things are hard right now," her mom whispered. "It'll get better. I promise. Your dad has a meeting next week with the hospital disciplinary board. I'm sure this whole thing will blow over. You know how charming he can be."

Dakota hated her mom like this—spineless. She'd rather her the other way, with a backbone of steel and a fistful of rage. "Hey mom . . . didn't you have a dog named Roscoe?"

She kept her eyes closed, heard the sharp intake of her mother's breath. "Yes. What made you think of that?"

"Oh, just this book I saw at the library. After I finished *Mindhunter*. There was a character named Roscoe in it. Whatever happened to him?"

Her mother didn't answer for a long time, and Dakota wondered if she'd left. But the bed still felt warm and sunken in beside her, so she didn't dare open her eyes. It would break the spell. "I thought I told you he ran away."

"Did he ever come back?" Dakota thought of the collar she'd hidden in her rain boot.

"It's not something I like to talk about. But you're getting older now, aren't you? I think you're old enough to understand. Your grandpa killed Roscoe. That's how sick he was. That's why I left there and went to live with my mom. And that's why I don't want him around you. He's dangerous, honey."

Dakota lay very still. Her heart sounded strangely muffled in her ears. Like it was buried under a mound of dirt.

"Are you sure?"

But her mother had already gone. On her desk, she found her mother's literary peace offering—*Silence of the Lambs*—with a note tucked in between the pages. *Do not read at bedtime.*

CHAPTER TWENTY-FIVE

BOYD waved at Dakota from across the parking lot. He must've gotten there early. She glanced around for anyone she recognized— anyone who could out her to her mom—before she waved back. She left the Napa Valley Swim Club behind her and headed for the VW, anxious to hear Boyd's news.

"Hi," he said, shuffling from one foot to the other. He opened the passenger door for her. "I got my AC fixed."

"I thought you couldn't afford it."

He shrugged, climbing in beside her. "Yeah. Funny story. One of my mom's friends needed some help building a website for her baking business, and she hired me. So . . ."

"Oh. Okay. Well, in that case . . ." Dakota leaned over and cranked the air to full blast. Boyd laughed a little harder than she did.

"*In that case,*" he repeated her words. "I sort of brought an early dinner. I thought we could take it to the park down the street. If you have time. And you're hungry. And you're not a vegetarian."

Dakota fidgeted with her seatbelt to avoid looking at him. He seemed different. Or maybe she was different, her heart still raw and bruised from last night. *Your grandpa killed Roscoe.* "That's a lot of ifs."

"It's okay if you don't want to. We can just talk here."

But she knew it wasn't okay by the way his voice deflated like a day-old party balloon. "It's fine. My mom's not coming to pick me up until five. I'm starving. And I'm about as vegetarian as Chewbacca."

"Actually, Chewie *is* an omnivore. He's not opposed to veggies. And a little-known fact, he loves fast food."

Ten minutes later, they were seated across from each other at a picnic table, with Boyd unveiling double cheeseburgers and fries in Styrofoam containers. Something about the way he looked at her, the way he gave her his extra ketchup, made it feel like a date. A supremely awkward one. Worse than the time Hannah's dorky cousin had asked her out.

Boyd held up a French fry. "Cheers," he said, tapping it to hers. "To Cagedbird and Chewie, the dynamic duo."

He smiled broadly, and Dakota shrank from the brightness of it.

"So what did you want to tell me?" she asked.

He removed a photograph from his wallet and laid it on the table in front of her with a sigh. "There's something I haven't told you. It's the reason I started with all this Shadow Snoops stuff in the first place. The reason I created Leia."

Dakota examined the picture. Two twin girls, her age, with side ponytails and matching striped sweaters and carbon-copy joy in their eyes.

"This looks like . . . uh, victim number four. Miriam Woodbury."

"Wow. You really know this stuff. It is Miriam. And that's her twin, Martha. My mom. This was taken just a week before Miriam went missing."

Dakota sat, stunned. She watched Boyd take another bite. "They had a dog too, right?"

Boyd nodded. "Bucky. They'd adopted him from the SPCA. My mom told me they'd just picked him up a few weeks before. Which got me thinking. So I looked back through everything on the site, plus some stuff my mom has in storage."

"And?"

"Not enough intel for Leia to work with. But there was this TV show clip about victim thirteen, Carrie Munroe. She had a basset hound named Buster. Her parents went on the news right after she disappeared, and they mentioned Buster had been a rescue dog. Apparently, he was fiercely protective of Carrie."

"Do you think all the dogs were rescues?"

Boyd shrugged. "No clue. I'm not even sure the SPCA keeps records like that, especially not for thirty-something years."

"We have to try, though, right?"

"I was hoping you'd say that."

Dakota polished off the rest of her fries, politely declining when Boyd offered his. He cleaned the table too, waving her off when she tried to help.

"Does your mom talk about it? About Miriam?"

"Not anymore. The media hounded her a lot back then. Everybody was fascinated by the whole twinless twin thing, wondering if Miriam talked to her in her dreams. Or maybe even ID'd Shadow Man. Plus, I think she blames herself. She was supposed to be with Miriam, walking to the park with Bucky. They went every day after school. But she had a stomach bug, and her mom made her stay home."

"I'm really sorry that happened to her. To your family. We're gonna take this guy down."

Boyd chuckled. "You really believe that, don't you?"

"Hell yeah, I do. We've got Leia—and Yoda."

"And Chewie," he added, pointing to himself.

Dakota frowned. "Who am I then? I feel left out."

"You're just you," he said, softly. "Dakota Roark, superstar investigative reporter. You don't need an intergalactic superhero name."

She laughed, but her stomach knotted. She wasn't sure what to make of it. Of him. The way he was acting.

"Hey, you know, you should give me your number, so we can talk offline. About Shadow Man stuff. If you want."

"Oh. I can't. My parents check my phone sometimes. They'd start asking questions." That used to be true at least. Before the Roark apocalypse.

"I can get you a burner phone. They don't have to know."

He spoke to his hands, never lifted his eyes. Dakota scooted off the bench and stood there, wondering what to do.

"I'm sorry," he said. "That was weird, wasn't it? I say stupid things sometimes."

"It's okay. Everybody does. I should probably get back to the pool though. My mom will lose it if I'm not there on time. She can be pretty scary when she's mad. It's not something you want to see."

Dakota started walking, knowing Boyd would follow. In a way, she felt powerful. In another, as small and disgusting as the spider in her grandfather's shed. Easily crushed by something bigger.

"What do you mean? She doesn't hurt you, does she?"

"It's not a big deal, Boyd. Just take me back, okay?"

"Not until you tell me."

He looked at her then. Not like half of a dynamic duo. Or Hannah's goofy cousin. But the pitying way an adult looks at a child. She felt ashamed for what she'd thought. What she'd accused him of in her mind. Not every guy was like her father.

"I know there's some stuff going on with your family," he said. "I saw the story about your dad on the news. You can talk to me about it if you want."

Dakota shook her head and kept walking until she reached the parking lot and Boyd's VW. She heard him behind her—his breathing, his heavy footsteps. He opened his door first, then reached across to hers. She got inside and waited for something to happen. She couldn't say what. Only that nothing did.

AFTER

CHAPTER TWENTY-SIX

(MONDAY, OCTOBER 8, 2018)

LUCIANA'S face speaks volumes.

Volume One: Confusion. When she opens the door to the student break room, her eyes dart between me and Cole. A man whose face she recognizes only because I'd once begged her—only half-joking—to fashion an ex-husband voodoo doll. *You need a picture for that, right?* I'd asked.

Volume two: Shock. Her jaw drops a little, and she mouths, *¡Ay, Dios mío!*

Volume three: Pity. Without so much as a scowl at Jane, she slinks into the room and takes the last seat in the Grieving Parents Group. It's the quietest entrance Luciana's ever made here. Possibly anywhere.

Pretending to check the clock—I'd felt every single second like a lash to my soul—I peek at Cole on my left. He's staring straight ahead, his face a blank slate. But he smells of cigarette smoke, and I suspect the work call he ducked out to make ten minutes ago involved a Mister Marlboro. So what if he's not the rubber ball I thought? He's still better at faking it than I am.

"Good evening, everyone. I'd like to start things off tonight. This is my ex-husband and Dakota's dad, Cole Roark."

I pause, but Cole stays mute. In the seat to my right, Sawyer shifts, and I try to steady my breathing, to match it to his, my own personal metronome. Jane fidgets with her wedding ring—she's still wearing it. Debbie, the newbie, gives me a small smile of encouragement. And Luciana raises a single eyebrow. It's as much of a statement as those M&Ms she'd crunched to death a few weeks ago.

I keep talking—that's my job as the Lead Basket Case—but I hold back, too.

What I say: "As many of you might have seen on the news, there were some developments in my daughter's murder case last week."

What I don't say: *There's a good chance my dad is the serial killer known as Shadow Man, and my daughter was his seventeenth victim.*

What I say: "It's been quite a whirlwind, and we're both still reeling."

What I don't say: *We spent Sunday reliving the awkward silent-treatment phase of our marriage and waiting in vain for DNA results to confirm said Shadow Man's identity.*

What I say: "Cole is visiting from Seattle."

What I don't say: *Where he started a new life with a woman who accused him of sexual harassment because he wouldn't leave me for her.*

What I say: "He asked to be here with us tonight."

What I don't say: *To keep tabs on me.*

"Cole, would you like to address the group?" I turn to him cautiously. All those unspoken words, bricks in a wall between us.

Just when I'm positive he's going to pass the grief baton, he surprises me. A sharp inhale and then, "I'm not exactly sure where to begin. Talking has always been Mollie's thing. I thought I had to be the strong one. That only she was allowed to break down. But I'm realizing that was a mistake—keeping it all bottled up. Because Mollie thought she was alone in this . . . in this nightmare . . . and I'm sorry for that. You think I would've handled it better since I'm a pediatric oncologist. I mean, I've lost my share of patients. I've seen grief. I thought I knew what this would be like. That I was some kind of expert. Hell, I had no fucking clue."

The room is quiet, save for the hum of the soda machine in the corner. When I look at Cole again, he reminds me of the man he used to be.

"The crazy part is I still see her sometimes," he says. "It's not her—not really. I know that. But a girl will catch my eye at work or the gym or the fish market downtown, and it'll punch me in the gut. I probably look like a total headcase, but in that split-second, I'll forget she's gone. That she's never coming back."

My eyes find Luciana's, and she nods. She's always told me I'm lucky to *see* Dakota. That it's a gift from her spirit. A sign she's okay. *Mi querida, there are no mistakes.* But me, I take it as a different sort of omen. That her spirit is restless and searching. For vengeance, for closure. Just like mine.

"It happens to me sometimes too," Debbie says, wiping a tear from her cheek. "Last week I was riding the bus, and there was this kid a few rows in front of me—he couldn't have been more than nineteen or twenty. He had the same cornrows as my Malcolm. I used to do his hair myself. Do you know I was so convinced it was him, I said his name? The kid never turned around, but I followed him for a block before I heard his friend call out to him. Wasn't my Malcolm after all."

Jane shares too. Since Scott moved out, she's convinced she's heard Harper crying. When Luciana offers her a tissue, I'm certain it must be laced with arsenic. But Jane gives her a grateful nod and blots her eyes without incident.

"I know what you mean," she tells Jane. "Isabella laughs sometimes when I do something crazy. Which is pretty much every day. You know me. *Muy loca.* How can anyone tell us that it's not real?"

The question is a dare to the universe for somebody to smack us back down to earth. When my cell buzzes in my back pocket, I already know. The same way I'd known when Dakota didn't come back that night. Or the next. When Gus had wandered back alone. When Cole had said, *Come home, Mol.*

"It's Detective Sharpe." I announce before I remember where I am. Who I'm supposed to be here.

"Answer it," Cole says. The group doesn't miss a beat, chiming in with their agreement. The chorus of voices thrums in my head, pushes me forward. Even as my own dread pins me to my seat. I'm still not certain, and never will be, which is worse. The knowing or the not knowing.

"Hello?" I'm half-standing when I answer, intending to bolt out the door. To preserve one last shred of dignity. But I stay there, hunched and frozen. Like Detective Sharpe's put a spell on me.

He says all the usual things. I'm sure he does. He must. But all I hear above the roar in my brain is this: "On Saturday, we obtained a sample of your father's DNA from the door handle of his pickup truck. The lab determined it's a match to the trace sample we collected from that discarded dog collar back in '92. We're in the process of executing a search warrant on the junkyard now."

Sawyer catches me by the arm, passes the phone to Cole, and guides me back to my chair. If not for him, the Lead Basket Case would've ended up on the floor. Stone-cold sober this time.

****

Dark and empty, the parking lot at Napa Valley College resembles the dreary landscape of my soul.

I've sent them all away. Luciana, home. Sawyer, to the Blue Rose. Cole, to his hotel room. It's only me and a thousand memories, thick as the cobwebs in my father's hunting shed. Fleeting as the shadows. Even Metallica is no match. So I silence the radio, close my eyes, and let them play my own warped home movie.

Six years old, I'd clung to my mother's hand as the judge addressed me. He'd reminded me of a king on his throne with his long robe. His gavel like a scepter.

"You say your father touched you on your private areas?"

I'd nodded, feeling like I might be sick. But I couldn't puke. Not here in the king's chambers.

"What were you wearing when that happened?"

This wasn't a question we'd practiced. I'd turned to my mother in a panic, certain the wrong answer would mean doom for the both of us. The king's dungeon. A hungry dragon. No prince to save us.

"Don't look at your mother. Just talk to me."

Instead, my eyes had veered across the aisle to the other bench, where my father sat with his shoulders slumped and his cheeks wet. *Was he crying?*

Right then, my mother's lie disintegrated inside me. The way witches in fairytales disappear in a puff of black smoke. Dad had never hurt me. He never would. Not unless I deserved it. Like the time I'd jumped out from behind the sofa and scared him. Of course, he'd shaken me so hard my teeth rattled. I'd reminded him of Charlie.

I'd believed that. I'd *actually* believed it. Until that day—fifteen years old and branded a spy. Stripped down to my bra and panties in the hunting shed.

I'd felt like an alien creature, the way he'd stared at me.

"What are you hiding?" he'd asked when I'd tried to cover myself. And he'd flinched when I'd whimpered.

He'd taken a step toward me. Then another and another. Grabbed my wrist and pulled me to him, his fingers twisting, burning me like a rope. Every whispered word came on a cloud of malt liquor, but at least he sounded like himself again. "Put your goddamn clothes on, Mol. And don't you dare ever let any man humiliate you again. Understand me?"

338

It's ironic, then, that when I open my eyes, Cole's face is in the driver's side window, frowning. His fist poised above it, about to knock. We both startle.

"Do you know how dangerous it is to fall asleep in your car? In an empty parking lot? God, Mollie."

"I wasn't sleeping," I say, rolling down the window. "What are you doing here anyway? I thought you went back to your fancy hotel to watch pay-per-view and call your girlfriend."

Sure, it's a cheap shot. Especially after his performance in group. Where he'd nearly convinced me that he had a real heart, not the Tin Man's pocket watch. But then he'd gone and done it, just like he always did. After group, he'd stood in the parking lot in front of everyone—Luciana, Sawyer, Jane, Debbie—and leveled me. *I told you. We should've had your father locked up a long time ago.* The implication: I'd dropped the proverbial ball. The ball being our daughter. After all, I'd been the one with Crazy Krandel for a father. I'd been the one who'd worked at the kind of place said crazy father belonged.

Cole throws up his hands at me. "Really? Why do you always want to pick a fight?"

"Why do you think? We both did this, you know. That summer we drove her away."

"You think I don't realize that? That I don't have a million regrets?" He crouches down beside the open window, his voice softening. "I'm not here to fight. I came back because I was worried about you. I thought Sawyer would've stayed."

"I told him and Luci to leave. I just needed some time."

"Yeah. Me too. Anyway, I'm sorry I said the thing about locking up your dad. You did your best to protect her from him."

"So—" My lungs squeeze shut as I try to say the words. "Did they arrest him?"

He nods. "Detective Sharpe said he tried to reach you. They took him down to the station for questioning, but they can only hold him for forty-eight hours. He said—"

A pair of headlights beam from behind Cole, and he turns to look, shielding his eyes as Sawyer steers his truck into the lot. A moment later, Luciana follows in Boludo. I imagine how we must look to them, Cole and me. Like it or not, this is what's left of our fragmented little family. The two of us.

"We couldn't leave you here," Luciana admits, practically pushing Cole aside to lean in to my open window. She slips a tarot card into my hand and whispers, "I got another jumper. It went straight out of my purse and onto Boludo's floorboard. Like it had to be seen."

I turn it over and lay it faceup on the seat, my blood whirring at the sight of it. The archangel, Gabriel, plays a golden trumpet as men, women, and children rise from their graves with outstretched arms.

Cole peers over her shoulder, addressing me. "Sharpe also said they found those hairs you were talking about. Fingerprints too. They sent it all to the lab."

When I don't respond, he moves closer. "What is that?" he asks.

I hold it up to him and read the name of the card. "Judgment."

BEFORE

CHAPTER TWENTY-SEVEN

"**HAPPY** birthday to me."

Dakota studied her work in the mirror. Not as good as Hannah would've done, but not bad for an amateur. She'd blown out her hair, even used one of the fancy styling products Hannah had left behind. But most importantly, she'd dyed it a vibrant rose gold again. She only wished changing her mood was that easy. Inside, she still felt like sad, faded pink.

Gus scratched at the bathroom door, and she let him inside, grateful for some company. He plopped onto the rug with a sigh, gazing up at her with his doleful brown eyes.

"Fifteen kinda sucks, doesn't it?" she asked him. "I know you were fifteen a long time ago and probably don't remember. Dog years and all. But trust me. Major suckage."

He cocked his head. Like he was contemplating her statement. Before the debacle of this summer, she'd planned to spend her birthday with Hannah at Six Flags, riding their new coaster and stuffing her face with way too much cotton candy and funnel cake. Instead, she'd be going to a lame dinner at some hoity-toity restaurant with parents who could barely stand to be in the same room. She hadn't even heard from Hannah. Such was the state of her universe.

"Hurry up in there! Your dad will be home any minute."

About time. After he'd eaten a few bites of birthday pancakes and kissed her on the forehead—*Happy birthday, sweetheart*—her dad offered up some excuse about meeting with his attorney and slunk out the door. Like the weasel he was.

"Big week for him this week." That's how her mother had explained it. Or excused it.

Dakota slipped into the simple black dress she'd worn for eighth-grade graduation—depressing how it still fit—and twirled for Gus. "Mom's gonna freak," she whispered to him, crouching to his level. He nearly caught her nose with his wet tongue.

Dakota opened the door to her mother lingering in the hallway mirror, pinning diamond studs in her ears. She'd really gone all out. Red dress by Trina Turk, Manolo pumps, Louie clutch. The earrings Dad had bought her last Valentine's. Same frown though, spoiling it all.

"Jesus, Dakota. Did you really have to dye it again? School's starting in a few weeks, and you know how strict Napa Prep is about stuff like this."

She shrugged. "What about Drake Gunderson? He dyed his black with white streaks and nobody cared."

"Don't they call him Dracula?"

"Exactly. The school just let it slide." She joined her mom in the mirror, making a goofy face. Tongue out, eyes crossed. *Nothing.* Not even a smirk. "At least I didn't get a tattoo."

"Not funny. If you get a tattoo, I'm taking you straight to Napa State Hospital and admitting you myself."

Dakota laughed. "Are there any patients like Hannibal the Cannibal? Because that'd be cool."

Finally, the glacial surface of her mother's face cracked. "Just keep Hannibal the Cannibal under wraps at dinner, okay? Your dad doesn't know I gave it to you. And he's got enough on his plate right now."

"Yeah, you're right, Mom. He probably doesn't like liver with his Chianti anyway."

****

Dakota had to hand it to her parents. They put on a good show for the patrons at Bouchon. Her dad even managed a compliment halfway through dinner—*Those earrings look great on you, Mol*—which lit her mother up like a Christmas tree. It was almost like old times, the three of them. When the cake arrived—a perfect little mound of chocolate drizzled with more chocolate and topped off with shavings, also chocolate—Dakota could see the light at the end of the tunnel. It looked a lot like a birthday candle.

Her dad cleared his throat and raised his glass for the annual birthday toast. "Fifteen years ago, right about now, you arrived in the world and made our family complete. We're so proud of you, sweetie. Pink hair and all. I know it hasn't been an easy summer— we've all struggled—but it's going to get better from here on out. Your mom and I hope this gift will be the start of a great fifteenth year."

Dakota opened the envelope he'd placed beside her plate. Inside the standard birthday card, she found a slick brochure plastered with smiling teens rappelling down the side of a rock face. Dakota's hands shook as she read.

Starry Sky Wilderness Retreat

Young adults face a unique set of challenges in our fast-paced society. Inundated with images from television and social media and lofty expectations from parents, friends, and teachers, teens often struggle with depression, anger, low self-esteem, and anxiety. At Starry Sky, we go back to basics, using a strengths-based approach and the healing powers of nature to ensure that teens grow into happy, successful, and independent adults. Starry Sky treats young men and women, ages twelve to eighteen.

Dakota tossed the brochure at her mother and watched it flutter to the ground. "What the hell is this? You're sending me away?" The words were out and wreaking havoc before she could contain them. Heads turned at the tables around them. Her father lowered his voice to a threatening growl.

"Language, Dakota."

Faking a smile for the onlookers, her mother retrieved the brochure. "It's only for two weeks before school starts. You'd be back by the third of September, right in time to start school on Monday. We just want to be sure you're solid, especially going into swim season. This place comes highly recommended."

She pointed to the shiny, well-adjusted models on the cover with their put-on excitement. "Look. It'll be an adventure. Plus, your dad and I need a little time to . . ."

"To what?"

Her mother's hands stirred the air between them. As if a gesture could explain the totality of this ambush. On her birthday, no less.

"Great. So I'll be learning to make fire and bury my poop while you and dad figure out your marriage. I'll save you the trouble. He's cheating on you. I saw him on prom night. There you go. Problem solved."

Dakota thought she'd feel relieved, stunning her parents into silence with her revelation. Casting it off like a straitjacket. Instead, her chest ached. Like she'd held her breath too long at the bottom. When the waiter came over to ask if they needed any help, Dakota inhaled before she answered.

"Yes. The mental kind, apparently."

****

Dakota saved her tears for later. After her dad paid the tab. After the funeral-quiet car ride home. After they'd all retreated to their respective corners. She buried her face in Gus's fur until a wet spot formed on the side of his stomach, darkening his golden hair.

The buzz of her phone—a text from Liv—drew her back to the land of the almost-living.

OMG did u c this???

Those three question marks seemed ominous, but Dakota clicked the link anyway.

Hannah had released a new vlog—*Guys Want To Be Hot Too*—featuring her newest subject, Tyler Lowry. Dakota watched as Hannah styled his hair—fauxhawked, slicked back, spiky, and mussed. At the end, Hannah perched atop Tyler's lap and turned to the camera. "So, guys, put a little effort in. I promise it'll pay off." Then she pressed her lips to Tyler's, leaving him breathless and red-lipped.

Dakota wished she could hate Tyler. But that she saved for Hannah. And it sat like a hot coal in her stomach, demanding release.

She scrolled to the bottom of the video and typed a comment in all caps. Then she copied it, pasted it, and pasted it again. Until her fingers got tired.

LIKE MOTHER LIKE DAUGHTER.
LIKE MOTHER LIKE DAUGHTER.
LIKE MOTHER LIKE DAUGHTER.

LIKE MOTHER LIKE DAUGHTER.

****

Dakota jolted awake, her face mashed against the screen of her cell phone, which glowed as bright as a curtainless window. Telling her two things: It was 1:30 a.m. And she'd missed two calls and thirteen texts. From Liv and from the group chat at Napa Prep.

She opened Liv's string first, dread growing as fast as a poison weed in her chest, tightening around her heart.

Damn girl. Hannah is super pissed.

U better call her.

Is this u?

The last text linked back to the group chat, forty-five members strong. Most of them Tyler's lacrosse buddies. At midnight, he'd sent out the photo. Of her. The one she'd deleted. He must've saved it somewhere.

But the photo had been altered. She could guess by who. Because Tyler couldn't photoshop his way out of a paper bag.

Dakota's face, all pouty and seductive and coached by Hannah, sat atop a very naked body. Definitely not hers. It could've been, though, with the budding breasts and the swimmer's shoulders. Even the summer tan lines were perfectly placed. A nice touch that left no doubt. This was Hannah's handiwork.

Tyler had written: *PSA on Dakota Roark: Total psycho, flat as a board. Hard pass.*

CHAPTER TWENTY-EIGHT

(SUNDAY, AUGUST 14, 2016)

"**SO** did you think any more about Starry Sky?"

Dakota sat at the kitchen table, her bare feet resting on Gus's stomach. She stared past her mother to the wall, stirring her Cheerios until they drowned, bloated in their milky bath.

"Well, I left the brochure on the coffee table just in case."

When Dakota's phone vibrated against the table, she flinched. Like it had become a part of her, her nerves hardwired to its circuit board. Maybe that's why she'd been buzzing all night and into the morning. She flipped it over and gazed into its face. It told her what she already knew. Everyone was talking. About her. Her and those naked photos.

"Are you even listening to me? You've been tethered to that thing all morning. Give it to me."

Panicked, Dakota eyes darted up to her mother, to her outstretched hand. "Where's Dad?"

"Phone. *Now.*" She watched helplessly as her mother laid the phone on the counter. "Relax. You can survive for a few minutes without it. What's so important anyway?"

Dakota shrugged. "Liv asked me to sleep over tonight. Her mom can pick me up from the library."

"I'm not sure that's such a good idea. I thought we could spend the day together. Talk, maybe. Like we used to."

"Why? Dad's not here. He's never here anymore. He's the one you need to talk to."

"After last night, he thought it would be best if he gave you a little space."

"Me? What about you? Did you even ask him if it was true?"

Her mother sighed. "I don't want you to worry about this stuff."

Dakota pushed back from the table, startling Gus. He pranced nervously between her and her mother. "I thought you wanted to talk. But you only want to talk about me. Like I'm the problem. The *identified patient.* Isn't that what you shrinks call it?"

"When did you get to be such a smart-ass?"

The cell phone buzzed again, reminding Dakota what was at stake. "I'm sorry, Mom. I just don't want to talk anymore. I'll go to the stupid Starry Sky thing if that's what you want. But until then, let me enjoy my last few weeks of summer. Okay?"

Without asking, she swiped the phone from the counter and tucked it away, safe in her back pocket. Her whole body hummed with relief. "So, Liv's tonight, if you're alright with it?"

"I guess so. I'm glad she's been a good friend to you lately. How's it been with Hannah? Has she said anything to you?"

Dakota realized then how wide the chasm had grown. Her mother on one side. Dakota on the other. A torrent of secrets and disappointments rushing between them, too dangerous to cross. "No."

Her mother frowned. "Really? No drama?"

Dakota laughed, but it hurt. And the chasm grew. "C'mon, Mom. You know I'm a no-drama llama."

✳✳✳✳

Grandpa Krandel parked the truck and pointed out the window. "I got an idea."

Dakota gaped at the storefront. *Bull's Body Art.* "Are you serious? Mom's head would literally explode. *Boom.*" She mimed sudden detonation with her hands, and her grandfather watched her fingers, transfixed.

"Back in Nam, we dropped a helluva lot of bombs. Cluster bombs. Chemical bombs. That was damn near the only thing we were good at. Blowin' shit up." He chuckled a little, and Dakota held her breath. She never knew when or where or why he'd turn into Crazy Krandel. "Now, you told me your birthday wasn't so good, right?"

She nodded.

"That some good-for-nothin' boy broke your heart?"

Another nod.

"And your mama wants to send you to sleepaway camp because your daddy can't keep it in his pants?"

"You know about Dad?"

"Hell, it's all over the papers."

Her mom had tossed the *Napa Valley Register*—probably before Dakota came down for breakfast—but she'd found it anyway, the headline covered with the scrambled eggs she hadn't touched. The Cheerios she'd sent to a milky grave.

Hospital Board Meets On Monday To Determine Fate Of Renowned Pediatric Oncologist

"I suppose it is."

"Alright, so I'm battin' one thousand on all counts. It sounds like what you really need right now is a great big ole bomb. Tell ya what, I'll get one too."

****

Dakota watched as Grandpa Krandel gritted his teeth. Even with his face scrunched in pain, he managed to wink at her. "This hurts worse than the damn punji pit."

Bull snorted so loudly, Dakota half-expected his nose ring to fly out. Which would have made him one piercing short of a half dozen. And those were just the ones she could see.

"You're lucky," he told her. "Your grandpa's hella cool. We met over at the VA."

Dakota nodded, watching the cage take shape on her grandfather's sinewy bicep.

"At the PTSD group," Grandpa Krandel added. Then he motioned to Bull. "Remind me what that stands for again."

Their voices chorused in unison, "Pretty Tired of Shit, Dude," and Dakota laughed.

Chuckling himself, Bull started up again. He filled in one of the cage's dark bars, and Grandpa Krandel winced, air hissing like steam from between his teeth. He made a show of grabbing Bull's arm, begging him, "No more. No more."

Bull stopped and turned to Dakota. "He does know this isn't the real thing, right?"

"Wait one gosh darn minute." Grandpa Krandel peeked up at them, trying to hide a smirk. "You mean to tell me this ain't a real tattoo?"

"You said you both wanted the semi-permanent ink." Bull looked from Dakota to the applicator in his hand and back again. "We don't tattoo minors. It's against the law."

Grandpa Krandel punched Bull's arm. "I'm kiddin'. Of course, we want the semi-permanent. This skin is too pretty to mark up with a goddamn needle." He smiled at Dakota. "Besides, we're going for firecracker level. Not the A-bomb. Right, Dakota?"

Bull shook his head, laughing to himself, before he returned his focus to her grandfather's shoulder, where he inked a small black bird.

"Right." In that moment, Dakota's heart soared, the highest bird in the sky.

****

Dakota studied Bull's handiwork in the small mirror he'd given her. "It looks so real," she said, already imagining her mother's stunned face. Her father's disgust. Tyler and Hannah's shock and awe.

"The ink will fade in about two weeks. But until then, you've got a tat, girl."

Grandpa Krandel cleared his throat and flexed his bicep in the floor length mirror.

"Yeah, yeah. You too, old man."

Her grandfather handed Bull a wad of cash and shook his hand. "Thanks, soldier. I'll see ya at Tuesday's group. And hey, if anybody calls here askin' questions, you didn't see me. You didn't hear me. You don't know me."

"Roger that," Bull said, giving him a stiff military salute. "I love a good covert op."

As they left the shop, Dakota snapped a picture of herself in front of the store's logo—a heavily tattooed bull with a studded ring in its nose. She grinned as she posted the photo online. It felt like a giant FU to the universe.

Beneath it, she typed: *Some birds aren't meant to be caged.*

AFTER

CHAPTER TWENTY-NINE

A lick from Gus's tongue is more effective than any alarm clock. I wipe my face and sit bolt-upright on the sofa, eyes wide. My fists clenched at my sides. My stomach knotted. As if I'm ready for a fight. Funny, I don't remember falling asleep, only the murmur of an infomercial, a mustached man in a silly chef's hat urging me to buy a set of knives that could halve a watermelon in midair.

Now, it's my father's face filling the screen. Not the father I know, though, the old scraggly man who eats wieners from a can. They've chosen a photograph from his Vietnam days. I'm not even sure it's him. But the caption beneath it assures me this strapping young fellow is Victor Krandel, person of interest in the murder of his granddaughter and possible suspect in the serial killings of sixteen other young women in Napa and Solano counties. He's wearing a war helmet and smiling like he's having a good time raping and pillaging a world away and a lifetime ago.

I find the remote on the floor, halfway hidden under the coffee table, and turn up the volume. Even though I'd rather listen to the screech of an acutely psychotic patient the moment before he gets an emergency Haldol injection.

Yesterday evening, Mr. Krandel was transported to the Napa County Jail, following questioning by the recently formed Shadow Man Task Force. He has been placed under arrest for several counts of criminal possession of a booby trap, after SWAT officers were called to disarm several traps, which impeded safe entry into his compound. According to the Napa County Sheriff's Department, Krandel is a person of interest in the murder of his granddaughter, Dakota Roark. Speaking off the record, staff from the Napa Valley Veteran's Administration confirmed Krandel has received treatment for severe mental illness, stemming from war trauma.

I cringe when the camera pans the campus of Napa State and takes us inside to an office I recognize. It belongs to Dr. Jackass. He's seated smugly in a chair where I'd once straddled him.

Doctor Peter Jacoby, Chief Psychologist at Napa State Hospital and expert in serial murder, has been following the Shadow Man case closely over the course of the last twenty years.

I laugh out loud when I spot the ink stain on the pocket of his shirt. I only wish it had been worse. Spinach in his teeth. Lipstick on his collar.

Mr. Krandel certainly possesses some characteristics similar to other serial killers. His history of military experience, for example. A background in law enforcement or the military may lend an advantage in gaining the compliance of a victim, and psychologically speaking, these men generally have a need to control others while simultaneously lacking an ability to control themselves. Mr. Krandel has been described by others as a loner who is fascinated by weapons and violent toward animals. These are signs of a seriously troubled person.

He frowns deeply—the way I'd done as Mollie of old, post-Botox to the forehead, admiring the way my skin had snapped back without a wrinkle in sight. He's trying to convince the audience of his own depth. Which is more kiddie pool than ocean.

Though it is not unheard of for serial killers to harm members of their family—for example, Edmund Kemper, the coed killer, murdered his mother and his paternal grandparents—it is much more common for them to maintain a façade of normalcy with those closest to them, such that their family and friends do not suspect the wolf in sheep's clothing. If—and I want to emphasize Mr. Krandel has not yet been charged of a crime—he did murder his granddaughter, this killing was likely more personal for him. Perhaps she had found him out and threatened to expose him.

He pauses, lowering his voice an octave.

In a way—the irony—perhaps she has.

I groan, silencing Dr. Jackass with a click of the remote. "What a prick."

Gus looks over his shoulder at me, wagging his tail. As if to voice his wholehearted agreement.

But Dr. Jackass's words stick, replaying in my head as I down a scalding cup of coffee way too fast, searing my throat.

More personal for him.

As I force myself to eat a piece of bread, a spoonful of peanut butter.

Perhaps she had found him out.

As I stand in the shower, dead-faced and unmoving, like a statue in the rain.

Threatened to expose him.

It comes to me suddenly. A conversation we'd had, Dakota and me. She'd asked about Roscoe and what had happened to him. Stupid me, I'd told her everything. Well, not everything, but enough.

Moving with purpose now, I toss on yesterday's clothes, still discarded on the bathroom floor, and squeeze the water from my hair. *Good enough.* Because I can't wait any longer to get the answers I need. From someone. Anyone. And I know where to start.

****

Martha Blackburn answers on the first knock. As if she's been expecting me. I'd given her fair warning, blasting Black Sabbath's "War Pigs" from my parking spot behind Boyd's VW, halfway up her drive. When Ozzy sings about bodies burning and the day of judgment, I see Dakota's green eyes.

Martha cracks the door, glowering.

"You lied to me," she says. Behind her, looming large on the television, Dr. Jackass. He's sitting next to a local news anchor, probably fielding questions he isn't qualified to answer.

At least he's been muted. "You're that girl's mother. Number seventeen."

"Dakota." It still hurts to say her name. But I can't imagine not saying it. That someday years will pass without it crossing my lips. "Did Boyd tell you he knew her?"

The familiar shadow of grief darkens her face. "This morning when the news broke. He told me about that website, Shadow Seekers. That he and Dakota had been trying to nail this bastard. For me. Me and Miriam."

"I didn't know either. Not until a couple of weeks ago when Boyd found me and told me what they'd been up to."

Martha finally acquiesces, moving her walker aside to let me in. But I feel her eyes boring into me. I imagine she must be looking for a sign. The mark of the devil. To confirm I'm Satan's spawn. "So that man on the news, Victor Krandel . . . he's your father?"

"He is." I think of all the things I could add. *We're estranged; I don't really know him; I wish he wasn't.*

But her gaze flits to the television, distracted, and mine follows. Five rows of photographs—smiles and bright eyes, ponytails and freckles—fill the screen. The seventeen victims. "Do you think he—?"

"Doctor Roark?" Boyd emerges from the basement. But it may as well be a grave. His skin is pale, his eyes murky pools of brown. He lingers near the sofa, running a hand along its plastic cover. "I—I don't know what to say. I'm sorry about . . ." He waves toward the television, the photographs. ". . . your dad getting arrested."

"Can we talk?" I ask him, peering into the space over Martha's shoulder. "In private."

He nods, and I trail him to the Overbridge. My clipped, determined walk following close behind those shuffling slippers.

Just before I descend the stairs, I glance back at Martha. Her face is a magic mirror. It shows me the past. Who I used to be. Because only a mother with someone to lose can look that worried.

****

Boyd paces in front of his whiteboard, the movie posters unfastened and dangling toward the floor. He'd put a large red *X* through all his suspects. At the bottom, in that same angry-red marker, he'd written: *Victor Krandel*. So he's sure then.

"You really think he did it?" I ask. The shock of it still raw as a cold-clock to the face. "He killed Dakota? And Miriam? And the others?"

"Well, the timeline matches up. He lives near the southeastern edge of the lake. He knew the area. He was in the military. The stuff they're saying about him . . . Anyway, it doesn't matter what I say. You knew him best."

The reel in my head unwinds, and I see my father telling ghost stories in the light of a Badlands campfire. Hunched over a rust bucket, wrench in hand. Aiming the barrel of his rifle. Drowning his sorrows in a can of Olde English. Cursing Charlie. Screaming bloody murder at me.

And rumbling up to the junkyard in his pickup with Roscoe, Waggles, Rex, riding shotgun.

Found another pup, Mol, he'd always say. *What are ya gonna call 'em?*

"Yeah. I guess I did."

I walk to Yoda's enclosure. She lies there, lethargic, a lump in the center of her belly. Where I'm certain some small rodent has met its end.

"Has Yoda ever escaped?" I ask.

"That's what you want to talk about?"

"Well, has she?"

"I figured you'd find out," he says. For a moment, I gape at him, confused. "About Yoda escaping. The cops picking me up. Yeah, it

359

happened. I was still working full time at the reptile store back then. They called me to cover a shift, and I forgot to lock her enclosure. When I came home that night, she'd disappeared. Just like the real Yoda in *Return of the Jedi*."

"And you coincidentally went looking for her in the bushes beneath a girl's window? In a neighborhood with a Peeping Tom? Sounds pretty unfortunate."

"I never said I was the luckiest guy on the planet." Boyd holds out his disfigured arm, half of his mouth lifting in an ironic smile. "Obviously."

I don't feel sorry for him. Because I know all about being unlucky. After the cops had linked Dakota's murder to the Shadow Man, I'd dragged myself out of bed in the middle of another sleepless night and typed a question into my computer's search bar, waiting wide-eyed for it to tell me exactly how unlucky I'd been. A silly pop psych article had provided the data, and I'd counted the zeroes. Three of them. As in, my daughter had a .00039% chance of being the victim of a serial killer. So yeah, unlucky.

"How did Yoda get out of the basement? To a house three blocks away?"

"I'm no expert, but I would surmise she slithered."

Yoda lifts her head, tasting the air with her forked tongue. If only I could speak snake, I'd ask her what happened. The same way I'd ask Gus to tell me about the day Dakota ran away. The day I'd driven her away with my lunacy, just like my father had done to me. Not that it matters. None of it matters now. The futility of it all is like gasoline to my lit match. The one that's always slow-burning at the heart of me.

"Cut the sarcasm, Boyd. I don't buy it."

"This isn't about Yoda. So why don't you go ahead and ask me what you really want to?" But his face tells another story. That my asking him the real questions is scary as hell.

"Did you hurt Dakota?"

"No."

360

"Were you attracted to her?"

He swallows hard, his Adam's apple moving beneath his neck like the prey in Yoda's stomach. "She was a pretty girl."

With a growl Gus would be proud of, I start toward him.

"Fine. *Yes*. I was. But I never touched her. Not like what you're thinking."

"You flirted with her though. I read your posts on the main page."

"She flirted back. It was harmless. I'm not like that. I promise. I'm just . . ." He spreads his long arms as wide as he can manage, nothing but a sad basement between them. "Lonely."

I glare at him, wishing I'd brought the bayonet.

"I want to see your messages. The ones she sent you."

Another strenuous swallow, but he shuffles to his computer anyway. He navigates the Shadow Seekers main page and logs in to Shadow Snoops, his hands shaking. Twice, he enters the wrong password.

"Sorry," he says. "I'm nervous."

"You should be."

Welcome, Chewie.

Your last login was October 8, 2018 11:35 p.m.

He opens his inbox and takes an audible breath. So do I. Because there's a folder called DAKOTA and a string of twenty or thirty messages inside.

"Give me a minute," I say, motioning him out of the seat. "But don't go far."

I move methodically through the bulk of them, reading and emailing each one to myself. The last outgoing messages, three of them, are timestamped at 6:30 p.m. August 16.

"What were you apologizing about?" I ask him.

"We had an argument about what to do next. After we'd found the dog license info."

"And she never responded?"

He shakes his head.

"What's this one?"

My heart scampers into the tall grass, shivering there as I click on the final message in the folder, addressed to DocSherlock.

Hi Doc,

I need your advice. I think I messed up with Birdie. And just when we were on to something big. What should I do?

Chewie

DocSherlock had responded a few minutes later.

An apology is a good place to start. But from one Shadow Snoop to another . . . any hints?

Boyd had written just one word in reply.

Dogs.

"That's all of them," he says. "I never heard from Dakota again."

I pretend to study the screen, trying to still myself. To think. "What about DocSherlock? Did you tell him anything else about what you and Dakota were on to?"

"No. I swear. I told you that I dropped off the site completely. I didn't want to be part of it anymore."

"When?"

"A little while after I went to Whitetails and Whoppers. I canvassed all of Allendale."

Boyd's wearing the carpet down to nothing. He's easier to read than any patient I've ever had.

"You just gave up. After all that. Why?"

He shrugs, his shoulders trembling.

"I got a message."

"On the site?"

"Yeah. A threatening one. It showed up in my inbox, along with a picture of my mom on the sofa. Whoever sent it had taken the photo through the window. And knew stuff about me . . . how old I was. Dakota's age too."

"What did the message say?"

"Let Dakota go. Or else. That was the gist of it. That and get off the site and don't go to the cops. I deleted it and tried to move on. For a while, I thought it might be from you. But the name didn't make sense. Now, it sorta does."

"The name?"

Boyd stops in front of the whiteboard and points to my father's name.

"MQKlinger."

****

Boyd didn't flinch when I'd told him I still had the bayonet. "I know where to find you," I'd hissed. Like a bad actor playing a Mafia hitman.

He'd only shrugged, resigned. "I hope you get the answers you need. I want them too."

I crank up the radio and lose myself in the shred of the electric guitar until I take the turn for home. I should've known. My fifteen minutes of infamy starts now.

The media vans are stacked two-deep on Ridgecrest, and if it wasn't for Gus, I'd drive right by and keep going. Pretend to be someone else.

Shielding my face with one hand, I continue past the turn for home, past the hoard of cameras watching me with their giant eyes, until I reach the sign for Roark Psychology Services. I figure now is as good a time as any to make my first pilgrimage across that fancy quarry stone.

I take the turn and hit the gas, nearly sideswiping a reporter with a NVMX station microphone. He stumbles back to the ditch and yells at me as the gravel makes a satisfying crunch beneath my tires.

"Doctor Roark, is your dad Shadow Man? How do you feel about the cops cutting him loose?"

It figures he's out. Cole told me they might not have enough to charge him.

"Were you in on it?"

My heart lurches when I slam on the brakes and jerk the gear into reverse.

They want a show? I'll give them a show.

"Hey!" I call out, waiting for the man to circle back with his microphone. A NVMX camera man swoops in after him. The two of them come at me like vultures on roadkill. Which is why it gives me the utmost satisfaction to raise my middle finger to the camera and tell them exactly where to shove their van, their microphone, their camera, and especially their goddamn moronic questions.

BEFORE

365

CHAPTER THIRTY

DAKOTA had a mission. In her mind, she'd named it O.P.B. *Operation Poke the Bear.* The bear in question, her mother. The poke, the temporary tattoo on her shoulder. Though she knew when her mother spotted it, as real as it looked, it would feel more like a steel-toed boot to the gut. But her mother deserved it. Because she had taken off work to accompany her dad to D-day, the board meeting at Seattle Children's to decide his fate. She actually had the nerve to ask Dakota to come along.

"You can wait outside the boardroom, honey," her mom had told her yesterday afternoon, after Dakota had bicycled back from the spot where Grandpa Krandel had dropped her off.

"Then why do I have to go at all?"

"Your father's attorney thinks it will make a difference. Please just do it for me and don't argue."

Dakota had decided, even as she'd nodded at her mother, avoiding her eyes. O.P.B. was a go.

The mission parameters were simple.

Time: This morning. The board would convene at 10 a.m., and they were set to leave for the hospital an hour before.

Place: The kitchen. She'd peeked downstairs. Both of her parents sat at the table, not speaking, per the usual.

Gear: A tasteful black skirt. And the perfect sleeveless blouse. Hannah had given it to Dakota for her birthday last year, telling her the royal blue accented her eyes. *Whatever.* What really mattered was it covered the tattoo completely until she extended her arm, revealing the tiny black cage on her shoulder.

Dakota folded a sweater across her arm, tucked her copy of *Silence of the Lambs* in her backpack, and glided down the stairs, as if she really did have wings.

Her father looked up from his sesame bagel. "You look nice. Very professional."

She took the seat to the left of her mother, a strategic position, fighting the urge to roll her eyes. To say something sarcastic. *Lucky for me, Hannah did a special episode on what-to-wear-to-your-dad's-misconduct-hearing*, for example. She smiled to herself and put a lid on it. O.P.B. wouldn't have the same impact if her parents were already fuming.

"Thanks, Dad. Are you nervous about today?"

"A little. But we're confident the truth will prevail."

Her mother didn't seem all that confident, even in her navy suit, which she wore every time she had to testify in court about some crazy patient needing to be forcibly medicated. When Dakota spotted the Tiffany necklace that she and her father had picked out only a few months ago, her chest ached.

"Hurry up and eat something," her mother said. "There's traffic, and we don't want to be rushed."

Dakota steeled herself. *Go time.*

She made a show of reaching for the last wheat bagel, certain her mother would spot her ink. But she'd already stood up from the table with her coffee cup and walked to the counter. Dakota watched as her mother emptied the rest of the cup into a thermos and topped it off with a generous splash of Bailey's liqueur left over from Christmas.

If her father noticed, he kept his mouth shut. Which was apparently the new normal for the Drs. Roark. Her mom let him get away with being a cheating slimeball, and he looked the other way while she drank like a fish.

Dakota took a few bites, washing her anger down with a swig of orange juice.

Time for Plan B. Every mission worth its salt had one.

"Mom, can you help with this top? I think there's a thread dangling back here." But just as her mother approached from behind, her father tugged at the thread she'd loosened that morning with a strategically placed safety pin.

"Got it," he told Dakota, giving her a smug pat on her non-inked shoulder. "See, your old dad's not so useless."

Her mother turned away and headed for the door, slinging the Louie over her shoulder like a weapon. Dakota joined her in the foyer, rethinking the whole mission. After all, when you really got down to it, she was all her mom had now. Well, her and the alcohol.

"Ladies first."

Her dad held the door open, and Gus bounded toward it. Without thinking, Dakota reached for him, snagging him by the collar just as he'd reached the threshold.

Behind her, her mother gasped. Not the sound of a poked bear but a wounded one. It didn't satisfy her the way she'd hoped. It saddened her.

"What's that?" her mother demanded, spinning Dakota around by her arm. "Where did you—"

"Mom, it's just—"

"Holy shit." Her father gaped at her, practically awestruck. She took her pleasure where she could. "Who did that to you?"

Dakota shrugged. "Some guy."

"When?" He leaned in closer, inspecting it. "It's not even red anymore."

"A few days ago, I guess. But hey, at least you guys can feel good about sending me away now. I'm a real rebel."

Red-faced, her mother stormed down the steps, hard-stopping at the bottom. O.P.B. had an expected outcome, and this was the moment Dakota had anticipated. The toss of the grenade. Her mom would yell at her to go to her room or tell her she was grounded. Maybe even charge back up the stairs and slap her across the face with a bearlike paw. Then, tonight, they'd cry about it together, and Dakota would confess. *It's fake, Mom.*

"Cole, deal with her. I can't even stand to look at her right now."

Leave it to her mother to toss a live grenade right back.

****

Dakota stayed in her room, where she'd been exiled by her father sans laptop and cell phone, which he'd locked in the bedroom safe. At least she couldn't read the comments on her photo, which had spread like a virus over the weekend. Instead, she huddled under the covers with Gus and Clarice Starling.

Even after she heard her parents come home. Especially then.

Because the board had decided in her father's favor, reinstating his pay. Hannah's mom had publicly rescinded the allegations against him. Well, her lawyer had, anyway. Dakota had watched the whole thing go down on the noon NVMX news broadcast.

My client wishes to retract the allegations of sexual harassment against Doctor Cole Roark and will not be pursuing legal or financial reparations.

369

We will be giving no further statement at this time.

She didn't know exactly what it meant. Only that it wasn't good. Because her mom kept yelling things like, "You paid her off, didn't you?" and "Is she your whore now?"

Her dad fired back the same old lines. "She told the truth. Nothing happened."

When the voices downstairs built to a crescendo—she barely recognized them anymore—something crashed against the hardwood. A door slammed. And Gus whimpered at her side.

Dakota couldn't focus. She tucked a Post-it between the pages, marking chapter three, knowing she'd have plenty of time at Starry Sky to get to know Hannibal Lecter.

CHAPTER THIRTY-ONE

DAKOTA spent the morning on her hands and knees. Someone had to do it. Otherwise, Gus would step on the glass shards and cut his paw pads. She swept the big pieces of the broken vase into the dustpan and used a wet towel to collect the slivers.

The Mercedes was gone, and her mom lay on the sofa, out cold and late for work. Dakota found the bottle of Baileys in the trash can, along with two mini-bottles of vodka, discarded beneath the coffee table.

She couldn't explain it, but seeing her mother slack-jawed and drooling and still wearing yesterday's clothes hurt worse than all of it. The affair, Starry Sky, even Tyler's stupid photo. It made her feel reckless. Like nothing counted anymore. Even being grounded.

She tore out of the drive on her bike and pedaled in a fury, her legs churning like a runaway machine. Leaving it all behind her, she headed for the library and took up her usual position at Storybook Corner.

Ten minutes of searching the internet and one local call on the library's free phone service, she'd found what she needed in Allendale. But she couldn't get there on her own. And she'd read too much about Ted Bundy to hitchhike.

She logged on to the Shadow Snoops forum and typed a public post. She'd give it ten minutes. Let the universe decide.

Cagedbird18: *There will come soft rains.*

She took a deep breath and held it, listening to the clock hanging near the circulation desk. She focused on the pain, the ache in her lungs. The way it made her feel alive. Eighty-three seconds later, eighty-three ticks, the universe decided.

Chewie: *Cryptic, Birdie.*

Cagedbird18: *I'll DM you.*

****

Boyd rambled nonstop on the drive to the warehouse. About the weather. *Wookiees aren't built for summer.* About Yoda's last meal. *Two frozen mice.* About the appropriate viewing order of the *Star Wars* series. *Chronological, obviously, and anybody who says to watch according to the release date is a heathen.* About the matching baseball caps he'd brought. *So we can go undercover, Lisa Ling style.* About anything but the last time they'd seen each other.

"Are you sure this is the place?" he asked as Dakota directed him into the parking lot. Empty, save for one beaten-up white van. The warehouse looked no better. Half its windows were boarded or broken or graffitied with spray paint.

She nodded, tucking her hair up into the black *Star Wars* hat. "Jeffrey said he'd meet us here at eleven. That's probably his."

"You mean that serial-killer van? *Great.*"

"Says the guy with the VW bug."

"At least my name isn't Ted. His is Jeffrey. As in *Dahmer*."

Dakota rolled her eyes at him, laughing. "Jeffrey Dahmer drove a blue van. Plus, he's dead. So I think we're safe."

But as they made their pilgrimage across the desert-hot pavement, Dakota's mind played tricks.

A face peeked out of a third-story window. *Just a shadow.*

Blood spotted the concrete. *Only paint drippings.*

A chainsaw buzzed from behind the dumpster. Probably Jeffrey waiting to take their heads.

"Do you hear that?" Boyd asked.

The high-pitched hum made her queasy.

As they drew nearer the door, Dakota located the source of the buzzing. Not Jeffrey after all. But flies. A swarm of them. She inched closer to Boyd.

They both leaned their heads, peering around the dumpster into the shadowy space where the sun didn't reach. Gristle and fur and a tiny skull. A horrible rotten stench. That's what was left of whatever had died there.

"Howdy, folks!"

Dakota stumbled back, bumping into Boyd's chest. His hands latched onto her arms and righted her, then lingered until she pulled away.

"I'm Jeffrey. And you must be Birdie."

She nodded and spoke a shaky *yes* over the drumbeat of her heart.

"This is my friend, Chewie." Her voice sounded better now. Steady.

"Sorry about the smell, guys. This little bugger—I'm thinkin' it's a squirrel—got himself trapped in the dumpster. Raccoons probably drug him out. They'll eat anything, you know."

Boyd elbowed Dakota, widening his eyes at her. "I didn't catch your last name," he said.

Jeffrey pointed to the badge hanging on a lanyard around his neck: SOLANO COUNTY, SHERIFF'S OFFICE, ANIMAL CARE RECORDS DIVISION, JEFFREY GOODFELLOW.

"Jeffrey *Goodfellow*, huh? As in good fellow." Boyd chuckled. "That's convenient."

****

Beads of sweat dotted the back of Boyd's neck like angry blisters. Dakota watched them fall into the collar of his T-shirt, leaving a wet spot down the back.

"I feel like I've lost ten pounds," he said. Wiping his forehead, he sifted through the last banker's box of records Jeffrey had pulled for them, marked 1990 A-G.

"Gunderson, Gustafsson, Gutierrez, Guttuso."

"Guzman!" They both shouted, their voices echoing eerily against the unfinished concrete walls. Jeffrey looked up from his desk, studying them for a moment—*blink, blink, blink*—before lowering his head back to his book.

"Seriously," Boyd whispered. "You don't think he's a little creepy?"

She put a finger to her lips and pointed to the file in Boyd's lap, trying not to think about Jeffrey and his reptile eyes and his well-worn paperback book. Which just happened to be a Stephen King.

"Maybe a little," she admitted, studying the Guzman's dog license application and jotting the details in her notebook.

Owner: Raul Guzman
Dog Name: Blondie
Breed: Golden Retriever
Adopted from Solano County SPCA: May 15, 1990

"Unbelievable," Boyd said. "Five of them. All adopted at the SPCA."

Dakota laid the file facedown on the copy machine, listening to its soft mechanical whir. "What do you think it means?"

"Sounds like you two are on the way to solving your caper."

Dakota jumped at Jeffrey's voice, calm as still water and suddenly right over her shoulder.

"No caper. Just a class project." Boyd took the folder from Dakota's hand and returned it to the box, affixing the dusty lid atop it.

"Right. A class project." Jeffrey twisted his mouth at them, taking a pointed glance at Dakota's notebook. SHADOW MAN INVESTIGATION printed in big block letters across the front. "I'll bet Birdie and Cheesy are your real names too."

"Chewie," Boyd corrected, with a crooked smirk.

"You know," Jeffrey said, stroking the yellowed pages of *Cujo*. "I always thought Shadow Man probably had a family or something. That's why he stopped. Or hey, who knows, he might've just passed the family business on to his kids. Maybe even his son."

****

Dakota couldn't stop laughing. She laughed so hard her stomach hurt and the tightness in her chest unwound. They'd run from the warehouse and Creepy Jeffrey, past the rotting squirrel carcass and across the pavement desert, and flung themselves, breathless, into the VW.

Boyd fired it up, just as Jeffrey emerged from the warehouse, waving at them, as if he really was a perfectly good fellow. They sped away, their giggles picking up steam as they drove.

"I don't want to go back yet," Dakota said, after their laughter had subsided. So Boyd took the exit for Glory Hole and parked at the overlook.

Dakota leaned against the railing and into the cool breeze, listening to the rush of water below. The last time she'd come here with her parents she'd done the same, savoring the magic of the place. Until her mom had pulled her back, worried. Like she might fall in and disappear forever into the swirling water.

When Boyd joined her there, letting out a howl into the wind, she started talking, unloading it all on him. The entire awful summer and more.

The stairs that led down to Hannah's basement and the end of the world as she knew it.

The first time her mother slapped her face.

The letter she'd mailed to Grandpa Krandel. And their trip to Allendale.

The worst birthday ever.

Even the fake tattoo that looked real.

Dakota decided Boyd listened better than any boy she'd ever met. But he had that look again, and it made her nervous. She wished he wouldn't do that.

"Can I see your tattoo?"

She didn't know how to say no, not without making him feel bad, so she pulled her T-shirt down over her shoulder. She flinched when he touched her, moving just out of his reach.

"I like it. It's totally you."

Her stomach roiled like the water below, but he seemed not to notice.

"I had fun today," he said.

"Me too."

"I like spending time with you."

She nodded.

"Do you like me?"

The question seemed impossible.

"I know I'm not that great looking, but you did say I wasn't ugly."

"You're not, but—"

"Is it the burns? They freak you out, don't they?"

The breeze turned to a sudden, whipping wind, burning Dakota's eyes till they watered. Scattering the magic of Glory Hole like the puff of a dandelion.

"I thought we were trying to solve this case. You know, Shadow Man? Crazed serial killer who murdered your aunt."

"Of course, we are." He twittered. "We're the dynamic duo."

"Well, it seems like you're . . . distracted. You're acting strange."

He sighed. And she had the sudden urge to wallop him. To hit harder than her mother ever had.

"You know the odds of us ID'ing Shadow Man are astronomical, don't you? I mean, you're fifteen and I'm a loser who lives in my mom's basement."

"So what are we doing then?"

"I thought we were hanging out, having fun together. You trust me, right? I know you do. You just told me all that stuff."

Dakota turned away from him. The car sat waiting to swallow her, to carry her wherever he wanted to go. The only witnesses here were the distant sycamores, waving to her the way Jeffrey had, yielding their bodies to the wind.

"Take me back to the library."

She felt ashamed when he hung his head. Because this was her fault. She'd been the one to let the universe decide.

"Okay," he said.

Halfway back to Napa, he started to speak. To say something about Shadow Man and the dogs and what they'd do next.

"Don't worry about it," she said. "I'll find Shadow Man without you."

AFTER

389

CHAPTER THIRTY-TWO

"SEE you in a bit," Sawyer says, taking a seat in one of the stiff-backed chairs in the lobby of the Sheriff's Office. I must look worried, because he squeezes my hand.

"Are you sure you don't have to get back to work?" I ask.

"The Blue Rose can survive a few hours without Grant Sawyer." Which is more than I can say. "I'll be here manning the extraction point. Ready for a counterattack if necessary."

Feeling lighter, I follow Detective Sharpe turn after turn, down a long, cold hallway. A circuitous route that seems designed to disorient me, though I have nothing to hide.

"So how have you been?" he asks. I'm grateful for the distraction. Because the click of his loafered heels against the tile unnerves me. Like a bomb counting down to explosion.

"Better. Now that the media vultures have scattered. Thanks for that, by the way."

After my unfortunate run-in with the NVMX reporter had been broadcast on every news station from here to China, Detective Sharpe had shown up in my driveway, threatening to arrest any remaining members of the media for harassment. *Have some respect. The woman's been through hell. She's hanging by a thread.* His words exactly. I'd heard him through the door, replayed them a hundred times. Deemed them absolutely true.

"No problem. I've got no patience for the way they feast on pain. It's inhuman."

I see myself, a cadaver, bisected and splayed down the middle. If they opened me up, I'd be hollow as a husk. All the good parts sucked away.

Detective Sharpe opens one of the nondescript doors lining the hallway and ushers me into a sparse interview room. One table. Two plastic chairs. It reminds me of Napa State. Even my office had been bare. Because furniture can be a deadly weapon.

I wait for him to speak. This is how my patients felt. Sized up by someone who holds all the cards.

"Have you heard from your father?"

"No. We're not exactly on speaking terms. I don't think he has my number. And he certainly doesn't own a cell phone."

"He said as much when we asked him." *See what I mean.* Holds all the cards. "He had a lot to say about you, though."

I'm not sure how to take that, so I don't. I just let it sit there between us.

"He feels bad about the way you grew up. The things you had to deal with."

My throat feels tight, but I shrug at him like it doesn't matter.

"It sounds like he had a pretty rough go of it himself."

"Is there a question here?" I hate the way my voice croaks.

"Wendall Grady." I'm certain I flinch. "Ever heard of him?"

"Not until last week when I read my father's sworn testimony before the Army C.I.D." The Wendall I know—lanky legs spread wide on my scornful sofa, black hat perched on his knee—is my secret to keep. Our sessions are confidential unless and until I decide otherwise. And right now, it feels like an ace in the hole I need to hold on to.

"So your father never mentioned him? You never met the guy?"

"I can't say for certain. There's a fair bit of my childhood I don't remember all that well." Except for the things I do. Those are more than enough.

Detective Sharpe makes a few scribbles in his notepad. If it's anything like the one I'd used, he's jotting words like *certifiable* and *kooky* and *unhinged.*

"What if I told you he worked at Napa State for a while as an orderly?"

I shrug off the fiery sting, the electrical prod to my heart. It goes with the territory of being caught in a lie to a detective. "There were a lot of orderlies, psych techs, nurses. It's possible."

"Those dogs you told me about, the ones you said matched up to Shadow Man's victims, where did your dad get those from?"

"I told you. He found them. Or that's what he said. Did he admit that at least?"

"He admitted you had those dogs. Confirmed your story exactly. Except . . ." Detective Sharpe leans forward, and so do I. "He said those dogs came from his old war buddy, Wendall Grady. That the guy volunteered at a shelter and smuggled out some of the dogs they were about to put down. Your dad didn't want to get Wendall in trouble, so he lied about where they came from. And he admitted to touching that collar, the one that belonged to Blondie. He said Wendall showed up with the dog outside of Mol's, and he refused to take her. Had a heck of a time getting her back in Wendall's car, though. He claims he never saw the dog again."

My thoughts pinball from Wendall to Dad to Wendall and back again. Sweat dampens my armpits, and suddenly the room that had been meat-locker cold is as stuffy and airless as a coffin. "If he's such good buddies with Wendall, why did he testify against him?"

Detective Sharpe nods sagely. As if all those cards he's holding reveal to him the secrets of the universe. "You tell me. You're the shrink."

I put my head in my hands, trying to fit pieces of a mixed-up puzzle. "Can you tell me what he said about Dakota?"

"Just that he cared for her. She visited him a few times, and they went out to the shed together once. The lab confirmed her prints were in the shed, and it was her hair you found. Of course, your father denies hurting her."

Hurting her. I repeat those words in my mind. Nice of Detective Sharpe to sugarcoat it.

"And you believe him? What if he runs?"

"We have to follow the evidence, Mollie. Belief is the least of it. I know it's hard, but I need you to steer clear of your dad for a while. Let us finish our investigation. We've got patrol watching Mol's round the clock."

"How can I just do nothing?" I have the urge to scream, to howl. To take my plastic chair and hurl it at someone. Anyone.

He looks at me and his eyes soften.

"There's something else I think you should know," he says, before leading me back to the world that I once believed I could control. The world I claimed to understand. The world that spit in my face and stole my daughter. "Your father begged us to keep him here. He's scared to death of Wendall Grady."

****

I call Cole on the drive back home to fill him in. Only because Sawyer tells me to. I have to summon the energy to explain it all.

"Where is this Wendall guy?" He sounds like he's gritting his teeth. "I'd like to pay him a visit."

"Detective Sharpe says he's pretty sick. Apparently, not well enough to leave his house anymore. He has a nurse."

"Well, have they talked to him? Jesus, Mollie. What if he dies?"

He's thinking what I'm thinking. We may never know. We'd turn into one of *those* families. Suspended in time. Our lives forever orbiting around the unknown.

Sawyer nudges me with his elbow. "You should tell him about the therapy," he loud-whispers.

"What therapy?"

I answer Cole with a groan. "Just come over to the house. I'll explain everything."

Sawyer parks in the driveway, and we sit on the steps, waiting for Cole. He puts his good arm around my shoulders, and I let myself lean in to him.

"I don't understand," I say, thinking of my father.

"Which part?"

"All of it. The harm he's done. He murdered that girl in Vietnam. Of all the things I'd heard about at Napa State—shootings, stabbings, rapes—I'd never heard anything like that."

"We don't know what happened over there. The fog of war is real shit. Especially in Vietnam. Hell, I'd go back to Afghanistan in a heartbeat before I'd want to be in those jungles. The first thing you learn in basic training is to follow orders. Obedience to something bigger than yourself. And to somebody with more bars and stripes on his uniform. For your dad, that was Wendall. For better or for a lot fucking worse."

****

The three of us are in my real office, examining the suspect wall.

Cole had gone straight for his picture, ripping it down without a word. He'd balled it in his hand and tossed it across the room into the corner. Where it still sat.

I'd taken Tyler's off too. Even though Luciana had sent me a link to an interview he'd done with some trash tabloid yesterday, telling them he'd met Dakota's grandfather. *The guy had killer eyes.* And that he'd never get over losing her, the love of his life. *Like, so far.*

That left Boyd and Victor and the Post-it where I'd scrawled *Wendall Grady/DocSherlock.*

Cole chews on the end of a pen. "So you're saying this guy, Wendall, worked at Napa State as an orderly for a while. He knew your dad. He started a goddamned Shadow Man website. And he just happens to show up to unburden himself in therapy and implicates Victor. I think we've got our man."

"What about the DNA?" I ask. "And the hair. You wouldn't dare argue with that. It's science."

Sawyer's eyes ping-pong between the two of us. "Do you believe your father is capable of killing Dakota?"

"He's right, Mol. Your dad's a nut, but c'mon."

"Really, Cole? On Monday, you were ready to execute him yourself. Now you're defending him?"

"That was before I knew about Wendall."

"Which I suppose is my fault too?"

"Well, yeah. Actually, it is."

Sawyer clears his throat. "I've got an idea. How 'bout we call a momentary truce and go pay Wendall another home visit?"

I'm already halfway out the door when I hear Cole.

"Another?"

✳✳✳✳

Cole heads up the sidewalk toward Wendall's house; Sawyer and I watch from the Jeep.

Cole is playing catch-up. Trying to make up for abandoning me here with my billboard and my suspect wall. My guilt too, and the unhealthy need to drown it in vodka.

Still, I want to be the one standing there, knocking. The one pushing my way past the stocky gray-haired woman who's appeared at the door.

"That must be Wendall's nurse," Sawyer says.

After a brief conversation, Cole turns around and shrugs. Like he's giving up.

Without a word, I bolt from the car and jog across the street before Sawyer can stop me. He calls after me, but I don't slow down. If anything, I run faster.

The nurse widens her eyes at me as I approach, huffing. I imagine I look scary, desperate. But I'm used to it now. *Sorry, Betty.* A clip-on name tag tells me to whom I should direct my silent apology. And my audible demands. "We really need to talk to Wendall, Betty."

"I'm sorry, but as I explained to your . . ."

Cole and I disagree, out loud, over each other. The story of our marriage.

"Ex-husband."

"Friend."

Nurse Betty presses her lips together in a thin pink line of defense against her judgments. But they find their way out regardless in the raise of her eyebrows. "As I said to this gentleman, Mr. Grady left about thirty minutes ago for a drive. I was about to head out myself. Grab some dinner. Lucky you caught me."

"A drive? I thought he was too sick to leave the house."

She shrugs. "I don't ask any questions. He's not the easiest fella to get along with, but the agency pays triple, and I fit the criteria, so I deal with it."

"Triple, huh?" Cole asks, incredulous. Meanwhile, I'm wondering if I should rethink a career as a home health nurse. "I imagine it's your extensive experience they value. Your bedside manner."

Betty's cheeks flush, and she makes a show of looking for an imaginary spy listening in on our conversation. The orange tabby cat is the only soul in sight, pressing his luck by tracking a grasshopper under Wendall's manicured bushes.

"Now don't go sharing this around, but Mr. Grady has had a few complaints against him in the past. He can be a tad demanding. There's not many of us left willing to deal with his shenanigans."

She winks at Cole. He's not half bad at this.

"So are you folks with the army too?"

Cole stammers—apparently his lying skills took a nosedive since we'd split—as Sawyer steps from behind me and shakes Betty's stubby hand. She teeters on the edge of swooning.

"Lieutenant Grant Sawyer, Army Rangers. You said my colleagues already stopped by?"

"I don't believe they were with the Rangers. But they left a business card. Come on in, and I'll find it for you." She motions us inside and disappears down the hallway, her cheery voice carrying. ". . . said they need to speak with Wendall urgently. I can't imagine why you're all still so interested in him. What with his dishonorable discharge a couple years back. His rank-stripping. That really set him off, the poor guy. It's none of my business, but what does it matter anyway what happened over there? It's all water under the bridge now."

I'm glad she can't see my face. The shock there. The outrage. The overwhelming desire to smack her skull against the wall. Because it would blow our thin story to smithereens.

By the time Betty returns to the living room, I pull it together enough to stand upright with my mouth closed like a good army flunky.

"Found it," she says, aiming her smile at Sawyer. "United States Army Criminal Investigation Command, Special Agent Bo Watley. An unpleasant fella. Real pushy. Cold as ice. You know the type."

"I do indeed." Sawyer examines the card with a faint smirk. "Unfortunately, sociopaths do make better soldiers."

"What happened to your arm?" Betty asks, extending a tentative hand toward Sawyer's prosthetic. Behind her, Cole circles Wendall's bag of medicines on the table, positioning himself for a better view. I spot his walker folded in the corner.

"Somebody whacked it off." Sawyer makes the sound of a blade slicing the air.

"Oh, my goodness. Were you held captive over there? A POW? Afghanistan? Iraq?"

"Vegas," he deadpans. "I lost a bet."

Betty's eyes widen, threatening to pop, until Sawyer laughs. "I'm just kidding. IED explosion, ma'am. Nothing glamorous. We appreciate your time today. I'll let Agent Watley know we stopped by."

Sawyer and Cole are already halfway back to the Jeep, but I linger at the door, unable to let go. "You said Mr. Grady went for a drive. Do you know where he went?"

Betty waves off the question before wielding her own axe. Half my heart lobbed off in two robust chops.

"Oh, some place up in Allendale, I believe. He's got a war buddy living there."

****

The only heavy metal on this drive is my lead foot on the accelerator. I don't let up until we're on the freeway and halfway to Mol's. Even then, it's just until the car in front of us mercifully glides into the right lane, the Jeep breathing down its bumper like a rabid wolf.

I'd said only what I needed to. Where we were going and why.

To my surprise, no one had argued. Meaning Cole, of course. In fact, he'd agreed my father might be in trouble. Because none of Wendall's medications suggested lung cancer. Organizing pneumonia, COPD, and vertigo seemed the worst of it.

And when Sawyer called CID, as we lashed down the highway fast as a whip, they'd said Wendall had been court-martialed and charged with two counts of murder related to war crimes in Vietnam.

I didn't tell them what Betty had said about Wendall's war buddy. How I felt *this* close to the answers I'd been chasing since the day Dakota stormed up the stairs, bleeding, and vanished from my life forever.

They wouldn't be able to see it. They wouldn't understand. In my lap, I held an empty box wrapped in shiny paper. A gift from the devil himself.

I'd started to hope.

CHAPTER THIRTY-THREE

DAKOTA lay in bed—she'd been awake and dressed for hours now—fingering the soapstone four-leaf clover her grandfather had given her for her birthday. After they'd left Bull's Body Art, he'd tucked it in her hand, along with a scrap of paper and his phone number, and closed her fingers around it with an affectionate pat.

"Seems like you need it more than me right now." He'd been right. Because when she'd finally made it home late yesterday afternoon, her mom had said nothing. Which could only mean one of two things: she'd been too hungover to care, or she'd been plotting Dakota's demise. The most horrible, truly awful, unfair punishment that her psychologist brain could conjure.

The knock on her door, measured but firm, turned Dakota's stomach. She tucked her grandfather's lucky charm into her pocket.

"Are you awake?" her father asked, without opening it. He was only being nice, softening the blows to come. It was nearly ten, and he wasn't at work yet.

"Yes."

"Come downstairs, please."

"Alright." Dread deepened her voice, weighed her down. So that every step felt like an effort.

Even Gus seemed subdued as he followed her into the lion's den, his tail dragging.

Her parents sat opposite each other, the coffee table between them. On it, smack-dab in the center, the worst thing she could have imagined. Her cell phone. Powered on and unlocked.

"Sit," her father directed.

Dakota could tell they had a plan. They never made plans anymore. Not like this. One where they'd teamed up against her. She couldn't decide whether to be furious or grateful.

"I don't even know where to start," he began.

"I do." Her mom stood up, tapped a few keys on Dakota's phone and held it out to her. "Explain this."

"It's not me. I mean, it's partly me. My face and all. But it's photoshopped."

"And this one?"

"I sent it to Tyler when we were dating. I begged him to delete it. I thought he had."

"So you're sending half-naked pictures to boys now? That's what you're doing? Did you have sex with him too?"

"No."

"I don't—*we don't*—trust you anymore." Her mom took another step toward her, looming over her now. So close, Dakota smelled the alcohol on her breath. Over her shoulder, Dakota searched out her father. But he seemed transfixed. Her mother's anger could do that. "That's not even the worst of it. *Ha!* I can't believe I'm saying that. That this is what it's come to."

Her mother fiddled with the phone again, cursing under her breath. She slammed it against the coffee table. Dakota winced when she saw the cracked screen.

"Mollie, calm down."

She spun around like she'd been lashed with a whip. "You don't get to tell me that, Cole. You haven't been here. Why do you think she's like this? Sneaking out, lying. Making me miss work. Letting me think she got a *real* tattoo. Embarrassing me on the phone with some guy named Bull. *Bull.* As if that's a reasonable name. He probably knows more about my own daughter than I do."

"I tried to tell you, Mom, but you—"

"But me, *nothing.* Your father and I have already decided. You're leaving early for Starry Sky. Go pack your shit."

"No."

"What did you say?"

"I'm not leaving. I'm not the one who needs help. Dad is having an affair with Hannah's mom. I can't believe you're too naive to see that. But it's as obvious as this tattoo. And you . . . you're just like Grandpa used to be. A total drunk."

Dakota saw it coming. She tried to duck. But some things are inevitable. Like the back of her mother's left hand—that big, meaningless diamond—against her cheek, harder than she'd ever felt it. So hard, she saw stars.

"What the hell, Mol!"

Her head buzzing, Dakota sprinted up the stairs to her room. Slammed the door. Locked it. She touched her fingers to her cheek. They came back wet and red and shaking.

Numb, she moved through the room on autopilot. If she stopped, if she thought, if she let herself feel anything at all, she'd start to cry. She couldn't afford to cry. Not now. Not yet.

She flung open her closet, her drawers. Grabbed her Grizzlies sweatshirt. A change of underwear.

She'd never run away before. But she stuffed her backpack with everything she didn't want her mother to find. Her Shadow Man notebook from under the mattress, Roscoe's collar from her rain boot.

Downstairs, World War who-knows-what-number had erupted. Dakota listened as the enemy combatants exchanged fire.

"She knows, Cole! Why can't you just be a man and admit it to her?"

"Because you told me not to tell her, goddammit. Then you haul off and hit her."

"She needs to learn some respect. Obviously, you're not teaching her."

"Like you are? Your dad hit you, right? Do you respect him?"

When the battle traveled up the stairs and into the master bedroom, Dakota slunk out, backpack on her shoulder. She tiptoed into the kitchen, shushing Gus, and stocked up on the essentials. Water and granola bars and a jumbo-sized bag of M&Ms.

"I can't believe you kissed that woman in front of our daughter. You destroyed her."

"Please. And you're perfect? I saw the way you looked at Peter Jacoby at the Fourth of July party. You're probably already fucking him, aren't you?"

Dakota cracked the door open and slipped out, barely shutting it behind her.

She never looked back. Not once.

****

Dakota pedaled faster than she ever had.

She'd already zipped down Ridgecrest and taken the dirt shortcut toward downtown, a narrow, bumpy trail that wound through the woods. With her slim street-bike tires, she usually avoided it. But it was the fastest route and the most secluded. She just wanted to be alone.

Huffing, she stopped at the edge of the trail. She laid her bike down and shrugged off her backpack, resting in the shade on a rotted stump. The bleeding had stopped, at least. She couldn't say the same for her tears, which kept flowing no matter how many times she told herself to stop.

Dakota closed her eyes and tried to think. One thought at a time. But they came in a rush, like demonic butterflies, each one intent on obliterating the other. So she gave up trying. Just sat there listening to the animals scurrying in the underbrush. But then it reminded her of Mol's. Of that angry rattler staked to the tree. Of her mother. The whack across her face. She couldn't sit still any longer.

Backpack in tow, she mounted her bike and rode toward the library.

****

At Storybook Corner, she logged on to Shadow Snoops. Three direct messages from Boyd.

I'm sorry.

So sorry.

Sorrier than the Dallas Morning News, circa 1977, when they forgot the second "e" in Wookiee.

A hollow laugh clunked from her throat. It felt raw, and her eyes welled again.

She reread Boyd's messages—all of them—from the very beginning. Then she deleted them one by one. She felt stupid for wanting to impress him. For thinking she could solve the Shadow Man case.

Well, it was over now.

Dakota logged out and studied her reflection in the screen, a bruise already forming on her cheek. At least her mom would have to look at it for a while. She gathered herself, the broken pieces, and headed for the exit.

When the door parted, a familiar face greeted her.

"Gus! What are you doing here?"

He stood there in the heat, his dripping tongue lolling at her. His tail swished like a windshield wiper against the ground.

"Did you sneak out behind me?"

She couldn't explain her relief. Only that his licking and tail wagging and dog smiling soothed something aching inside her. She knew what she had to do.

"Let's go home, buddy."

AFTER

CHAPTER THIRTY-FOUR

(FRIDAY, OCTOBER 12, 2018)

MY headlamps spotlight the fence line, and Cole's voice wavers.

"Are those squirrels?" he asks as I park the Jeep in the turnaround next to my father's pickup. There's no sign of the regular patrol Detective Sharpe had promised me. But Sawyer spots Wendall's empty Cadillac in the nearby tree cover, sitting smug as that black cowboy hat atop his head.

"Welcome to Mol's Junkyard, where we kill anything that moves."

Cole lets out a breath, shakes his head like he's trying to convince himself he's not dreaming.

"Jesus, Mollie. You grew up here?" He knows I did. So he may as well add *no wonder* or *that explains a lot.*

Sawyer cracks his door, letting in the familiar sounds of twilight, and I latch onto his prosthetic arm, suddenly wishing we could spin out, spitting gravel, as fast we came and leave this scrap heap forever.

But Luci was right. Cole too. I can't let go. I never will. Not until I stare down the truth, unblinking at its ugliness. Not until I know for certain what happened to my daughter.

"Be careful," I say. "The whole place is rigged. Assume everything is a trap." Because I'd once seen my dad rig a single punji pit in thirty minutes flat. Who knows what tricks he's managed to pull out of his camouflage sleeve in the last twenty-four hours?

"I thought the cops disabled all the—"

A distant *crack* pierces the stillness, silencing Sawyer mid-sentence. The birds take to the air, flecking the purple sky like confetti. I wait for them to settle in the grove of sycamores, but they keep flying until they vanish against the dark horizon.

Cole ducks behind the Jeep, wide-eyed. "Tell me that was engine backfire."

I shake my head.

"Fireworks?"

When my eyes meet Sawyer's, it's confirmation of what I already know. Because once you've heard the sound of gunfire, there's no mistaking it.

Stay here, Sawyer mouths, gesturing with is hand. Then whispers, "I'll check it out."

He points to the junkyard, to Dad's trailer rising up from the refuse like the Loch Ness Monster. But unlike that elusive creature, it hides nothing. Its homemade curtains splay open. Its lit windows look back at us, winking. The oddest part of all, the gate is unlocked. There's no mystery here, only an invitation that makes my stomach churn.

Sawyer slips inside the confines of my youth. The weeds, the beer cans, the lunacy. I'm still not sure how I made it out alive. But he moves like a soldier, careful and steady, arming himself with a rusty tire iron he retrieves from the bed of the burned-out jalopy. He turns back to us—*thumbs up*—before pressing on toward the perimeter of the trailer.

"We should call the cops," Cole whispers.

I nod. "Here. Use my phone. But do it quietly."

When Cole slinks inside the Jeep and out of sight, I gaze up at the sky. It's nearly dark, but the limbs of the sycamores wave to me, calling.

Certain the gunshot came from the grove, I run toward it.

****

When I reach the end of the fence line and skirt beneath it, it's as if I've awakened in my dream. In my past life. The one that lives inside me. That makes me who I am.

I'm chasing Roscoe again, his stubby legs galloping faster than they ever have. He's up ahead, dodging sycamores like enemy soldiers. I do my best to keep up. But it's nearly dark now, and the ground can't be trusted.

The trees are different tonight. They sense me coming. Their limbs part for me like lover's arms and gently push me forward. Until I see a faint glow escaping from between the shed's dilapidated planks, a swatch of light from beneath its doorframe.

The bowling ball has fallen to the ground, its wire severed under its weight. The mouth of the punji pit is open and waiting, uncovered. The way I'd left it. If I squint my eyes, let the dark play its tricks, I see Roscoe digging there, his white paws sullied with dirt.

"Who's in charge now, Grady?"

My father's voice booms from the tiny shed, threatening to blow it over. I cower in its wake but keep moving like a small, determined animal through the grass.

"You think you can come on my property? Sneak up on me? You're lower than a goddamned VC spy!"

I drop to my knees and crawl to the side of the shed. Press my eye to a dime-sized hole in the board where the woodworms have tunneled through. What I see, I hold in my throat, a silent scream.

Wendall's arms are rope-bound behind his back and strung up from a tool hook on the wall, his gaunt shoulders threatening to pop from their sockets under his weight. His feet, still clad in those snakeskin boots, are tied at the ankles. Above his eyebrow, a gash gapes open, a stream of blood coloring his eye red. And there's more blood spreading from a hole in his pant leg.

"Tell me what you were doin' out here, rummagin' around, before I make you wish Charlie had caught ya and given ya a one-way pass to the Hanoi Hilton."

Clad in his army fatigues, dog tags clinking round his neck. Crazy Krandel stalks in a circle around Wendall, his .22 in one hand and a riled-up gopher snake in the other, its head secured in a snake hook.

"Private Krandel." Wendall croaks, coughs, spits blood onto the dirt floor. "I came to apologize, soldier. They're takin' me away, court martial. Damn military police. It wasn't your fault, the things you did. The things *we* did. I wanted you to know."

My father lunges at Wendall, shaking the poor snake in his face, and Wendall screams, a sound so shrill, so pathetic, I cringe. He probably thinks it's a rattler.

"What were you doing with these, Grady? You tryin' to set me up?"

The board is flush against my forehead, the thin splinters pricking my skin. I know I'm not dreaming. But still. I must be.

My father holds up an old rucksack, emptying its contents in one fell swoop. Dog collars. Fifteen at least.

"I saw you. You were nosing around in here. With these. *Trixie. Buster.* Funny, those are some of the same damn dogs the cops were asking me about. I'd never heard of 'em."

My mouth is dry as dirt. My breath, suspended. Only my heart keeps going—it has to—thudding against my chest like the march of a wayward platoon. Headed for certain death.

"Mollie!"

I whip around to Cole, stumbling well off the trail in the darkness, and gesture to keep him quiet with one swift hand across my neck. He keeps coming, clumsy as a fawn, tromping through the underbrush.

Until he trips, cries out. A punji pit swallows him whole.

****

My father glares at me down the barrel of his rifle. Under his eyes, two streaks of black mud. His war paint. "What in tarnation are you doing here, Mol?"

The words gather strength in my throat until there's nothing to do but let them out.

"What are *you* doing? You've got a man strung up in there like some kind of prisoner of war."

"You bet I do. But he's not a man. He's a lying snake in the grass. And you're probably workin' with him, the way you ran outta here last time, accusin' me of things. You think I don't know you're the one who turned me in. Told the police I might've hurt Dakota. That I'm the goddamned Cloud Man."

"Shadow Man, Dad."

I give in to a fit of hysterical laughter, but when he nudges my cheek with the rifle's bore, I sober up fast. "Get up and get in there. Before I take you outta this world."

Casting a desperate glance at the spot where Cole disappeared, I step into the shed.

My father sets the lantern atop his footlocker, a circle of light stretching across the dirt floor. At its edges, I spot the gopher snake coiled in the shadows. Wendall's black hat discarded in the corner. The collars, scattered.

404

"Sit." My father directs me to the end of the trunk.

"I tried to warn you, Doc. Your daddy is one of them soldiers who didn't heal right. He's messed up in the head. Beyond savin'.'"

"Because of you," I say. "You made him do unspeakable things over there. How could he heal from that?"

"I'm real remorseful. It's the whole reason I came here. To say sorry. To try to help him, even though he's crazier than a June bug. Doc, you know you can't make nobody do nothin' they weren't born for. Ask your daddy how many pretty VCs he blew up over there. Ask him who shot your doggie, Roscoe."

My father points the rifle to the ceiling and fires a round, sending down a shower of splintered wood.

"Shut your pieholes. The both of you. I'm the one doing the talkin' here. The next round is goin' in your other knee." Under his breath, he mutters *Roscoe* as he turns his fiery gaze to me. "I did shoot that damn dog. Grady told me I had to. That the cops would see him in that picture in the newspaper. That they'd know he stole him from the shelter."

"Is that true?" I ask Wendall. "Did you tell him to shoot Roscoe? Did you bring those collars here to set him up?"

But he doesn't answer. His wide eyes trail the gopher snake slithering toward his boots. Like it's Charlie himself come to end him in the worst possible way.

He presses his lips together, shakes his head. "I'd never hurt a doggie. You know that, Doc. They say dogs are the best judge of a man's character. Your goldie, Gus, he liked me a whole bunch, didn't he?"

The scene replays in slow motion. Me running after Gus. Gus leading me to the office. To Wendall standing there, grinning and waiting. Had I told him Gus's name?

"Ain't nothin' worse than a lyin' SOB." My father aims the gun at Wendall's kneecap. "You made me shoot that dog. You told me the shelter would come lookin' for him. Maybe lock me up. Take Mol away. She loved ol' Roscoe. We both did."

I meet his eyes, two simmering stones of coal. Beneath the fire, it's all pain. I should know.

"I kept his collar, Mol. Did Dakota tell you she found it?"

Wendall answers for me. "See there, Doc. Your daddy saved the collar. A twisted little memento from his kill. And every time he looked at it, he lived it again."

My father fires off a shot into Wendall's kneecap, evoking a pitiful cry. Then he pulls his army green T-shirt over his head and stomps toward him, baring his teeth and the wiry gray hairs on his sun-spotted chest.

"Burns, don't it?"

He wraps the shirt around Wendall's fresh wound. It's soaked through in an instant.

"This here's a tourniquet," he says. "Because your death is gonna be slow. Real slow. Mol, how long do you think it'll take this here snake to swallow up a man as big as Grady?"

I can't answer. I'm transfixed by the tattoo on my father's bicep. A caged bird, identical to Dakota's, except for this written beneath it: R.I.P. Dakota. "Is that real?" I ask my father. "Your tattoo?"

He turns to me, shrugs, as Wendall speaks through gritted teeth.

"Looks like you've got two matching cuckoo birds in your family, Doc. Both of 'em desperate to fly the coop. Well, just one now, I suppose. May Dakota rest in peace."

I retrieve the hook, snag the gopher snake, and hold it up to Wendall's pale face. Blisters of sweat bead up on his forehead, like he's burning on the inside. In his rheumy blue eyes, I see my own reckoning. The police never publicized Dakota's tattoo. The detectives held the information back, waiting. For a suspect. For a moment like this one. Something only her killer would know.

"So you wouldn't hurt a dog," I say, inching the snake closer to his hawk nose. "What about a girl? Would you hurt a girl like Susana Donnelly? Like Miriam Woodbury? Jacqueline Pierce? Jessica Guzman? Would you hurt a girl like my daughter?"

My father stands beside me, rage wafting from him in waves. Together, we're radioactive.

"Do you mean to tell me this rat bastard killed Dakota?"

I nod at him through blurry eyes. Heat, not tears.

"Say it," I demand of Wendall. "I want to hear you admit it."

"Wouldn't you, now? I'm always takin' the blame. Like with that bitch, Sister Frances. She found a whole bunch of strangled chickens one Sunday mornin'. Had the nerve to accuse me of doin' it. Like it was any worse than what she did. Too bad she slipped down the rectory stairs and broke her back. She never did walk right after that. And your little friend, Nurse Dalton. I could've had my way with her fifteen times till Sunday, and not even a thank you. Then, there's your daddy. He killed them gooks same as me. Killed Dakota too and those other girls. But I'm the one sufferin'. It ain't right."

Wendall's head droops. He's breathing hard with the effort of it all. As if he's giving birth to a demon baby. We're on fire—all three of us—and I wait for the whole shed, the whole world, to burn.

"I'll make him say it." Snatching the hook from my hand, my father opens the shed door and drops the gopher snake into the grass. When he returns, he dips the hook into an old plastic bucket. "You think a couple shots to the kneecap and a little gopher snake was all I got planned?"

He lifts the hook slowly, teasing Wendall. At its end, a fighting mad rattlesnake. "This one here's the real deal. Yes siree."

Wendall screams again, twisting and squirming against the ropes that bind him. His teeth chatter as my father stretches the hook toward his face. So close, the snake's black tongue flicks against his cheek. Once, twice, three times.

"Alright!" Wendall shouts. "I didn't plan on hurting her. I thought I was done with all that mess. Cured. Damn if she wasn't just like the both of you and that loser Chewie. Stickin' her nose where it didn't belong. I figured one last time for the road, ya know. I ain't got that many years ahead of me."

"So you knew she and Boyd were onto something? Or should I say *DocSherlock* knew? Who else did you pretend to be? MQKlinger? Jojo?"

"I never pretended to be anybody. Those fools trusted me. That's on them."

Even now, bloodied and wincing and strung up like a ham in Crazy Krandel's shed, Wendall thinks he's getting one over.

"Your arrogance," I say, the snake's rattle chattering behind me. "That's your weakness. You came to me. Laid it all out. Did you really think you'd pin this on my dad and get away with it?"

"I didn't need to pin a damn thing. I expected more from ya, quite frankly. I expected a worthy opponent. A bit of a challenge at least. Somethin' to get my blood pumpin'. Turns out you were just as gullible as the next fella. Come to think of it, your girl was a helluva lot smarter than you are. You would've bought whatever I sold about ole Crazy Krandel."

My father drops the snake into the bucket and retrieves his rifle. "You deserve somethin' slower, Grady, but it's all I got."

"Wait, Dad."

I push the barrel of his rifle aside and slide the bayonet from my waist, where I'd tucked it that afternoon before we'd left for Wendall's house. I walk toward him, calm as I've ever been. When I hear the shed's door creak open behind me, I don't even glance over my shoulder. Cops, Sawyer, God himself, whoever it is, I don't care who sees this.

"Kill, kill, kill. Kill without mercy," I whisper to Wendall, the blade at his throat. "C'mon, you know this one."

"Do it," he hisses back. "Go on now. Just be careful you don't like it too much."

A hand joins mine on the knife's battle-worn handle. It's a hand I recognize, though it's scratched and muddy. A hand that's clawed its way up from somewhere dark, dirt beneath the fingernails. A hand that had once placed a gold band on my own. That had once held our daughter with reverence.

My father had said war hones you to a sharpened point. Grief is a kind of war, the kind you fight alone. It hones you too. Sharper than the finest blade.

Together, Cole and I step behind Wendall and guide the knife across his throat, from one hinge of the jaw to the other, his blood pooling onto the dirt floor.

That's the spirit of the bayonet.

****

Sirens wail. Or is it me?

"C'mon, Mol," my dad says, coaxing me from the ground, where I've fallen, the bayonet shaking in my hand. "We gotta hurry. I know what to do."

Crazy Krandel's in charge now.

Cole and I don't look at each other. We follow orders and move with purpose—covering our hands with our shirts to transfer the collars to the infamous black duffel, then hiding it in the footlocker's secret compartment. Hoisting Wendall's body onto my father's tarp, as he rakes up the dirt floor, concealing the blood we'd let. Dragging the tarp through the sycamore grove and across the fence line.

My father trails behind us with Wendall's rucksack. Inside it, the bayonet, the ropes, and a can of gasoline.

"You remember that abandoned well I told you about?"

I feel myself nod, numbly. For an entire year, he'd been convinced Charlie lived inside it, crawling out and wreaking havoc when the sun went down. Finally, we'd secured it with a slab of cement. Too bad Charlie couldn't be kept down by a concrete block.

"Up and over," Dad says, after we slide the cover to one side, grunting with the effort of it. "Down he goes. Where he stops, only Satan knows."

I turn away when Dad lights the match. But Cole won't let me.

"It's for Dakota," he tells me. "For our girl."
But I know better. This is for us.

****

My hands are clean.

I washed Wendall's blood away in the deer trough my father built. Before the smoke began to billow, Cole and I re-covered the well, sealing Wendall inside to burn forever. Though I don't think of him as Wendall now, but Shadow Man. Only fitting he should be buried in darkness.

"Hey, Mollie!" Sawyer's voice carries through the sycamores, and I wave my father's lantern, signaling from the front of the shed. Detective Sharpe leads the cavalry behind him. "Are you alright?"

"We're okay," I answer as my father lays down his rifle and proudly points out his booby traps, steering the officers safely toward us.

I collapse against Sawyer, and he holds me there, cupping my head to his chest.

"Your dad had that trailer rigged with a trip wire and dynamite," he whispers. "I nearly ended up as No-Arm-Jack."

Detective Sharpe leaps the last punji pit, shaking his head at it, marveling. He eyes my father with the same kind of fearful wonder as I do.

"What happened out here, Mr. Krandel?"

My father steps forward, shoulders back like he's ready to salute. "Grady came after me, that's what. He said it was my fault he'd been court-martialed. Wanted me to change my story. I've got a lot of faults, sir. I'm sure Mol told you that. But I ain't no liar. When I refused, he lunged at me. We tussled at bit, and he got away."

"And the gunshots?"

"My trusty twenty-two. I won't deny I tried to put him down like an ole dog. But some dogs are damn hard to kill, if you know what I mean."

With a kiss to the forehead, Sawyer releases me and wanders off toward the shed. He disappears inside.

"Mollie? Cole? Did you two see anything?"

I shake my head. "Cole fell into that pit over there. It took a while to get him out. And then Dad came running up. Told us the same story. That he'd lost Wendall."

"Which way did he go?"

My father points to the house with a steely-eyed glare. "We were on our way back there. I was hopin' my trip wire might blow him to smithereens."

"He's probably heading to his car," I add, widening my eyes at my father. Crazy Krandel never did know when to quit. "We saw it parked in the trees out front."

"You're right, Mol. A rat bastard like that would run off with his tail between his legs."

Sawyer emerges from the shed and levels me with a look. It feels as if I've slipped right out of my skin again. All of it—muscle, bone, blood, truth—there for only him to see.

"All clear in here," he shouts.

Detective Sharpe waves the troops onward, the same way they'd come, directing his flashlight into the sycamore grove. "He couldn't have gotten too far with his pneumonia, his COPD . . ."

Cole and I exchange a glance. No mention of lung cancer. God, I had been a fool. *Had been.* But no longer.

"Let's check the house one more time." Detective Sharpe takes a few steps, then stutters to a stop.

I go cold, thinking he must know. That I'm about to be pinned to the ground, a knee in my back. Handcuffed and carted away. Locked in a box with other women like me. Women capable of ending life. Surely, there's something backwards about that.

"Mr. Krandel, if it's all the same to you, I'd like to leave here with all my limbs intact. You lead the way."

They walk on ahead, my father in front. Cole and the others following carefully in his footsteps. I lag behind in the darkness, waiting for Sawyer to catch up.

"Forget something?" he whispers, holding Wendall's black hat out to me.

I take it from him and crush it like a bug beneath my foot.

BEFORE

CHAPTER THIRTY-FIVE

DAKOTA played out the scene in her mind as she pumped the pedals up the hill toward Ridgecrest, Gus trailing on her right.

For starters, she'd have to apologize.

She'd tell her mom everything. Like she used to. About Hannah and Tyler and the photos. About Grandpa Krandel. Boyd too. Maybe if she hadn't deserted her mom on the battlefield, she wouldn't have stopped trusting Dakota. Wouldn't have started drinking. Wouldn't have ever hit her at all.

She'd leave for Starry Sky today, if that's what they wanted.

And she'd go back to pretending she'd never seen her dad that night. Because no good had come from her telling the truth. Only bad, bad, and worse.

Dakota felt the sudden heat of an engine behind her. It seemed to come from nowhere.

She waved it past. It didn't move.

She pedaled harder. It matched her speed.

She moved left. It moved with her.

The car accelerated; its tire aimed straight at Gus's hind legs. That she couldn't bear.

"Gus! Watch out!"

The dog ducked into the ditch.

Dakota swerved—too late.

A last panicked glance over her shoulder. The car's long silver jaw jutted out toward her, ready to crunch her between its teeth.

It nipped her back tire and she went down.

****

Dakota lay on the ground, her left side throbbing. Her backpack had fallen from her shoulders and tumbled into the ditch. The blue sky spun above her; the sun, an orb of fire at the center of it all. It was too bright to keep her eyes open, so she shut them tight and listened.

To the soft purring of the car's engine.

A door yawning open.

A swingy song—sax and trumpet and a chorus of men's voices singing about watching girls go by.

Footfalls on the pavement. Someone was coming.

Then a sound she'd never heard. Not even at the dog park when Frankie the Great Dane had postured with raised hackles and a curled lip.

Gus growled. And she had to look, if only for a moment, afraid he'd been hit. She called to him, but his eyes were fixed beyond her, behind her. To the someone.

The quiet someone who made kissing noises to summon Gus. His tail low and barely waving, he whined a little but walked past her.

"Is he okay?" she asked, hoping the someone would answer.

"Right as rain, aren't ya, boy? Crackers make it all better. Now you get on home. Go on now. I've got some nasty business to take care of. You don't want to see it."

Dakota watched the fine hairs on her arms raise. She rolled onto her right side, planning to run, but found herself frozen. Fear could do that.

"Don't ya be thinkin' about runnin'. I got a bullet with your goldie's name on it. Gus, ain't it?"

Grandpa Krandel's soapstone clover had skittered from her pocket. It sat on the hot pavement, bright as a penny. It seemed essential not to lose it.

"Now what do we have here?" the someone asked, calmly unzipping her backpack, rifling through its contents. "Shadow Man Investigation. Ain't that a hoot?"

She realized then. She knew this someone.

"Oh. And a collar for a doggie. *Roscoe.* How sweet."

She called for Gus again, her voice barely a whisper, and reached for the clover, ignoring the sharp twinge in her shoulder. Her fingers touched it, wrapped around it, cradled its warmth in her palm as a shadow, long and dark as a knife's blade, blocked the sun.

****

Dakota steeled herself. She thought of her mom and dad. Of Grandpa Krandel. And Gus. She wore their love like armor. Surely, it would protect her. Love could do that.

She waited until he knelt beside her. *Too long*, she realized. Because he had something in his hand. A rag that smelled sickly sweet and made her woozy even before it reached her mouth.

She did the only thing she could as his old man's face drew nearer. She bit down hard, first on his fingers beneath the foul-tasting rag. And then, as her whole world slipped beneath the horizon, she sunk her teeth into the dark heart of him, leaving a perfect sickle on the brim of his black hat.

AFTER

CHAPTER THIRTY-SIX

(MONDAY, OCTOBER 22, 2018)

I fidget with the sterling silver heart around my neck, tracing the engraved letters beneath my thumb. **M-O-M**. I almost wish Cole could see me wear it again, but he swam for Seattle this morning. Both of us free fish now.

I watch the group members file in from the safety of the Jeep. It's the first time I feel nervous. But I don't blast the radio to lose myself in a screaming guitar. Instead, I read.

Manhunt For Shadow Man Wendall Grady Enters Tenth Day

The Napa County Sheriff's Department and the Federal Bureau of Investigation announced yesterday that disgraced military officer Wendall Grady has been officially identified as the prime suspect in the Shadow Man killings, which began decades ago and terrorized the Bay Area. After the Shadow Man Task Force received an anonymous tip last week, their search of Grady's house revealed human remains in a soundproof underground bunker, as well as numerous dog collars hidden beneath his bed, many of which belonged to the dogs of Shadow Man's known victims. Given the number of mementos found, authorities speculated there could be more than five additional unknown victims. It is believed that Grady selected his victims while volunteering for several local animal shelters, because nearly all identified victims had either adopted a pet or visited a shelter prior to their abductions.

Grady also founded a website, Shadow Seekers, where he maintained several fictitious profiles in order to closely monitor any developments in his case. Police now suspect that victim seventeen, Dakota Roark, encountered Grady on the site and was targeted due to her investigatory efforts, as well as Grady's long-standing feud with her grandfather, Victor Krandel. Forensic computer analysts believe Grady pinpointed the girl's location by using IP-tracking software.

Grady was last seen on Friday evening, October 12, at Krandel's compound, Mol's Junkyard. Grady reportedly made criminal threats against Krandel, who police had previously suspected in the killing of Dakota Roark. Consistent with his elusive moniker, Shadow Man abandoned his vehicle and disappeared into a heavily wooded area outside the compound.

Napa PD spokeswoman Helen Yi issued a statement indicating the department has devoted all available resources to finding the serial killer, including relying upon special checkpoint procedures developed in 2016, after Clive Cullen successfully escaped from San Quentin State Prison and went on a violent rampage. Like Cullen, Wendall Grady is considered armed and highly dangerous, though police will not rule out the possibility Grady may be injured.

According to Peter Jacoby, Chief Psychologist at Napa State Hospital, Grady fits the profile developed by Napa psychologist in the mid-1980s. "By all accounts, Grady blended seamlessly into the fabric of society. He was happily married for twenty-three years. Until recently, he was a decorated military veteran. He even volunteered in the community, donating a good portion of his veteran's benefits to the SPCA. Wherever he is, he's unlikely to stand out. He may even be your next-door neighbor.

Luciana parks Boludo in the spot next to mine. She knocks on the window, frowning at the paper in my hand.

"Any news?"

"Nada."

"He'll get what's coming to him. Se siega lo que se siembra." I smile, because I know this one. It's about reaping what you sow.

I think of the well. I'll go there one day, when all the hoopla blows over. Push the cover aside myself. Toss in the last remnants of the Shadow Man, the treatment agreement he'd signed on our first day of therapy. Then I'll get Dad to help me fill it in with concrete, and I'll walk away forever. Leave his soul in the exact opposite of peace to reap all the rotten seeds he'd planted.

Luciana and I walk into the break room, arm in arm. When I spot Debbie with three packages of M&Ms on her lap, a gift from the vending machine gods, I'm certain it's a good day.

I take the seat that's been saved for me next to Sawyer. He's dressed in jeans and a clean T-shirt, and I inhale the earthy scent of him. Later tonight, I fully intend to shove my tongue down his throat. Again. If he'll let me. But only after we've had our first dinner date. Only after I've gotten to the bottom of that story about how he really broke his jaw.

"Hello, everyone, and welcome to the Grieving Parents Group. I'm sure all of you are aware of the developments in my daughter's case in the last week and a half, and I'm eager to tell you all about it. But first, I want to share an announcement. After careful consideration, I've decided to take over as group facilitator on a permanent basis. If you'll have me."

I listen to their applause. Feel the warmth of Sawyer's hand on my knee.

It turns out being the Lead Basket Case suits me after all.

****

I'm not ready to go inside yet. I'm still giddy from our first real date, from truths told. Turns out Sawyer had jumped from the roof of his high school on a dare with a bedsheet as a makeshift parachute. *That's when I knew I wanted to be a Ranger*, he'd said, laughing.

I let Gus run in the yard, watching him frolic from the porch steps. When his tongue is hanging, we walk together to my real office.

I turn on the lights and go to my suspect wall. Rip it down piece by piece until there's nothing left.

The white paint is a blank canvas. I'll put something nice here. Something Dakota would've liked.

Gus snuffs at the box in the corner, the one marked Napa State. He scratches at the edge of it, making long claw marks down the side, and my hairs stand on end.

I look behind me, but the room is empty. The night as quiet as falling snow.

Pushing Gus aside, I open the dusty flaps and scour the refuse of my career. Books, papers, a *Keep Talking, I'm Diagnosing You* mug. At the bottom, beneath it all, I find it. It's Shadow Man's last gift to me. I'm certain of that.

It's Roscoe's collar.

EPILOGUE

TYLER Lowry is as predictable as a rat in a cheese maze. *A numbskull,* my dad would say. And I've tailed that numbskull to the Napa Prep lacrosse field every evening since he'd arrived back at his parents' house in Napa on Christmas vacation, sporting his Duke gear like he owned the place.

"Alright, hand me the goods," Dad says, flashing a mischievous grin. He's been taking his meds again, but all the risperdal in the world isn't enough to contain Crazy Krandel when he sets his mind to something. "Careful though. They ain't nothin' to mess with."

I pass him the box from Reptiles 'R' Us, a special order courtesy of Boyd Blackburn, and take a step back for my own safety.

Dad leans over the pit we'd dug in front of the gate and empties the contents.

"Now we camouflage it. Just like I taught you."

The leaf cover in place, we hightail it to my dad's old rust bucket to wait before the field lights come on. The night is a cold one, and we huddle together over a can of Beanee Weenees, clinking spoons before the first bite.

"Cheers!"

I wash down the salty sweetness with a swig of coke from Dad's cooler. It's no Olde English. Certainly, no Macallan 18. But we're both off the sauce, earning our two-month bronze chips together at the Allendale AA meeting a week ago.

"Dakota was somethin' special," he says, staring off for a moment. "Just like her mama."

"I'm sorry I didn't let you see her more. I should have found a way to make it work."

"You did the best you could, Mol. That's what we do as parents. The best we know how. Even if it ain't worth a hill of beans. I hurt you. I hurt Roscoe. You only wanted to protect her from that. You weren't wrong."

I smile at him, letting my eyes well. "Thanks for helping me with this, Dad. It feels like old times. But better."

"What kind of daddy would I be if I didn't help my girl get some good ole-fashioned revenge? Let me see that list. What other numbskulls we got on there?"

Dad reads the names exactly as I'd written them. I wish I could take credit, but I'd stolen the first nickname from Dakota's phone records. "Dickface Tyler. Backstabbing Hannah. Doctor Jackass."

I'd given Joanna Montgomery a pass. She'd have to deal with Cole. That was punishment enough.

At exactly 7:01 p.m., Tyler squeals into the parking lot in his little black Jetta, the official car of pricks everywhere. He cracks the door and struts out, lacrosse stick balanced against one shoulder. He's headed straight for the punji pit.

"Here it comes," Dad says. "In three, two, one . . ."

Now that you've finished *Shadows Among Us*, please consider leaving a review. Reviews and star-ratings may not seem important, but to an author they are essential. They help readers like you discover my books! And they give an author a little "street cred" for those browsing for their next read.

So what's the best way to feed an author? Leave a review, of course. You can find all the links to review *Shadows Among Us* on my website ellerykane.com.

ACKNOWLEDGMENTS

Some writers say every book is easier to write than the last. I wish that was true! For me, each book is different in its own way and no less challenging than the one that came before. With that said, completing Shadows Among Us would not have been possible without the AnnCastro Studio team who provided all editing services for book, including developmental editing/line editing by Ann Castro; proofing via an editorial eye by Emily Dings; and test reading/evaluation by Katrina "Kat" Martin; Giovanni Auriemma who produced the mysterious and intriguing cover; and Mallory Rock who designed the book's interior. As always, I owe a debt of gratitude to my friends, family, and work colleagues— my cheerleaders—who are always there telling me to keep writing and keep dreaming big. And of course, to you, dear readers, for devouring every sinful bite of the Doctors of Darkness series!

I never intended to write a book about the Vietnam War, but when Victor Krandel came to life in my mind he told me he was a Vietnam vet, and thus a major portion of the storyline was born. In 1968, the Pentagon established the Vietnam War Crimes Working Group to investigate the veracity of allegations of war crimes committed by United States forces in Vietnam, in light of the My Lai Massacre after which Charlie Company's Lieutenant William Calley shouldered the blame for the methodical killings of more than five hundred unarmed victims, as well as the sexual assaults of women and young girls, mutilation of the dead, and burning of homes and villages. My Lai was once believed to be an isolated incident, the crazed actions of a disturbed ranking officer; however, over time, numerous more war crimes have been documented by journalists like Nick Turse, who penned *Kill Anything that Moves: The Real American War in Vietnam*, which inspired many of the scenes in this book. It is an intense, moving, and eye-opening read that I highly recommend.

I'll end this one the way I always do, because it is just as true as the first time I wrote it: We all have a space inside us that we keep hidden from the world, a space we protect at all costs. So many people have allowed me a glimpse inside theirs—dark deeds, memories best unrecalled, pain that cracks from the inside out—without expectation of anything in return. I couldn't have written a single true word without them.

ALSO BY ELLERY KANE

Shadows Among Us is the fourth in the *Doctors of Darkness* series of psychological thrillers by forensic psychologist and author, Ellery Kane. Look for the next book, How to Disappear, coming soon. If you want to be the first to know when new books are released, sign up for Ellery's newsletter at ellerykane.com.

If you enjoyed *Shadows Among Us*, look for these other great reads from Ellery Kane.

Doctors of Darkness Series
Daddy Darkest
The Hanging Tree
The First Cut
Shadows Among Us
How to Disappear (coming soon!)

Legacy Series
Legacy
Prophecy
Revelation
AWOL

ABOUT THE AUTHOR

Forensic psychologist by day, novelist by night, Ellery Kane has been writing--professionally and creatively--for as long as she can remember. Just like many of her main characters, Ellery loves to ask why, which is the reason she became a psychologist in the first place. Real life really is stranger than fiction, and Ellery's writing is often inspired by her day job. Evaluating violent criminals and treating trauma victims, she has gained a unique perspective on the past and its indelible influence on the individual. And she's heard her fair share of real life thrillers. An avid short story writer as a teenager, Ellery recently began writing for enjoyment again, and she doesn't plan to stop anytime soon!

Ellery's debut novel, Legacy, has received several awards, including winning the Gold Medal in the Independent Publisher Book Awards, young adult, e-book category, and the Gold Medal in the Wishing Shelf Independent Book Awards, teenage category. In 2016, Ellery was selected as one of ten semifinalists in the MasterClass James Patterson Co-Author Competition.

Printed in Great Britain
by Amazon